China's Education Policy Review

(2018—2021)

中国教育政策评论

袁振国 ◎ 主编

陈霜叶　游　蠡 ◎ 副主编

华东师范大学出版社
·上海·

图书在版编目（CIP）数据

中国教育政策评论／袁振国主编；陈霜叶，游蠡副主编. —上海：华东师范大学出版社，2022
ISBN 978 - 7 - 5760 - 3430 - 1

Ⅰ.①中… Ⅱ.①袁… ②陈… ③游… Ⅲ.①教育政策—研究—中国 Ⅳ.①G520

中国版本图书馆CIP数据核字（2022）第224713号

中国教育政策评论

主　　编	袁振国
策划编辑	龚海燕
责任编辑	顾晨溪
责任校对	时东明
装帧设计	刘怡霖

出版发行	华东师范大学出版社
社　　址	上海市中山北路3663号　邮编200062
网　　址	www.ecnupress.com.cn
电　　话	021 - 60821666　行政传真 021 - 62572105
客服电话	021 - 62865537　门市（邮购）电话 021 - 62869887
地　　址	上海市中山北路3663号华东师范大学校内先锋路口
网　　店	http://hdsdcbs.tmall.com
印　刷　者	上海昌鑫龙印务有限公司
开　　本	787毫米×1092毫米　1/16
印　　张	25.75
字　　数	410千字
版　　次	2022年12月第1版
印　　次	2022年12月第1次
书　　号	ISBN 978 - 7 - 5760 - 3430 - 1
定　　价	128.00元

出版人　王　焰

（如发现本版图书有印订质量问题，请寄回本社客服中心调换或电话021 - 62865537联系）

Preface

China is a major player in the field of education and is striving to become an education powerhouse. Although Chinese education has its own historical and cultural traditions, its current educational system and educational ideology clearly originated from its Western counterpart. Since the adoption of the reform and opening-up policy in the late 1970s and early 1980s, China has broadened the horizons and discovered that the world had moved toward modernization. Once again, the country eagerly introduced the advanced ideas and best practices of Western education, and initiated another period of rapid development in China's education industry. It was not until the first decade of the new millennium and Shanghai's repeated outstanding achievements in the PISA test that we realized that China had gradually shifted from the role of importer to exporter in education. Indeed, an increasing number of countries around the world are beginning to pay close attention to Chinese education in an attempt to learn from its experience of achieving exemplary performance in the field.

Previously, we noted how one must be familiar with **three types of discourse** in order to engage in scientific educational research, namely, *scholarship as discourse*, *policy as discourse*, and *practice as discourse*. One must also have a good grasp of the **three forms of education** to understand Chinese education: *education as presented by theories*, *education as constructed by policies*, and *education as implemented and developed in practice*. All three forms are indispensable for obtaining an authentic and comprehensive understanding of Chinese education. With regard to education as presented by theories, Chinese educational researchers are focusing on the storytelling about Chinese education through the use of scientific and empirical methods. Education as implemented and developed in practice is being highlighted by the continuous expansion of Sino-foreign educational exchanges at the grassroots level. However, there remains insufficient emphasis on education as constructed by policies, despite the important influences the related policies have actually achieved. Better or worse, policies have significantly influenced Chinese education from practice to research. Indeed, it is neither realistic nor possible to understand Chinese education without reference to its policy features and governance model. Similarly, the Chinese experience and wisdom at the policy level cannot be ignored in discussions of learning from China.

In light of the foregoing, a special column entitled "Policy Review" was introduced to the journal of *ECNU Review of Education* (hereinafter, *ROE*) in its inaugural issue. This journal is the first international journal on Chinese education published in English, fully managed by East China Normal University, and published with East China Normal University Press and the SAGE publishing house. The "Policy Review" column aims to introduce current and important education policies in China to readers who are interested in the development of Chinese education. The introduction of this column echoes *ROE*'s own mission and vision to provide a unique platform for global scholars to launch sustained and dynamic dialogues on important issues in Chinese and international education, to harness educational research to generate new knowledge and ideas for the prospects of human being and shared future of the world, and to promote far-reaching reforms in the field of education.

By July 2021, *ROE* has published 4 volumes 13 issues. The special column has been a regular feature of *ROE* since the journal's launch in April 2018. The September issue of 2020 focused on some important changes in policies governing social science research evaluation in China. Not long after, the related policy review articles were mentioned in a special column in the *Times Higher Education*, which has proved *ROE*'s growing international influence. We thus considered it was time to revisit *ROE*'s previous attempts to introduce China's education policies, which brought out the current edition entitled, ***China's Education Policy Review (2018 – 2021)***.

The selected articles in this collection are primarily drawn from the "Policy Review" column. They are categorized into three sections according to the education level steered by these policies: namely, overall, basic, and higher education policies. The first section on overall education policies also includes "Dual Priority Agenda: China's Model for Modernizing Education" authored by Professor Zhenguo Yuan from East China Normal University, and "Chinese Educational Policy Research: The Arduous Formation of a Research Paradigm" by Professor Xiaoying Lin from Peking University. These two research articles seek to help readers better understand the modernization process of China's education and the current status of research on Chinese education policies from the macroscopic perspective. What we aim to do is to provide a compass and a map for our readers to rely upon as they venture through the dense forest of Chinese education policies. The rest are specific policy review articles on the general topics of lifelong education, educational exchanges with foreign countries, education informatization, K-12 curriculum reform, faculty development, regulatory policies on private supplementary tutoring, the Double First-Class initiative in universities, and the evaluation of scientific research. With the abundant variety of topics covered, readers have the option to select policies in which they are personally interested for further reading.

Finally, it must be pointed out that these articles cover the most recent Chinese education policies, and encompass various areas ranging from basic to higher education, and from school governance to curriculum instruction. Additionally, all contributions were made by first-rate leading scholars or industry experts in the related fields. This comprehensive collection provides readers with a full dimensional introduction to education policies landscape in China, including their specific contexts, core content, historical trajectories, and future prospects. The papers in this collection serve to document and record policies likely to significantly impact the future of Chinese education. We hope that this collection will provide an easy reference and a quick guide for our international readers and friends to better understand Chinese education and its policies. If there are any education policies or data that you would like to know more about, please feel free to contact us via e-mail: **roe@ecnu.edu.cn**. We would like to sign off by expressing our heartfelt gratitude to all!

Zhenguo Yuan
Editor-in-Chief of *ECNU Review of Education*
Dean of Faculty of Education at East China Normal University

Shuangye Chen
Executive Associate Editor of *ECNU Review of Education*
Associate Dean of Faculty of Education at East China Normal University

Li You
Managing Editor of *ECNU Review of Education*

Contents

Preface ... 1

Introduction

Dual Priority Agenda: China's Model for Modernizing Education ... 3
Zhenguo Yuan

Chinese Educational Policy Research: The Arduous Formation of a Research Paradigm ... 36
Xiaoying Lin

Overview of Education

New National Initiatives of Modernizing Education in China ... 57
Yiming Zhu

Post-PISA Education Reforms in China: Policy Response Beyond the Digital Governance of PISA ... 67
Wenjie Yang and Guorui Fan

China's Experiences in Developing Lifelong Education, 1978 – 2017 ... 81
Zunmin Wu

China's Preschool Education Toward 2035: Views of Key Policy Experts ... 98
Yong Jiang, Beibei Zhang, Ying Zhao and Chuchu Zheng

China-Africa Education Cooperation: From FOCAC to Belt and Road ... 122
Kenneth King

Higher Education for International Students in China: A Review of Policy From 1978 to 2020   138
Yuting Zhang and Yu Liao

Comparison of Female Teachers in Primary, Secondary, and Tertiary Education: China and the World   155
William Anderson

Basic Education

Making Teaching an Enviable Profession: New Epoch-Making Teacher Policy in China and Challenges   163
Tingzhou Li

Review of Regulatory Policies on Private Supplementary Tutoring in China   170
Junyan Liu

School Choice in China: Past, Present, and Future   181
Hui Dong and Lulu Li

Competence for Students' Future: Curriculum Change and Policy Redesign in China   192
Tao Wang

From Scale to Quality: Experiences and Challenges in Teacher Education in China   204
Bin Zhou

Accelerated Move for AI Education in China   213
Xiaozhe Yang

Refreshing China's Labor Education in the New Era: Policy Review on Education Through Physical Labor   219
Guorui Fan and Jiaxin Zou

China's New Laws and Policies on Nongovernmental Education: Background, Characteristics, and Impact Analysis 230
Shengzu Dong

Education Informatization 2.0 in China: Motivation, Framework, and Vision 241
Shouxuan Yan and Yun Yang

Education Quality Assessment in China: What We Learned From Official Reports Released in 2018 and 2019 261
Danqing Yin

Moral Education Curriculum Reform for China's Elementary and Middle Schools in the Twenty-First Century: Past Progress and Future Prospects 276
Hanwei Tang and Yang Wang

Higher Education

The "Double First Class" Initiative Under Top-Level Design 297
Xiao Liu

The Composition and Evolution of China's High-Level Talent Programs in Higher Education 303
Junwen Zhu

Policy-Driven Development and the Strategic Initiative of One-Million Enrollment Expansion in China's Higher Vocational Education 311
Xiaoxian Fan

***Suzhi* Education and General Education in China** 319
Haishao Pang, Meiling Cheng, Jing Yu and Jingjing Wu

Review and Critique on the New Higher Education Policy Promoting "The First-Class Major Programs" in China 336
Xiaodong Lu

Evaluation of Scientific and Technological Research in China's Colleges: A Review of Policy Reforms, 2000 – 2020   344
Junwen Zhu

China's SCI-Indexed Publications: Facts, Feelings, and Future Directions   350
Weishu Liu

Reflections on the Use of SSCI Papers in Evaluating Social Sciences Research in Chinese Universities   357
Li Liu, Huilin Xue and Jing Li

The Greater Bay Area (GBA) Development Strategy and Its Relevance to Higher Education   363
Ailei Xie, Gerard A. Postiglione and Qian Huang

Eight-Year Medical Education Program: Retrospect and Prospect of the High-Level Medical Talent Training in China   375
Hongbin Wu, Ana Xie and Weimin Wang

Notes on Contributors   397

Introduction

Forty years ago, China made a critical decision to reform and open up, achieving sustained economic growth. Simultaneously, China continued to center efforts on achieving its education modernization goals. It succeeded in the unconventional development of education, consolidating a population of nearly 1.4 billion into a powerful human-resource-centered nation and creating favorable interactive relationships with social and economic development. This article aims to explore how these achievements were gained and how these relationships were made. Based on the policy documents and development practice, this article proposes a model of Dual Priority Agenda (DPA), whereby the government prioritized education development, and this development focused predominantly on promoting national development. This article contributes to a new conceptualization of the reciprocal relationship between the state and educational modernization and also helps us to appreciate the significant role education policies played, play, and will play in Chinese education development.

Dual Priority Agenda: China's Model for Modernizing Education [1]

Zhenguo Yuan

A critical decision to reform and open up was made during the 3rd Plenary Session of the 11th Central Committee of the Communist Party of China (CPC) held in December 1978. Since the implementation of China's economic reform policy, the economy has sustained a 40-year growth, rising to 70th in global ranking for GDP per capita from 171st [2] and 2nd for gross GPD from 9th [3]. China's global contribution rose from 3.05% in 1978 to 31.53% in 2016 [4]. This economic advancement was a miracle in the history of both China and the world.

China's education is a primary component of this miracle and a major driving force behind it.

---

1   This article was published on *ECNU Review of Education*, 1(1), 5–33.
2   Source: United Nations Statistics Division (UNSD; https://unstats.un.org). Branch: GDP per capita (current USD). 187 countries were surveyed in 1978, and 212 countries were surveyed in 2016. The statistics presented in the article do not include three regions of China—Hong Kong SAR, Macao SAR, and Taiwan—unless otherwise specified.
3   Source: UNSD (https://unstats.un.org). Branch: GPD (current USD). 187 countries were surveyed in 1978, and 212 countries were surveyed in 2016.
4   Source: World Bank Open Data (https://data.worldbank.org.cn/indicator). Branch: GDP (constant 2010 USD). Calculated based on China's contribution to global economic growth = China's GDP growth/global GDP growth * 100%.

The pre-primary gross enrollment rate (GER) increased from 12.62% in 1981 to 77.4% in 2016, surpassing the average GER of moderate-to-high-income countries by 5%. The consolidation rate of nine-year compulsory education reached 93.4% in 2016, surpassing the average rate of high-income countries. High school GER rose from 39.56% in 1981 to 87.5% in 2016, surpassing the average GER of moderate-to-high-income countries by 5%. Tertiary education GER rose from 1.6% in 1981 to 42.7% in 2016, surpassing the average GER of moderate-to-high-income countries by 6%.

In the same period, China has performed quite well in the Program for International Student Assessment (PISA) and various rankings of global universities. China's significant development in education has transformed the human resource structure. The average years of education for Chinese people between the ages of 16 and 59 rose from below 5 years in 1981 to 10.35 years in 2016. In addition, the percentage of the population with a college degree or higher rose from 0.58% in 1982 to 12.44% in 2015 [1]. The expected years of schooling in China was 8.8 years in 1990, ranked 119th in the world. By 2015, it rose to 13.5 years, elevating China to 8th [2].

Scholars are interested in probing the reasons of such dramatic changes after the implementation of China's economic reform. John King Fairbank, a prominent American academic on the history of China, published *The United States and China* in 1948, which was the first publication from a Western author to compare the United States and China. Fairbank (1983) stated in his book that China was amidst a modernization movement; the most evident characteristic of this movement was China's decision to abandon all existing traditions and systems and then reference to the edifications and systems (including languages) of Western societies. Therefore, the modernization of China can be characterized as a process whereby China continually responded to the encroachment of the West (Fairbank, 1983). Over time, this impact-response model became recognized as the start of modernization in China among Western scholars. However, in *China: A New History*, Fairbank (1992) realized that the modernization of China may not be the result of Western impacts and China's responses. Instead, it might be the product of internal genetic change and intrinsic development impulse.

---

1 Source: Statistics presented in the 1982 Census announced by the National Bureau of Statistics of China (http://www.stats.gov.cn/tjsj/tjgb/rkpcgb/qgrkpcgb/200204/t20020404_30318.html) and statistics presented in the 2015 1% National Population Sample Survey (http://www.stats.gov.cn/tjsj/zxfb/201604/t20160420_1346151.html).

2 Source: Statistics on the expected years of schooling announced by the United Nations Development Program (http://hdr.undp.org/en/data#); 172 countries were surveyed in 1990, and 191 were surveyed in 2015.

Ronald H. Coase (2012), a Nobel Prize winner in Economics in 1991, argued from his observation of China's reform that China's economic development could not be explained using conventional Western economics theories, and the success of China's economic reform was the unintended consequence of human behavior.

Therefore, modernization neither follows a fixed development process nor does a set of "universal standards" exist. The success of China as a country and in modernizing education proves the multidimensionality of modernization and highlights the global significance of China's modernization success.

This paper aims to attribute the success of China in modernizing national education to the creative formulation of a model of Dual Priority Agenda (DPA) in education modernization (see Figure 1) by drawing on its strengths, promoting traditions, and learning from international experiences. The DPA is a model conceptualizing complementary and reciprocal relationships between the state and education development, in which simultaneously the state prioritizes education to promote national development.

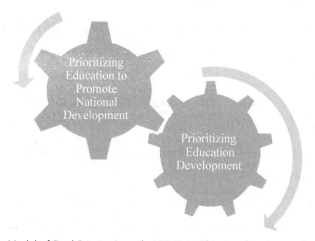

Figure 1. Model of Dual Priority Agenda (DPA) in China's education modernization.

Prioritizing education development

Prioritizing the development of education over employment, social security, healthcare, hygiene, sports, and culture is the national policy and historical practice of China's education reform and development.

Education first

The Chinese leadership believes that human capital and education are key to expediting economic development and catching up to developed countries. Only by prioritizing the development of education can modernization be quickly achieved.

Shortly after the return of Deng Xiaoping in 1977, he took the initiative in promoting education development, stating, "To catch up to advanced global standards, we must focus on science and education" (Deng, as cited in He, 1998, p. 1573). Deng (1993) firmly believed that science and technology are the foremost powers of productivity, stating, "to achieve modernization, we must improve our science and technology. To do this, promoting education is key" (Deng, as cited in He, 1991, p. 1573).

The 3rd Plenary Session of the 11th Central Committee of the CPC was held in December 1978. The ideology of "adopting class struggle as guidelines" was abolished during the meeting, and national operations were steered toward economic development. Thereafter, the status and effects of education modernization gained increased awareness, which coincided with the following statement of Deng (as cited in He, 1998), "The Four Modernizations are only empty words without science and education development" (p. 1577).

The *Decision of the CPC Central Committee on Education System Reform* was published in 1985. It was one of the most crucial documents to be published during the reform and opening-up of education in China, stating, "Human capital is the key to future success. To resolve the problem of human capital, education must improve significantly amidst economic development" (CPCCC as cited in He, 1998, p. 2285).

"The development of science, technology, and education must be prioritized, allowing technological advancement and increased labor quality to facilitate economic development," was an idea first proposed in the 13th National Congress of the CPC held in 1987.

In response to the immense workload and financial limitations after implementing the economic reform policy, the ideology of "education must be set aside for the economy to grow" rose in popularity for a period in China. Supporters of this ideology believed that education was a consumption and advocated for the prioritization of funding for economic development. Unwavering, Deng Xiaoping (1993) stated, "At all costs, we must tolerate certain aspects and sacrifice some speed to resolve the education problem." He criticized those that undervalued education as "those without foresight" (p. 121).

The *Outline of Education Reform and Development in China* in 1993 regulated, "Various levels of government shall abide by the provisions in the *Decision of the CPC Central Committee on Education System Reform* that stipulates 'The increase in education appropriations by the central and local governments shall be higher than that of regular revenue, the average education expenditure per student enrolled shall increase steadily, and teachers' salaries and average public expenditure per student shall increase annually'" (as cited in He, 1998, p. 3473).

As the economy continued to develop, government officials began to understand the necessity of prioritizing education development. They came to realize that education is a basis and a driving force for economic development, and that it imposes fundamental, comprehensive, and pilot effects on the modernization of the entire country.

The strategy to prioritize education and adopt science education-centered national development policies as China's foremost national policies was first proposed in the 14th Congress of the CPC, held in October 1992. Jiang Zemin (2006) asserted when addressing the assembly, "We must prioritize education development and strive to enhance the ideological, moral, scientific, and cultural standards of our people, and this is the fundamental plan to modernize China." He continued,

> Scientific education-centered national development refers to adopting an ideology that science and technology are the foremost powers of productivity. We must adhere to an education-centered system and incorporate science, technology, and education into the key processes of economic and social development, thereby strengthening China's ability to convert science and technology into tangible productivity and improving people's science, technology, and cultural competency. Moreover, we must allow technological advancement and increased labor quality to facilitate economic development, expediting national prosperity. (Jiang, 1995)

In the 3rd National Education Working Conference held in 1999, Jiang proposed for the first time,

> We shall adopt education as a key item of strategic development; incorporate education into the overall layout of modernized infrastructure; view education as a precursor and a global and fundamental task; and place education as a priority in our strategic development plan ... Party and government leaders at all levels must fulfil education objectives, ensure that education is ahead of development when formulating their economic and social development plans, ensure that the three aspects of growth

concerning education funding are met when formulating financial budgets, increase the proportion of education spending in overall financial spending, and provide material guarantees for prioritizing education development. (Jiang, 1999)

As international competition exacerbated, the Chinese leadership further emphasized the aggressive implementation of strategies to strengthen China through human resource development and ensure national security and the future of the Chinese people.

During the National Talent Working Conference held on December 19, 2003, Hu Jintao asserted that national competition is basically human capital competition and proposed the Strategy of Reinvigorating China Through Talent Development. In the 34th Collective Learning Session held by the Central Politburo of the CPC in 2006, He asserted,

> In today's world, knowledge is an increasingly crucial factor in enhancing overall national power and international competition, and human resources are an increasingly crucial strategic resource in promoting economic and social development … Human capital is at the root of the future development of China and reinvigoration of its people, and education is the basis for cultivating human capital. (Hu, 2006)

Hu Jintao (2007) further requested in a national educational meeting,

> More effort and financial resources must be invested into education; education development must be prioritized in economic and social development plans; financial budgets must chiefly guarantee education investments; and public resources must chiefly meet the requirements for education and human resource development. (Hu, 2007)

During the One-Year Anniversary Event of the United Nations Global Education First Initiative held in September 2013, Xi Jinping (2013) reaffirmed, "China shall firmly implement the Strategy to Invigorate China Through Science and Education and always prioritize the development of education." The report of the 19th Congress of the CPC held in October 2017 stated, "Strengthening education is fundamental to our pursuit of national rejuvenation. We must give priority to education." [1] This is the latest statement and it fully reflects the policy continuity of the Chinese governmental agenda of prioritizing education.

---

1 The report is titled as "Secure a decisive victory in building a moderately prosperous society in all respects and strive for the great success of socialism with Chinese characteristics for a new era," delivered by Xi Jinping at the 19th National Congress of the CPC, *People's Daily*, 18 October 2017.

"The three priorities"

Prioritizing education development in the modernization of China is a grand feat of social systems engineering. Based on national conditions, the Chinese government created "three priorities," namely prioritizing education development in economic and social development plans, prioritizing government funding for education expenditure, and prioritizing public resources for education and human resource development. These three measures of "three priorities" have firmly ensured the implementation of "prioritizing education development."

Prioritizing education development in economic and social development plans

Characterizing education as a key item in national economic and social development plans. A key governance approach adopted by the Chinese government is the formulation of a development plan every 5 years. Deng Xiaoping (1978) asserted for the first time in 1978, "Education must coincide with the requirements of national economic development," and "the State Education Commission, Ministry of Education, and other government departments must collectively center efforts to shape education into a vital component of the national economic plan." Thereafter, education development became a key component in the formation of national economic and social development plans. The following part lists how education development has characterized in the national plan from 1986 to 2015.

- The *Seventh Five-Year Plan for National Economic and Social Development of the People's Republic of China* issued in 1986 requested, "within five years, the national spending for education shall reach 116.6 billion CNY, for a 72% increase compared with the Sixth Five-Year Plan period, and the growth of education spending shall surpass that of regular revenues."
- The *Outlines of the Ten-Year National Economic and Social Development Plan and the Eighth Five-Year Plan of the People's Republic of China* issued in 1991 mentioned, "central and local governments at various levels shall gradually increase their education investments and center efforts in creating Chinese features and a socialist education system fit for the twenty-first century."
- The *Outlines of the Ninth Five-Year Plan for National Economic and Social Development of the People's Republic of China and the 2010 Long-Term Goals* issued in 1996 mentioned, "government departments at various levels shall govern education by law and increase education spending."
- The *Outlines of the Tenth Five-Year Plan for National Economic and Social Development of the People's Republic of China* issued in 2001 instructed, "adhere to appropriately exceeding the

development of education and serving national economic and social development."

- The *Outlines of the Eleventh Five-Year Plan for National Economic and Social Development of the People's Republic of China* issued in 2006 contained a dedicated article that discussed the prioritization of education development.
- The *Outlines of the Twelfth Five-Year Plan for National Economic and Social Development of the People's Republic of China* issued in 2011 stated, "accelerating education reform and development ... guarantees that citizens exercise their right to education, and satisfies people's education needs."
- The *CPC Central Committee Recommendations for the Thirteenth Five-Year Plan for Economic and Social Development* issued in 2015 requested, "enhancing education quality, promoting the balanced development of compulsory education, promoting equal education, and enhancing teaching and innovation standards of high schools, enabling high schools and disciplines to reach or approximate world-class standards."

Formulating education-centered development plans and programmatic policy documents. Education development was not only characterized in the 5-year national economic and social plans, but also mentioned in several other crucial documents, such as the *Decision of the CPC Central Committee on Education System Reform* issued in 1985, *Outline of Educational Reform and Development in China* issued in 1993, and the *Outline of the National Medium- and Long-Term Program for Education Reform and Development (2010 – 2020)* issued in 2010. These documents stipulated concrete regulations for the prioritization of education, serving as critical guidelines for education development.

Prioritizing government funding for education expenditure

Allocating 4% of government funding to education. During early stages of reform and opening-up, China's economic and social development performance was relatively poor, and education severely lacked funding. In the first decade of reform and opening-up, the education budget declined. Between 1980 and 1993, education spending dropped from 3.17% to 2.97% of the overall GDP, among which, the percentage of government-allocated funds for education dropped from 2.94% to 2.43% of the overall GDP. To ensure that education development was prioritized, the Chinese government proposed a goal in 1993 to increase educational investment to 4% of GDP by the end of 2000. Thereafter, the Chinese government centered its efforts on achieving this goal. It surpassed 4% of GDP for the first time in 2012 (4.28%) and maintained a percentage over 4% for 5 consecutive years.

Ratifying the "three growths" to ensure the continued growth of education funds. To ensure the stable growth of education funds, the *Decision of the CPC Central Committee on Education System Reform* issued in 1985 mentioned, "The increase in education appropriations by the central and local governments shall be higher than that of regular revenue, and the average education expenditure per student enrolled shall increase steadily." The *Outline of Education Reform and Development in China* issued in 1993 further asserted, "teachers' salaries and average public expenditure per student shall increase annually." These regulations completed the construction of the three growths model for government investment in education.

Table 1 shows the changes in public education investment in China from 1980 to 2016.

Table 1. Changes in public education investment in China (1980-2016).

Year	GDP (100 million CNY)	Total education spending (100 million CNY)	Financial funds (100 million CNY)	Percentage of education spending in GDP (%)	Percentage of government funds in GDP (%)
1980	4,587.6	145.5	134.9	3.17	2.94
1985	9,098.9	306.7	262.9	3.37	2.89
1990	18,872.9	659.4	564.0	3.49	2.99
1995	61,339.9	1,878.0	1,411.5	3.06	2.30
2000	100,280.1	3,849.1	2,562.6	3.84	2.56
2005	187,318.9	8,418.8	5,161.1	4.49	2.76
2010	413,030.3	19,561.9	14,670.1	4.74	3.55
2011	489,300.6	23,869.3	18,586.7	4.88	3.80
2012	540,367.4	27,696.0	22,236.2	5.13	4.12
2013	595,244.4	30,364.7	24,488.2	5.10	4.11
2014	643,974.0	32,806.5	26,420.6	5.09	4.10
2015	689,052.1	36,129.2	29,221.45	5.24	4.24
2016	743,585.5	38,888.4	31,396.3	5.23	4.22

Source. China Statistical Year Book 2017 and *China Educational Finance Implementation Statistics Bulletin.*

The growth of the government's education budget exceeded that of regular revenue. Over 35 years (1981 - 2015), the increase in fiscal appropriations for education was higher than or approximate to that of fiscal revenue in most years, which met the requirement that the growth of education appropriations by government departments at various levels shall exceed that of regular revenue (see Figure 2).

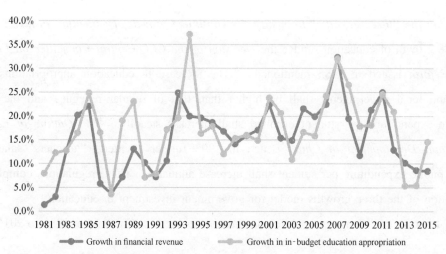

Figure 2. Changes in the growth of fiscal revenue and in-budget education appropriations in China between 1981 and 2015.

Source. China Statistical Year Book and *China Educational Finance Statistical Yearbook.*

The average education expenditure per student enrolled gradually increased. Between 1993 and 2014, in addition to negative growth in the in-budget average education expenditure per student of secondary vocational education and general tertiary education, the in-budget average education expenditure per student at all other levels of education increased annually (see Figure 3).[1]

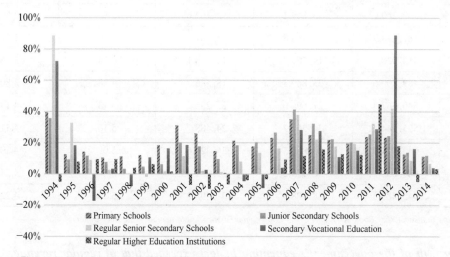

Figure 3. Changes in the growth of in-budget average education expenditure per student at various levels of education in China between 1994 and 2014.

Source. China Educational Finance Statistical Yearbook.

---

1. To ensure data availability and statistical consistency, the in-budget average education expenditure per student statistics and average public expenditure per student statistics between 1993 and 2014 were used. The teacher salary statistics between 1998 and 2014 were used.

Teacher salary and average public expenditure per student increased annually. Between 1993 and 2014, the growth of teacher salaries and average public expenditure per student at various levels of education in most years were higher than zero, suggesting positive annual growth (see Figures 4 and 5).

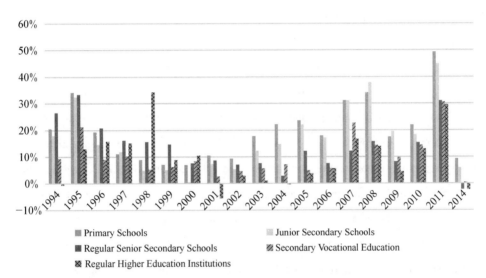

Figure 4. Changes in the growth of average public expenditure per student at various levels of education in China between 1994 and 2014.

Source. China Educational Finance Statistical Yearbook.

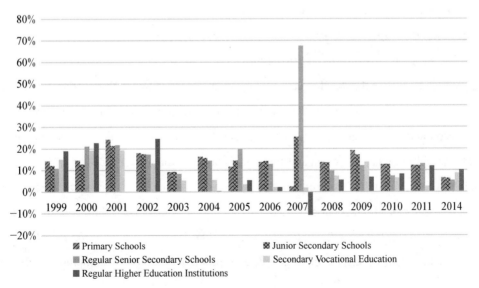

Figure 5. Changes in the growth of teacher salaries at various levels of education in China between 1999 and 2014.

Source. China Educational Finance Statistical Yearbook.

Elucidating the responsibilities of the three levels of government concerning financial investment in education. Prior to the reform and opening-up, China's education budget was managed by a central authority. Over 40 years of education and school, management, and investment systems reform, China's funding system for compulsory education gradually shifted to an allocation model [1] wherein funds are provisioned by the central and local governments on project or pro rata bases (State Council of the People's Republic of China, 2015).

According to the *Outline of Education Reform and Development in China* issued in 1993 and the *Decision on Education Reform and Development in Basic Education* issued by the State Council in 2001, funds for higher education shall be budgeted by city governments or lower, whereas provincial governments shall be responsible for overall planning. The three-level schooling system that involves the central government, provincial governments (autonomous regions and municipalities), and major city governments is adopted for budgeting tertiary education, whereby the central government is primarily responsible for the provisioning of tertiary education funds to the various central ministries, and local governments are responsible for the provisioning of funds to local colleges and universities. This system provides a clear classification system for the appropriation of education funds at various levels of education and the responsibilities of various levels of government, facilitating longterm and stable growth in financial investment in education in China.

Reinforcing the supervision of education appropriation. To ensure that local governments fulfil their education investment responsibilities, continue to increase education appropriations, and appropriately exceed the development of education in accordance with the education investment obligations of government at various levels, the central government constantly increased its efforts in supervision and inspection, thereby ensuring that the government at all levels strictly abided by relevant laws and regulations to expand their financial investment in education.

After 1986, the Standing Committee of the National People's Congress conducted six large-scale national enforcement inspections to determine the implementation conditions of the *Compulsory Education Law of the People's Republic of China* and the *Education Law of the People's Republic of China*. A key item of inspection was the appropriation of funds to compulsory education at

---

1　The funds required to meet average public expenditure per student shall be budgeted by the central and local government on a pro rata basis. The proportion of Western and Central China shall be based on the county (city, district) ratio of 8∶2 ratified in the Policy of Grand Development in Western China, that for other central regions is 6∶4 and for Eastern China is 5∶5.

various levels of governments. In addition, a budget and final account management system as well as an information transparency system were established to urge various levels of government to adopt education as a key domain for public expenditure and guarantee education expenditure by the government. These systems requested that local governments list budget items independently and submit the list to their local people's congress for approval and public announcement. Each year, an annual statistical report on the national and local education funding and expenditure conditions is compiled by a dedicated party and made available to the public, allowing people to supervise the growth and implementation of education funds. This process has provided an institutionalized supervision and management mechanism for ensuring the adherence of various levels of government to their education investment obligations and continually increasing financial appropriations.

Prioritizing public resources for satisfying the requirements of education and human resource development

Adequate financial investment is at the core of prioritizing education development. Nonetheless, relying solely on financial resources for prioritizing education development is insufficient. Only by reasonably combining human capital, financial resources, land, information, and other public resources to form a system that supports education reform and development can the prioritization of education development be truly fulfilled.

Valuing teachers

Enhancing teacher employment standards. The quantity and quality of teachers are the foremost factors in education. Discussions on establishing a teacher qualification system began in China in the 1980s. In 1995, the *Teachers Law of the People's Republic of China* and its implementation regulations were announced, providing a set of standards for the recognition and classification of teacher qualifications and the periodic review of teaching certificates. In addition, the Ministry of Education issued a number of policy documents requesting that teachers continually advance their educational level. The issuance of these documents prompted middle and elementary school teachers to meet national academic standards[1]. The *Suggestions for Strengthening Teacher Training Programs* announced in 2011 mentioned, "As of 2012, a clear

---

1 For example, the *Outline of Education Reform and Development in China* issued by the State Council in 1993 announced the achievement of a fundamental objective, "at the end of the last century, most middle school and elementary school teachers in China met national academic standards through supplementary and in-service training. The number of middle school and elementary school teachers with college or university undergraduate degrees is gradually increasing."

progression of elementary school teachers' education level toward college undergraduate level can be observed. A similar trend can be exhibited in middle school teachers toward university undergraduate level, and the proportion of high school teachers with a graduate degree or higher has increased significantly." In 2015, the proportion of elementary school teachers in China with a college degree or higher reached 91.9%, the proportion of middle school teachers with an undergraduate degree or higher reached 80.2%, the proportion of general high school teachers with an undergraduate degree or higher reached 97.7%, and the proportion of general high school teachers with a graduate degree or higher reached 68.4%. These statistics suggest an exponential overall improvement in the standards of China's teaching resources.

Adjusting teacher staffing standards. Staffing standards govern the number of positions and teacher allocation. Staffing standards were proposed for the first time in 1984 with the release of *Suggestions for the Staffing Standards of Teachers in Middle Normal Schools and Full-Day Middle and Elementary Schools*.[1] The *Suggestions for the Staffing Standards of Teachers in Middle Schools and Elementary Schools* was re-issued in 2001[2], changing staffing ratios from classroom-teacher ratios to student-teacher ratios, and modifying the standards for balancing urban and rural staffing standards to three-tiered staffing standards for cities, counties, and villages. The *Notice on Unifying the Staffing Standards for Elementary and Middle School Teachers* issued in 2014 formed a unified set of staffing standards for elementary and middle school teachers in urban and rural areas. The teacher-student ratios in high schools, middle schools, and elementary schools were 1 : 12.5, 1 : 13.5, and 1 : 19, respectively. Based on the teacher quota standards, national and regional staffing, human resource, and social security

---

1 According to the *Suggestions for the Staffing Standards of Teachers in Middle Normal Schools and Full-Day Middle and Elementary Schools* issued in 1984, the number of students per classroom in urban elementary schools was between 40 and 45, the number of teaching staff per classroom was 2.2, and the number of classroom teachers per classroom was 1.7. The number of students per classroom in rural elementary schools was between 30 and 35, the number of teaching staff per classroom was 1.4, and the number of classroom teachers per classroom was 1.3. The number of students per classroom in urban middle schools was between 45 and 50, the number of teaching staff per classroom was 3.7, and the number of classroom teachers per classroom was 2.5. The number of students per classroom in rural middle schools was between 40 and 45, the number of teaching staff per classroom was 3.5, and the number of classroom teachers per classroom was 2.5. The number of students per classroom in urban high schools was between 45 and 50, the number of teaching staff per classroom was 4.9, and the number of classroom teachers per classroom was 2.8. The number of students per classroom in rural high schools was between 45 and 50, the number of teaching staff per classroom was 4.0, and the number of classroom teachers per classroom was 2.8.

2 According to the *Suggestions for the Staffing Standards of Teachers in Middle Schools and Elementary Schools* issued in 2001, the teaching staff-to-student ratios in city, county, and village elementary schools were 1 : 13.5, 1 : 16, and 1 : 18, respectively. Those in city, county, and village middle schools were 1 : 13.5, 1 : 16, and 1 : 18, respectively. Those in city, county, and village high schools were 1 : 12.5, 1 : 13, and 1 : 13.5, respectively.

departments began coordinating and allocating teachers to their positions in elementary and middle schools, relieving the shortage of teachers and modifying teacher structures, and thereby optimizing staffing and ensuring that basic education schools continue to operate normally and that the basic requirements for education and learning are satisfied.

Improving teacher salaries and status. Respecting both teachers and education is a Chinese tradition. To promote respect for teachers and education nationwide, the Chinese government proclaimed September 10th to be the Teachers' Day in 1985, reinforcing the legal status of public elementary and middle school teachers as civil servants (State Council of the People's Republic of China, 2018) as well as guaranteeing that teachers were paid an average salary of no more or less than the average salary of a public servant and that their salaries would gradually increase over time (Ministry of Education of the People's Republic of China, 1993). According to the statistics released by the National Bureau of Statistics of China, the average salary of employees in urban education industry ranked 12th among the 19 major industries in 2007, rising to 8th in 2016 (see Table 2).

Table 2. Average wage of employed persons comparison in urban units in various industries between 2007 and 2016 (Unit: CNY).

Industry	2007		2016	
	Average salary	Rank	Average salary	Rank
Information transmission, software and information technology	47,700	1	122,478	1
Financial intermediation	44,011	2	117,418	2
Scientific research and technical services	38,432	3	96,638	3
Production and supply of electricity, heat, gas and water	33,470	4	83,863	4
Cultural, sports and entertainment	30,430	5	79,875	6
Mining	28,185	6	60,544	13
Transport, storage and post	27,903	7	73,650	9
Health and social service	27,892	8	80,026	5
Leasing and business service	27,807	9	76,782	7
Public management, social security and social organization	27,731	10	70,959	10
Real estate	26,085	11	65,497	11
Education	**25,908**	**12**	**74,498**	**8**
Manufacturing	21,144	13	59,470	14
Wholesale and retail trades	21,074	14	65,061	12

Continued

Industry	2007		2016	
	Average salary	Rank	Average salary	Rank
Services to households, repair and other services	20,370	15	47,577	17
Construction	18,482	16	52,082	15
Management of water conservancy, environment and public facilities	18,383	17	47,750	16
Hotels and catering services	17,046	18	43,382	18
Agriculture, forestry, animal husbandry, and fishery	10,847	19	33,612	19

Implementing preferential policies to meet the educational needs of public resources. To promote the national and local development of education industry, the government not only increases appropriations, but also levies education surcharges and prioritizes the revenue for improving education and teaching facilities. In addition, the government implements preferential policies for coordinating and allocating school land and schooling resources; implements prioritization and preferential policies for publishing and issuing textbooks and teaching materials as well as producing and supplying teaching instruments and equipment; and provides teacher and student discounts to libraries, museums, sports centers, cultural venues, and other public cultural and sports facilities, historical and cultural sites, and revolutionary memorial halls (sites), thereby enhancing access to educational content.

The promulgation of the *Education Law of the People's Republic of China* in 1995 legally regulated the inclusion of school infrastructure into urban and rural construction plans as well as the responsibilities of local governments to plan and allocate land and resources to building this school infrastructure, in addition to the implementation of prioritization and preferential policies. The *Notice of Education Tax Policies* proposed by the Ministry of Finance and State Administration of Taxation in 2004 further clarified the scope and magnitude of tax exemptions for school land, guaranteeing the physical and mental fulfillment of prioritizing education development. Relevant key national documents regarding prioritizing education development are summarized in Appendix A.

Prioritizing education to promote national development

Education is multifunctional. Prioritizing education to promote national development is the government's means to define China's education functions. This policy coincided with that of prioritizing education development, becoming an internal driving force for China's positive education development.

During the National Education Working Conference held in 1978, Deng Xiaoping (1990) stated, "Education must coincide with the requirements of national economic development" (p. 62). How well adapting to national economic development has always been an indicator of education development performance in China.

On a plaque given to a school in Beijing in 1983, Deng Xiaoping inscribed, "Education must advance toward modernization, the world, and the future," which essentially reflected the government's expectations for education and confirmed the strategic goals and working principles for China's education development.

The *Outline of Education Reform and Development in China* issued in 1993 summarized the main principles for creating a socialist education system with Chinese features, mentioning, "education is the basis for the modernized socialist development," and "we must continue to invest in education to facilitate modernized socialist development, combine education with production and labor, consciously abide by and serve in this hub of economic development, and promote comprehensive social advancement."

At the 3rd National Education Working Conference held in 1999, Jiang Zemin mentioned, "during the initial stages of China's socialist development, adopting education as a basis for economic, political, and cultural development provided the human capital and intellectuals required for modernization development. Human capital must be directly invested into various development projects, thereby encouraging contribution."

In 2017, *Suggestions on the Further Reform of Education Systems and Mechanisms* issued by the State Council comprehensively and systematically presented the requirements for prioritizing education to promote national development, stating, "education should serve the people and the state administration of the CPC. It should serve the reinforcement and development of socialist systems with Chinese features, economic reform of China, and modernized socialism."

"Strengthening education is fundamental to our pursuit of national rejuvenation" (Xi, 2017). This statement was made in the 19th Congress of the CPC, and it perfectly summarizes the concept of dual priority agenda.

Education must serve socialist development, and socialist development must rely on education

The *Decision of the CPC Central Committee on Education System Reform* issued in 1985 mentioned, "Education must serve socialist development, and socialist development must rely on education." This sentence concisely illustrates the independent relationship between prioritizing development and prioritizing satisfaction. Prioritizing education to promote national development has both historical implications and realistic requirements in China.

Confucian tradition

Since ancient times, China has developed a tradition of respecting mentors and teachers. One of the earliest books on education, *Book of Rites: Xue Ji*, mentioned, "Rulers that wish to govern their people effectively and form favorable customs must prioritize education." This ideology became a major feature of the Confucian culture and was adopted by founders as a core value. "Governing people with benevolence" was already advocated during the Wenjin Period of the Han Dynasty, whereby people were taught democracy to maintain national security. Emperor Wu of Han adopted the recommendation of Dong Zhongshu to establish an imperial academy to educate the country. During the Southern Song Dynasty, the leading figure in the School of Principle, Zhu Xi, mentioned, "Education is the foremost aspect of national prosperity and diplomacy." He cited the *Book of Rites: Xiangyin Jiuyi*, "People must learn to respect and care for their elders before they are able to respect their parents and siblings at home. People that respect their parents and love their siblings at home and respect and help elders outside will form morality. Once morality is formed, the security of the country is ensured," promoting "the formation of morality to ensure national security" to the extreme. During the Ming-Qing transition, the ideologies of "practical learning" and "practical application" were popularized in education. They centered on cultivating human capital that benefited the country. More recently, Sun Yat-sen mentioned, "Scholars are a core component of a country. Without immediate amendment to existing laws and the promotion of education, how are we able to cultivate human capital and national resources?" This emphasized that education is the foundation of building a country. Tao Xingzhi firmly asserted, "When people receive adequate education, come to each other's aid, and take responsibility for their country, the foundation of the country would inevitably be strong" (Tao, 1991, p. 693). Tao began one of the largest movements for mass education in China's modern history, fully reproducing the historical tradition of embedding national development requirements into education.

Red gene

Li Dazhao, one of the founders of the CPC, has long advocated that educators spread the seeds of light in society, stating, "Knowledge is a candle guiding people to the light and truth" (Chen, 1984, p. 8). Li believed that wholly embracing education would "open up a new road for people's lives" (Chen, 1984, p. 176).

Mao Zedong passionately advocated that education should serve China's reform and the country. During the Chinese Soviet Republic era of 1934, Mao stated, "The Soviets must undergo cultural education reform, lift the constraints that the reactionary ruling class has imposed on the morale of farmers and laborers, and create a new Soviet culture centered on farmers and laborers" (Mao, 1934/1991, p. 282). Mao proposed a general principle for cultural education, stating, "Cultural education must serve reform and class conflict, facilitate the integration of education and labor, and allow the Chinese public to enjoy a happy and civilized society" (Mao, 1934/1991, p. 285). In 1942, Mao asserted that the economy and education were the two focal aspects during the crisis at the Shaan-Gan-Ning Border Region, stating, "Discussing education or learning without accounting for the economy is nothing more than empty words" (Mao, 1942/1986, p. 565). A popular work of Mao published in 1957, *New Democracy*, mentioned, "Our education policy should focus on the moral, intellectual, and physical development of learners, helping them grow into cultural laborers with a consciousness for socialism." This statement became a consistent education ideology of the CPC.

International competition demands

In 1980, Deng Xiaoping provided a brief assessment of the international situation in the 1980s, stating, "the various tasks for building a powerful and modernized socialist nation are interrelated" (Deng, 1993), emphasizing that human capital and education are fundamental aspects.[1]

1　Deng Xiaoping emphasized "vigorously fostering science and technology talent" during the opening ceremony of the Science Conference of China held in 1978, stating, "education is the foundation for the fostering of science and technology talent."

Confronted with the changes in international conditions in the 1990s, national leaders realized,

> Amidst changes in today's political climate, increasing intensity in international competition, and rapid technological advancement, global economic competition and overall national competition are essentially the competition of science, technology, and national quality ... In this context, whoever controls education will have a strategic competitive advantage in the 21st century. Therefore, we must have foresight and plan for China's education early to meet the challenges of the 21st century. (He, 1998, p. 3467)

Entering the 21st century, Chinese leaders further emphasized human capital is the key to the development and reinvigoration of China, and education is the foundation for fostering human capital. Therefore, they requested the deepening of education reform, allowing education to more effectively meet national development and competitive advancement needs.

Three stages to meet national development requirements: Upscaling, structural adjustment, and quality enhancement

Upscaling education and resolving insufficient placement problems

During early reform and opening-up, the years of education received by the working population were fewer than 5 years. Nearly 10% of children attended preschool, 60% attended middle school, 20% attended high school, and 1% attended university. Chinese families hoped that their children could attend school, and the country hoped to "foster more and better professionals" (He, 1998, p. 2285). Upscaling education and increasing the GER at all three levels of education were the foremost education-related challenges faced by China during the early period of reform and opening-up. In response, China first focused on establishing a 9-year compulsory education system while simultaneously developing secondary and tertiary education.

Universalizing compulsory education. In 1980, the State Council announced the *Decisions on Resolving the Issues Concerning the Universalization of Primary Education*, stating, "In the 1980s, the historical mission of universalizing primary education shall be achieved nationwide, with able regions universalizing secondary education." In 1985, the State Council further announced the *Decision of the CPC Central Committee on Education System Reform*, stating, "basic education in China remains lagging, which shows a stark contrast with other modernized socialist countries." In response, the State Council asserted, "the implementation of 9-year compulsory education should be strongly associated with the improvement of national standards and prosperity."[1] *Compulsory Education Law* was passed in April 1986. The government used legislature to ensure implementation of the 9-year compulsory education system in China. Since then, China has made great strides in universalizing compulsory education.

First, the 14th National Congress of the CPC held in October 1992 mentioned, "at the end of the last century, illiteracy among teenagers had been essentially eliminated, and implementation of 9-year compulsory education has been achieved in China." Furthermore, the "double 85%" objective was achieved in 1994. At the end of the twentieth century, the 9-year compulsory education system was implemented in regions that accounted for 85% of the population, and the GER at the secondary education level achieved 85%.

Second, the *Two Basic Action Plans on Education (2004 - 2007)* centered on the western regions of China were implemented in 2004. The plans were fulfilled at the end of 2007. The population coverage of the plan achieved 98% in 2007. In November 2011, all of the county administration departments and provincial administrative divisions in China conducted a full-scale survey to evaluate the universalization of the 9-year compulsory education system, and the elimination of illiteracy among teenagers and young adults, completing a historical strategic task.

Third, an announcement was made that, "all tuition and fees for compulsory education in urban public schools shall be exempted as of fall 2008," achieving the objective of free education.

Increasing the universalization of high school education. Because of a large population and relatively poor education structure, the government was only able to promote a few high-priority high schools when universalizing the 9-year compulsory education system. Subsequently, the lag in general high school education became increasingly evident. In response, the *Outline of Education Reform and Development in China* issued in 1993 mentioned, "actively universalizing high school education concurrently with the implementation of the 9-year compulsory education system in metropolitan and developed coastal regions" for the first time. Thereafter, enrollment and attendance at general high schools have increased annually. The advancement rate from middle to high school increased from 40.6% in 1990 to 51.2% in 2000, and graduation and advancement rate in high schools increased from 27.3% in 1990 to 73.2% in 2000.

---

1 The document defined compulsory education as the guarantee of national education necessary for the development of modern production and social survival of school-age children and adolescents by the country, society, and family by law. Such education is a symbol of modern civilization.

Entering the twenty-first century, the development of high school education in China has shifted into the fast lane. The State Council announced the *Decision on Education Reform and Development in Basic Education* in 2001, providing instructions to, "vigorously develop high school education, promote the coordinated development of high school education, and systematically universalize high school education in large and medium cities and economically developed regions." In 2016, the high school GER rose to 87.5%, and in the same year, the Ministry of Education and three other government departments jointly proposed the *Guideline for Popularizing High School Education (2017–2020)*, proclaiming an objective to achieve a high school advancement rate of 90% by 2020.

Achieving the universalization of tertiary education. Between the 1980s and mid-1990s, the GER for tertiary education in China was roughly 5%. The *Outline of Education Reform and Development in China* issued in 1994 mentioned that, "6.3 million students enrolled in general and adult universities and colleges in 2000. Among this number, 1.8 million were undergraduates, and 4.5 million were college students. The enrollment rate for students between ages 18 and 21 years rose by roughly 8%." The outline accelerated the development of tertiary education; however, at the end of the 1990s, the pressure of employment and further education among tertiary-level students rose exponentially. In response to rapidly changing trends, the Chinese government implemented a plan in 1999 to expand the enrollment rate of colleges and universities, expanding the enrollment rate of general colleges and universities by roughly 50%, from 1.08 million in 1998 to 1.59 million in 1999 (see Figure 6). The enrollment rate continued to rise incrementally by another 45% over the next three years. With the sequential rise in the enrollment rate in the several years that followed, the scale of enrollment for general colleges and universities reached 3.20 million in 2002. The GER for tertiary education rapidly increased by over 15%, verifying the initial universalization of tertiary education [1]. The GER for tertiary education in China continued to rise into the twenty-first century, reaching 42.7% in 2016. However, a decline in population at the tertiary level occurred because of China's family planning policy. Nonetheless, by 2020, the GER for tertiary education is expected to surpass 50%.

---

1   Historically, the United States, Korea, Japan, and Brazil respectively spent 30, 14, 23, and 26 years promoting their GER in tertiary education from 5% to 15%. China roughly spent a decade raising its GER in tertiary education from 3.4% (1990) to 15% (2002).

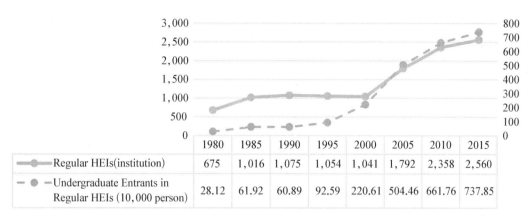

Figure 6. Number of regular higher education institutions and number of undergraduate entrants in regular higher education institutions between 1980 and 2015.

Adjusting the structure and adapting to changes in the national economic structure

During the initial period of reform and opening-up, China was a leading country in agriculture, and 70% of its population resided in farming villages. In the early 1980s, primary, secondary, and tertiary industries accounted for 30.1%, 48.5%, and 21.4% of China's overall GDP, respectively[1]. Amidst advancements in production quality and the progression of urbanization over 4 decades, China's urbanization rate surpassed 55% in 2016. This changed the proportions of primary, secondary, and tertiary industries in China's overall GDP to 8.6%, 39.8%, and 51.6%, respectively. The requirement for human resources in economic development changed concurrently with the adjustment of industrial structures. To meet these requirements, the education structure in China is constantly changing.

Adjusting general vocational school structures. In the early 1980s, the secondary education structure was fairly unitary. "Besides a few high school graduates advancing to university, millions of graduates entered the labor force without specialized knowledge or skills each year. Simultaneously, industries were in dire need of skilled professionals. However, newly employed workers had to undergo apprenticeship for 2 to 3 years, which hindered labor production" (He, 1998, p. 1855).

In 1980, the Ministry of Education and the Ministry of Human Resources and Social Security jointly announced the *Report of the Reform and Development of Technical and Vocational Education*, mentioning, "In order for high school education to conform with the requirements of

---

[1] Source: *China Statistical Year Book*; ratio of the three education levels in corresponding year.

socialist modernization development, general education and vocational/technical education must be promoted concurrently, full-time schools and part-time/spare-time schools must be promoted concurrently, and national education and sales departments/factories and mining enterprises/community schooling must be promoted concurrently." The education system reform of 1985 requested that the enrollment rate of high school-level vocational and technical schools match that of general high schools and that establishing reasonable structures and vocational education systems that communicate with general education be adopted as the primary objectives for adjusting general vocational structures. By the end of 1990, the number of secondary-level vocational schools increased from 4,773 in 1978 to 8,173, and enrollment rate between general high schools and secondary vocational schools increased from 3.7 : 1 in 1980 to 1.1 : 1 (see Figure 7).

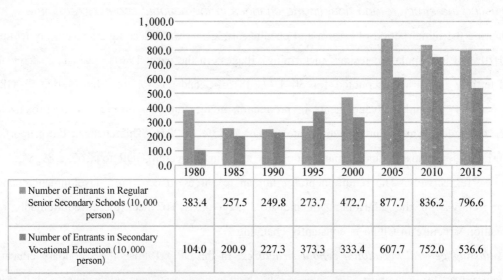

Figure 7. Number of students enrolled in regular senior secondary schools and secondary vocational education between 1980 and 2015.

In the same period, tertiary vocational education rapidly developed. By 2016, the number of vocational (technical) colleges reached 1,359, which was roughly 52.3% of all general colleges and universities, suggesting that vocational education accounted for half of all tertiary education in China.

Adjusting university specialization structures. Vital adjustments to specialization structures in tertiary education were conducted concurrently with the structural adjustment of secondary education. After the initial reform and opening-up, China underwent four major adjustments to specialization structures at the tertiary education level.

The first adjustment of specialization structures occurred in 1984, focusing on "resolving the over-classification of professions and expanding the scope of specialization operations to reinforce scientific foundations, improve education quality, and strengthen talent adaptability" (He, 1998, p. 2202). After the adjustment, the number of professions in colleges and universities reduced from 1,039 in 1980 to 870 in 1988. In addition to an increase in the number of professions under the teaching, liberal arts, law, sports, and art specializations, the number of professions in the remaining six specializations decreased.

The second adjustment of specialization structures occurred in 1989, focusing on "valuing investment and social performance, correctly handling quantitative and qualitative relationships, forming reasonable specialization structures and networks, avoiding unnecessary repetitive settings, and ensuring stable development while guaranteeing quality and performance" (He, 1998, p. 2854). After the adjustment, a batch of specializations were adjusted and consolidated, and specialization content was enriched and expanded, forming a total of ten disciplines, 71 categories and 504 specializations. The number of specializations was 309 fewer than before the adjustment. Among them, 56 were interdisciplinary specializations urgently required in China, including those in information engineering, computer science, and computer software.

The third adjustment of specialization structures occurred in 1997, focusing on changing the over-emphasis of specialization-vocation matching to all-round development, which had a positive effect on expanding the specializations of colleges and universities, enhancing adaptability, strengthening professional development and management, and improving educational standards and talent development quality.[1] Compared with the previous directory, the specialization directory of 1998 adjusted the number of disciplines and specializations to 11 and 249, respectively, for a downward revision of 50.6%. A comparison between the old and new directories showed that the new directory not only added, adjusted, or removed professions to meet immediate national requirements but also added new high-tech specializations, which promoted the development of material science and construction, marine science, environmental engineering, electrical science and technology, and information and computer technology.

The fourth adjustment of specialization structures occurred in 2010. The 2010 specialization

---

1 Based on the *Notice on Amending the Undergraduate Profession Directory in General Colleges and Universities* issued by the Ministry of Education in 2010. http://www.moe.gov.cn/srcsite/A08/moe_1034/s3882/201012/t20101206_112726.html.

directory retained a batch of professions that were more mature, in stable demand, offered in more locations, and were more inheritable; adjusted a batch of specializations that were unclear, unstandardized, and less distinct; and added a batch of emerging specializations that were strategically beneficial to industrial development and the improvement of livelihood as well as being highly applicable and industry specific, such as logistics management and engineering, e-commerce, and rail transit signal and control.

From the initial adjustment and optimization of undergraduate specializations in 1987 to 2016, the number of specializations concerning primary industries reduced from 69 to 35, those concerning secondary industries reduced from 505 to 251, and those concerning tertiary industries increased from 276 to 309.

Enhancing quality to adapt to national economic restructuring

Rapid advancements in science and technology and the advent of the information era have constantly posed new challenges for people's qualities and demands. As the Chinese government channeled its efforts into increasing enrollment rates at various education levels, it also continually increased the quality and specifications of fostering human capital, changed the content of talent qualities, and prompted the transition of an extensive, labor-based economy into an intensive, knowledge-based economy.

Restoring order to education and fulfilling the two basic action plans on education. At the end of the 1970s and following the Cultural Revolution that lasted a decade, China's education system was left in complete ruin, and students lacked basic knowledge and training. China began rebuilding its education system in 1977, gradually restoring order to school education. In January 1978, the Ministry of Education announced the *Full-Time Ten-Year Primary and Secondary School Teaching Plan*, mentioning, "We must reinforce cultural education and teach students to diligently study for the revolution. Students should acquire a basic knowledge of advanced cultural science and its theoretical implications, gradually developing self-learning and self-analysis abilities" (He, 1998, p. 1593). In the same year, the Ministry of Education implemented a draft version of the *Temporary Working Regulations for Full-Time Middle School Education* and the *Temporary Working Regulations for Full-Time Elementary Education*. The objective for fostering full-time middle school students was to "allow students to expand the knowledge acquired in elementary school to continue fostering their basic language, mathematics, and foreign language knowledge and skills, gradually developing self-learning, self-analysis, and problem-solving abilities; gaining production knowledge; and forming the habit of enjoying, learning, and using science" (He, 1998, p. 1630); the objective of fostering full-time elementary school students was "to foster students' preliminary reading, writing, and calculating abilities; general knowledge concerning nature and society; and positive learning habits" (He, 1998, pp. 1635 - 1636).

In addition, the working regulations stipulated that mathematics classes should aim to strengthen the teaching of basic mathematics and the training of fundamental skills. School works gradually improved, and a quality education system was established.

Overcoming the one-sided pursuit of education and achieving all-rounded development. With the comprehensive restoration of order to fundamental education and learning as well as college and university entrance examination systems, an unprecedented rise in the pursuit of education by long-suppressed Chinese students occurred. Schools began "focusing on advancement rates rather than preparing students for employment, and on test scores rather than ethical and physical education and the fostering of basic knowledge and skills" (He, 1998, p. 2148). In response, the Ministry of Education issued *Suggestions on Further Improving the Quality of Education in General Middle Schools* in 1983, requiring, "reforming and strengthening students' ideological and political works" and "alleviating students' burden, allowing them to actively learn and foster intelligence and capability; teaching content shall more suitably meet labor and further education needs." The *Decision of the CPC Central Committee on Education System Reform* issued in 1985 further indicated that the personnel required by the country must "exhibit ideals, morals, culture, and discipline; be passionate about the socialist motherland and socialist operations; be willing to sacrifice themselves for the prosperity of the country and its people; and demonstrate a scientific mindset for constantly pursuing new knowledge, seeking truth, thinking independently, and boldly creating." The *Outline of Education Reform and Development in China* issued in 1993 mentioned that schools at various levels must train participants of and successors to the socialist cause who develop morally, intellectually, and physically, emphasizing, "Middle and elementary schools shall steer the 'examination-centered education' toward enhancing quality and comprehensively fostering the ideological and moral, cultural and scientific, labor and skill, and physical and mental qualities of all students, thereby allowing students to develop actively and vividly." These documents reflect the renewed requirements for quality and competence from economic and social development.

Emphasizing key competences. *Decisions on Deepening Education Reform and the Comprehensive Implementation of Quality Education* was issued by the State Council in 1999, which asserted,

> In today's world, science and technology are rapidly advancing, knowledge economies are emerging, and national competition is intensifying. Education is a fundamental component in the formation of national power, and national power is becoming increasingly dependent on the quality of the workforce and the quality and quantity of human capital. These trends have created new and urgent demands for fostering and promoting new professionals in the twenty-first century. ... With the emergence of new trends, our existing subjectivities and objectivities have caused our education ideologies, education systems, education structures, talent cultivation methods, education content, and education methods to lag behind those of other countries, hindering our youths from all-round development and our ability to meet national standards. (State Council of the People's Republic of China, 1999)

It proposed a key ideology of "implementing quality education," which emphasized "the development of students' creative spirit and practical abilities." The *Outline of the National Medium- and Long-Term Program for Education Reform and Development (2010 – 2020)* issued in 2010 further emphasized that the key to implementing quality education was "the comprehensive development of all students, enhancing their sense of duty toward serving their country and its people, and cultivating their creative spirit for bold exploration and practical skills to solve problems." The *CPC Central Committee Recommendations for the Thirteenth Five-Year Plan for Economic and Social Development* issued in 2015 provided instructions to, "deepen education reform and prioritize the enhancement of students' sense of social responsibility, creative spirit, and practical abilities in national education," which further emphasized fostering people's qualities. A list of key national documents on prioritizing education to promote national development is included in Appendix B.

Concluding remarks

Since 1978, China has focused on achieving modernization of its education system. By being led by reform and opening-up, rooting in the national context, and referencing the experiences of advanced countries, China formed an interactive and reciprocal model to prioritize both education development and education to promote national development, paving a path to pursue and surpass international standards.

Understanding and handling the relationships between national and social development are challenges shared by all leaders, and frequently discussed in academia. Fagerlind and Saha (1983) classified the relationships between education and national development into four types: developed capitalist countries, underdeveloped capitalist countries, developed socialist countries, and underdeveloped socialist countries. Moreover, they analyzed the associations between education and national development in two dimensions: economic levels and social systems. They believed that the most prominent differences in the relationships between education and national development in capitalist countries and socialist countries are that capitalist countries promote education for individual achievement, focusing on the intrinsic value of education, whereas socialist countries promote education for collective achievement, focusing on the instrumental value of education (Fagerlind & Saha, 1983, p. 208).

Associating socialism with planning economies and collective goals, as well as associating capitalism with market economies and individual goals, forms a common ideological model in both Western and Eastern countries. However, this model cannot fully reflect modern situations. The goal to construct a socialist market economy system was clearly proposed for the first time in the 14th Congress of the CPC in 1994, proposing the merging of a fundamental socialist system with a market economy to establish a socialist market economy system. A socialist market economy is primarily a state-owned economy that prioritizes collective interests and protects private assets, respecting individual interests, encouraging market competition, and motivating individual activity. Since its reform and opening-up, China has centered its efforts on minimizing the tension between individual development and collective objectives in education. Tsang (2000) clearly highlighted that after reform and opening-up, the CPC centered party efforts on economic development; however, these efforts caused a conflict between social fairness and justice as well as political theory development, which constituted the broad social and historic environment for the development of the education system. The historical economic and political achievements of the CPC reflected its ability to adapt to social reform. In the future, it may further expand its control over the government and society, affecting the direction and pace of future social reform. Education remains the source of the science, technology, and human resources required for national development. Education policies should clearly highlight the "who, how and what" of education. Therefore, education has the potential to affect the agencies and departments involved in the formation of national development policies.

China has a historical tradition of respecting teachers and education. Regardless of prosperity or crisis, China has always valued personnel training and education development. After the reform and opening-up, China proposed a model comprising "three priorities" and "three growths" to prioritize education development, to supply the country with the human resources required to achieve national modernization, and to convert immense population burden into social wealth. Similarly, China has always valued the social value of education, setting the satisfaction of social and national development as the foremost objective of education. Social development requirements are immediately reported to education authorities, which then propose work requirements and formulate relevant policies that coincide with the priority development policies.

The model of DPA was neither created on the first attempt nor simply developed linearly. Rather, it gradually materialized as China endured numerous major social changes. Furthermore, the complementary effects of the DPA were formed through incremental adaptation and development. During the past decade, the DPA and its complementary effects have become more apparent. The DPA can be anticipated to continue facilitating national development and accelerating the modernization of China's education system in the future.

References

Chen, D. (1984). *A compilation of selected works of Chen Duxiu* (Vol. II) [in Chinese]. SDX Joint Publishing Company.

Coase, R. H., & Wang, N. (2012). *How China became capitalist*. Palgrave Macmillan.

Deng, X. (1978). *Speech at the National Education Working Conference* [in Chinese]. http://www.jyb.cn/info/jyzck/200602/t20060227_11491.html

Deng, X. (1990). *Deng Xiaoping's works on education* [in Chinese]. People's Education Press.

Deng, X. (1993). *Selected works of Deng Xiaoping* (Vols. 2 - 3) [in Chinese]. People's Publishing House.

Fagerlind, I., & Saha, L. J. (1983). *Education and national development: A comparative perspective*. Pergamon Press.

Fairbank, J. K. (1983). *The United States and China* (4th ed.). Harvard University Press.

Fairbank, J. K. (1992). *China: A new history*. Harvard University Press.

He, D. (Ed.) (1998). *Major education documents of China* [in Chinese]. Hainan Publishing House.

Hu, J. (2006, September 1). *Speech at the 34th collective learning session held by the Central Politburo of the CPC* [in Chinese]. http://www.most.gov.cn/yw/200609/t20060901_35754.htm

Hu, J. (2007, September 1). Speech at the Forum of Outstanding Teachers [in Chinese]. *People's Daily*.

Jiang, Z. (1995, June 5). Speech at the Academicians Conference [in Chinese]. *People's Daily*.

Jiang, Z. (1999, June 16). Speech at the National Education Working Conference [in Chinese]. *People's Daily*.

Jiang, Z. (2006). *Selected works of Jiang Zemin* (Editorial Committee on Party Literature of the Central Committee, Ed.) [in

Chinese]. People's Publishing House.

Ministry of Education of the People's Republic of China. (1993). *Teachers law of the People's Republic of China* [in Chinese]. http://old.moe.gov.cn/publicfiles/business/htmlfiles/moe/moe_619/200407/1314.html

Mao, Z. (1934/1991). Report and conclusion on the second All China Congress of Soviets by the Central Steering Committee and People's Committee of the Chinese Soviet Republic [in Chinese]. In *Soviet China*, Chinese Modern History Editorial Committee.

Mao, Z. (1942/1986). Benefits that people can see. In Editorial Committee on Party Literature of the Central Committee (Ed.), *Selected Works by Mao Zedong* (Vol. II) [in Chinese]. People's Publishing House.

State Council of the People's Republic of China. (1999). *Decisions on deepening education reform and the comprehensive implementation of quality education* [in Chinese]. http://www.moe.edu.cn/jyb_sjzl/moe_177/tnull_2478.html

State Council of the People's Republic of China. (2015). *Notice on further perfecting the funding guarantee system for urban & rural compulsory education drawn by the State Council of the People's Republic of China* [in Chinese]. http://www.gov.cn/zhengce/content/2015-11/28/content_10357.htm

State Council of the People's Republic of China. (2018). *State Council of the People's Republic of China suggestions on deepening the establishment and reform of new generation teacher teams* [in Chinese]. http://www.gov.cn/xinwen/2018-01/31/content_5262659.htm

Tao, X. (1991). *Advocating mass education* [in Chinese]. Sichuan Education Publishing House.

Tsang, M. C. (2000). Education and national development in China since 1949: Oscillating policies and enduring dilemmas. *China Review*, 579–618.

Xi, J. (2013, September 27). Speech at the one-year anniversary event of the UNGEFI [in Chinese]. *People's Daily*. http://cpc.people.com.cn/n/2013/0927/c64094-23052930.html

Xi, J. (2017, October 18). Speech at the 19th National Congress of the CPC [in Chinese]. *People's Daily*. http://www.xinhuanet.com/2017-10/27/c_1121867529.htm

Appendix A

Table A1. National documents containing statements related to prioritizing education development.

Year	Document name	Description
1985	Decision of the CPC Central Committee on Education System Reform	From this day forth and in a specific amount of time, the increase in education appropriations by the central and local governments shall be higher than that of regular revenue and the average education expenditure per student enrolled shall increase steadily.
1987	Report of the 13th National Congress of the CPC	The development of science, technology, and education must be prioritized, allowing technological advancement and increased labor quality to facilitate economic development.
1992	Report of the 14th National Congress of the CPC	We must prioritize education development and strive to enhance the ideological, moral, scientific, and cultural standards of our people. This is the fundamental plan to modernize China.
1993	Outline of Education Reform and Development in China	Legislation was passed to ensure the stable provision and growth of education funding.

Continued

Year	Document name	Description
1995	Education Law of the People's Republic of China	Education is the basis of the socialist modernization drive, and the State ensures priority to the development of educational undertakings.
1997	Report of the 15th National Congress of the CPC	Education and science development is the basis of cultural development. The development of education must be prioritized in relevant strategies.
1999	Decisions on Deepening Education Reform and Comprehensive Implementation of Quality Education	Party and State Council members shall fully ensure the prioritization of education development, increase education investment, and gradually increase financial spending on education to 4% of the overall GDP.
2002	Report of the 16th National Congress of the CPC	Education is the foundation for scientific and technological advancement and personnel training. Playing a vanguard role and having an overall bearing on the modernization drive, education must be placed on our development agenda as a strategic priority.
2010	Outline of the National Medium- and Long-Term Program for Education Reform and Development (2010–2020)	The prioritization of education development is a major long-term plan proposed by the CPC and the government to ensure the prioritization of education development in national economic and social plans, government funding for education, and public resources for satisfying the requirements of education and human resource development and increasing the proportion of financial spending on education in the overall GDP (achieving 4% by 2012).
2012	Report of the 18th National Congress of the CPC	We must attribute a high priority to developing education, fully implement the Party's education policy, and ensure that education serves socialist modernization and the people.
2017	Report of the 19th National Congress of the CPC	Giving priority to developing education: Strengthening education is fundamental to our pursuit of national rejuvenation. We must attribute priority to education.

Appendix B

Table B1. National documents containing statements of prioritizing education to promote national development.

Year	Document name	Description
1982	Report of the 12th National Congress of the CPC	We shall ensure that education serves socialist modernization, improve education structures, and enhance education quality according to actual requirements, thereby ensuring that education meets realistic expectations, not just the one-sided pursuit of academic advancement.
1993	Outline of Education Reform and Development in China	We must enhance labor quality, foster immense human capital, and construct education systems that coincide with the economic systems and politics of socialist markets and technology system reform, thereby serving the development of socialist modernization more effectively.

Continued

Year	Document name	Description
1997	Report of the 15th National Congress of the CPC	The key to achieving socialism in the twenty-first century is fostering billions of high-quality laborers and millions of dedicated professionals to coincide with modernization requirements and maximize China's immense human capital advantage.
1999	Decisions on Deepening Education Reform and Comprehensive Implementation of Quality Education	We shall endeavor to close the gap between education and the economy and technology, thereby integrating education, economics, and technology.
2010	Outline of the National Medium- and Long-Term Program for Education Reform and Development (2010 – 2020)	We shall ensure that education serves socialist modernization and the people, combine with productive labor and social practice, and train participants of and successors to the socialist cause to develop morally, intellectually, physically, and aesthetically.
2012	Report of the 18th National Congress of the CPC	We shall ensure that education serves socialist modernization and the people, make fostering integrity and promoting rounded development of the people the fundamental tasks of education, and train participants of and successors to the socialist cause who develop morally, intellectually, physically and aesthetically.
2017	Suggestions on Deepening Education System Reform	Education should serve the people and the state administration of the CPC. It should serve the reinforcement and development of socialist systems with Chinese features, China's economic reform, and modernized socialism.
2017	Report of the 19th National Congress of the CPC	We must attribute priority to education, speed its modernization, and develop education that people are satisfied with.

As one of the earliest scholars engaged in the study of Chinese education policy, the author attempts to sort out the efforts made and lessons learned by researchers in the field of education policy in China in this article. Based on the academic publications, symposia, and thematic research, the article argues that there is now a correspondence among the ideas, themes, forms, and frameworks of the educational reform promulgated by the government in recent years that have appeared in educational policy research, but there is no clear demarcation of what makes an educational policy researcher; no stable academic community has been formed that might strive together toward the foundation of a disciplinary paradigm, the rational organization of academic ideas, and the establishment and handing over of a theoretical framework to a succeeding generation. In a word, a paradigm for Chinese educational policy research is still nascent in the arduous process of formulation. This article contributes to the understanding of the current states of Chinese education policy research.

Chinese Educational Policy Research: The Arduous Formation of a Research Paradigm[1]

Xiaoying Lin

Chinese educational policy research in the 40 years since reform and opening-up may be examined in two periods: the first 20 years and the latter 20 years. In the first 20 years, a host of articles were published dealing with promulgation of the new policy, general policy suggestions, and retrospectives of policy studies; innovative theoretical framework construction or actual research on policy phenomena were rare. In the latter 20 years, however, educational policy research has gradually become a hot educational research topic. Internationally, educational policy research has been developing very quickly as a new field of educational research since the 1980s, becoming the most prominent component of international education research and the focal point generating the most attention.

---

1   This article is partially based on the authors' recent review of Chinese educational policy studies, which was published as a Chinese-language article in the journal *Educational Research Monthly* (*Jiaoyu Xueshu Yuekan*) in December 2018 pp. 3 – 11. The use of this version has been authorized by *Educational Research Monthly* and acknowledged by *ECNU Review of Education*. It was published on *ECNU Review of Education*, 2(4), 544 – 560.

This phenomenon is not unique to education. It is a reflection on the entire social discipline of where social science applications are heading. Since the 1980s, an integrated discipline has been developing with unusual alacrity: public policy ... Strictly speaking, this is not really a course of study so much as it is a developmental trend which almost all social sciences are exhibiting, an applicable shift in emphasis from theoretical speculation on the 'What is it?' to the 'How is it done?' Internationally, prominent researchers in every discipline now almost all participate in policy research pertaining to those disciplines. In both theory and practice, the most influential research findings have nearly all been related to policy. (Yuan, 2000, pp. 1-2)

It is precisely with this understanding, together with the development toward an empirical and experiential orientation in education research, that educational policy research has asserted the need to utilize first-hand experience, collect empirical data, construct logical evidence chains, and draw clear conclusions that can be made into policy suggestions or that have policy implications, all of these forming an essential component of educational policy research and a new paradigm of empirical orientation in educational policy research that has begun to spring up with the criticism of analytical and commentary policy research. Around the year 2000, China published a number of textbooks and monographs all identically titled *Educational Policy Studies*, but the research topics mentioned in these works do not today seem to have developed into individual branches of academic study. As the government has introduced all manner of education reforms, almost none concerning educational policy research in the field of academia have crossed the threshold. Among more and more keyword lists and "research interests" presented in theses and curriculum vitae from educational researchers, the word "policy" has appeared with increasing frequency. This has caused "educational policy research" to seem even more like a chance result of changes in educational practice, rather than a natural evolutionary development in the course of academic or disciplinal progress, and it is difficult to frame it as an independent and serious theme for research.

Thus, this essay intends to clarify, organize, and summarize the relationships that have been established between the ideas, themes, and methods that appear in all manner of educational policy research and the various forms and styles of educational reform that have been promulgated in our time.

Calling for policy-oriented research and research-oriented policy

In the past 20 years, works in China dealing with educational policy have been mostly compilations of policy documents intended for the use of researchers in various fields studying historical evidence of the administration of education by the government of a particular time period, for instance, the *Anthology of Laws and Decrees on Primary and Secondary Education Policy* (1949 – 1966) put out by Institute of Educational Science Research of Beijing Normal University, the *Anthology of Foundational Laws on Foreign Education* from the State Council's Office for Research and Discussion of Educational Affairs, or *Key Studies on Education Policies and Regulations* from the Shaanxi Primary School Principal Training and Continuing Education series, as well as some practical works discussing education policy regulations in other countries. The research literature on educational policy from this period in China's history was still made from a perspective within government administration, with the intent being to increase the quality and efficiency of key policies. In 1996, Yuan published *Educational Policy Studies*, systematically transplanting and recommending theories and patterns in the field of public policy, and categorizing the policy process into formulation, implementation, and evaluation stages, individually categorizing and introducing mid-level and microlevel concepts and theories. In subsequent editions, the author intentionally introduces policy research methods such as ethnographical discussions and investigations of the relationship between researchers and policymakers and asserts that both sides have a need to mingle and communicate (Yuan, 1996). Following this path, Yuan in 2000 published a book called *On Changes of Chinese Educational Policy: A Case Study on the Relationship between Equality and Benefit in Key Middle Schools*, in which he empirically discusses experiential research on acclimation to the peculiarity of the Chinese circumstance using a Western public policy theory framework. The author brings up the question of whether the emphasis of education should be on outstanding talent or on the masses, or in other words whether nurturing a few exceptionally talented individuals or the entire school-age population of young people should be the core aim; this is a problem encountered in any country when setting education policy, and the theoretical issue behind this decision is that of equality and benefit in education. This research when it was published not only echoed the core theme of the government's education reform to "equalize school conditions for compulsory education," but the focus of the theory behind this research—the conflicting relationship between "fairness and efficiency"—made conspicuous the value dilemma of what was most important in education reform during the previous 20 years. Looking at it from the perspective of establishing China's education policy research paradigm, the greater import of this research is that it reveals the author's growing conscientious understanding of method and research standardization and opens an age of positivism in China's education policy research.

From the year 2000, Zhenguo Yuan has been chief editor for 17 volumes of *Chinese Education Policy Review*, gathering thematic dissertations on education policy research, publishing book format periodical collections and in appendices laying out a timeline of important developments in Chinese education policy research for the past year (Yuan, 2000 – 2017). The project is useful as a weathervane and signpost for China education policy research of the past 20 years, allowing us to glimpse the paths Chinese educational policy has followed and the corresponding changes in research themes. From Volume 1 of 2000 through Volume 5 of 2004, every volume collected research theses into two modules: discussion of theory and commentary on practice. In the theory discussion section of every issue, the effort on the parts of both the editor and contributing researchers in the disciplinal and academic aspects of educational policy research is plain to see. In the "How to better design education policy" section of Volume 1 of 2000, a group of education policy research pioneers discuss topics including the relation between key education policy decisions and policy research, the value foundation of education policy, the cost of education policy decisions, uncertainties in policy activity, factors influencing education policy, and the extent of such policies' power. These all point to the principal problem layer of education policy research and offer a deep and detailed discussion of general problems that permeate the process of policy determination. We can see how researchers facing the imminent emergence and application of results from the theoretical field of public policy research upon the actual circumstances of Chinese education practice might in academic aspiration engage in accommodative changes, critical evaluation, or theory construction.

However, comparing the research on education practice of these first five volumes with the research on policy after 2005 makes it clearer that these may be classified as critical and discursive research styles. When engaging in research on education policy introduced by the government, researchers are not actually adhering to the reciprocity in the roles of "policy researcher" and "research policymaker" that the chief editor later strongly advocated, but are instead playing the detached role of a pure researcher standing outside his field of study. Moves since 1999 such as the policy to increase high school enrollment, measures to spur the economy through education, private school development and regulation, the industrialization of education, and the "3+X" *gaokao* reform program have for the most part been analyzed objectively and rationally.

As chief editor, Yuan's critical demarcation of "policy culture" from "academic culture" in educational activity caused a swift upsurge in educational policy research of the "key policy consultation" variety which directly faces the government. And actually, in Volume 2 of *Chinese Education Policy Review* in 2001, policymakers in the department of educational administration often directly authored pieces to advocate one educational policy or another. This kind of article became especially numerous after 2004, far exceeding the number of so-called scientific policy research. Just a few examples are "We Must Pay More Attention to Rural Compulsory Education" by Lianning Li, Director of the Ministry of Education's Basic Education Department; "Preliminary Discussions on Policy Direction for Character Education" by Ning Kang, deputy director of General Office of the Department Education, and the direct interview with the author which follows it, "The Societal Import of Lightening Students' Burden and Promoting Character Education"; "A Policy Analysis of the Development of Our Country's Basic Education and A Few Related Issues" by the deputy mayor of Suzhou, Yongxin Zhu; "Teambuilding among Middle and Elementary School Teachers: A Policy Analysis and Outlook for the Millennium" by Peijun Guan, assistant director of the personnel department of the Department of Education; and "Thoughts on Rural Tax Reform and Work in Education in Anhui" by Hanjie Jin, associate director of the Anhui Office of Education.

After this point, the essays in each volume of *Chinese Education Policy Review* turned to the second pathway advocated by Qiquan Zhong (see the "Disciplinization efforts in educational policy research" section of this article), articles specifically addressing one policy issue or another in the field of education: teacher education (2002); supervision and direction (2003); educational development and shrinking the rural-urban education gap (2004); modern education systems, higher education, and Chinese educational development (2005); Sino-foreign joint educational ventures (2006); reform of the university scientific research system (2007); fairness and efficiency in education (2008); the growth of innovative talent (2009); standards for educational quality (2010); basic public education services (2011); the modern university system (2012); internationalization of education (2013); and higher education performance assessment (2014). By 2015, issues of *Chinese Education Policy Review* no longer had distinct themes, and the articles collected for each issue very strongly echoed current policies coming from the government that year. The previous effort at an empiricist and regulated research paradigm influenced by the concept of a core principle of "process" in the field of public policy became increasingly rare. Volumes of 2016 and 2017 both concentrated on the relationship between fairness in education and related ancillary themes, which was precisely the greatest public education problem faced by the Chinese government in these years.

Disciplinization efforts in educational policy research

Meanwhile, efforts by researchers in institutions of higher learning toward the disciplinization of education policy research are comparatively apparent. In a piece titled "A New Direction for Education Politics: Education Policy Analysis," Zhong gives a comprehensive survey of the formation, maturation, and changing direction of education politics and uses a few representative examples from U.S. public policy studies in establishing "education policy research" as an "academic field," proposing that policy research might be classified into "analysis of policy" and "analysis aimed at policy." The former is primarily description and analysis of the experiential and empirical value of policy itself, done for the purpose of explaining policy through laws and regulations, with the emphasis on "objective" understanding; the latter is aimed at "improving" policy, with the emphasis on topics like the establishment of new policies, collecting information, and assessing the value of policy programs. From this basis, he continues to position educational policy research below education politics, believing that the foremost characteristic of current-generation educational policy is emphasizing experiential and empirical research, including normative and prescriptivist research making policy value judgments, policy criticism, proposals for replacement policies, and the provision of policy information. The value put on this kind of normative research is exactly the source of the "novelty" of new policy research and is one thing separating new education politics from old education politics. A second characteristic of new education policy analysis is apparent in how his research interest is not only the policy process discussed in old education politics but also policy content and policy resolution. He borrows the viewpoint of Western scholars in thinking that the categories of research themes in education policy analysis are opportunity equalization in education, a fair field, administrative systems in education, and economics and finance in education. He refers to these as specific policy issues discussed in the new politics of education. Zhong believes that in this way the disconnect of the old politics of education from real problems might be brought under control, making the field face up to specific policy topics, promoting practical research, and establishing an academic foundation for communication on the relationship between theory and practice (Zhong, 2001, pp. 247 – 258).

More seasoned education researchers hope to define the position of educational policy research from the standpoint of the politics of education, hope to find new territory for traditional education research, and hope that this new positioning and purpose might bring new life to a field so full of methodology but devoid of consciousness. But if an independent and unique disciplinal paradigm does not take shape as hoped, then the new position will just be putting old wine in a new bottle. This kind of educational policy research centered on policy process is expanding to classical pedagogy, education economics, education finance, and such themes; while the disciplinization of China education policy research remains incomplete, it not only makes the boundary of the discipline even less clear, but also dilutes the contributions researchers have made to education policy process research in terms of concept, principle, and method, obscuring the progress made in education policy research disciplinization.

Xie's (2001) "Discussion of Education Policy Research Classification and Theoretical Foundations" clarifies and classifies several types of Chinese and foreign education policy research as follows: researching how more ideal education policy can be set, how an education policy is determined, specifically researching one particular education policy, analyzing the theoretical framework of education policy and differentiating different types of education policy. This kind of classification is based on but distinguished from research methods and contexts already in use, though it lacks the inspiration this segment needs for further development. Similarly, education policy research abroad has for a long time been borrowing theories from other fields of discipline, and some researchers have done some enumeration of theories appearing with relatively higher frequency in policy research literature. China's education policy researchers face a similar quandary: Exactly what principles are behind or underlying education policy research? Xie invokes the related work of policy researchers abroad, proposing that the principles of education policy research are roughly sixfold: rational synthesis, progressive theory, political systems theory, group theory, elite theory, and critical theory (Xie, 2001, pp. 288 – 298). Each of these is relatively common in the literature of the public policy field, and accordingly the Chinese translation of Paul Sabatier's *Theories of the Policy Process* quickly became an indispensable desktop volume for education policy researchers. Actually these principles are not unique to the field of policy research, but have been borrowed and adapted by public policy researchers from sociology, political science, management, economics, and other mainstream social science disciplines.

When the field of educational policy research was first being created, most research into actual Chinese education policy by researchers in institutions of higher education adopted a critical stance. Feng in "Positioning Analysis of Current Chinese Basic Educational Policy" cites the improbable altitude and attitude of today's researchers and asks how it can be that even as Chinese basic education moves steadily toward universal compulsory education, policy positioning can still be so unclear. China is a lately developing country; its education system remains very outdated. This outdatedness is comprehensive: Basic education needs to be updated, vocational education needs to be updated, and higher education also needs to be developed. Under such circumstances, in order to attack this on all fronts, how should policy for developing basic education fit in? One section title of this article is direct—"An Error Analysis of the Positioning of China's Current Basic Education Policy"—and it cites four errors present in Chinese basic education policy: an inverted foundation (basic or specialized?), an imbalanced elite education model (operation or broader promotion?), an ossified unity (fairness or differentiation?), and polarized examinations (is the goal modeling or a variety of intellects?). The research direction revealed in this piece has an obvious discrepancy in intention with the research style displayed after many institutes of higher education set up education knowledge bases aimed at key policy consultation around 2008 (Feng, 2001, pp. 280 – 285). Education policy research from this time was still engaged in an attempt to make it into a social science, with work at democratization in the policymaking process, the question of delegation and agency, environmental analysis of educational policy distortion, policy value conflicts, and so on; research was focused on quitting specific cases and moving toward theoretical description of a generalized, broadly applicable policy process. But this kind of effort is primarily manifest in the assertion of research direction; it is scarce in actual empirical research, and the quality of the research has clear room for improvement as well.

From the mid-1990s, the Chinese government began a broad acceptance of educational assistance from international organizations and developed countries. The foreign experts hired to these assistance programs and the Chinese researchers in especially western region development program surveys and on-the-spot project promotions in China could distinctly see that "almost all the education research programs supported by the World Bank and other international funding organizations were policy research studies" (Yuan, 2000, p. 2);

almost all the big-name universities added colleges, departments, or areas of study related to education policy research, some simply renaming their colleges or departments of education into the 'College of Education Policy Research', the 'Education Policy Research Department' or similar names. New journals titled after one area or another of education policy research and monographs related to education policy research cropped up like bamboo after a spring rain. (Yuan, 2000, p. 2)

This direction of development was quickly seized upon by Chinese researchers, and institutes of higher education adopted education policy research as a new field for doctoral training within the education discipline. Beginning in about 2010, when some colleges and universities began specifically including "education policy research direction" in their doctoral faculty hiring advertisements, these efforts in disciplinization could be considered to have shown concrete results.

Empirical research on theory-guided educational policy

Many researchers feel this is not enough and only unwillingly accept a place under the authority of academic discussion on public policy, maintaining a practical and realistic approach, and garnering many valuable results. The "empirical research on theory-guided educational policy" topic represents these efforts and trials.

As in the development of American education policy research, the lack of basic research on the policy process cannot help improve and increase the efficacy of education. It keeps us from having the wisdom and foresight to make changes to that could spur new policies, from having the ability to confidently conjecture the potential effects of the suggestions we might make if they were to be realized, from having the ability to make timely adjustments and rectifications to policy process (Nagel, 1983). It is precisely through this kind of understanding, Chen et al. say, that basic research on education policy is largely focused on the actual condition of the education policy process, and only through probing into the actual condition of education policy can we reveal its true nature, understand its workings, and forecast the appearance, effects of, and changes to new policies. But the true condition of policy process is often quite complicated, requiring the support and guidance of theory to clarify and understand. More than speculative research, literature research, normative research, or empirical research, innovation in education policy research requires a kind of pathway combining both theoretical exploration and substantive research; this is what we mean by empirical research on theory-guided educational policy (Chen et al., 2011, p. 1). Combining the word "innovation" with basic research allows us to walk much more solidly but also laboriously down this pathway. Because it is empirical research, the collection of empirical materials is of great importance, however in an actual political environment and actual administrative departments, it is far from easy for a researcher outside the government policy process to follow the empirical path of the social sciences to engage in "policy field research." It becomes clear that the respective teams led by Xuefei Chen and Zhenguo Yuan began at the same time but moved in different research directions.

Around 2010, the contributing authors of Chen's book series of *Peking University Education Policy Research Series*[1] brought out, following the direction of theory-guided empirical research on education policy, important research on our country's higher education policy process since reform and opening-up, with research on the policy space for changes in private (*minban*) higher education policy, the agenda setting process in Chinese education policy using the example of that on state student loans, advocacy coalitions and the policy process (i.e., policy directing construction priorities in Chinese higher education), the process of setting the Non-state Education Promotion Law of the People's Republic of China, the promulgation of the policy on national educational discipline centers, the gradual changes in China's graduate education system, resource dependency and the development of graduate education (case studies of how China's government policy to invest in technology affected graduate education), and the formation of and changes to U.S. policies on subsidizing veterans' education, along with analysis of the beneficiaries of educational policy assessment for China's graduate students and other topics. Through this research series, considerable progress has been made in foundational research on education policy using empirical materials and especially abstract theoretical work in the Chinese context.

Throughout this series, in introductions and epilogues, researchers nearly all described

---

[1] *Peking University Education Policy Research Series* is a book series to publish the research results of the educational policy research team led by Professor Xuefei Chen of Graduate School of Education at Peking University. It was published in Peking University Press since 2010, including *Muddling-through Changes in Graduate Education System*, *Research on Key Construction Policies of Higher Education*, *Research on Policy Diffusion of National Discipline Bases*, *Research on the Formulation Process of Private Education Promotion Law*, *Higher Education Policy Production*, *Strategic Space in the Changes of Educational Policies*, *University and the Army: Research on Manpower Policy Coordination*, and *Chinese Online Education Policy Change*.

experiencing a similar moment: having meticulously refined concepts borrowed from public policy theory, upon entering the education policy process, whether in the design or implementation stages, there is a possibility that nothing will be gained. Obtaining policy documentation is also difficult. In truth, the difficulty in collecting these documents is precisely like that encountered in making sociological surveys and field research in the humanities. The difference is education policy researchers must provide theoretical analysis of actual policy process, which makes them feel the concepts and theories taken from the field of Western public policy fall somewhat flat. We therefore face the task of restructuring concepts and building theories for the context of Chinese education.

Similar to the two pathways of the researchers described above, scholars advocating empirical research on theory-directed education policy realize that policy science may be categorized as that researching the public policy process itself, policy analysis to provide government departments with policy plans, consultative research providing policy departments with References for deciding policy, and comparative research on the public policy of other countries. Clearly, they feel, the cornerstone is policy research on the public policy process itself, and from this have come three areas of achievement.

First, using the policy case studies already made, they have amassed a wealth of knowledge on how important education policies in China were actually set and revised, and from this they have built a substantial foundation for the construction of a native Chinese education policy theory. Second is the testing, revision, and proposal of related education policy theory. The theory of education policy research comes mainly from many disciplines in the field of Western social sciences research. As a country where the social sciences have developed more recently and having more lately established groups of researchers, it is quite natural that China should see arise an ambition to surpass Western theories. In empirical research on the education policy process in China, they have tried to utilize institutional theory, organizational theory, network information theory, policy theory, and so on, as a research framework to analyze the educational policy situation in China and have found some theories can explain it very well, some require a little rectification, and other phenomena cannot be explained using existing theories, and new concepts must be introduced, such as the "policy space" that exists frequently in China's education policy process, and the way it forces policy actors to take "strategic action" and thereby drives substantive change in education policy. Third, Chen does not believe that theory-driven education policy research is unable to deliver a consultative effect in the setting of government policy, but rather the opposite: He believes that theories going beyond singular policy themes are the most valuable, and the most broadly applicable; he is not seeing himself as a government worker who directly considers policy in the government's stead. The primary function of the departments setting and implementing policy is action, not research, and their understanding of issues in the policy process is often of an experiential nature. Empirical research on theory-guided educational policy, on the other hand, has the potential to discover some more obvious deficiencies in the policy determination and implementation system, for example, in the process for setting and implementing education policy for private education, policy departments often have too much administrative freedom and discretion, policy regulation could be more thorough, policy resources could be exchanged, and so on. As policy on disciplinal centers is spread, there is an obvious tendency to "*YiChu WeiZheng*" (defer to "governance by the street-level bureaucracy"), and in graduate education policy assessment, there is an obvious uniformity in the body of critique and a lack of position for those who would benefit the most. They feel that progress for the education policy system will have to be based on research, but this kind of foundation is exactly what empirical research on theory-guided education policy can provide (Chen, 2012, pp. 15 – 16).

To make some order of this recently emergent education policy process theory, Chen's team published a new set of teaching materials in 2011 for China's 11th Five-Year Plan, *Foundations of Educational Policy Research*, an attempt to escape from the disciplinary paradigm of earlier education policy studies, emphasizing clarification and application of foundational concepts in education policy research, expunging some underused or even unused concepts, and offering a basic framework distinct from that for public policy process research. The writing of this volume lasted the whole duration of the national Five-Year Plan. During this time, the number of education policy research articles carried in many academic periodicals continued to increase. The textbook strove to distill the unique place or influence of the "education" component of policy process, but unfortunately the authors were unable to provide a clear conclusion.

Thus, one of the biggest shortcomings of this research was the failure to return to an education standard. In the "conclusions" section, the pieces all echoed standard themes from the field of public policy research, without strong critical explanation of the uniqueness of the "education" in education policy. Just as with the fate of education research, adopting a sociological orientation by taking the empirical social sciences branch of the academic road and positioning oneself in the grand category of the social sciences is not conducive to gaining recognition as a mainstream discipline, and in fact makes the shortcomings more evident: They have not convinced those working in education practice. The reality of education is intricate and complex, with too many difficult problems to be solved; when one asks an educational researcher the way, it is not often that he gets a resolute or even very useful reply. Discussion and contention over whether education is an independent academic discipline was already disorderly and confused in the 1980s; today, education reform in countries all over the world seems to no longer require strict academic discussion, the attention being instead given to resolving issues in educational practice. The tragic fate of the Department of Education at the University of Chicago shows that if education research does not take into account the real needs of academic practice but instead single-mindedly follows the path of academia, it will be chasing its own destruction. What education researchers really need to do is pursue the path of practice and provide real support for educators, not fall in to the mainstream of the social sciences (Zhou, 2010). A similar fate befalls our young Chinese education policy researchers, brief though their story has been thus far. After working hard at building up a theoretical framework for more than 10 years, working out to which branch of the thick forest of academia the final research results belong is still a problem plaguing researchers looking at the academic transformation of education policy.

Those working their hardest to explore the academic path being taken by education policy research tend to view the policy process—including the setting of agendas, the formation of policy, legalization, policy execution, policy assessment, and policy documentation—as an object of study, and the content of the policies then comes to be treated individually as if it were an external characteristic. In the first 10 years as this field was emerging, most researchers' effort was concentrated here, awkward though it may be. If we consider it as policy process research, then education policy process research is an applied field of Western public policy research, and the collected data primarily act to verify or refute Western theory in the circumstance of China. What is awkward is that there is no one within the overall discipline of education with whom this facet of research findings can be discussed on an academic level. If we consider it as applied education policy process research, then the research findings are not attractive enough to policymakers, who view it as a sort of idealized description or critical evaluation of the process of government administration, while educators care more about the content of policies, not their operating procedure. Policy process research is often simplified by frontline educators along the lines of a Western proof of the old Chinese popular adage: "The government has its policies, and people down below have their own ways of getting around them." For Chinese education policy researchers, who have a pragmatic view of scholarship deep in their bones, this awkwardness is as close as a shadow and just as impossible to dispel.

After more than 10 years of hard work, the way to address this embarrassment is to be satisfied with individual case research and not try to promote it into deep theoretical consideration or methodology. Distilling out a particular thematic field of focus from among research on education policy published in the last 5 years is difficult. Owing to the continuing nature of education reform, an education policy research theme can be constructed directly just by appending "policy" to the end of certain content. When the concept of "policy" is applied as broadly as this, its meaning has all but disappeared. With the increasing proliferation of journal articles on education policy research, it becomes difficult to make use of a mutually exclusive and complete system of categorization to give a general survey of the field, and even harder to have effective academic debate, but these are precisely the conditions needed to establish a stable branch of study.

Guidance of major educational policy research topics and think tanks for educational policy decisions

Beginning in 1999, facing a new millennium, the government introduced a series of structural education reform measures, mostly through the document *A Plan of Action for Promoting Education in the 21st Century*, promulgated in February that year. This was a working blueprint for Chinese education reform and development as it transitioned from one century to the next, setting out clear goals for education development over 2000 – 2010. From here, China will continue to advance education policy along such a path, and the focus and direction of education policy research will be determined by a policy model of similar 10-year schemes. Education policy researchers are gradually moving away from researching practical education issues and instead looking to government education policy decisions for more currently popular research topics. "Attendees showed a great degree of sincere passion, engaging in earnest discussion and broad idea exchange on the national influence of major education policy, the issue of making policy decisions more scientific, and the establishment of education policy research as a discipline" (Yuan, 2000, p. 308); these remarks are typical at the closing of education policy forums.

In June 1999, the Party Central Committee and the State Council held the third national conference on education since reform and opening-up, promulgating a *Decision on Deepening Education Reform and Comprehensively Promoting Quality Education*. The meeting called upon "the whole Party and country, upon Chinese of all ethnicities" to work more vigorously at improving national civility and the ability to innovate, strengthen the systematic and structural reform of the education system, comprehensively promote character education, and reinvigorate the education industry as part of a national science and education-oriented revitalization strategy. In the 20 years since, the ideal for Chinese education policy has been education aimed at the overall person, and all manner of reforms revolving on character education have begun in the various branch fields. The archetypal policy example is the Eighth Curriculum Reform of the People's Republic of China which was first put into practice in 2001, also known as "NCR" for "new curriculum reform." Since then, topics addressing this aspect have generated a large volume of education policy research advances.

Work to make education policy research its own discipline in the beginning borrowed the dichotomy of policy research: study *of* policy and study *for* policy. The former has been interpreted as using the method of empirical research with supplementary attention to descriptive or theoretical research on policy, putting it in the category of foundational research; the latter is standard research, with a secondary emphasis on applied research. What government departments actually want most is policy assessment, which Dunn has placed between the two (Dunn, 2011, p. 73). Those who study Chinese education policy understand that the research orientation of Dunn, who enjoys a fine reputation in the field of American public policy, views academic research and government education policy decisions and policy topics as being intimately related. This choice has an obvious effect on the determination of topics in this field. Education is one of the most important issues for everyone, the hope of course being that policy which most directly affects the livelihoods of those within education obtains fundamental and legal support from academic research. Two voluminous collections of thematic reports that are classic examples of academic research supporting government education policy are 2003's *Stride from a Country of Tremendous Population to a Country of Profound Human Resources: A Report on Chinese Education and Human Resources Issues* (China Education and Human Resources Report Group,

2003) and 2005's *Narrowing the Gap: A Key Issue in China's Educational Policies* (Case Study Group on Major Education Policies in China in the Transitional Period, 2005). The body of education policy researchers has expanded from higher education researchers to government policymakers and executors; in fact, the field of education policy has from the beginning been able to develop at high speed thanks to being in this region of fusion where it may benefit from both these sets of resources.

The similarity between the word "policy" and the word "political" is not without reason, and policy researchers naturally work closely with policymakers. In 1999, with the support of the Ministry of Education's personnel department, the First High-Level Education Policy Analysis Symposium was held at East China Normal University (ECNU). Participants included representatives from the National People's Congress (NPC) Committee on Education, Science, Culture, and Public Health, the Policy Research Department of the State Council, the General Office of the Ministry of Education and related departments, and the National Office for Educational Science Planning, along with experts in education policy and theory from several normal universities around the country (Yuan, 2000, p. 308). For a university-held academic conference to be so well attended by this many central government departments means that from the very beginning education policy research has had a different origin and path of development from other education disciplines, with academic research and policy consultation blended together. Taking a positive interpretation, "This symposium has made a very significant step toward promoting the research of education policy science, and marks a successful beginning for communication between education policymakers and scholars." (Yuan, 2000, p. 308) Looking at it negatively, work at the disciplinization and academization of education policy research has never been unadulterated. Most theoretical resources for education policy research come from public policy research, and Western public policy research at that; in the eyes of policymaking officials in important government departments is akin to trying to scratch an itch through boot leather: It doesn't really solve the problem. As can be seen from annual project applications, education policy research that is not directed at application is not very often funded.

The current scope of national policy is greater than it has ever been, and the existence of a "policy accumulation law" is especially true for education, the numbers accumulating as unsuccessful policies require replacement. We might also give another "policy tool" theory, the "policy ineffectiveness law": The continual introduction of new policies entails weaker and weaker intended results, and increasingly apparent unintended results (Peters & Van Nispen, 1998). Thus, government demand for policy consultation has reached an all-time high. Just as Yuan has emphatically advanced at the High-Level Education Policy Analysis Symposium and in many articles,

> As the educational policy environment and key policy factors become increasingly complex, setting policy becomes increasingly challenging. In order to make policy decisions more scientifically, more democratically, more effectively, we are entirely justified in demanding that those in charge of setting policy should be researchers, and should make a concerted effort to become 'researching policymakers.' Because the social function in which social science research is so rich is growing in importance, the associated social responsibility is also greater, so in order to ensure that academic research can have a greater impact, we are also justified in demanding that researchers should be participants in policy, and should themselves take action to become 'policy researchers.' (Yuan, 2001, p. 363)

Recommendations and endeavors like this often cite a basis in "foreign experience," and the typical example is the influence of human capital theory on government education policy.

After human capital theory in Western countries began to broadly influence education policy, as the field of education economics became more well-known in China in the 1990s, it came to have a direct consultative function for the government. As a more lately developed country, China found an extraordinary motivation to study other already developed countries' experience with setting policy. For example,

> After the 1960s, spurred by 'human capital' theory, it was felt that investment in education had the highest rate of return. Countries in Asia, Africa, and South America, out of an urgent wish to modernize and at the same stroke change their appearance of being poor and backward, invested as much as 20% or even 40% of national income into education, from which they hoped to reap great rewards, without considering the background or conditions behind these great rates of return. As a result, some countries are still shrouded beneath the influence of mistaken policy decisions made at the outset. (Yuan, 2000, p. 2)

Beginning in 2010, institutions of higher learning began to gradually establish education policy knowledge banks which were set up precisely to serve a consultative function for government education policy. In 2011, the Ministry of Education began promoting its "Collaborative Innovation" plan, driving knowledge bases to not just propose research relevant to government policy agenda but also function to award research topic contracts, further shepherding and strengthening the tendency of education policy research toward being a service for government policymaking. This tendency is supported by new theories in the technology policy field in other countries, a sort of knowledge production "Mode 2." In Gibbons's view, Mode 2 is in contrast to Mode 1, which refers to a style of knowledge production which encompasses concept, method, value, and standards together. In many circumstances, Mode 1 is essentially the same as "science," where knowledge and societal standards determine which problems will be viewed as important, who is permitted to engage in scientific work, and what constitutes "good science." The style of practice that accords with these standards is defined to be "scientific," that which goes against them viewed as "unscientific"; the words "science" and "scientist" appear frequently. In Mode 2, however, more generally encountered are the terms "knowledge" and "workers." In Mode 1, the settings and arrangements for resolving issues are determined primarily by a certain group with a shared academic interest, while in Mode 2, information processing is undertaken in an applied setting (Gibbons, Trow, Scott, & Schwartzman, 2011, pp. 2 – 3). The Mode 2 method of knowledge production is often invoked as proof of the value of the knowledge that can be produced from an education policy knowledge base. The effective application of human capital theory to policy making and this Mode 2 pathway to technological innovation are now used as a direct endorsement of researchers serving government policy decision-making, showing how difficult and how vacillatory the process of education policy research paradigm formation can be.

This explains the internal government logic behind the establishment of so many education policy knowledge bases and reveals an answer to the question "What is an education policy researcher?"—there is no clear demarcation of what makes an educational policy researcher; no stable common body of academics has been formed that might strive together toward the foundation of a disciplinary paradigm, the rational organization of academic ideas, and the establishment and handing over of a theoretical framework to a succeeding generation. Researchers in any discipline within the field of education—or even in any discipline within the social sciences—can magic themselves into dedicated education policy researchers. Even though the division of disciplines was not the result of a logical evolution within disciplines to begin with, but rather something humans formalized in order to more conveniently understand the world, and even though any discipline is not the sole territory of any one person or group of researchers, the haphazard entry or exit of various individuals does mean that the disciplinization of education policy has already faltered before it has even taken shape.

A paradigm for Chinese educational policy research is still mired in the arduous process of formulation.

References

Case Study Group on Major Education Policies in China in the Transitional Period. (2005). *Narrowing the gap: A key issue in China's educational policies* [in Chinese]. People's Education Press.

Chen, X. (2012). Actively carrying out theoretically oriented educational policy empirical research [in Chinese]. In X. Lin (Ed.), *A space for the strategies in educational policy process* (pp. 15 – 16). Peking University Press.

Chen, X., Lin, X., & Cha, S. (2011). *Foundation of educational policy research* [in Chinese]. People's Education Press.

China Education and Human Resources Report Group. (2003). *Stride from a country of tremendous population to a country of profound human resources: A report on Chinese education and human resources issues* [in Chinese]. Higher Education Press.

Dunn, W. N. (2011). *Public policy analysis: An introduction* [in Chinese] (4th ed.) (M. Xie, Y. Fu, & X. Zhu Trans.). China Renmin University Press.

Feng, Z. (2001). Positioning analysis of current Chinese basic educational policy [in Chinese]. In Z. Yuan (Ed.), *Chinese education policy review 2001* (pp. 280 – 285). Education Science Press.

Nagel, S. (1983). *Encyclopedia of policy studies*. Marcel Dekker.

Peters, B. G., & Van Nispen, F. K. M. (1998). *Public policy instruments: Evaluating the tools of public administration*. Edward Elgar Publishing.

Xie, S. (2001). Discussion of education policy research classification and theoretical foundations [in Chinese]. In Z. Yuan (Ed.), *Chinese education policy review 2001* (pp. 288 – 298). Education Science Press.

Yuan, Z. (1996). *Educational policy studies* [in Chinese]. Jiangsu Education Press.

Yuan, Z. (2000). *On changes of Chinese educational policy: A case study on the relationship between equality and benefit in key middle schools* [in Chinese]. Guangdong Education Press.

Yuan, Z. (2000 – 2017). *Chinese education policy review (Volume 1 – 17)* [in Chinese]. Education Science Press.

Zhong, Q. (2001). A new direction for education politics: Education policy analysis [in Chinese]. In Z. Yuan (Ed.), *Chinese education policy review 2001* (pp. 247 – 258). Education Science Press.

Zhou, Y. (2010). The tragic fate of the department of education at the University of Chicago [in Chinese]. *Reading*, (3), 82 – 91.

Overview of Education

This piece of analytical policy review aims to shed light on a latest education policy blueprint in China, titled *China's education modernization 2035*, which was issued by the Central Government of China in February of 2019. The author argues that this new Chinese educational policy was driven by three factors: UN 2030 Agenda, China's national strategy, and Chinese educational reform and improvement. In *China's education modernization 2035*, eight key principles were rooted in the Chinese context and also recognized by international society. According to this policy initiative, 10 specific strategical tasks are outlined to reform Chinese education toward 2035. This article will be useful to learn and understand the new directions and the future approaches of Chinese education development and reform toward 2035.

New National Initiatives of Modernizing Education in China[1]

Yiming Zhu

In February 2019, the Chinese central government officially issued an educational development plan entitled, *China's education modernization 2035* (Ministry of Education of the People's Republic of China [MOE], 2019). Developed over the course of 3 years, the plan is intended to serve as the framework for China's education reform and development in the coming period. As such, it systematically describes the concepts, goals, and tasks of this reform and development. This article briefly reviews *China's education modernization 2035*: namely, its background, core concepts and main content, features, and potential risks.

Background

Since China implemented its reform and opening-up policy in 1978, educational development has been guided by the idea that "education needs to be modernized, oriented to the world, and oriented to the future" (Gu, 1998, p. 1309). As such, *China's education modernization 2035* was initiated in the new era of educational development, both at home and abroad.

---

1 This article was published on *ECNU Review of Education*, 2(3), 353 – 362.

Response to UN's **The 2030 agenda for sustainable development**

Released in 2015 and endorsed by all United Nations Member States, the *Transforming our world: The 2030 agenda for sustainable development* set out 17 Sustainable Development Goals (SDGs) for achieving sustainable human development in economic, social, and environmental dimensions. Of these, SDG 4 is related to education and seeks to "ensure inclusive and equitable quality education and promote lifelong learning opportunities for all" (United Nations, 2015).

In conjunction with the United Nations Children's Fund (UNICEF), the World Bank, the United Nations Population Fund (UNFPA), the United Nations Development Programme (UNDP), UN Women, and the United Nations High Commissioner for Refugees (UNHCR), the United Nations Educational, Scientific and Cultural Organization (UNESCO) held the World Education Forum in Incheon, Korea, in May of 2015. Attracting more than 1,600 delegates from 160 countries, the Forum released the *Education 2030 Incheon declaration and framework for action: Towards inclusive and equitable quality education and lifelong learning for all* (UNESCO, 2015a). In 2015, UNESCO published *Rethinking education: Towards a global common good?*, reiterating its position on the development of education (UNESCO, 2015b). The same year, the Organisation for Economic Co-operation and Development (OECD) launched the *OECD future of education and skills 2030* project (OECD, 2018).

These documents, reports, and actions have shaped China's education planning in some way. In early 2016, Chinese policymakers began developing a medium- and long-term plan for education development. In this process, "ensuring inclusive and equitable high-quality education and promoting lifelong learning opportunities for all" were assimilated into the goals of China's education modernization.

Response to the Chinese government's demand to build a moderately prosperous society

In October of 2017, the National Congress of the Communist Party of China proposed that after the country's reform and opening-up, the Chinese government should make strategic arrangements for socialist modernization. It thus proposed the strategic goals of "three steps." The first step involves solving the problem of subsistence for the people. The second step entails achieving the two goals necessary to create a moderately prosperous society, both of which have been accomplished. The third step involves building a modern socialist nation by the centennial year of the founding of the People's Republic of China.

On the basis of a comprehensive analysis of the current international and domestic situation and China's development conditions, the Chinese government will organize the 2020–2050 period in two stages. The first stage, 2020–2035, will involve the achievement of socialist modernization. The second stage, 2035–2050, will involve building China into a modern socialist country that is prosperous, strong, democratic, culturally advanced, harmonious, and beautiful (Xi, 2017).

Therefore, *China's education modernization 2035*—not 2030—was created to respond to the requirements of China's national modernization development strategy. The educational plan is to build a powerful education system, which is a fundamental project to bring about a great rejuvenation of the Chinese nation. Moreover, developing education is intended to serve as the support for the fundamental modernization requirements of the country in 2035 and realize the development of socialism with Chinese characteristics in the new era. Consequently, China will be a modern, harmonious, and creative society (World Bank and the Development Research Center of the State Council, P. R. China, 2013). The modernization of education in China is believed to contribute significantly to realizing such goals in 2035.

Meeting the requirements of educational transformation and improvement in China

In China, industries typically formulate a development plan envisioning over a 5- or 10-year period, such as "Made in China 2025" and "Healthy China 2030." In 2010, the Chinese government formulated the *National medium- and long-term education reform and development plan (2010–2020)*. With 2020 fast approaching, new plans are necessary. China has become the second largest economy in the world and achieved remarkable progress in educational development. Indeed, indicators show that China is moving closer to the global advanced level of education (see Table 1).

Table 1. Major indicators of education development in China, 1978 and 2017.

Indicator	1978	2017
Preschool education gross enrollment rate	10.6	79.6
Primary schools net enrollment ratio	94	99.91
Lower secondary level gross enrollment ratio	66.4	103.5
High school gross enrollment ratio	—	88.3
Tertiary education gross enrollment ratio	2.7	45.7

Source. MOE (2018).

However, China's educational development still faces many problems and challenges. In this regard, educational development needs to shift from a focus on quantitative expansion to ensuring a higher quality of education. Such development should guarantee the right to education and learning for all, while providing people with a strong sense of fulfillment, happiness, and security.

Moreover, educational development should help establish a more pluralistic and transparent system of education governance in order to stimulate the enthusiasm, initiative, and creativity of every school and teacher.

China's education modernization 2035 plan was developed within this context and to address these broader aims. In addition to proposing solutions to the current problems facing educational development, the plan provides a blueprint for the modernization of education in China. In doing so, it emphasizes the goal of achieving high-quality education in China, as detailed in the following section.

Core concepts and main content

China's education modernization 2035 comprises five parts: strategic background, overall thinking, strategic tasks, implementation path, and guarantees. This section provides a brief overview of the plan's core concepts and main content.

The concept of development is rooted in Chinese practice while incorporating international consensus on education

China's education modernization 2035 sets out eight basic concepts emphasizing ethics as the priority of education, well-round development, people-orientation, lifelong learning, personalized teaching, integration of knowledge and practice, integrated development, and co-construction and sharing.

These concepts reflect the series of education proposals by General Secretary Xi Jinping since he took office in 2012. According to Xi, both virtue and leadership should be fostered through education, educational development should be rooted in China's system, and focused on people-centered development. Claiming that education should facilitate the great rejuvenation of the nation, Xi further advances the need to deepen educational reform and innovation. In this regard, he notes that teacher development is a fundamental domain of educational development (Xi,

2018). These beliefs are fully reflected in *China's education modernization 2035*.

In developing *China's education modernization 2035*, the Chinese government considered the views of the international community in numerous ways, including holding thematic discussions at UNESCO headquarters, inviting World Bank experts to provide technical support reports (World Bank, 2016), and organizing international symposiums. New ideas such as educational equity, quality of education, lifelong learning, and integrated development—to which the international community attaches great importance—are fully reflected in *China's education modernization 2035*.

Reflecting the characteristics of education modernization in China

China's education modernization 2035 proposes that the overall modernization of education will be achieved by 2035, resulting in China entering the ranks of the most powerful countries in terms of education. Consequently, China will become known for its learning, human resources, and talent, thereby laying a solid foundation for the creation of a prosperous, strong, democratic, culturally advanced, harmonious, and beautiful socialist nation by the middle of the 21st century.

The main development goals of educational modernization in China include the establishment of a modern education system that provides lifelong learning for all, the universalization of quality preschool education, the achievement of high-quality and balanced compulsory education, the complete universalization of upper secondary education, the significant improvement of vocational education services, marked improvement in the competitiveness of higher education, the provision of the appropriate education for disabled children, and the formation of a new pattern of education management involving the participation of society. These development goals fully demonstrate the characteristics of a powerful educational system.

Specific strategic tasks to ensure faithful implementation

China's education modernization 2035 sets out the strategic tasks, implementation paths, and guarantee measures required for the realization of China's educational reform and development by 2035.

The strategic tasks focus on the following areas: education development concepts, advanced quality of education, the universalization of education at all levels, balanced educational system services, lifelong learning systems, talent development, the development of a teaching force, the informationization of education, the opening-up of education, and educational governance systems. These areas comprise specific tasks and content requiring further reform and development. The implementation paths emphasize the need to consider local conditions in the step-by-step advance, implementation, and exploration of reforms intended to stimulate reform and innovation in education modernization. These measures place significant emphasis on strong leadership at all levels of government, an institutional guarantee of sufficient educational expenditure, and a mechanism ensuring the participation of the whole society.

It is worth noting that *China's education modernization 2035* clearly identifies the specific requirements for "raising the level of education input." These requirements include improving the long-term mechanism for ensuring the sustained growth of financial investment, as well as guaranteeing that the general public budget for expenditure in education increases each year, that the average cost per student in school increases each year, and that the national fiscal education expenditure is at least 4% of the gross domestic product. These requirements, which were never clarified in the past, demonstrate the determination and courage of the Chinese government to develop high-quality education as well as the strong economic basis for this development.

Key features

Chinese characteristics of education development

In the past 70 years since the founding of the People's Republic of China, China has always paid attention to the integration of national development and personal development in education. According to *China's education modernization 2035*, the guiding philosophy of education modernization is " uniting the hearts of the people, comprehensively developing integrity, developing manpower, nurturing talents, benefiting the people as the goal, foster all-round moral, intellectual, physical and aesthetic grounding with a hard-working spirit in the socialist builders and successors" and "serving the great rejuvenation of the Chinese nation as an important mission of education, consolidate and develop a socialist system with Chinese characteristics, and to serve as a driver for reform and opening-up and socialist modernization" (MOE, 2019).

Clearly, these ideas reflect both China's adherence to the people-centered concept of development and the contribution of education to the development and prosperity of the country.

They are also indicative of China's self-confidence in building a socialist education system with Chinese characteristics.

Experience of China prioritizing educational development

Following its reform and opening-up in 1978, China adopted a strategy of prioritizing the development of education. This prioritization of education has made significant progress over the past four decades (Yuan, 2018).

At the 19th National Congress of the Communist Party of China in 2017, Xi once again emphasized that:

> We must give priority to education, further reform in education, speed up its modernization, and develop education that people are satisfied with. The establishment of an educational power is a fundamental project for the great rejuvenation of the Chinese nation, so education must be given priority. (Xi, 2017)

In 2018, the People's Republic of China held the first "National Education Conference" (formerly the "National Education Work Conference"). During the conference, Xi once again stressed the need to prioritize educational development in the new era as a gambit to advance the endeavors of the Party and state in all areas. He also stressed the need to constantly adapt education to the requirements of the Party and state, ensuring that it aligns with the expectations of the people, as well as supports China's comprehensive national strength and international roles. A core strategy of China's modernization, the prioritization of educational development is clearly reflected in *China's education modernization 2035*.

Innovation-driven Chinese educational development

Innovative reform is the fundamental driving force in the modernization of education in China. Indeed, "adherence to innovative reform" constitutes one of the basic principles of *China's education modernization 2035*.

At present, China's educational development remains unbalanced and inadequate. It is not fully adapted to the new expectations of the country's socioeconomic development and the growing demands of the people. As such, *China's education modernization 2035* identifies the actions required to adapt and improve the country's educational development. This includes establishing a modern education governance system by deepening comprehensive educational reform, fully utilizing new technologies and mechanisms, and innovating in both educational services delivery systems and school running and management systems. Three strategic tasks are directly related to these actions: "upgrading first-class talent development and innovation skills," "building a team of highly qualified professional and innovative teachers," and "accelerating education reform and innovation in the era of ICT" (MOE, 2019).

However, *China's education modernization 2035* is not a refined design procedure or project but a development guideline and outline. Chinese provinces and cities have begun developing corresponding *Local education modernization 2035* plans, which are intended to implement the national requirements and achieve the national goals set out in *China's education modernization 2035*.

Open development of education in China

As an active participant in the UN's *The 2030 agenda for sustainable development*, China has proposed initiatives to build a community with a shared future for mankind, including the "Belt and Road" initiative. In this regard, *China's education modernization 2035* proposes that

> it is necessary to provide a higher level and more open education, to strengthen educational and humanistic exchanges, to promote the exchange of hearts and minds among people for civilized exchanges, and make greater contributions to the creation of a better future for mankind. (MOE, 2019)

One of the strategic tasks of *China's education modernization 2035* is to "create a new prospect of opening-up to the outside world in education" (MOE, 2019). This will actively contribute to the "Belt and Road" initiative; comprehensively strengthen cooperation with all countries and international organizations; enrich the meaning of openness, as well as increase the level of openness and its international influence; and contribute to the building of a community with a shared future for mankind. To this end, China seeks to comprehensively enhance international exchange and cooperation in education, attract outstanding international teachers to teach and students to learn in China, and actively participate in global education governance.

As such, in addition to focusing on education in China, *China's education modernization 2035* places significant emphasis on exchange and co-development in the international context.

Potential risks

In the current fast-changing world, it is not easy to grasp changes and trends. *China's education modernization 2035* fully reflects China's current understanding and requirements for the development of national education. Appropriateness and feasibility of such understanding and requirements will be tested in practice. In any case, however, the development of such systematic policy planning in the context of rapid change carries a certain degree of risk.

Uncertainty about future education development and change

It is not entirely clear what kind of changes will emerge in the future of education and what form of education will take in China. In addition to ensuring external conditions for educational development, the modernization of education should consider the impact of changes in teaching and learning on school development and individual development. Indeed, the scale of China's educational system makes it even more necessary to diversify educational development.

During the third Global Conference on Education and Research (GLOCER) in May 2019, the topic of "Education Think Tank 2030" asked the following questions: "Will the professors be replaced by artificial intelligence-supported robots? Will universities disappear? Will the traditional transfer of information in the form of lectures be a thing of past? Will universities only offer online courses?" However, there is a significant difference between *China's education modernization 2035* and the international academic community in terms of the potentially revolutionary impact of modern technology—such as artificial intelligence—on education.

Caution of youth engagement in the future

China's education modernization 2035 focuses on guaranteeing equitable and quality education, learning, and development for everyone. This understanding is based on national development needs and traditional cultural perceptions of education. At present, the modernization of education in China needs to move beyond the traditional thinking of a "poor country running big education," pursuing the concept of a "great country constructing strong education" instead. With the rise of China, the Chinese people have become more proactive, active, open, and enterprising. The living and development conditions and needs of young people in a globalized world are unpredictable. Moreover, an open China may be attracting an increasing number of international youth with educational requirements.

It is clear that *China's education modernization 2035* does not fully grasp the engagement and development needs of the youth in a globalizing world. As such, educational planning needs to work with and for the youth (Hopma & Sergeant, 2015).

References

Gu, M. (1998). Three orientations [in Chinese]. In M. Gu (Ed.), *Dictionary of education* (supplementary ed., p. 1309). Shanghai Education Press.

Hopma, A., & Sergeant, L. (2015). *Planning education with and for youth*. UNESCO, IIEP.

Ministry of Education of the People's Republic of China. (2018). *National statistical bulletin on the development of education in 2017*. http://www.moe.gov.cn/jyb_sjzl/sjzl_fztjgb/201807/t20180719_343508.html

Ministry of Education of the People's Republic of China. (2019). *The Communist Party of China Central Committee and the State Council recently issued China's education modernization 2035* [in Chinese]. http://www.moe.gov.cn/jyb_xwfb/s6052/moe_838/201902/t20190223_370857.htm

Organisation for Economic Co-operation and Development. (2018). *OECD future of education and skills 2030*. http://www.oecd.org/education/2030/

United Nations. (2015). *Transforming our world: The 2030 agenda for sustainable development*. https://sustainabledevelopment.un.org/post2015/transformingourworld

United Nations Educational, Scientific and Cultural Organization. (2015a). *Leading education 2030*. https://en.unesco.org/education2030-sdg4

United Nations Educational, Scientific and Cultural Organization. (2015b). *Rethinking education: Towards a global common good?* UNESCO.

World Bank. (2016). *Policy note on international trends and experience in education. Technical assistance to China education strategy 2030 (for internal discussion only)*. China Education Team, Education Global Practice, the World Bank.

World Bank and the Development Research Center of the State Council, P. R. China. (2013). *China 2030: Building a modern, harmonious, and creative society*. World Bank.

Xi, J. (2017). *Secure a decisive victory in building a moderately prosperous society in all respects and strive for the great success of socialism with Chinese characteristics for a new era—Delivered at the 19th National Congress of the Communist Party of China* [in Chinese]. People's Publishing House. http://www.china.com.cn/19da/2017-10/27/content_41805113.htm

Xi, J. (2018). *Following the path of socialist education with Chinese characteristics to nurture generations of capable young people well-prepared to join the socialist cause* [in Chinese]. http://www.moe.gov.cn/jyb_xwfb/s6052/moe_838/201809/t20180910_348145.html

Yuan, Z. (2018). Dual priority agenda: China's model for modernizing education. *ECNU Review of Education*, 1(1), 5–33.

This article mainly examines the impact of the large-scale international assessment on China's education governance and discusses the influence of digital governance on the education reforms. It conducts a text analysis of materials related to China's education system, including PISA data and analytical reports published by OECD since 2009. PISA test results did reflect the main problems facing China's educational sector, while it also causes the excessive pursuit of the digital governance effect, that is even highly consistent with the China's desire of efficiency, emphasis on scores, and the rate of students entering higher level schools. According to the discussion of the impact of digital governance on the education reforms in other countries, this study provides suggestions that China's post-PISA education reforms should be implemented by complying with its own cultural traditions and social realities as well as by referencing and using PISA data with care and prudence.

Post-PISA Education Reforms in China: Policy Response Beyond the Digital Governance of PISA[1]

Wenjie Yang and Guorui Fan

Background

Developed by the Organisation for Economic Co-operation and Development (OECD), the Programme for International Student Assessment (PISA) is an international test assessing the knowledge and skills that 15-year-old students should master in order to engage with society. The program has had a wide and profound impact on major countries around the world. With PISA's global influence, the OECD has become the "arbitrator of global education governance" (Meyer & Benavot, 2013, p. 9). The design concept of the PISA indicates that it connects various key factors to ensure comprehensive analysis, including students' test scores, their personal characteristics, and factors affecting learning within and outside schools. It identifies the differences between results of students from various backgrounds, schools, and education systems. It then determines

---

1 This article was funded by the Major Project (Education) of the National Social Science Foundation of China in 2016 "Research on Modernization Strategy of Educational Governance System and Governance Capacity in China" (No. VGA160003). It was published on *ECNU Review of Education*, 2(3), 297–310.

the characteristics of the schools and education systems in which students achieve good results and which practice the equitable distribution of educational opportunities. Consequently, the assessment data can answer the following questions: "What policies are effective?" "Why are these policies effective?" and "What types of policy reforms may be the most effective?" (Lu, 2010).

In 2009, Shanghai represented China in participating in the PISA for the first time, emerging as the champion for 2 consecutive years. Represented by Shanghai, the Chinese education system has since replaced Finland as "the new cover poster for excellence" (Kamens, 2013, p. 131). China's growing educational achievements pose a challenge to the U.S., leading to a rivalry akin to when the Soviet Union launched the first artificial satellite during the space race of the 20th century (Dillon, 2010; Kristof, 2011). After the computer-based version of the PISA was launched in 2015, 540,000 fifteen-year-old students from 72 countries and regions participated, with students from Singapore achieving the best overall performance. The combined Chinese team from the four provinces/cities of Beijing-Shanghai-Jiangsu-Guangdong (B-S-J-G) dropped to the 10th position; more specifically, the Chinese team was ranked 10th for science, 27th for reading, and 6th for mathematics. Although these results were significantly poorer than previous results, the Chinese team's performance kept the country in the top echelon of the 72 participating countries.

Digital governance (Lingard, 2011) is a common perspective used in contemporary education policymaking. This is because numbers have made comparisons the new form of governance model across countries and on the global scale (Nóvoa & Yariv-Mashal, 2003; Simola, 2005), and policies are used as leverage to influence the education reforms of various countries. The outstanding performance of Chinese students in mathematics, reading, and science has prompted many countries around the world to shift the focus of their education policy reform toward the East (Auld & Morris, 2014; Crossley, 2014; Waldow, 2012; You & Morris, 2016). Although countries such as Australia, the U.S., and the United Kingdom (UK) have prioritized China as the reference template for their school systems and national education reforms (Alexander, 2012; OECD, 2014b; Sellar & Lingard, 2013), few studies have considered China's views toward its PISA achievements.

The relevant literature has mainly (i) analyzed the rationality of China's education reforms by connecting PISA data with current education reforms (Tan, 2017; Zhang & Alexander, 2012), (ii) excessively mythologized the Chinese education system represented by Shanghai (Tan,

2013; Waldow, Takayama, & Sung, 2014), (iii) paid attention to media and policy discussions triggered by PISA, or (iv) focused on the responses of education decision-makers rather than the other stakeholders (Baird et al., 2016). There is a lack of overall analyses of the problems faced by China regarding the reforms of its education system as a result of digital governance triggered by PISA. This study systematically analyzes China's education problems as reflected by the PISA as well as the education reforms developed to address these issues. This study also addresses the impacts of the tendency toward digital education governance triggered by the PISA on China's education reforms in order to counter the future challenges of digital governance.

Mirror images: PISA and China's education issues

Students' performances in PISA are measured by their abilities to complete increasingly complex tasks. The test results are categorized into one of seven ascending levels from 1b to 6. Of these, Level 2 is the baseline and represents the minimum basic skills required to participate in social activities. Only students with scores at Levels 5 and 6 are considered the best in science, reading, or mathematics. Presenting results by ranking student scores, PISA reveals the weaknesses and blind spots in the education systems of various countries. Despite receiving good PISA results in the past, the unsuccessful performance of Shanghai students in more recent PISA has exposed the weakness of the municipal government's approach to education (Tan, 2017). As such, the superficial glory of China's PISA high rankings reflects some of the deeper issues within its current education system.

Overburdening of Students at Schools

The PISA 2012 report indicates that students in Shanghai spent more time on homework than their peers, spending approximately 13.8 hr a week on homework compared to the OECD average of 4.9 hr (OECD, 2014c). In 2015, PISA surveyed the students' average amount of time spent in class, total duration spent in classes per week, and the respective number of hours spent on science, reading, and mathematics. Table 1 presents a comparison of the weekly learning times of students from the top-ranking countries in PISA 2015.

Among OECD countries, students reported an average learning time of 26 hr and 56 min per week. The breakdown of hours per week for science, language learning, and mathematics courses

Table 1. Learning hours for relevant subjects in representative countries and regions according to PISA 2015.

Country & Region	Hour per week				
	Science	Math	Reading	Other subjects	Total time in school
Finland	3	1	2	15	24
Singapore	6	6	3	12	27
B-S-J-G	6	4	4	19	33
Korea	3	4	3	22	31
OECD average	3.30	3.39	3.36	15.51	26.56

Source. Adapted from OECD (2016b).
Note. The weekly learning times for the various subjects in Finland, Singapore, B-S-J-G, and Korea were estimated on the basis of the results of PISA2015. PISA = Programme for International Student Assessment; B-S-J-G = Beijing-Shanghai-Jiangsu-Guangdong; OECD = Organisation for Economic Co-operation and Development.

was 3 hr and 30 min, 3 hr and 36 min, and 3 hr and 39 min, respectively (OECD, 2016b). On average, Finnish students spent approximately 24 hr a week learning in school, and their weekly learning time for the three subjects were the shortest. In contrast, students from China had the longest learning week among all countries participating in PISA 2015, averaging at 33 hr per week—approximately 9 hr longer than that of Finnish students and significantly higher than the OECD average.

Emphasis on knowledge transfer during the teaching process

The PISA 2000 results show that a small proportion of students who scored below Level 2 entered higher education, with the majority joining the low-wage labor market (OECD, 2016a). Taking the reading literacy test as an example, the PISA 2009 results show that nearly 20% of the participating Chinese students scored lower than Level 2, indicating that almost one fifth lacked basic reading skills. Students in this age-group who lack basic skills are likely to drop out of the education system without completing high school and end up joining the low-skilled workforce (OECD, 2010b). Table 2 shows the proportions of students at the different PISA 2015 reading levels. Compared to students from the top three countries—namely, Singapore, Canada, and Finland—a relatively high proportion (21.8%) of Chinese students did not attain the baseline score. This means that among the Chinese students tested, the reading literacy of approximately one in five failed to meet the minimum standard. Moreover, the proportion of Chinese students who scored below Levels 1b and 1a was as high as

8.3%. This figure is approximately 3 times that of the top three countries and 1.8% above the OECD average.

Table 2. Proportion of students at different reading levels in some countries and regions according to PISA 2015.

Country & Region	Students sampled (%)							
	Below Level 1b (<262)	Level 1b (262 – 335)	Level 1a (335 – 407)	Level 2 (407 – 480)	Level 3 (480 – 553)	Level 4 (553 – 626)	Level 5 (626 – 698)	Level 6 (>698)
B-S-J-G	2.1	6.2	13.5	20.9	25.4	20.9	9.1	1.8
Singapore	0.3	2.5	8.3	16.9	26.2	27.4	14.7	3.6
Canada	0.4	2.1	8.2	19.0	29.7	26.6	11.6	2.4
Finland	0.6	2.6	7.8	17.6	29.7	27.9	11.7	2.0
OECD average	1.3	5.2	13.6	23.2	27.9	20.5	7.2	1.1

Source. Adapted from OECD (2016a).
Note. PISA = Programme for International Student Assessment; B-S-J-G = Beijing-Shanghai-Jiangsu-Guangdong; OECD = Organisation for Economic Co-operation and Development.

PISA 2012 tested students' creative problem-solving abilities. The results indicate that in China and other countries, approximately one in five students could only use traditional problem-solving methods, reflecting a lack of creative thinking ability (OECD, 2014b). While there are many reasons for this failure to cultivate creative thinking, the main reason may be that this capacity has not been effectively addressed through teaching and learning approaches in the classroom (Beghetto & Plucker, 2006, pp. 316 – 332). As a result of the impact and interference of evaluation indicators such as school performance, as well as teacher and student evaluations, Chinese teachers pay more attention to knowledge and rote learning in classroom teaching process. Moreover, knowledge-based learning oriented toward examination-based education is emphasized at the expense of training students' creative thinking and problem-solving abilities. The existing college entrance examination system has also been influential in this regard, with scores and ranking used as the bases for talent selection. Ultimately, students' abilities to think and learn have been stifled by factors at various levels, impacting the training of their thinking abilities.

An analysis of the proportion of Chinese students at the various PISA 2015 reading literacy levels reveals that their cognitive levels were average and below. While students had superficial abilities to read and comprehend text, they were unable to establish connections between different texts, explore the deeper connotations behind those texts, understand changes in levels when cognizing text, or demonstrate high cognitive levels. These results reflect China's teaching practices, namely "the students learn whatever the teacher teaches." Teachers predominantly focus on knowledge transfer and rote learning, emphasizing knowledge-based learning that is examination oriented and paying less attention to the cultivation of thinking abilities. Consequently, students may be able to understand the text literally but do not know how to answer questions using their life knowledge. The reading method at which Chinese students are most adept is summarizing the central ideas by segment—in other words, they generalize based on the segment's meaning. Chinese students are also good at understanding the general meaning of the entire text in chronological order and generally tend to have one reading style. Contextual analysis of text exposes their weaknesses in the mastery of knowledge and application ability. Reading has become merely a tool for learning and is not related to the improvement of comprehension abilities.

Prevalence of extracurricular tuition

In many countries, a significant proportion of students attend extracurricular tuition classes, especially in mathematics and language learning. Among OECD countries, 35%, 48%, and 41% of students attend such classes in science, mathematics, and language learning, respectively (OECD, 2016b). Chinese students also engage in a high rate of extracurricular tuition as a result of the demands for academic achievement and parental expectations. In 2014, 48.9%–58.1% of elementary and 66.8%–74.4% of middle school students in Shanghai attended extracurricular tuition. Meanwhile, in Beijing, 60.5% of elementary students in Grades 5–8 and 58.4% of middle school students engaged in extracurricular activity in 2015 (Li, 2019). Indeed, it is not uncommon for students to wake up at 7 a.m. and continue studying until past 10 p.m. in order to finish their homework (Tan, 2019).

The PISA 2009 survey shows that, although Shanghai students ranked first in reading, mathematics, and science, they spent 34.8 hr a week studying in and outside of class (OECD, 2010a). The PISA 2012 questionnaire reveals that the teaching time in Shanghai schools was roughly equivalent to that of other countries or regions. This means that students' academic burdens are mostly associated with after-school assignments. PISA data show that 15-year-old students in Shanghai spend an average of 13.8 hr a week completing assignments, with private tuition and remedial classes comprising an average of 3.3 hr per week. The total time spent on extracurricular learning per week amounts to 17.1 hr (OECD, 2014a). According to the PISA 2015 Survey, students spent an average of 3.2 hr on science, 3.8 hr on mathematics, 3.1 hr on language learning, 3.1 hr on foreign language, and nearly 4 hr on other subjects (OECD, 2016b). Students in B-S-J-G (China) spent more than 25 hr a week learning after class, whereas students in Finland, Germany, Iceland, and Japan spent less than 15 hr per week on average.

Effects: PISA-triggered digital governance and the root cause of China's education issues

The PISA results are based on numbers, and its premise is to describe national school education systems and the "truth" of children's education. This way of thinking is used to distinguish and categorize countries on a global scale (Popkewitz, 2011, pp. 32 – 36). Although this approach of constructing and representing the world based on digital information seems objective and nonvalue laden, it obfuscates PISA's theoretical hypothesis (Poovey, 1998, p. 237). This approach has caused numerous countries to comprehensively reform their education systems in the hope of improving their rankings. As a result, such countries have focused on economic growth and pursued the utilitarian value of education, thus ignoring the intrinsic values of education, which is to educate people. More specifically, some countries have adopted the education policies of countries with good PISA performances in a bid to demonstrate the ranking and strength of their national education system at the global level, thereby elevating the international status of their system.

In the UK, the test results of British students were unsatisfactory following the implementation of PISA. Although the overall trend is stable, it has dips. When the PISA 2009 results were about to be released, the British government issued a white paper titled *the importance of teaching*, which proposed the importance of teacher quality to the overall quality of education (Department of Education, UK, 2010). Inspired by Shanghai's excellent performance in PISA, the UK's Department of Education launched the "England – Shanghai Mathematics Teacher Exchange Program"[1] in 2014. This program selected excellent math teachers for a study tour to Shanghai in

---

1 The mutual education and training exchange program between math teachers from the UK and China (Shanghai) was jointly led by China's Ministry of Education and the UK's Department of Education and jointly implemented by the Shanghai Municipal Education Commission, Shanghai Normal University, and UK's National Centre for Excellence in the Teaching of Mathematics. It is one of the key projects under the high-level Sino-British humanities exchange mechanism. The UK sent its outstanding teachers to learn, study, and receive training in China, while Chinese teachers were invited to teach in the UK and share their knowledge and experiences (Department for Education, UK, 2015).

order to understand the latter's advantages in (mathematics) education. Subsequently, *The Shanghai Maths Project*—a series of supplementary teaching materials in China—was introduced to British elementary and middle school curricula in the UK's strive to achieve good PISA results. Such rank-pursuing policies neglect the unique cultural, historical, and economic backgrounds of the country. This type of education reform is akin to impatiently taking shortcuts, only to receive adverse results: The learning burdens of teachers and students in the UK were increased, resulting in new educational problems.

PISA's narrative for the present and future is premised solely upon numbers. It describes the truth about education and social progress/regression based on "facts." In addition to PISA, numbers are an important part of contemporary societies (Popkewitz, 2011, p. 35). Studies have pointed out that the main reason for the overburdening of Chinese students is the expectations of parents and other educational stakeholders who insist on the college entrance examination constituting the sole or main criterion for evaluating a school's quality (Tan, 2019). In fact, this evaluation system is merely symptomatic of a deeper lying issue. Examining the underlying cause, issues of comparative and digital forms of governance presented by PISA align with the country's ideas and practices regarding socioeconomic development and its pursuit of efficiency in education development. There are rational aspects to scores, rankings, and other quantifiable indicators, such as fairness—at least on the surface—and operational simplicity. For a long period of time, this tendency toward digitalization had a positive effect on educational development and benefited the promotion of educational equity. However, after an education system becomes sufficiently developed, it tends to obstruct scientific development (Ma, 2019).

During China's education reform, there was a period where the educational pursuit of "serving the development of socialism" echoed the economic development model, which centered on gross domestic product growth. These reforms promoted the development and progress of the Chinese society to some extent. The development method was based on the doctrine of efficiency, relied on scores as the single evaluation standard, and was represented by the lopsided pursuits of educational certificates and students' rates of entering higher level schools. The problems with this method became apparent when all levels and types of education started becoming fully popularized, and the overall quality level had generally improved. This led to the disorderly and uneven development of education, harmed students' physical and mental health, and violated the original intention of education reform.

Examples of negative aspects include the adoption of a cookie-cutter approach to evaluating students and schools, with scores constituting the only criteria used to determine merit; making entry to higher level schools the ultimate target of education to the detriment of other meaningful goals; using academic qualifications to determine an individual's career and prospects for promotion and evaluating graduates solely on their certificates; pegging job titles to the papers published and evaluating teachers quality based on authorship; and determining people's remunerations and assessing their talents according to superfluous accolades.

Going beyond: Practical explorations of China's education reforms

The PISA automatically collects and reproduces the educational information of various countries in a digitalized format and describes the results in the form of rankings. This has produced numerous negative effects. Although standardized testing has been used in many countries for decades, PISA has resulted in the extended application of this testing method and greatly exacerbated the reliance on such quantitative measures. For example, the U.S. recently used PISA as a primary indicator in the "Race to the Top" project. This has increased the use of standardized testing tools to assess the weight attributed to students, teachers, and education authorities. Characterized by the cyclical global test periods, the PISA describes the current status of education in different countries by ranking, exacerbating the high pressures already faced by schools. This led to the appearance of more curricula that are formulaic and by the book as well as teachers who lack autonomy. Finally, by emphasizing a relatively small range of measurable factors in education, PISA diverts attention away from educational goals that are difficult or impossible to measure, such as physical, moral, civic, and artistic developments. PISA's method of measuring contents has limited people's visions of what education is and should be.

The best example of PISA results being utilized as a form of control is when analyses and interpretations of data and the factors affecting change are used to influence policy formulation. This has been described as a form of governance through data or indicators (Bogdandy & Goldmann, 2012). China has used the information provided by PISA to achieve two main objectives: (i) highlight Shanghai's existing educational problems in order to validate the need for reform and (ii) provide support for ongoing reform measures in order to redefine the goals and nature of education in Shanghai (Tan, 2019). Unlike many other countries obsessed with

PISA rankings, even as China explores the reasons for its shortcomings in education, it is proactively improving the current situation through education reform while breaking through the shackles of digital governance. This is because the educational problems reflected by PISA are rooted in the fact that academic achievements are the only evaluation indicator, while the cultivation of students' abilities is ignored. In this regard, Shanghai drew upon PISA's advanced ideas, theories, and techniques of examination evaluation in developing its own "scientific assessment system" (Cao & Yan, 2014). In March 2011, the city gradually formed a set of green indicators for the comprehensive evaluation of academic quality. The set of indicators considers 10 different aspects: students' academic level, learning motivation, academic burden, teacher-student relationship, teaching methods, the principal's curriculum leadership, the impact of students' socioeconomic backgrounds on their academic achievements, students' moral conduct and behavior, students' physical and mental health, and student progress across multiple years.

Following the implementation of the green indicators, education management analyzed the evaluation results to comprehensively understand the students' academic situation at the regional and school levels, discover the effective experiences and shortcomings of education and teaching, explore the factors impacting scores, as well as guide schools to further understand the connotations of the green indicators in order to change teaching methods and optimize teaching behaviors. In regard to teaching research, the evaluation reports are interpreted and the evaluation information subjected to in-depth analysis, thereby providing schools and teachers with specific, detailed, and targeted teaching recommendations. For teaching in schools, the evaluation information is applied to the next stage of teaching improvement, thus forming a virtuous cycle of "standards → teaching → evaluation → improvement" that gradually forms a school-based guarantee system for education quality. The application of green indicators is based on the evaluation of multiple indicators related to students and relevant stakeholders. It goes beyond the previous singular evaluation criteria of students' academic achievement and rates of entering higher level schools, thereby realizing the innovation of educational evaluation methods.

The next step is to find ways to integrate the evaluation concepts and methods of the green indicators into (i) the local education system for administrative decision-making, teaching, and research; (ii) the daily academic tests and reforms of the entrance examinations for senior high schools and colleges; (iii) assessment of schools' development; (iv) monitoring and supervision of the developmental status of government education; and (v) realizing the reform of the entire education evaluation system by learning from Shanghai's experience. These are all green indicator-related application problems awaiting solutions. Moreover, the indicators for physical and mental health, as well as moral conduct and behavior, are insufficiently developed in terms of content and evaluation methods, necessitating further and in-depth research.

While facing the fact that the performance of Chinese students in PISA 2015 was worse, it should be noted that this ranking does not represent the country's educational level as a whole nor does it imply that the standard of Chinese education has declined. On the contrary, China has gradually moved beyond the use of PISA's digital governance as an education policy tool. Instead, the PISA is combined with the country's current economic, cultural, and historical background. The internal and external environments of the education system constitute the bases from which to review and reflect upon current education problems, and the transformation of education governance is promoted through internal and external educational innovations.

Conclusion

In the global economic system, the educational success of a country or economy is not only an indicator that national standards have been achieved but also an indicator of an education system with the best performance and most rapid improvements (OECD, 2014b). PISA plays an increasingly significant role in global education governance. This is commonly attributed to three factors: (i) its acceptance as a universal measure of education quality, (ii) its perceived economic significance, and (iii) the promise of policy solutions to educational problems in the form of prescriptions of "best practices" (Grey & Morris, 2018).

The response of China to the disappointing PISA performance of Shanghai's students was reflective, measurable, and self-critical. The students' performance only related to a narrow definition of success and did not represent the current state of the entire education system in China (Tan, 2017). Through quantification, simplification, and measurability, PISA has demonstrated that its statistical inference represents the traditional partial construction of complex, complicated, and varied contexts, while reflecting the objective facts of education "performance." PISA has created a global domain for education policies through digitalization and statistical data. Although PISA researchers have warned policymakers against focusing on rankings, it is easy and convenient for decision-makers to use the numbers and tables provided by PISA when formulating policies (Therese & Kristine, 2017). With the gradual rise of new technologies such as cloud computing and big data, the informatization process of human societies has gradually moved from the eras of computers and the Internet to that of big data. From small to massive amounts of big data, and the basis for education decision-making moving from experiences to digits, data are being used to "speak." Data are also being categorized and transformed into the basis for policies. To a certain extent, policy concepts based on evidence realize the substantive connection between microscopic data and macroeconomic policies. In terms of real significance, big data have become a policy concept for practical operations (Chen, Meng, & Zhang, 2014). Education governance based on big data is the inevitable result of the development trends in information technology. Even as the modernization of the education governance system is being promoted, education governance itself relies on numbers for characterization and encompasses an inherent tendency for digitalization. In doing so, the ways of governance based on ranking and results are further entrenched.

As an evaluation system, PISA should not become the driving force for countries to compete against one another for achievements and rankings. Instead, the role of PISA should be more like that of a mirror—a means by which a country can better understand the existing problems of its own education system through comparisons with other countries or regions. The advantages and innovations in the educational field demonstrated by high-performance countries can also be used as References to further enhance educational possibilities and experience. The PISA results are no longer the targets of various countries but an important frame of reference for the reform of their education systems and education policies. Going forward, the common trend of global education governance should be moving beyond global education quality assessments characterized by numbers. To this end, countries must hold the prudent view of PISA and transcend PISA-trigged digital governance. The combined efforts and long-term commitment of all countries are needed to address and solve the global governance problem caused by data.

References

Alexander, R. (2012). Moral panic, miracle cures and educational policy: What can we really learn from international comparison? *Scottish Educational Review*, *44*, 4–21.

Auld, E., & Morris, P. (2014). Comparative education, the 'New Paradigm' and policy borrowing: Constructing knowledge for education reform. *Comparative Education*, *50*, 129–155.

Baird, J.-A., Johnson, S., Hopfenbeck, T. N., Isaacs, T., Sprague, T., Stobart, G., & Yu, G. (2016). On the supranational spell of PISA in policy. *Educational Research*, *58*, 121–138.

Beghetto, R. A., & Plucker, J. A. (2006). The relationship among schooling, learning, and creativity: "All roads lead to creativity" or "you can't get there from here?" In J. C. Kaufman & J. Bear (Eds.), *Creativity and reason in cognitive development* (pp. 316–332). Cambridge University Press.

Bogdandy, A. V., & Goldmann, M. (2012). Taming and framing indicators: A legal reconstruction of the OECD's Program for International Student Assessment (PISA). In K. E. Davis, A. Fisher, B. Kingsbury, & S. E. Merry (Eds.), *Governance by indicators: Global power through quantification and rankings* (pp. 52–85). Oxford University Press.

Cao, J., & Yan, W. (2014, February 8). PISA, Viewing basic education from a new perspective [in Chinese]. *Guangming Daily*, 7.

Chen, S., Meng, L., & Zhang, H. (2014). Evidence of education policy in the age of big data: Enlightenment of evidence-based concept on modernization of China's education governance and scientific decision-making [in Chinese]. *Global Education*, *2*, 121–128.

Crossley, M. (2014). Global league tables, big data and the international transfer of educational research modalities. *Comparative Education*, *50*, 15–26.

Department of Education, UK. (2010). *The importance of teaching: The schools white paper 2010*. TSO (The Stationary Office).

Department of Education, UK. (2015). *Experts to visit Shanghai to raise UK mathsstandard*. https://www.gov.uk/government/news/experts-to-visit-shanghai-to-raise-standards-in-math

Dillon, S. (2010). Top test scores from Shanghai stun educators. *The New York Times*. http://www.nytimes.com/2010/12/07/education/07education.html?pagewanted=all

Grey, S., & Morris, P. (2018). PISA: Multiple 'truths' and mediatized global governance. *Comparative Education*, *54*, 109–131.

Kamens, D. H. (2013). Globalization and the emergence of an audit culture: PISA and the search for 'best practices and magic bullets.' In H.-D. Meyer & A. Benavot (Eds.), *PISA, power and policy: The emergence of global educational governance* (pp. 117–140). Symposium Books.

Kristof, N. (2011). China's education system. *The New York Times*. Retrieved January 15, 2011, from http://kristof.blogs.nytimes.com/tag/pisa-test/

Li, J. (2019). "Substitution" or "supplement"—Examining the quality of school education from the development of shadow education—An analysis based on PISA 2015 data of four provinces and cities in China [in Chinese]. *Social Science of Beijing*, *5*, 57.

Lingard, B. (2011). Policy as numbers: Accounting for educational research. *The Australian Educational Researcher*, *38*, 355–382.

Lu, J. (2010). Analysis of the policy guidance of PISA research [in Chinese]. *Research in Education Development*, *8*, 20.

Ma, L. (2019, March 26). Replacing 5 single quantitative evaluation ways with comprehensive quality assessment [in Chinese]. *Guangming Daily*, 13.

Meyer, H.-D., & Benavot, A. (2013). Introduction. In H.-D. Meyer & A. Benavot (Eds.), *PISA, power and policy: The emergence of global educational governance* (pp. 7–26). Symposium Books.

Nóvoa, A., & Yariv-Mashal, T. (2003). Comparative research in education: A mode of governance or a historical journey? *Comparative Education*, *39*, 423–438.

Organisation for Economic Co-operation and Development. (2010a). *PISA 2009 results: Executive summary*. https://www.

oecd.org/pisa/pisaproducts/46619703.pdf

Organisation for Economic Co-operation and Development. (2010b). *PISA 2009 results: Volume II, Overcoming social background: Equity in learning opportunities and outcomes.*

Organisation for Economic Co-operation and Development. (2014a). *PISA 2012 results: Creative problem solving. Vol. V: Students' skills in tackling real-life problems.*

Organisation for Economic Co-operation and Development. (2014b). *PISA 2012 results in focus: What 15-year-olds know and what they can do with what they know.* https://www.oecd.org/pisa/keyfindings/pisa-2012-results-overview.pdf

Organisation for Economic Co-operation and Development. (2014c). *PISA 2012 results: What students know and can do— Student performance in mathematics, reading and science* (Vol. I, Rev. ed.).

Organisation for Economic Co-operation and Development. (2016a). *PISA 2015 results (Volume I): Excellence and equity in education.*

Organisation for Economic Co-operation and Development. (2016b). *PISA 2015 results (Volume II): Policies and practices for successful schools.*

Poovey, M. (1998). *A history of modern fact: Problems of knowledge in the sciences of wealth and society.* University of Chicago Press.

Popkewitz, T. (2011). PISA: Numbers, standardizing conduct, and the alchemy of school subjects. In M. A. Pereyra, H. G. Kotthoff, & R. Cowen (Eds.), *PISA under examination: Changing knowledge, changing tests, and changing schools* (pp. 31–46). Sense.

Sellar, S., & Lingard, B. (2013). Looking East: Shanghai, PISA 2009 and the reconstitution of reference societies in the global education policy field. *Comparative Education, 49*, 464–485.

Simola, H. (2005). The Finnish miracle of PISA: Historical and sociological remarks on teaching and teacher education. *Comparative Education, 41*, 455–470.

Tan, C. (2013). *Learning from Shanghai: Lessons on achieving educational success.* Springer.

Tan, C. (2017). Chinese responses to Shanghai's performance in PISA. *Comparative Education, 53*, 209–223.

Tan, C. (2019). PISA and education reform in Shanghai. *Critical Studies in Education, 60*, 391–406.

Therese, N. H., & Kristine, G. (2017). The politics of PISA: The media, policy and public responses in Norway and England. *European Journal of Education, 52*, 192–205.

Waldow, F. (2012). Standardization and legitimacy: Two central concepts in research on education borrowing and lending. In G. Steiner-Khamsi & F. Waldow (Eds.), *World yearbook of education 2012: Policy borrowing and lending in education.* Routledge.

Waldow, F., Takayama, T., & Sung, Y.-K. (2014). Rethinking the pattern of external policy. Referencing: Media discourses over the 'Asian Tigers' PISA success in Australia, Germany and South Korea. *Comparative Education, 50*, 302–321.

You, Y., & Morris, P. (2016). Imagining school autonomy in high-performing education systems: East Asia as a source of policy referencing in England. *Compare: A Journal of Comparative and International Education, 46*, 882–905.

Zhang, C., & Alexander, A. (2012). PISA as a legitimacy tool during China's education reform: Case study of Shanghai (TranState Working Papers No. 166). Retrieved June 9, 2016, from http://econstor.eu/bitstream/10419/64810/1/727146068.pdf

This article systematically reviews China's progress in lifelong education (LLE) policies, theories, and practices in the 40 years since its reform and opening-up. It analyzes the characteristics of Lifelong Education (LLE) in China through a review of its developmental process and prospects at the policy, theoretical, and practical levels. Following the goals of LLE set by the UNESCO, China has developed and implemented LLE with distinctly Chinese characteristics, focusing on protecting citizens' learning rights, improving civic literacy, and enhancing human resources. Four aspects of China's experiences of LLE development are revealed to provide some guidelines for developing LLE going forward. In addition to suggestions for the creation of an LLE system with Chinese characteristics, this study also reveals several core theoretical topics of LLE development in China that warrant further research.

China's Experiences in Developing Lifelong Education, 1978 – 2017[1]

Zunmin Wu

The history of the People's Republic of China (PRC) since its reform and opening-up is not only one of entrepreneurship by which the country became prosperous and achieved economic growth but the modernization of its education system and development of lifelong education (LLE). After four decades of promotion and implementation, LLE has carved a developmental path with unique Chinese characteristics. Achieving remarkable results that have attracted worldwide attention, China's LLE has also served as an important practical foundation and provided valuable experiences for global LLE development.

However, despite the impressive results it has achieved, China is facing practical dilemmas and a theoretical bottleneck in further LLE development. For example, there is an ambiguous relationship between the LLE and traditional national education systems, the direction of the

---

1 This article is based on the research findings of "China's experiences in developing LLE: A 40-year historical review since the reform and opening-up, and future prospects" (Project No. 2017BHA020), under the "40th anniversary of the reform and opening-up, 70th anniversary of the PRC's founding, and 100th anniversary of the CPC's founding" series organized by the Shanghai Planning Office of Philosophy and Social Sciences. It was published on *ECNU Review of Education*, October 13, 2020.

transformation of adult education has yet to be clarified, and institutional barriers hinder the interchange and integration of various educational resources. Moreover, some educational forms of the traditional education system are in decline, while emerging forms of off-campus education have yet to establish a clear position. Interest disputes and competition between various educational forms have also impacted new resource integration and caused difficulties in system building. It is necessary to learn from history and experiences of success and failure to overcome these obstacles and develop a clear vision of the future.

This study reviews the historical evolution and experiences of China's LLE development since its reform and opening-up. LLE development in China over the past four decades can be divided into four periods, as follows:

i. The introduction period, 1978 – 1987: During this period, LLE was transformed from a concept to policy. Theoretical research primarily focused on the translation and dissemination of ideas on LLE, while its implementation was manifested in the growth of various activities related to adult education.

ii. The start-up period, 1988 – 1997: During this period, ideas on LLE were gradually reflected in policies and there was an initial push toward LLE legislation. Adult education and the Open University of China (OUC), formerly the Central Radio and Television University of China, gradually grew in popularity. Community education also began emerging as a new education form.

iii. The trial-and-error period, 1998 – 2007: During this period, policies and legislation related to LLE were advanced and implemented. Together with greater emphasis on education for the elderly, continuing education in the form of community education and off-campus training was strengthened. Concurrently, there was a significant increase in theoretical discussions in the academic community. New popular keywords for research included "lifelong (LL) learning," "learning society," and "LLE systems."

iv. The intensification of LLE development, 2008 – 2017: During this period, LLE was elevated from an education policy to a national development strategy. While local regulations were promulgated one after another, there was an active push for national legislation. LLE development was characterized by the establishment of open colleges and credit banks, as well as new ideas in community education propelled by experimental projects. The depth of theoretical research gradually deepened, leading to the formation of a core theoretical research team. Research on LLE legislation also became a popular topic.

Examining these periods, this study identifies key factors from relevant policy, theoretical, and practical dimensions that helped establish China's historical experiences and provided a realistic foundation from which to gain a clear understanding of the basic direction of LLE development—especially in terms of path selection and the institutional dilemma faced in the building of an LLE system. Based on an in-depth analysis of the historical background and social realities underpinning these problems, this study proposes policies to support effective LLE development going forward, thereby facilitating China's goal of "learning for everyone, anywhere, anytime."

The introduction period, 1978 – 1987

In December 1978, the 3rd Plenary Session of the 11th Central Committee of the Communist Party of China (CPC) saw the formulation of the principles and policies for the country's reform and opening-up. While these principles and policies facilitated political and economic stabilization, the education situation—damaged during the "Cultural Revolution"—also began recovering. In particular, the country's opening-up promoted both intranational and international political, economic, and cultural cooperation and exchange. Meanwhile, educational research perspectives were broadened, with notions of LLE finally introduced to China—albeit some 15 years after its conception (Guo, 2013).

With the stabilization of the social order, work in the various fields could be carried out normally. This made it possible for the study of educational theories, including the introduction of important international education concepts like lifelong learning. In 1979, the People's Education Press published *Formulation of and Measures for Spare-Time Education*, which included an article by R. Zhang entitled, "LLE: A Trend of Thoughts Worth Noting." This was the context in which the first paper on LLE was disseminated. A year later, Liang (1980) published "Issue of LLE in Japan"—the first locally written paper on LLE development in another country.

This study used CiteSpace, a visualization analysis tool, to analyze data in the China National Knowledge Infrastructure, specifically papers published between 1978 and 1987 that contained the keyword "LLE." Only 26 papers related to LLE were published in China during this period. They primarily focused on the introduction of the LLE concept and background analysis. For instance, W. Zhang's (1984) paper, "Important Contemporary Thoughts on Education: LLE," systematically introduced the background, development, and basic contents of LLE. In "Progress of LLE in Japan," Sun (1981) provided a detailed introduction of the theoretical foundation upon which Japan promoted LLE as well as the status of related policy. The paper also analyzed the reform and institutional mechanism of Japan's education system.

The keyword search of CiteSpace during the 1978 – 1987 period also revealed that the distribution of publications was scattered in terms of the authors, their organizational affiliations, and journals. A cohesive disciplinary research force had yet to be formed (Figure 1), while theoretical research on LLE core characteristics was in its primary stage.

Figure 1. Analysis of collaboration among LLE researchers, 1978–1987.
Note. Translation of the Chinese characters are available in the Online Appendix.
LLE = lifelong education.

Despite the attention of some scholars, when notions of LLE were initially introduced, China lacked the conditions necessary for their comprehensive implementation. With one of the goals of LLE being the provision of educational opportunities to adults without formal education, various forms of adult education were introduced and flourished. This was especially true after the State Education Commission (SEC)—the predecessor of the Ministry of Education (MOE)—held a national working conference on adult education in Yantai, Shandong province, in 1986. For the first time, adult education was listed as an important component of China's national education system, along with basic, higher, vocational, and technical education (Wu, 2003).

Adult education went on to achieve significant success under the guidance of the LLE concept and as a specific element of LLE implementation. At this stage, adult education activities primarily centered on the large-scale development of distance education. This included the creation of the OUC and the self-study and examination system (SES) for adult higher education, the implementation of supplementary cultural and technical education for youth employees, and the establishment of correspondence and evening/night colleges supported by general colleges. In contrast to the unreceptiveness and rigidity of traditional education, adult education was welcomed by people from all walks of life as a result of its flexible and free format, as well as its focus on practical results. In addition to facilitating the accumulation of experiences for the implementation of off-campus education, the development of adult education laid the foundation for the subsequent construction of the LLE system.

With the proliferation of practical activities related to adult education, signs of LLE's transformation from concept to policy started appearing in the 1980s. More specifically, in 1980, the MOE published a policy document in which the term "LLE" appeared. Titled *Opinions on Further Strengthening Training for Elementary and Middle School Teachers*, the document noted that

> Colleges of teacher education bear the responsibility of LLE for in-service elementary and middle school teachers. They are important components of China's teacher education system and will continue to exist for a long time. Therefore, its importance must be accorded due recognition and its status must be made clear. (China Education Yearbook Editorial Department, 1984, p. 761)

Thereafter, the term "LLE" appeared in various speeches on educational work by the CPC and state leaders, as well as in the MOE's annual working documents.

While the LLE concept had yet to appear in any concrete way, the *Constitution of the PRC* had already established education as the right and obligation of all citizens and clarified the state's responsibilities in providing education. As such, although LLE terminology had appeared in some related government documents and begun emerging as an item on the policy agenda, relevant policies had yet to be introduced. Essentially, between 1978 and 1987, LLE was still in the process of being formulated into policy.

The start-up period, 1988 – 1997

The field of education was restored to normal working order between the late 1980s and the early 1990s. Subsequently, the call for educational reform became stronger in response to the need for social development. With the intensification of China's reform and opening-up, as well as the development of policies directed toward a market economic system, education was assigned the dual task of cultivating the talents necessary for the modernization of socialism and improving China's human resources, while transforming the economic growth model in anticipation of the era of the knowledge economy. Originating in the early 1990s, this education policy focused on the reform of China's education system and structure. It was also completely aligned with the concepts advocated by LLE. This period also created excellent opportunities for the promotion of LLE policies.

During this period, the concept of LLE gradually moved toward policy implementation and legalization. In 1993, "LLE" was officially adopted by the CPC's Central Committee and the State Council in formulating the *Outline for the Reform and Development of Education in China*. This was an important marker in the transition of LLE from concept to policy. The document clearly stated that "adult education is a new type of education system that facilitates the development of traditional school education toward LLE and plays an important role in continuously improving the quality of the nation's people and promoting socioeconomic development." In short, LLE was identified as a basic policy and strategic decision in the development of national education.

The first indicator of LLE's entrance into legislation was its inclusion in the *Education Law of the PRC* in 1995, specifically Article 11, which asserted that

> the state is promoting education reform and facilitating the coordinated development of different levels and types of education, and establishing and improving the LLE system, so as to adapt to the needs of the socialist market in terms of economic development and social progress. (The Eighth National People's Congress, 1995)

In addition, Article 41 noted that "the state encourages schools and other educational institutions and social organizations to undertake measures at creating conducive conditions for citizens to have LLE." (The Eighth National People's Congress, 1995). As such, LLE was highly valued by the CPC and included in the legislative framework as a basic national policy.

Implementation advanced at a steady pace during this period. As a new type of education in the transition to LLE, adult education was consistently improved upon and standardized. In December 1988, the State Council approved the SEC's restructuring proposal to determine the functions, institutions, and establishment of LLE. This resulted in the merger of the former Department for the Management of Adult Education, the three SEC divisions in charge of higher education, and the Office of the Steering Committee for SES in Higher Education into the Adult Education Division (Dong, 2008). Issued by the SEC in 1993, *Opinions on the Further Reform and Development of Adult Higher Education* was China's first government document providing comprehensive guidance on adult higher education. Consequently, the OUC and SES grew in popularity and strength, while adult education classes organized by general institutions of higher learning (IHLs) proliferated. Indeed, adult education even gained popularity in rural areas.

A noteworthy phenomenon at this stage was the emergence of community education—a new educational form—on the historical stage of China. This development was marked by the concurrent establishment of community education committees in the Xinjiang and Pengpu Streets of Shanghai's Zhabei District in March 1988. These were the earliest local communal organizations under the label of "community education." Led by their respective street offices, each street saw the joint participation of factories, shops, military units, administrative institutions, schools, and local police stations in educational endeavors. The following year, the Zhabei District People's Government established a district-level community education committee.

In addition to leading to the development of grassroot communal education activities in Shanghai, the formation of local community education organization had nationwide impacts—sparking instantaneous and wide-ranging activity across the country. Community education has multiple functions, including "cultivating and enlightening the people," maintaining social stability and unity, and promoting the building of social and interpersonal relationships. It thus received significant attention from and approval by local governments and general public across the country.

With the strengthening of policy support and further intensification of implementation activities, theoretical research on LLE in China also advanced. The publication of literature reviews progressed in terms of quantity and quality, particularly after 1995. Indeed, 34 related papers were published in 1997 alone. The growth of research interests in this field was also reflected by improvements in the quality of both the papers and the source journals. However, keyword analysis of CiteSpace reveals that a research community facilitating collaboration between authors and institutions had yet to develop. Despite substantial progress in LLE in terms of theory and implementation during this period, research output was relatively low and lacking in in-depth analyses. No institution or expert team undertook comprehensive and specialized research on LLE during this period.

Analysis of the co-occurrence chart of LLE keywords in the 1988–1997 period (Figure 2) reveals that a portion of research content was merely the continuation of popular topics from the previous period. These were basically think-pieces and theoretical commentaries on LLE, including discussions of LLE concepts and elaborations on the implementation of LLE in other countries. Other research examined the relationship between LLE and adult and continuing education, including the impact and significance of LLE ideas on adult education, as well as the relationship between LLE and adult education. Against the backdrop of the educational reform of the 1990s, researchers were inclined toward examining the connection between LLE and adult education connection, as well as the significance of LLE for educational reform.

Figure 2. Co-occurrence chart of keywords in LLE research, 1988–1997.
Note. Translation of the Chinese characters are available in the Online Appendix. LLE = lifelong education.

The trial-and-error period, 1998–2007

In the early 21st century, reform and opening-up—now deeply ingrained in China's political and economic framework—continued to improve China's socialist market economy. Meanwhile, education reform had facilitated the relaxation of external conditions. As the fruits of economic development improved living conditions, people's spiritual needs and educational awareness grew. The consequent advance of educational reform provided the opportunity and foundation to formulate LLE policies.

Steered by Former General Secretary Hu Jintao, on July 28, 2003, the Central Committee of the CPC proposed the timely concept of governing the country with a scientific outlook of development, producing a new direction for education reform. The government began paying more attention to various aspects of education, including its public benefits, balance, and equality. This established the foundation from which LLE ideas were transformed into policy and legislation, as well as its further theoretical and practical development.

Essentially, the CPC recognized that to realize the prioritization of education and rejuvenation of China, the prevailing education system and mechanism had to be reconstructed. This involved establishing an education system comprising both basic and adult education, and capable of integrating the various educational forces by facilitating their mutual convergence and assimilation. The creation of an LLE system thus came into view. In March 2001, the 4th Session of the 9th National People's Congress (NPC) approved the revised *Outline of the 10th Five-Year Plan for Socioeconomic Development in the PRC* (The Ninth National People's Congress, 2001). The report reiterated the need to "develop adult education and various forms of continuing education so as to gradually construct an LLE system." This was also the first time that LLE was included in the national 5-year plan.

At the 16th CPC Party Congress held in November 2002, a report entitled *Establishing an All-Round Moderately Prosperous Society and Creating a New Phase in the Socialist Cause with Chinese Characteristics* similarly reiterated that the goals under the strategic decision for educational development should include "establishing an LLE system" and "forming a relatively complete modern national education system" (Jiang, 2002). Although the dual-system theory was controversial, this was the first time that the establishment of an LLE system appeared in any of the major documents of the CPC Party Congress.

In his report to the 17th CPC Party Congress in October 2007, Former General Secretary Hu Jintao advanced a more refined notion of dual-system education: "The modern national education system is further improved, the LLE system has basically been formed, and the people's general education level and the level of cultivating innovative talents have improved significantly" (Hu,

2007). The resolution made at this party congress facilitated the rapid advancement of the LLE policy in the early 20th century and set important guidelines and goals for the building of an LLE system.

The implementation of LLE practices at the local level made significant progress with the support of national policies and in response to social needs. Published by the CPC Shanghai Municipal Committee and Shanghai Municipal People's Government, *Guiding Opinions on Promoting the Establishment of a Learning Society* argued that building a learning society that supported learning for all and LLE was essential to the comprehensive development of the people, implementation of the scientific outlook of development, and creation of a harmonious society. The document also proposed the goal for the initial establishment of a learning-oriented social framework by 2010 under the banner of "learning for everyone, anywhere, anytime." Additionally, it noted the need to build a new type of college, one that was diversified, multilevel, and open, and which provided academic education, vocational training, as well as leisure and cultural education. These opinions reflect the popularization of the idea of LLE in China during this period. There was general consensus that developing LLE was integral to China's social development, and the central and local governments focused on the construction of a learning society and LLE system. As such, in addition to clarifying the specific requirements and theoretical orientation of building a learning society in China, the aforementioned documents provided a policy basis for the implementation and popularization of LLE activities.

Between 1998 and 2007, community colleges oversaw the rapid development of community education, vocational training, and cultural education. With the aging of society, more attention was paid to the elderly population when implementing LLE. Incorporating education for the elderly as a goal of building a learning society and practicing LLE also objectively promoted the establishment and development of colleges for elderly citizens.

Theoretical research on LLE entered a period of rapid development between 1998 and 2007, and the number and quality of related papers increased sharply. Analysis using the CiteSpace visualization tool reveals the formation of a small group of core researchers and authors, namely, Nailin Chen, Zunmin Wu, Qing Wang, and Kongyi Sun. The more influential governmental agencies and cooperative groups were represented by the Jiangsu Radio and Television University, Jiangsu Institute of Educational Science, and Jiangsu Province Education Commission. The initial formation of this group of scholars and research institutions marked the emergence of a core force for theoretical research on LLE (Figure 3). This research group brought popular topics of LLE research into greater focus through in-depth studies of LLE policies and the pace of their implementation. In short, LLE, learning society, and the LLE system became popular research topics.

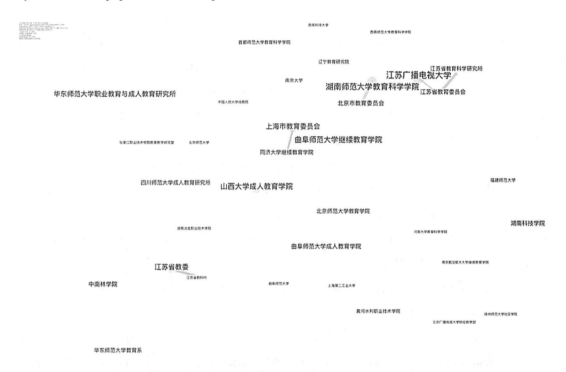

Figure 3. Analysis of collaboration between institutions that published papers on LLE research, 1998–2007.

Note. Translation of the Chinese characters are available in the Online Appendix. LLE = lifelong education.

Others focused on the difficulties of establishing China's LLE system and suggested countermeasures. For instance, Xu and Li (2001) revealed that establishing an LLE system was a huge social system project requiring specialized institutions to exercise the duties of centralized planning and management coordination. They also called for LLE legislation and the establishment of a corresponding safeguard mechanism (Xu & Li, 2001). Some scholars drew on the experiences of developed countries and regions such as Japan, Europe, and the United States in providing recommendations for the construction of China's LLE system. For example, Luo and Zhang (2007) recommended that the methods used to implement community education in Europe and the United States be adopted in promoting the development of community education in China, arguing that community education would provide the foundation upon which to build an effective LLE system.

The intensification of LLE development, 2008 – 2017

In the second decade of the 21st century, there were signs that the process of LLE related policymaking and legislation was accelerating in China. From 2010, the development of LLE was elevated from an educational policy to a national development strategy, frequently appearing in central documents on macro education policies and receiving substantial government support. During this period, several policies with greater practicality and more target measures were introduced. In the prelude to LLE legislation, numerous local legislative regulations were promulgated one after another, while national legislation was prepared.

In 2010, the State Council promulgated the *Outline of the National Medium-to Long-Term Plans for Reforming and Developing Education (2010 – 2020)*. The document asserted the need for China to "build a comprehensive LLE system" (The CPC Central Committee and the State Council, 2010) by 2020. This developmental goal essentially elevated LLE from the level of education reform to a development strategy. On December 27, 2015, the *Decision of the Standing Committee of the NPC on the Proposed Amendments to the Education Law of the PRC* was officially adopted by the 18th Session of the Standing Committee of the 12th NPC. This was the first amendment to the *Education Law of the PRC* since its promulgation in 1995. The phrase "establishing and improving an LLE system" was amended to "perfecting the modern national education system, improving the LLE system, and elevating the level of educational modernization." "Preschool education" was also incorporated into China's current education system under the newly introduced Article 18. These developments heralded the transformation of the modern national education system into the LLE system.

In the revised Article 20, "adult education" of Provision 1 was replaced by "continuing education," Provision 2 remained unchanged, and Provision 3 was extended to include "facilitating mutual recognition between and convergence of different types of learning outcomes, and promoting LL learning for all people (The Twelfth National People's Congress, 2015)." Both legislative provisions indicate the great importance that the party and government attached to LLE development, building a learning society and improving the national education system. At the national level, legislative research on LLE and the related drafting work were commencing; at the local level, LLE legislation achieved substantial progress in Fujian, Shanghai, Hebei, Taiyuan, and Ningbo.[1] The introduction of local LLE regulations not only guaranteed the advancement of legislation at the local level but served as the reference and source of learning for national legislation.

Several new characteristics were evident during this LLE implementation stage: Namely, (i) the appearance of open colleges, which constituted a new form of LLE practice; (ii) the founding of the Shanghai Academic Credit Transfer and Accumulation Bank for LLE, which was the country's first credit bank; and (iii) new progress in community education, as reflected by the successive emergence of various experimental and innovative projects. The need to establish open colleges was clearly mandated in *Outline of the National Medium-to Long-Term Plans for Reforming and Developing Education (2010 – 2020)*. Shanghai immediately used the Shanghai TV University as the foundation for open education and gradually integrated various educational resources, including the existing colleges of continuing education and online colleges set by IHLs, as well as independently established IHLs for adult education. Officially founded on July 23, 2010, Shanghai Open University was positioned as a new type of IHL intended for any individual. Compared to earlier radio and television colleges, open colleges are characterized by being more open—that is, they did not require entrance exams or registration for enrolment—and placing more emphasis on the development of disciplines, particularly professions urgently needed by society.

Issued by the MOE in January 2016, *Opinions on the Proper Management and Operation of Open Colleges* advanced the need to "explore an operating model for open colleges that reflect the characteristics of both China and the current times, so as to meet the learning and LLE needs of all the people and to build a learning society." In addition to providing an important practical platform for the building of an LLE system and learning society, the establishment of open colleges contributed to meeting the multicultural needs of the general public.

With the continuous advancement of LLE policies and practical activities, theoretical research on LLE in China entered a relatively stable period of intensification between 2008 and 2017. This was primarily reflected in the number of LLE-related studies published as well as the increasing

---

1 The dates on which various provinces/cities passed their respective *Regulations on the Promotion of LLE* were as follows: Fujian Province, 2005; Shanghai City, 2011; Taiyuan City, September 2012; Hebei Province, May 2014; and Ningbo City, October 2014.

consistency of their quality. CiteSpace analysis reveals that a professional and authoritative group of core authors—represented by Zunmin Wu and Nailin Chen—had formed in the field of LLE (Figure 4).

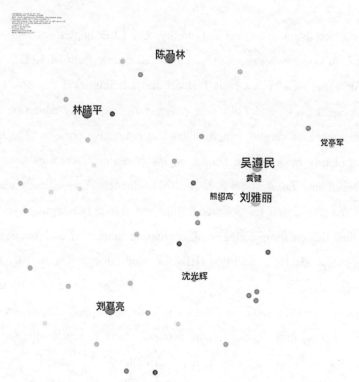

Figure 4. Core group of authors engaged in LLE research, 2008–2017.
Note. Translation of the Chinese characters are available in the Online Appendix.
LLE = lifelong education.

The core institutions of LLE research included the East China Normal University and several radio and television colleges. The co-occurrence chart of keywords illustrates that research on the LLE system and learning society remained popular topics. However, a new topic of "research on LLE legislation" emerged. Related studies contained in-depth reviews of LLE legislation in China, comparisons of similar legislation promulgated in other countries, as well as commentaries on and the identification of learning points from the experiences of these countries (Figure 5).

Conclusion

Summarizing the developmental process of LLE in China over the past 40 years, implementation

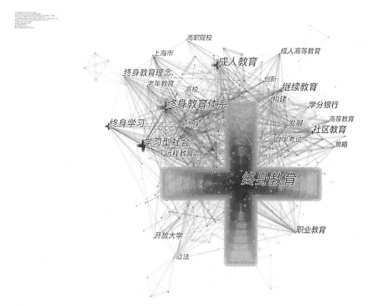

Figure 5. Co-occurrence chart of keywords in LLE research, 2008-2017.
Note. Translation of the Chinese characters are available in the Online Appendix. LLE = lifelong education.

moved from adult education to LLE and then lifelong learning. Under the guidance of and direction set by China's reform and opening-up, LLE was able to catch up to Europe, the United States, Japan, and Korea—taking just 30 years to establish what other countries took nearly half a century to achieve. In terms of building a learning society, China implemented the value orientation and target foundation of LLE and LL learning set by the United Nations Educational, Scientific and Cultural Organization, which included protecting the learning rights of citizens, improving civic literacy, and developing human resources. These achievements resulted from four conditions and factors that facilitated the localization of the international LLE trend in China.

China's LLE development had specific characteristics. First, the government played a prominent role in LLE development, providing guidance and leadership, as well as the vigorous promotion of LLE. Second, the enthusiastic response and strong expectations of the Chinese people. As a result of economic development, the Chinese people began thinking about the connotations of being moderately prosperous. In the process of enhancing their spiritual cultivation and refining their quality of life, they established the practical status of LLE. Third, the socioeconomic and political context of China's reform and opening-up consolidated the value and foundation of LLE development. While advancing China's economy and prosperity, the fundamental purpose of promoting LLE was nonutilitarian: It was intended to improve the personality and humanity of individuals to ensure the cultivation of qualified, proactive, and responsible citizens. In China, LLE became linked to improving human nature and cultivating qualified citizens. Fourth, the positive responses and research of the academic community. Indeed, regardless of the initial introduction of LLE after reform and opening-up or its subsequent development through policy promotion, academia was always at the forefront of implementation. Researchers actively studied and interpreted policies and conveyed the voices of the people in a timely manner, thereby ensuring that LLE development progressed in a way that consistently connected and united China's leaders and its people.

In the four decades since its reform and opening-up, China has made significant progress in LLE development, fostering a system of lifelong learning unique to the country. Looking forward, policy support and legislative guarantees are still necessary for the implementation of LLE. This includes elucidating the relationship between LLE and the national education system as well as removing the institutional barriers hindering the merging of educational resources through top-level design, thereby facilitating LLE interchange. It is also necessary to speed up the process of national LLE legislation to boost the healthy development of LLE in China and meet the growing need for high-quality education.

References

China Education Yearbook Editorial Department. (1984). *China education yearbook (1949 – 1981)* [in Chinese]. Encyclopedia of China Publishing House.

Dong, M. (2008). *Thirty years of reform and the development of adult education in China* [in Chinese]. Higher Education Press.

Guo, H. (2013). *Policies on LLE in China* [Doctoral dissertation, East China Normal University] [in Chinese].

Hu, J. (2007). *Holding high the great banner of socialism with Chinese characteristics and striving for new victories in establishing an all-round moderately prosperous society* [in Chinese]. http://www.npc.gov.cn/zgrdw/npc/xinwen/szyw/zywj/2007 – 10/25/content_373528.htm

Jiang, Z. (2002). *Establishing an all-round moderately prosperous society and creating a new phase in the socialist cause with Chinese characteristics* [in Chinese]. http://www.moe.gov.cn/jyb_sjzl/moe_364/moe_258/moe_44/tnull_5009.html

Liang, Z. (1980). Issue of LLE in Japan [in Chinese]. *Journal of Education in Japan*, (1), 9 – 11.

Luo, J., & Zhang, X. (2007). Community education in Europe and the United States: Revelations for the building of an LLE system in China [in Chinese]. *Distance Education in China*, (1), 72 – 74.

Sun, S. (1981). Progress of LLE in Japan [in Chinese]. *Journal of Northeast Normal University (Philosophy and Social*

Sciences), (5), 100-105.

The CPC Central Committee and the State Council. (2010). *Outline of the national medium- to long-term plans for reforming and developing education (2010 - 2020)* [in Chinese]. http://www.moe.gov.cn/jyb_xwfb/s6052/moe_838/201008/t20100802_93704.html

The Eighth National People's Congress. (1995). *Education Law of the PRC* [in Chinese]. http://www.moe.gov.cn/s78/A02/zfs_left/s5911/moe_619/201512/t20151228_226193.html

The Ninth National People's Congress. (2001). *Outline of the 10th five-year plan for socioeconomic development in the PRC* [in Chinese]. http://www.npc.gov.cn/wxzl/gongbao/2001-03/19/content_5134505.htm

The Twelfth National People's Congress. (2015). *Decision of the standing committee of the NPC on the proposed amendments to the Education Law of the PRC* [in Chinese]. http://www.gov.cn/zhengce/2015-12/28/content_5029900.htm

Wu, Z. (2003). *Theories on LLE in modern China* [in Chinese]. Shanghai Education Publishing House.

Xu, M., & Li, X. (2001). Difficulties in building an LLE system in China and the countermeasures [in Chinese]. *Educational Research*, 22(3), 59-63.

Zhang, W. (1984). Important contemporary thoughts on education: LLE [in Chinese]. *Social Sciences Abroad*, (3), 13-14.

2020 is the concluding year of the basic preschool education popularization policy in China and marks the beginning of *China's Education Modernization 2035*. This study focuses on the top-level design and the prospect of the development plan of China's preschool education toward 2035. The study interviewed 11 experts, including policymakers, educational administrators, scholars, and practitioners in the education, aiming to clarify the focus to have an impact on China's preschool education toward 2035. According to the article, to develop China's preschool education, we need to integrate macro-level, meso-level, and micro-level contents: focusing on public welfare as the development concept, furthering the reform of the educational system and mechanism, making quality improvement the plan's key goal, and forming a new preschool education development mode with Chinese characteristics.

China's Preschool Education Toward 2035: Views of Key Policy Experts [1]

Yong Jiang, Beibei Zhang, Ying Zhao and Chuchu Zheng

Context

Since preschool education has a great impact on the development of individuals, families, and countries (Edwards, 2001; Yu & Miao, 2015), the quality improvement of preschool education has become a global trend. Countries and relevant organizations worldwide have designed plans for the development of preschool education. Through the integrated analysis of the *Incheon Declaration for Education 2030* (UNESCO, 2015), *Statutory Framework for the Early Years Foundation Stage* (U.K., 2017), *Every Student Succeeds Act* (U.S., 2015), *Investing in the*

---

[1] The article was fully funded by major projects of the National Social Science Fund of China (Project #: 18ZDA336). It was published on *ECNU Review of Education*, May 26, 2021. All experts were informed about this study and agreed to give public statements in this article. Suggestions from different experts: (1) Yong Jiang and Liping Guo; (2) Liping Guo; (3) Bingcheng Gao and Xiaohui Xu; (4) Lijuan Pang; (5) Sujing Zhu and Pingzhi Ye; (6) Pingzhi Ye; (7) Xiumin Hong; (8) Lijuan Pang; (9) Xiumin Hong; (10) Yong Jiang; (11) Yong Jiang and Liping Guo; (12) Yong Jiang; (13) Rong He; (14) Sujing Zhu; (15) Yong Jiang and Liping Guo; (16) Sujing Zhu; (17) Sujing Zhu; (18) Rong He; (19) Jinlong Sang; (20) Jianhui Xiong; (21) Liping Guo; (22) Bingcheng Gao; (23) Xiaohui Xu; (24) Xiumin Hong; (25) Bingcheng Gao; (26) Bingcheng Gao and Jinlong Sang; (27) Jianhui Xiong; (28) Xiumin Hong; (29) Jianhui Xiong; (30) Yong Jiang and Xiaohui Xu; (31) Yong Jiang and Liping Guo.

Early Years—A National Early Childhood Development Strategy (Australia, 2009), *Pathways to the Future: Nga Huarahi Arataki* (New Zealand, 2002), *Hakutulokset hakusanalla: Education and research development plan 2011 – 2016* (Finland, 2011), and *Major Policies and Plans for 2016* (Korea, 2016), it is found that they all emphasize high-quality preschool education, paying attention to preschool education equity and disadvantaged children, improving the quality of teachers, and so on. In addition, the application and gradual popularization of the Internet, Internet of Things, Big Data, cloud computing, artificial intelligence, sensor technology, robotics, virtual reality, and other new technologies in the field of education (Yang, 2019) has also injected fresh vitality into the development of preschool education, leading it toward the intelligent age.

Achievements of preschool education in China since 2010

In China, the development of preschool education is being led by the government (Hou, 2016), which mainly relies on policies to promote it. In 2010, *the National Outline for Medium and Long Term Education Reform and Development (2010 – 2020)* and several statements made the State Council on the current development of preschool education were issued. Starting in 2011, all regions in China have formulated and implemented *Three-year Action Plans for Preschool Education* to promote the standardization and quality development of preschool education.

With the development of society and promotion of policies, preschool education, as the foundation of basic education in China has undergone tremendous changes. Various indicators show a rapid growth trend and remarkable achievements of the preschool education in China (see Table 1). For example, the popularization rate of preschool education has increased significantly. In 2018, the gross enrollment rate of preschool education was 81.7%, which was 25.1% higher than that of the gross enrollment rate in 2010. The growth rate of the number of school-age children attending preschool and the gross enrollment rate of disadvantaged children attending preschool education (especially in the central and western outlying areas, along with the poverty-stricken areas) is also relatively high (He et al., 2018). Preschool education resources have expanded geometrically. After the preschool education data of 2018 and 2010 is compared, it is observed that the total number of preschools in China increased by 77.29% in 2018, number of classes increased by 72.81%, number of full-time preschool teachers increased by 125.60%, and number of childcare workers increased by 467.79%. Financial investment in preschool education has increased significantly. By 2017, financial investment in preschool education in China's public budget increased from 21.874 billion RMB to 154.607 billion RMB, more than 6 times as compared to 2010. The education level of preschool teachers has also developed steadily. Since 2010, the Ministry of Education has successively issued *Kindergarten teacher professional standards* (2012), *Kindergarten staff allocation standards (Provisional)* (2013), *Kindergarten director professional standards* (2015), and other documents, which specify conditions of eligibility for preschool teachers and directors, and give clear directives with respect to staffing and other aspects. As of 2018, out of the total number of teachers, the percentage of preschool teachers with a junior college degree or a higher education background reached 80.98%. This figure shows that the number of teachers having a higher educational background have tripled since 2010. At the same time, the number of teachers participating in various types of training programs at all levels has continued to increase. Owning to the current implementation of the National Training and Provincial Training of Basic Education Teachers, the level of training of preschool teachers is relatively high (Hui & Chu, 2015). Thus, China's preschool education has entered a period of rapid development.

Table 1. Some indicators of China's preschool education development in 2010 and 2018.

Indicators	2010	2018	Growth rate (%)
The gross enrollment rate of preschool education (%)	56.6	81.7	25.1
Number of preschools (N)	150,420	266,677	77.29
Number of classes (N)	971,525	1,678,924	72.81
Number of full-time preschool teachers (N)	1,144,225	2,581,363	125.60
Number of childcare workers (N)	160,330	910,332	467.79
Financial investment in preschool education in China's public budget (RMB)	21.874 billion	154.607 billion	606.81
Number of preschool teachers with a junior college degree or a higher education background (N)	689,952	2,090,076	202.93

Note. The data involved in this table and "Short Board in the Development of Preschool Education in China" part are from the education statistics and the financial investment bulletin of the Ministry of Education of China in relevant years.

Weak points in the development of preschool education in China

However, there are some problems that hamper the development of preschool education in

China, such as regional and urban-rural differences in the quality of education (Luo & Li, 2017; Ye & Zhang, 2015). Some of these differences concern the curriculum and reflect the different stages of education development in different regions. Furthermore, a long-term funding guarantee mechanism for preschool education has not yet been established. As China's preschool education funds implement the "county-based" investment system, large-scale differences exist in areas due to insufficient county-level financial investment (Bu et al., 2011). Moreover, the amount of investment is too low, and the local government's financial investment in different types of preschools is significantly different in different areas (Hong & Jiang, 2018). In addition, the number of preschool education teachers still needs to be increased, as there is a high children-teacher ratio. In 2018, the children-teacher ratio was 18∶1 in preschools and the proportion of teachers with professional titles and ranks was 75.67%, far higher than that of primary and secondary school teachers. Moreover, the overall treatment of preschool teachers is poor, and the serious shortage of staff in public preschools (Wu et al., 2018), such as part of the preschool teachers' salaries, can only meet the basic needs of life, and their work is massive and complicated. These problems adversely affect the stable development of preschool teachers.

The year 2020 is of great significance as it is the concluding year of the *National Outline for Medium- and Long-term Education Reform and Development (2010–2020)* and the 13th Five-Year Plan. It is also the opening year of *China's Education Modernization 2035* (proposed in 2019) and the preschool education legislation.

In the report of the *19th National Congress of the Communist Party of China*, it was proposed that steady progress should be made to ensure people's access to childcare and education. To accomplish the basic tasks of education development, modern educational governance thought has focused on reforms in preschool education, emphasizing children's sustainable development, valuing every child's interest and hobbies, and placing importance on the growth in the happiness of children. We should adhere to the fundamental task of assisting the people to cultivate virtue, and this task is also a new requirement of the times for the development of preschool education. The problem of "difficulty to access the preschool" has become the "difficulty to access the public preschool" in some areas (Du, 2016; Liu, 2018). The needs of parents have changed from "preschool for all children" to "good preschool for all children," reflecting new needs and aspirations. These needs are closely related to the explicit and realistic interests of the masses.

Based on the above-mentioned background and expectations, this study aims to carry out top-level design and the prospect of the development plan of preschool education and uses expert interview method to integrate the suggestions and ideas of 11 experts (including policymakers, educational administrators, scholars, and practitioners) and puts forward the development plan of China's preschool education toward 2035. And the analysis of the interviews is carried out to have an impact on the practice and theoretical research of preschool education in the policy field, the practice field, and the research field and to provide suggestions for the strategic planning of preschool education development in other countries.

Method

Expert interview is a widely used qualitative interview method often aiming at gaining information about or exploring a specific field of action (Doeringer S., 2020), which is in line with the research needs of this study, so this study used the method of expert interview. Through the analysis of existing studies, we found that researchers focus more on the strategic planning of preschool education development using the research method of policy text analysis. We found that researchers pay more attention to meso-level contents, such as financial investment in preschool education and construction of teaching staff, or the micro-level contents, such as the gross enrollment rate of preschool education, the number of public preschools, and the number of accessible preschools with low prices (Bao, 2018; Huang, 2011). They seldom put forward relevant suggestions from the perspective of the macro system (Cao, 2017). This study interviewed experts from different professional backgrounds, scholars from different units, administrative personnel, and practitioners in order to interpret the practical views of different stakeholders on the development of preschool education from multiple perspectives to accomplish the set goals of development of preschool education by 2035. This study aimed to suggest changes to make the preschool education system more reasonable and reliable and to have a certain impact on the sustainable development of preschool education in the policy domain.

As a part of the expert interview approach, researchers visit or organize interviews with highly qualified and representative experts for specific topics, record the interview contents, and then conduct comprehensive content analysis to draw conclusions (Zhang et al., 2016). This approach is widely used in the fields of education, medicine, and so on. This approach is also used in the process of government policy planning, decision-making, and implementation (Broda et al., 2017; Vidal-Hall et al., 2019).

Selecting interviewees

This study selected 11 experts. We looked for potential interviewees from different research institutes, universities, and government institutions in the fields of education theory research, education policy research, and preschool education by taking into account policymakers, educational administrators, scholars, and preschool directors. Timeliness and foresight are needed to understand the current situation and needs of preschool education development in China from the perspectives of policymaking, formulation and implementation of policy, theoretical research, and practical exploration. These two qualities are needed to think deeply about the accomplishment of the development plan of preschool education in China by 2035. To this end, we selected 11 experts (see Table 2) including policymakers and educational administrators who can effectively influence the formulation and implementation of preschool education policies. We also included university scholars and preschool directors who have rich theoretical research and practical research experience. Because of the differences in the interviewees' locations and times, we adopted different interview forms. After communicating and coordinating with the interviewees, the interviewees located in the same city participated in a group interview. We conducted a telephonic interview or a face-to-face interview with the interviewees who were located in the same city but could not participate in the group interview. The interviewees who were not in the same area participated in a telephonic interview.

Structure of the interview

The basic framework of the interview included the opinions of experts on the current situation, policies, and existing problems of preschool education and the main challenges and future planning in the face of the development of preschool education toward 2035 (see Table 3).

Analysis

Data analysis consisted of two stages. In the first stage, thematic analysis was conducted. The advantage of this method lies in its flexibility and compatibility. In the second stage, Bacchi's "What's the problem represented to be?" (WPR) policy analysis method was used, which takes

Table 2. Basic information of the experts.

Name	Unit	Title/position	Identity	Research field
Lijuan Pang	BNU	Vice Chairman of Minjin Central Committee; Member of the Standing Committee of the National People's Congress; Vice Chairman of the Standing Committee of Beijing Municipal People's Congress; Professor	Researcher; Committed to the promotion of preschool education legislation	Preschool education; educational theory and management; psychology
Jinlong Sang	Beijing Academy of Educational Sciences	Vice President; Researcher	Researcher, participating in the formulation of education policy in Beijing	Education theory and management; higher education; secondary education
Jianhui Xiong	National Center for Education Development Research	Researcher	Researcher; staff member of the Ministry of Education; participating in domestic and international education research; participating in formulating the 14th 5-year plan for education	Education theory and management
Rong He	Shanghai Municipal Education Commission	Instructional Coach	Researcher; supporting government staff, administrators, directors, and service providers of Shanghai preschool education	Preschool education
Xiumin Hong	BNU	Director, Institute of Preschool Education, Ministry of Education, BNU; Professor	Researcher; participating in the formulation of preschool education policy through subject research, university consultation reports, and so on	Preschool education; educational theory and management; demography and family planning
Yong Jiang	ECNU	Professor	Researcher; participating in the formulation of preschool education policy through subject research, government consultation report writing, and so on	Preschool education policy; preschool teacher education

Continued

Name	Unit	Title/position	Identity	Research field
Liping Guo	ECNU	Professor	Researcher; having original opinions on the application of information technology in preschool education	Preschool education; psychology; educational theory and management
Bingcheng Gao	National Institute of Education Sciences	Associate Research Fellow	Researcher; The Institute is a national comprehensive education scientific research institution directly under the Ministry of Education and is the first national education think tank	Preschool education; educational theory and management; psychology
Xiaohui Xu	Capital Normal University	Associate Professor	Researcher; paying more attention to the "difficulty of entering the preschool" and education equity	Preschool education; educational theory and management; psychology
Pingzhi Ye	Guangzhou University	Professor	Researcher; holding positions in many academic organizations; member of the state training expert group of the Ministry of Education	Preschool education; higher education; educational theory and educational management
Sujing Zhu	Soong Ching Ling Kindergarten	Director	Practitioner; Researcher; reflecting on problems in preschool education practice through CFA	Preschool education

Note. CFA = China Welfare Institute; ECNU = East China Normal University; BNU = Beijing Normal University.

Table 3. Basic structure of the interview.

Code	Description
Current situation	What do you think of the current development of preschool education in China? What achievements have been made?
Current policies	How does the state stipulate the character, development direction, and basic requirements of preschool education from the perspective of macro-level?
Urgent issues	What are the outstanding problems that need to be solved for the development of China's preschool education?
Policy barrier	What are the main difficulties and obstacles faced by the government and policymakers in promoting the national preschool education? What efforts and attempts need to be made by stakeholders to resolve these difficulties?
Changes and challenges toward 2035	What changes have taken place in the government and policymakers' understanding of the character and functions of preschool education? What new requirements and expectations have been put forward for preschool education toward 2035?
Future planning	In your opinion, what are the future directives on national preschool education development by 2035? How will the role of the government change in the development and management of preschool education? How do you consider the future planning of preschool education development?

policy as the premise of discourse, and uses models to perform a critical analysis of the preschool education decision-making process (Bacchi, 2009). This method enables analysts to question how to express specific meaning through discourse in policy design. Similar to the statement that "policy is both text and action, words and deeds, it is what is enacted as well as what is intended" put forward by Stephen Ball (1995), the intention of policy recommendations can be understood through the review of the experts' interviews by analyzing their key considerations in the process of policy formulation.

Findings

Through the integration analysis of the key points of preschool education in 2035 mentioned by policymakers, education managers, scholars, and kindergarten directors, we found that (see Figure 1) their opinions clarify the development concept of public welfare and benefits, embody the product attributes of preschool education public service, reform the educational system and mechanism at its core, make quality improvement as its key focus, emphasize the construction of teaching staff, and take into account the rapid development of information network. A new model of preschool education incorporating Chinese characteristics has been designed to play a leading role in the development plan. The entire planning picture takes into account the contents of macro-, meso-, and micro-levels [1] and embodies the unity of concept and practice.

Figure 1. The Planning of China's preschool education toward 2035.

Intelligent class: Information technologies and artificial intelligence

Information technology. The construction of intelligent preschools corresponds to the vision to "accelerate the educational reform in the information age, build an intelligent campus, and build an integrated intelligent teaching, management and service platform" clearly put forward in the text of *China's Education Modernization 2035*. Focusing on the construction of databases and intelligent preschools, the text emphasizes the cultivation of humanistic qualities in the students

---

1 The macro-level emphasizes the contents related to thinking from the national level and the overall development of preschool education, such as "Accessible with low prices" services, "Service-oriented" preschool education system and Chinese characteristics: A new preschool education model. The mesolevel emphasizes the contents related to institutions and mechanisms, such as optimization and upgradation of institutions and mechanisms. The micro-level emphasizes the contents related to the improvement of kindergarten and its education quality, such as Intelligent class and "High-quality" platform for talent gathering for teachers.

and the return of the true essence of education. Following directives can provide guidance in using IT and AI in preschool education.

1. Improve the level of informatization and strengthen the construction of the database

With the development of IT, academic circles are paying increasing attention to the construction and management of children's information databases (Lin & Xu, 2018). Some experts have proposed establishing an electronic information platform system to store each child's scores and carry out data mining work related to children's learning and development research. They have proposed using the data provided by the platform to record, analyze, monitor, and support children's learning and development in the form of "identity authentication." (1) In addition, the experts propose a two-way opening of the data system, strengthening the systematic construction and transformation of government functions, strengthening the legal construction of information management, and ensuring personal information security.

2. Carry out the construction of intelligent preschools and pay attention to the cultivation of humanistic qualities

Information and communication technology (ICT) plays an important role in the construction of intelligent preschools. It has great potential to develop preschool teachers' information literacy, organize educational activities, and stimulate the growth and development of young children. It also plays an important role in the joint education of families and kindergartens (Nazarenko & Andriushchenko, 2019). The 2035 development plan of China's preschool education should focus on the construction of science and innovation centers, strengthen the comprehensive application of artificial intelligence technology in the field of preschool education, carry out the construction of intelligent preschools, and develop intelligent teaching assistant systems. The plan should use intelligent technology to speed up the reform of teaching methods and build a new education system that includes intelligent learning and interactive learning. (2) In addition, it is important to note that when carrying out AI supported science education for preschool teachers, children, and their parents, attention should be paid to the cultivation of the humanistic spirit in the children. Preschool teachers should also consciously cultivate their own morality, which is rarely mentioned in the existing research.

"Accessible with low prices" services: Balanced development and fair access

Inclusive development. The purpose and motive of preschool education development is to support public welfare and provide accessible preschools with low prices (Hu et al., 2016; Liu, 2009). Out of these set goals, a sufficient number of accessible preschools with low prices has become the focus of policymakers, educational administrators, and scholars. Effective promotion of the construction and development of accessible private preschools with low prices (Zhuang & Cheng, 2012) is also the key goal of *Three-year Action Plans for Preschool Education* in various regions. Following directives can provide guidance in ensuring accessible preschool education.

1. Narrowing the gap between public and accessible private preschools with low prices (3) and promoting the construction of inclusive private preschools

In order to enable the vast majority of children to enjoy inclusive preschool education services, some experts proposed that we should adhere to the policy of integrating public and inclusive preschools, explore the method of calculating the average cost incurred by students in accessible private preschools with low prices, formulate the financial subsidy standard and charging standard, and adopt methods such as water and electricity pricing, land preference, rent reduction and exemption, appointment of public teachers, free teacher training, maintaining education quality, and compensation by awards to transform private preschools. (4) At the same time, we should ensure that private preschools have the same status as public preschools in classification, grading, evaluation, guidance, teacher training, and professional title evaluation. All regions should carry out the proposed changes step-by-step and ensure orderly promotion by taking into account the actual status of local preschool education.

2. Reforming the grading system of preschools and realizing the balanced development of education

Preschool rating plays an important role in the development of private preschools. However, a vast majority of accessible private preschools with low prices are facing problems with the current grading system (Lei, 2014). Therefore, some experts have proposed canceling the original preschool rating and reward system, reducing parents' preference to high-quality demonstration preschools, and promoting balanced and fair allocation of educational resources. (5) In the specific implementation of the reform in the rating system, we should shorten the evaluation time of preschools, simplify the evaluation process and content, reduce the requirements for summary materials and written work, and adhere to the evaluation concept of "promoting quality by evaluation." (6) In addition, pre-assessment training should be provided to supervisors and assessors to ensure the professionalism of the assessment. (7)

"Developmental" pattern: Optimization and upgradation of institutions and mechanisms

Institutions and mechanisms. The institutions and mechanisms are the bottleneck restricting the development of preschool education and are the fundamental reason behind problems such as the difficulty and high cost of entering preschool (Yu & Liu, 2017). Promoting reforms in the current preschool education system and mechanism is the key to realizing the sustainable development of preschool education and the development of China's preschool education toward 2035, including mechanisms such as policy guarantee, financial guarantee, management guarantee, and social security. (8) At this stage, the supervision system and school system reforms are the key areas to optimize and upgrade the system and mechanism. The following directives can provide guidance in reforming the preschool education system.

1. Reforming the supervision system and liberating teachers

China's Education Modernization 2035 emphasizes the need to improve the system and mechanism of education supervision, improving the authority and effectiveness of education supervision, and stresses that the education management department should issue the preschool education quality evaluation standard (9) as soon as possible. Preschool is the place where preschool education supervision is implemented. We should fully trust and empower the director of kindergartens to carry out internal innovations. Under the "Internet plus education" ecosystem, we should change the way of supervision and use information technology to build online supervision and assessment platforms to understand the real education and teaching situation in kindergartens. Teachers, parents, principals, evaluators, and education administrative departments can upload information and communicate and interact with each other in real time through the platform. This communication will help to liberate teachers, realize the transparency and humanization of assessment, (10) promote the establishment of a third-party public welfare evaluation institution independent of the government and preschools, select high-quality evaluation institutions through competition, and manage the institutions scientifically. (11)

2. Carrying out reforms in school system and promoting a smooth, stable, and high-quality connection between preschools and primary schools

For the past 2 years, the theme of the national preschool education publicity month focused on the connection between preschools and primary schools. Solving the problem of education transition from kindergarten to primary school has become a major research focus (Yu, 2017). Some experts, in accordance with the existing research, pointed out that to scientifically and effectively solve this problem, it is necessary to integrate resources, open up the system, make preschool teachers follow primary school classes or primary school teachers follow preschool classes, and teach the teachers transitional and balanced allocation of educational resources (Pei, 2015). In areas like Shanghai, where preschool education development is at the forefront of national policy, experts suggest that we can try to reform the school system, change the previous "3 + 5" model of the primary school system, move the first grade of primary school down to preschool, and change it into a "4 + 4" school system. (12) At the same time, a cooperative community of teachers between preschool and primary school should be established to jointly formulate curriculum objectives, contents, and forms for children in their early childhood to help children smoothly realize the transition from preschool to primary school. (13) In addition, the government should formulate practical and coherent policies for preschool and basic education.

"High-quality" platform for talent gathering: A team of talented preschool teachers

Teachers' development. China has always attached great importance to the construction of preschool teachers' identities. *Opinions of the State Council on the current development of preschool education* (*2010*) and *On strengthening the construction of kindergarten teachers* (*2012*) proposed multiple ways to strengthen the construction of preschool teachers' identities, such as focusing on teacher training, professional identity, wages and salaries, establishing of professional titles, and so on. *China's Education Modernization 2035* plan proposed to "build a team of high-quality professional and innovative teachers." The plan proposed to achieve this goal by taking into account the actual needs of preschool teachers' development, and strive to improve teachers' political, social, and professional status, and enhance their sense of professional identity and professional well-being. The following directives can provide guidance in preschool teachers' development.

1. Improving the overall salary of preschool teachers, enhancing the value of teacher's qualification certificate, and implementing the teacher identity credit certification system

In order to elevate the quality of preschool teachers, it is necessary to bring reforms in the recruitment system of preschool teachers, implement equal pay for equal work policy, and balance the allocation of educational resources. (14) To improve the treatment and welfare of preschool teachers, we have to raise the minimum wage standard for preschool teachers and ensure that it is basically the same as that of primary and secondary school teachers. It is also important to design plans to double the income of preschool teachers. (15)

Improving the value of preschool teachers' qualification certificates: With the qualification certificate, preschool teachers can avail benefits such as purchasing a house or a car and they can enjoy travel and other benefits. The availing of such benefits enhances the teachers' sense of professional identity. Teacher's qualification certificate is linked with the teacher's morality, which means that a teacher's teaching certificate will be revoked immediately once he/she acts against teaching ethics. (16) With the credit certification of "teacher's identity," we can realize the connection between teacher's qualification certificate and credit mechanism and standardize teacher's morality.

2. Strengthening the moral construction and professional training of preschool education

Many studies have focused on the participation of preschool teachers in training programs (Hui & Chu, 2015), with few suggesting the idea of appointing an instructional coach. Some experts pointed out that the idea of the appointment of an instructional coach for preschool education should be encouraged and implemented. In the process of selecting an instructional coach, we should abandon the mechanism of selecting an instructional coach only from among practitioners in the education field, and instead should seek the coach from other professional fields. (17) There needs to be a clarification of the division of responsibilities among departments' staff and instructional coaches, an effort to carry out project-based management and reduce the bureaucratic processes of education administration. The training of instructional coaches of preschool education needs to be carried out in a planned way to establish the concept of equality; to realize scientific, efficient, humanized, and comprehensive evaluation in the course of action; (18) and to establish an effective incentive mechanism to link the title evaluation, salary, and bonus of the instruction coach with their scientific research and work achievements.

3. Promoting the diversity of the constitution of preschool teaching staff, innovating the system of teacher training, and strengthening the comprehensive management and cultivation of teachers

The construction of teaching staff is closely related to the training of teachers. These two aspects correspond to the requirements of *China's Education Modernization 2035* for the organic connection to vocational education, connotation development of higher education, and preservice and post-service development. From the perspective of preservice training, we should encourage people of a diverse range of backgrounds to study early childhood education to become preschool teachers, strengthen the cultivation of preschool education major in normal universities, (19) and support the reform and planning of local normal schools. We should also adopt various models such as "3+2" and "3+4" for the enrollment of undergraduate and secondary students in vocational training to train the students as preschool teachers, encourage surplus teachers and normal graduates in primary and secondary schools to enter preschool after professional training, gradually improve the entry threshold of preschool teachers, and form professional preschool teacher teams that consist of full-time undergraduate students. (20) From the point of view of post-service training, we should strengthen post-job training, change training methods, adopt credit systems, and let teachers choose courses according to credit requirements, so as to enhance the merit and relevance of teacher training. (21)

"Service-oriented" preschool education system: Open, tolerant, and inclusive

Public service. *Opinions of the State Council on the current development of preschool education (2010)* proposed to "strive to build a public service system of preschool education covering urban and rural areas with a reasonable layout." Local governments should focus on building such a public service system as it will continue to be the main area of focus for a period of time in the future. To include the concept of a life-long education development in the construction of public service system of preschool education, it is necessary to uphold an open and inclusive attitude, to pay attention to children with special needs, to pay attention to the needs of children who move with their parents and the left-behind children, and to integrate the nurseries and kindergartens for children aged 0 – 6 year(s). The following directives can provide guidance in ensuring that children receive the right to participate in an inclusive preschool education system.

1. Paying attention to the children with special needs and improving the overall level of inclusive education

With the development of information technology, experts have stated that all regions can rely on grid management to gradually smoothen the mechanism of finding and reporting special children, improve the evaluation system of special children, and refine the classification standards. It can also provide support for the survival, development, and learning of children with special needs by means of the distribution of goods, living subsidies, family guidance, and intervention. (22) It is necessary to improve the rules regarding the implementation of teacher training, accessibility of training, enrollment, and placement related to special children's education. (23) It is important to actively build integrated education demonstration schools and promote the application of artificial intelligence in this field.

2. Guaranteeing the right to receive fair and high-quality preschool education to the children who move with their parents and the left-behind children

With the development of urbanization, the education of children who move with their parents and that of left-behind children has become a major problem in China. By taking into account the experience of relevant regions in the preschool education stage, we can gradually promote the implementation of the policy of "tenants enjoying the same rights as home buyers" in the city, endow the children of the lessee (who fulfill the necessary conditions) the right to enter a nearby preschool, and ensure that all children have the right to receive quality preschool education. At the same time, we should pay close attention to the ratio between population change and resource allocation. This ratio reflects a dynamic adjustment: how to meet the resource demand when the numbers of preschool children are increasing or how to relocate these resources when the number of children decreases to avoid wasting the resources. (24)

3. Establishing community service centers and parent schools for preschool education to meet the diversified parenting needs

We should actively promote the establishment of community service centers for preschool education and further strengthen the overall planning of family education. Similar to existing research (Lv, 2015; Stanova & Mitova, 2015), we should consider the construction of a new mode of joint education for families and kindergartens as an important breakthrough. In areas like Shanghai, where preschool education is relatively advanced, we should try our best to build parent schools. We should make full use of existing resources, improve the preschool education service website platform and resource base, support the development of large-scale public welfare activities for children, and provide comprehensive, detailed, and targeted education services for parents. The effective implementation of these suggestions has now become the focus of the government's attention and research focus.

4. Actively promoting the integration of nurseries and kindergartens for children aged 0–6

With the development of parents' educational concepts and changes in educational service demands, the integration of nurseries and kindergartens for children aged 0 – 6 has become a new trend. (25) Based on Shanghai's trial of the trend, the experts proposed that in the process of construction of educations institutions, we should establish a cooperative operation mechanism between education, health, family planning, and the community. (26) We should strengthen the construction of professional service teams and promote the training of professionals such as nursery teachers, early childhood teachers, child health-care teachers, and nutritionists. We should also provide parents with family education instruction manuals for children aged 0 – 6 to improve their childcare abilities. (27) For children aged 0 – 3, we should regularly track the performance of early education services in various communities and focus on the quality of parent-child preschools, early education centers, and other institutions. (28) For preschools, we should pay attention to the development of connotation, avoid the development of homogeneity, and advocate personalized development. (29)

Chinese characteristics: A New preschool education model

Characteristic development. At the *18th National Congress of the Communist Party of China*, it was put forward that "morality is the fundamental task of education." Later, the reports of the *19th National Congress of the Communist Party of China and China's Education Modernization 2035* and other important documents reaffirmed this important education concept. This concept has far-reaching implications and has been adapted to the requirements of the times (Wu et al., 2019). At the same time, we should build a preschool education development model by incorporating Chinese characteristics, stick to the original aim in the multicultural world wave, increase influence, and show cultural confidence. Following directives can provide guidance in incorporating Chinese characteristics in the preschool education system.

1. Adhering to the fundamental task of moral education and bringing traditional culture into the focus of basic education

We should adhere to the fundamental task of assisting the people to cultivate virtue, taking this task as the basic idea and value orientation of preschool education, and further commit to thinking about what kind of sample morality, values, core literacy, and ability should be cultivated in the children participating in China's preschool education. At the same time, amid the wave of multiculturalism and cultural integration in the world, we should think about how to incorporate Chinese characteristics in the preschool education and increase the popularity of Chinese characteristics by showcasing their advantages to other countries. (30) We should pay special attention to the position of traditional culture in basic education and focus on the fundamental task of fostering virtue through education. By following the rules of children's learning and development, we should integrate Chinese traditional culture into children's moral education, cultural knowledge education, art and physical education, social practice education, and so on.

2. Facing China's Education Modernization 2035, building a preschool education model with Chinese characteristics

Few studies have mentioned the construction of preschool education model with Chinese characteristics. To promote the development of China's preschool education by 2035, we should think about how to overcome difficulties and to break the bottleneck of preschool education development. Some experts have proposed that we should establish brand awareness, analyze the development trend of preschool education in the world, and summarize the experience, characteristics, and advantages of preschool education development in China. (31) Based on China's situation, using top-level design, we will make key breakthroughs in resource allocation, development structure, system and mechanism, connotation quality, social function, and brand creation. We will build, from the micro to the middle level and then to the macro-level, a preschool education model incorporating Chinese characteristics that adheres to public welfare, openness and diversity, high quality and balance, and which is full of vitality (Samuelsson et al., 2019).

Reflections

One of the advantages of this study is that it brings the important contributions of scholars and experts from different research institutes and universities who are engaged in educational theory and preschool education research to one platform. Based on the analysis and integration of thoughts of 11 experts on the planning of China's preschool education toward 2035, we found that the construction of preschool education model which incorporates Chinese characteristics is an important direction for future development. This direction closely focuses on the nature of public welfare's provisions for preschool education (Pang & Han, 2010) to promote the development of inclusive preschool education, focus on the standardized development of preschool education, paying close attention to quality development and the fairness of education, actively building and improving the public service system of preschool education. At the same time, the development of ICT is closely integrated with the development of preschool education under the trend of "internet plus education."

Based on the achievements and existing problems in the development of preschool education in China, combined with the planning for the development prospects of China's preschool education toward 2035, we propose the following considerations.

Respecting local differences and promoting the development of preschool education step-by-step

As mentioned earlier, there are great differences in the development levels of preschool education in different regions of China. Since there are too many problems in the development of preschool education in China, deep-seated contradictions still exist, as local conditions are special and are closely related to the local funding support level, policy implementation level, and so on (Hong & Jiang, 2018). Thus, we cannot make up for all the past debts all at once. Based on such a situation, the proposed planning scenario is not only far from reality but is also difficult to put into practice. We should respect the development differences of each region, and at the same time, each region should follow the principle of "step by step" progress, formulate feasible plans, and implement them in stages and steps. In addition, while solving the existing problems, we should also promote the development of preschool education moderately and allow some regions to experiment first to keep pace with developed countries and their excellent preschool education. We should also allow regions with serious historical arrears to develop preschool education qualitatively and quantitatively so as to avoid a "one size fits all" situation.

Thinking comprehensively and taking advantage of the situation to modernize China's education

In *China's Education Modernization 2035*, the development of each education stage is not separated, but connected with each other. The development of preschool education 2035 is closely connected to the development of other education stages. Therefore, we need to comprehensively consider the relationship between education development and preschool education. For example, the connotation development of vocational education and higher education is closely related to the cultivation of preschool teachers and staff at early childhood education institutions. It involves encouraging preschool education students to undertake vocational education. The progress of preschool students to undergraduate and graduate stages is closely related to the output quality of preschool teachers and staff. In addition, *Plan for the Revitalization and Development of the Middle and Western Regions* and "*Three districts and three prefectures*" *poverty alleviation plan for deep poverty areas* provide opportunities for the development of preschool education. Therefore, the development of preschool education should be based on the background of the development of the times, the policies issued by the state, and taking advantage of various plans to seek a way for the development of preschool education.

Focusing on people's needs and emphasizing "people-oriented" education

To achieve the goals of preschool education toward 2035, it is necessary to focus on "peopleoriented" education. Planning at macro-, meso-, and micro-levels is based on the purpose and value of people (Li & Yang, 2017), which is consistent with the fundamental purpose of the CPC to serve the people wholeheartedly. The foothold of the development of preschool education lies in early childhood and in the needs of early childhood development. Facing 2035, the development of preschool education finally returns to the question "what kind of person to cultivate, how to cultivate, and for whom to cultivate." To provide "people-oriented" preschool education, the key focus should be to ensure the effective implementation of the policy. The preschool education policies issued in China are more comprehensive. Therefore, connecting policy and practice, truly benefiting the masses, and providing satisfactory preschool education to the people require the political wisdom of governments and the support of kindergartens, parents, and other stakeholders.

Conclusion

In a word, compared with the strategic goals and plans of Preschool Education issued by the world organization or other countries, the key words of "equity," "quality," "resources," and "kindergarten teachers" are also highlighted in the development of China's preschool education toward 2035, which is consistent with the international trend of the development of quality preschool education (Alieva, T. I. et al., 2013). At the same time, we should highlight Chinese characteristics in the construction process, actively cooperate with the country to build a moderately prosperous society in 2020, build a modern country in 2050, and adhere to the goal-oriented, reform-oriented, and problem-oriented principle.

References

Alieva, T. I., Trifonova, E. V., Rodina, N. M., & Vasyukova, N. E. (2013). The development and validation of models for assessing the quality of preschool education. *Psihologičeskaâ NaukaI Obraz-ovanie*, 5(3). http://psyedu.ru/journal/2013/3/3408.phtml

Bacchi, C. (2009). *Analysing policy: What's the problem represented to be?* (p. 2). Pearson Education.

Bao, B. (2018). Constructing high quality public service system for preschool education—Based on the investigation of the third-stage preschool education action plan in Guizhou [in Chinese]. *Journal of Teacher Education*, 5(2), 53–62.

Broda, A., Bieber, A., Meyer, G., Hopper, L., Joyce, R., Irving, K., Zanetti, O., Portolani, E., Kerpershoek, L., Verhey, F., Vugt, M., Wolfs, C., Eriksen, S., Røsvik, J., Marques, M. J., Gonc, alves-Pereira, M., Sjölund, B. M., Woods, B., & Jelley, H., & the ActifCare Consortium. (2017). Perspectives of policy and political decision makers on access to formal dementia care: Expert interviews in eight European countries. *BMC Health Services Research*, 17(1), 518. https://doiorg/10.1186/s12913-017-2456-0

Bu, Z., Hou, Y., & Wang, Y. (2011). County-level education expenditure adequacy of China: An empirical analysis with evidence based approach [in Chinese]. *Tsinghua Journal of Education*, 32(5), 35–41+67. https://doiorg/10.14138/j.1001-4519.2011.05.005

Cao, Q. (2017). Development orientation and tendency of preschool education [in Chinese]. *Journal of Shaanxi Xueqian Normal University*, 33(10), 129–135.

Doeringer, S. (2020). 'The problem-centred expert interview'. Combining qualitative interviewing approaches for investigating implicit expert knowledge. *International Journal of Social Research Methodology*, (4). https://doiorg/10.1080/13645579.2020.1766777

Du, L. (2016). The preschool education public service based on parents satisfaction survey [in Chinese]. *Forum on Contemporary Education*, 4, 43–49. https://doiorg/10.13694/j.cnki.ddjylt.2016.04.006

Edwards, M. E. (2001). Home ownership, affordability, and mothers' changing work and family roles. *Social Science Quarterly*, 82(2), 369–383. https://doiorg/10.1111/0038-4941.00029

He, H., Li, H., Bao, B., & Zhang, J. (2018). One village, one kindergarten: exploration of the reform of the publicization and development of preschool education in remote rural area—Based on the experience of village Kindergarten in Tongren [in Chinese]. *Journal of Shaanxi Xueqian Normal University*, 34(7), 119–123.

Hong, X., & Jiang, L. (2018). The problem, causes and countermeasures of the development of Chinese early childhood education under the two-child policy—An analysis of phase II three-year action plan for early childhood education [in Chinese]. *Journal of Beijing Normal University (Social Sciences)*, (5), 53–61.

Hou, L. (2016). Challenges and opportunities: Review on the development of government-dominating preschool education [in Chinese]. *Journal of Guangxi Normal University (Philosophy and Social Sciences Edition)*, 52(6), 106–110. https://doiorg/10.16088/j.issn.1001-6597.2016.06.017

Hu, Y., Zhang, Y., & Wang, Y. (2016). Research on the development of inclusive preschool education in China [in Chinese]. *Education Exploration*, (5), 49–53.

Huang, J. (2011). The strategic goal analysis of "making preschool education universal" and its implementation [in Chinese]. *Research in Educational Development*, 33(24), 7–13. https://doiorg/10.14121/j.cnki.1008-3855.2011.24.012

Hui, J., & Chu, Y. (2015). Characteristics of "quality" preschool teachers' training [in Chinese]. *Education Exploration*, 6, 142–145.

Lei, F. (2014). On the building of inclusive private kindergartens in Changsha, Zhuzhou and Xiangtan Cities [in Chinese]. *Studies in Early Childhood Education*, (11), 23–28. https://doiorg/10.13861/j.cnki.sece.2014.11.005

Li, Y., & Yang, Z. (2017). Research on pedagogy implication of the "human-centered education" [in Chinese]. *Journal of Schooling Studies*, 14(2), 14–24.

Lin, Y., & Xu, L. (2018). Research on the construction of intelligent kindergarten under the background of information technology [in Chinese]. *The Chinese Journal of ICT in Education*, (1), 64–66.

Liu, Y. (2018). An impressive kindergarten—A case study of the difficulties in entering a kindergarten under the background of "comprehensive two-child" policy [in Chinese]. *Theory and Practice of Education*, 38(17), 27–29.

Liu, Z. (2009). Preschool education must maintain the two basic characteristics of instructiveness and public interest [in Chinese]. *Educational Research*, (5), 32.

Luo, M., & Li, K. (2017). An investigation on the quality gap of early childhood education between urban and rural areas based on a national sample of 428 classrooms [in Chinese]. *Studies in Early Childhood Education*, (6), 13–20.

Lv, X. (2015). A mode of three-dimensional interaction between kindergarten and family [in Chinese]. *Journal of Ningbo Institute of Education*, 17(5), 123–124+140. https://doiorg/10.13970/j.cnki.nbjyxyxb.2015.05.035

Nazarenko, H. A., & Andriushchenko, T. K. (2019). Information and communication technologies as an instrument for preschool education quality improvement. *Information Technologies and Learning Tools*, 69(1), 21–36. https://doiorg/10.33407/itlt.v69i1.2688

Pang, L., & Han, X. (2010). Legislation of China's pre-school education: Reflection and progress [in Chinese]. *Journal of Beijing Normal University (Social Sciences)*, (5), 14–20.

Pei, R. (2015). On the effective strategy of kindergarten going to "primary school" [in Chinese]. *Liaoning Education*, (10), 66–67.

Samuelsson, I. P., Li, M., & Hu, A. (2019). Early childhood education for sustainability: A driver for quality. *ECNU Review of Education*, 2(4), 369–373. https://doiorg/10.1177/2096531119893478

Stanova, K., & Mitova, D. (2015). The family and kindergarten — The main factors supporting educational environment and personal development of the child. *PEDAGOGIKA-PEDAGOGY*, 87(7), 1010–1014.

Stephen, B. (1995). Education reform: A critical and post-structuralist approach. *Journal of Social Policy*, 24(3), 448.

Vidal-Hall, C., Sakata, N., & Higham, R. (2019). Editorial: Methodological innovations in qualitative educational research. *London Review of Research*, 17, 249–251. https://doiorg/10.18546/LRE.17.3.01

Wu, D., Song, Y., & Liu, W. (2019). Establishing morality and cultivating people is the fundamental task of the development of socialist education with Chinese characteristics in the new era [in Chinese]. *Leading Journal of Ideological & Theoretical Education*, (1), 66–70. https://doiorg/10.16580/j.sxlljydk.2019.01.024

Wu, Z., Huang, X., & Qu, L. (2018). Reflections on the legislation of preschool education law in China [in Chinese]. *Fudan*

Education Forum, *16*(1), 35–41. https://doiorg/10.13397/j.cnki.fef.2018.01.007

Yang, X. (2019). Accelerated move for AI education in China. *ECNU Review of Education*, *2*(3), 347–352. https://doiorg/10.1177/2096531119878590

Ye, P., & Zhang, C. (2015). On the influencing factors of preschool education development in developed regions [in Chinese]. *Educational Research*, *36*(7), 23–33.

Yu, H., & Miao, R. (2015). On the important value of preschool education in present China [in Chinese]. *Research of Modern Basic Education*, (1), 53–58.

Yu, W. (2017). The performance and countermeasure of the tendency of kindergarten education toward primary school [in Chinese]. *Vocational Technology*, *16*(7), 99–101. https://doiorg/10.19552/j.cnki.issn1672-0601.2017.07.039

Yu, Y., & Liu, Y. (2017). The main problems and reform directions of preschool education systems [in Chinese]. *Studies in Early Childhood Education*, (12), 3–11. https://doiorg/10.13861/j.cnki.sece.2017.12.001

Zhang, X., Wu, H., Chen, Y., Sun, L., Wang, W., & Pharmacy, S. O. (2016). Establishment of evaluation model of o2o platform service quality based on SERVQUAL scale [in Chinese]. *China Pharmacy*, *27*(7), 1005–1008.

Zhuang, X., & Cheng, L. (2012). On the development of generally-benefit-kindergartens [in Chinese]. *Studies in Early Childhood Education*, (11), 45–49.

This is the first article explicitly to compare the human resource development (HRD) pledges of the Forum on China-Africa Cooperation (FOCAC) with those associated with Education Action Plan of the Belt and Road Initiative (BRI). The article draws upon discourse analysis of both the FOCAC VI and VII documents and the key Chinese Ministry of Education (MOE) 2016 Action Plan, aiming to discuss the relationship between the human resource traditions of FOCAC and the BRI. Given the trans-continental coverage of the BRI, it is suggested that its ambitious pledges in respect of education and HRD actually complement or even exceed the commitments made by FOCAC VI and VII.

China-Africa Education Cooperation: From FOCAC to Belt and Road[1]

Kenneth King

The Forum on China-Africa Cooperation (FOCAC) has encouraged wide-ranging engagement with Africa since its foundation in 2000. Arguably, FOCAC is the formalization of China's links with Africa that go back to the founding of the People's Republic of China (Taylor, 2011).[2] Across its very wide spread of cooperation, social and development commitments have been substantial, and within this focus, Education and Human Resources, have always constituted a major element. There has consistently been a common core of scholarships and short-term training within the human resource development (HRD) package, but there have been additional, institutional elements depending on the particular FOCAC conference or summit. Although school building has featured in two of the FOCAC Action Plans, the main focus of the commitments has generally been in the area of higher education (King, 2013). Capacity building or more recently capacity cooperation have been key elements in the FOCAC pledges, and these have not of course been limited to the education sector, but have been widely applied to other sectors, such

---

1 This article was first presented in the International Seminar on Sino-Africa Education Policy Reform and Institution Innovation, November 26, 2018, University of Dar es Salaam and was published on *ECNU Review of Education*, 3(2), 221–234.
2 Taylor's book on FOCAC only treats the first four FOCAC summits.

as health, environment, science and technology, and infrastructure.

One of the other core elements in the FOCAC packages has been the claim of mutuality or of common development between China and Africa. In other words, China has always talked of these agreements in terms of mutual benefit or mutual support rather than employing the language of donors and recipients. These constitute, therefore, forms of South-South cooperation (SSC). Thus, there has frequently been a description of some of the FOCAC pledges as illustrating people-to-people and cultural exchanges. In this way, the FOCAC discourse underlines the sense that the agreements are two-way or win-win; it is, therefore, commonplace for the text to talk of "the two sides agreed ..." or other similar expressions. This affirms the role of African agency in the agreements, and this is supported by the activity of the senior officials' meetings and of the African diplomatic corps in Beijing in the preparations of FOCAC documentation. Despite this discourse of two-way collaboration, it is clear that the bulk of the HRD pledges are in reality one-way provision of scholarships and training awards.

This context means that this short article is a small contribution and a corrective[1] to the literature on SSC (Kragelund, 2019) as well as adding to the growing literature on China-Africa research cooperation.[2] It is noteworthy that although Education and Human Resources development are constant features of the FOCAC Action Plans, there has been relatively little academic research on these dimensions. For instance, in a recent volume on *New Directions in Africa-China Studies*, none of the 21 chapters examine the history or contemporary aspects of Africa-China studies in education (Alden & Large, 2019). There is a parallel with studies of India's cooperation with Africa. Despite HRD and capacity building being central to India's program of support to Africa, there are very few critical studies of the role of education (King, 2019a; Mawdsley & McCann, 2011).

A key question for this article is how these and other FOCAC traditions of support to HRD are reinforced by the Belt and Road Initiative (BRI), and in particular by the *Education Action Plan for the Belt and Road Initiative*, issued by the Chinese Ministry of Education (MOE) in 2016 (MOE, 2016). Given the trans-continental coverage of the BRI, does this mean that its pledges, especially in respect of education and HRD, actually complement or even overlap with the

---

1 Despite education and HRD being central to SSC, it often receives little attention. See just two pages in Kragelund (2019).
2 See the Chinese in Africa/Africans in China Research Network. http://china-africa.ssrc.org/about/. See also the China Africa Project. https://chinaafricaproject.com.

commitments made by FOCAC? Unlike FOCAC, where virtually all 54 African countries are now represented, BRI's African partners have grown dramatically from just 6 in 2018 to 32 at the time of the Second BRI Forum in Beijing in April 2019.

Another international dimension that will be touched upon is whether the Belt and Road or FOCAC may connect at any stage, or be contrasted, with the Asia-Africa Growth Corridor (AAGC), promoted by India and Japan since May 2017.

From FOCAC VI to FOCAC VII

Johannesburg Summit, 2015

Given that the only accessible study in English on FOCAC (Taylor, 2011) treats only the first four FOCACs (from 2000 to 2009), it will be appropriate to focus attention on the fifth and sixth FOCAC in this analysis. In doing so, it may be useful to bear in mind Taylor's (2011) final comment on this set of fora:

> Symbolism and spin then is at the root of the whole FOCAC enterprise and works at various levels and is directed both toward Africa, toward the world *and* toward the Chinese population [*sic*]. (p. 103)

The Johannesburg Summit [1] in December 2015 covered many different dimensions of capacity building and HRD. Historically, as mentioned above, China's cooperation with Africa has not usually focused narrowly on schools or on formal education, even if two earlier FOCACs did support the development of a small number of schools (total 150). [2] Instead, the support to HRD in FOCAC VI can be found under very many different titles, including capacity building, training opportunities, scholarships, cultural partnerships, mutual learning, knowledge sharing, research, and people-to-people exchanges. The overall focus remains higher education. [3]

Education and HRD are principally treated together in FOCAC VI under "Social development cooperation" along with medical care and public health, and other issues, but this should not be regarded as the only focus on capacity building in the FOCAC VI Action Plan; many different

---

1 Every second FOCAC summit is held in Africa, so far in Ethiopia, Egypt, and South Africa. For the South African FOCAC meeting, see also King (2015).
2 For all the past FOCAC conferences, see https://www.focac.org/eng/zywx_1/zywj/.
3 See for the Johannesburg Summit (FOCAC VI): https://www.focac.org/eng/zywx_1/zywj/t1327961.htm.

dimensions of training and capacity development are also covered under the various sections of "Economic cooperation" such as agriculture, industry, infrastructure, information, energy, tourism, investment, and trade. In these economic investments, there is a constant reference in the text to human capacity development, technology transfer, and skills training. Beyond this, there are institutional development pledges—including the building of five "transportation universities" and a "China-Africa Aviation School."

Specifically, under the section on "Social development cooperation" are some of the largest and most ambitious training numbers FOCAC has seen so far. Again, these pledges are not restricted to the sub-section termed "Education and human resources development," but there are major training initiatives in the sub-section on "Medical care and public health," including the training of doctors, nurses, public health workers, and administrative personnel from African countries, as well as the building of an African Union Disease Control Center and regional medical research centers.

Similarly under the "Exchanges of experience on poverty eradication strategies," China pledged to provide degree programs on poverty eradication and to help train specialized personnel in this field. Equally, under the sub-section on "Science and technology cooperation and knowledge sharing," there are a whole series of joint building projects for research and demonstration, as well as plans for sending "outstanding African youths and technical personnel to participate in exchanges to and training in Africa."

Specifically under the section "Education and human resources development," China pledges to provide some 32,000 government scholarships to Africa. This is almost twice as many as the 18,000 offered in the previous FOCAC V of 2012.

Given the alleged bottleneck on skills development in Africa, it is noticeable that China intends to renovate as well as build more vocational and technical training facilities in Africa, including an unspecified number of regional vocational education centers. Intriguingly, the provision of "colleges for capacity building in Africa" is mentioned, though nothing more is said about these. Beyond this, there is the promise of training no less than 200,000 local technical and vocational personnel, and of providing 40,000 training opportunities for African personnel in China. It must be assumed that this latter figure of 40,000 is for short-term training of some 2–3 weeks of the kind that has been offered traditionally through the FOCAC HRD process. This, too, is much larger than the 30,000 provided through the previous FOCAC V. Equally under this same heading of education and HRD, there is the pledge to build an SSC and Development Institute in China for the benefit of senior African professionals.

Still, under education and HRD, there is a continuation of China's support to the UNESCO-China Funds-In-Trust which had been running at US $2 million annually in FOCAC V. There is also a promise of more support to African countries wishing to establish Confucius Institutes and Classrooms. Equally, at the university level, there is a financial encouragement to African universities to establish China research centers "and vice versa." Presumably, these last three words are meant to encourage Chinese universities to open more African research centers.

Under the separate section termed "Cultural cooperation and people-to-people exchanges," there is a whole series of proposals covering culture, media, academia, think tanks, youth, volunteers, women, trade unions, and Non-Government Organizations (NGOs). It is noticeable that the agreements proposed here are mainly (21 of them) prefaced by the term "The two sides ..."; only six are prefaced by "The Chinese side ...." This suggests that there is more of a symmetrical, two-way set of proposals in this key section of the Action Plan. China does, however, plan to build five more cultural centers in Africa, but parallel African centers in China are also encouraged.

China is very aware of the negative way in which its presence and activities in Africa are often portrayed by much of the Western media. It is suggestive, therefore, that China is offering to train no less than 1,000 African media personnel annually. It is also planning to run "training and capacity building for African countries" news officials and reporters.

Still under "people-to-people exchanges," there is the planned continuation of cooperation between think tanks and academia on both sides, with encouragement to do more research, and invite African scholars to China.

Youth exchanges are a further dimension of collaboration, with no less than 500 going annually for study trips from Africa to China. From the Chinese side, volunteers are also mentioned as continuing, but no numbers are given.

In reviewing these many pledges, it should be noted that they are announced at a Pan-African level in the FOCAC conventions, but they are not, at the fora, allocated to specific countries across the continent. That process is carried out bilaterally between China and a whole series of specific countries. Thus FOCAC V promised support to more Confucius Institutes, but bilaterally there is an agreement completely to renew the Confucius Institute in the University of Dar Es Salaam and to provide the University with a state of the art library.

As far as evaluating these pledges and action plans is concerned, there is a Chinese Follow-up Committee and this works in conjunction with the Senior Officials' Meeting and representing the corps of African ambassadors in Beijing. Thus, FOCAC is by no means just "symbolism and spin"; there are mechanisms for judging delivery.

This Chinese mix of Pan-African pledges with bilateral agreements differs markedly from the India-Africa Forum Summits (IAFS) which India supported from 2008, and again in 2011 and 2015. The pledges made at the IAFS were left to the African Union to distribute to specific countries. Arguably, this made for much slower implementation, since the African Union allocated the pledges according to its view of the needs of the Regional Economic Commissions (King, 2019b).

Beijing Summit, September 2018

FOCAC VII took place in Beijing in early September 2018. One of the most obvious changes between FOCAC VI and VII is that the Silk Road was only mentioned once back in 2015, in a telling phrase of Africa welcoming China's championing "the 21st Century Maritime Silk Road" "which includes the African continent" (FOCAC, 2015, section 3.5.1). By contrast, in FOCAC VII, the terminology of the BRI and of the Silk Road was used many times, as will be seen after analyzing the HRD pledges of this Beijing Summit.

As is usual in the FOCAC Action Plans, the Education and Human Resources' agreements fall in a different section from the Cultural and People-to-People Exchanges. There is a reference back to some of the pledges made in Johannesburg. One of the more significant of these, under Education and Human Resources, is the establishment of the Institute of South-South Cooperation and Development. This was duly set up in the National School of Development of Peking University. It is presented in the iconic language of mutuality: "as a platform for South-South cooperation featuring equality, mutual trust, mutual benefit, solidarity, and mutual support, and support other developing countries in their exploration of development paths suited to their own national conditions" (FOCAC, 2018a, section 4.3.2).

Another item that was mentioned in Johannesburg was Colleges for Capacity Building. Though there is no specific mention of these in the text of the 2018 Action Plan, there is an affirmation for the construction of an African Capacity Development Institute, to be headquartered in the African Capacity Building Foundation in Harare.

Still under Education and Human Resources, the FOCAC VII Action Plan reinforces the positive comments made in FOCAC VI about the increasing role for Confucius Institutes and Classrooms, as was seen above, but there is no further mention in FOCAC VII about the setting up of China research centers in African universities and their African counterparts in China.

One of the areas within the education pledges that is keenly followed in each FOCAC Action Plan is whether China will really be able to continue to improve on the total number of long-term scholarships and short-term training slots from the previous triennium. Here the key sentence is that "China will provide Africa with 50,000 government scholarships and 50,000 training opportunities for seminars and workshops and train more professionals of different disciplines for Africa" (FOCAC, 2018a, section 4.3.3). This betters the Johannesburg numbers of scholarships by almost 20,000, and of short-term professional training by 10,000. In addition, it is mentioned that there will be a special "tailor-made programme to train 1,000 high-caliber Africans" (FOCAC, 2018a, section 4.3.3). There is no further detail on this, but it is possibly a scheme to bring potentially influential "high flyers" to China.

A further item carried over from the commitments in Johannesburg involved research centers supported by China in the continent. One of these is supported by both sides in the FOCAC VII Action Plan and is termed the China-Africa Joint Research Center; its concern covers a wide range of scientific research and professional training, including ecology, health, and renewable energies. This particular research center will have responsibility for selecting 150 African students for masters or doctoral training in China.

As in the previous FOCAC Action Plans, Cultural and People-to-People Exchanges are treated separately from Education and Human Resources. FOCAC VII repeats some of the promises of FOCAC VI, such as opening more Chinese Cultural Centers in Africa—though it is not clear if there are now more than the five centers that were in operation in 2015 (Mauritius, Nigeria, Benin, Egypt, and Tanzania).

But of more direct interest to our concern with the links between FOCAC and BRI is that there is quite a range of developments in the cultural and people-to-people sphere that use the new Silk Road discourse. Thus the following invitation suggests an expansion of the cultural world to the one which just talked of an African Arts Festival in 2015 to a broader vision: "China welcomes Africa's participation in the Silk Road International League of Theatres, the Silk Road International Museum Alliance and the Network of Silk Road Art Festivals" (FOCAC, 2018a, section 5.1.5). Similarly, there is perhaps the incorporation of the NGO activity mentioned in Johannesburg in 2015 into a wider network: "The two sides value the role of the Silk Road NGO Cooperation Network in promoting friendly exchanges and cooperation between China and Africa" (FOCAC, 2018a, section 5.4.4).

There are many other parallels in cultural and people-to-people cooperation between FOCAC VI and VII. One of the intriguing developments is that where FOCAC VI had mentioned large-scale support to local vocational training in Africa, as was seen above, the FOCAC VII talks about specific institutional development for the first time for vocational training: "Ten Luban [1] Workshops will be set up in Africa to provide vocational training for young Africans" (FOCAC, 2018a, section 5.5.2).

In respect of the implementation of this 2018 pledge, it should be noted that the first of the 10 Luban workshops was opened in Djibouti in March 2019, doubtlessly linked to the China-funded railway linking Addis Ababa and Djibouti. A second was being established in Cairo's Ain Shams University. [2]

Looking over both FOCAC VI and FOCAC VII, however, it is clear that there is a very strong emphasis on training, not just vocational training and skills development, but capacity building and capacity cooperation. [3] This is, of course, in line with China's desire to present its support as cooperation and not as conventional aid. The confirmation of this discourse of cooperation is that the terms "mutual" and "joint" appear as many as 33 and 37 times, respectively, in the Action Plan, and the whole document emphasizes that these are shared agreements and actions. Hence the phrase "the two sides" (i.e., African and Chinese) occurs no less than 130 times in the Plan.

Overall, the Action Plan pays more attention to the African Union's Agenda 2063 than to the UN's Agenda 2030, but that is perhaps understandable given the continental focus of the document.

From FOCAC VI and VII to the BRI

It is valuable to have available an English version of the *Education Action Plan for the Belt and Road Initiative* (MOE, 2016). Even though the BRI was unveiled in September 2013, this

---

1 Lu Ban is said to have been the father of Chinese architecture.
2 See Yang (2019), 10 Luban workshops to provide training in Africa.
3 "Training" appears no less than 43 times in the FOCAC VII Action Plan.

Action Plan had become accessible in July 2016, between the dates of FOCAC VI and VII, and just over a year before the opening ceremony in Beijing for the BRI in May 2017. By the time of FOCAC VII in September 2018, it was possible to reflect on the eight major lessons of FOCAC VII, but put them in the context of several other policy documents, including from BRI, the UN, and the African Union: "China and Africa: Toward an Even Stronger Community with a Shared Future through Win-Win Cooperation" [FOCAC VII Declaration]

> pools the strength of the Belt and Road Initiative, UN 2030 Sustainable Development Agenda, AU Agenda 2063, and the development strategies of individual African countries, places emphasis on fostering indigenous growth capacity for Africa, create new ideas and ways of cooperation, and will bring China-Africa cooperation to new heights [sic]. (BRI, 2018, p. 1)

It is noteworthy that one of the eight major lessons of FOCAC VII was "capacity building activities" (BRI, 2018, pp. 13 - 15). This summarized all of the major dimensions of HRD, education, and people-to-people exchange, many of which have been mentioned, but it is significant that the document appears on the Belt and Road Portal, suggesting that there is convergence between the thinking about human resource for FOCAC and for the Belt and Road.

The *Education Action Plan for the Belt and Road Initiative* will offer further evidence of the extent of the overlap in the thinking about FOCAC and BRI. It has already been noted that the terminology of the Silk Road had begun to be used in some of the cultural pledges of FOCAC VII, but this becomes much more evident in the large ambitions for educational cooperation among the countries of the New Silk Road. It will be seen that many of the new initiatives are now termed "Silk Road."

Not surprisingly, the discourse of the *Action Plan* has resonance with the discourse of FOCAC. This is true of its plans for education collaboration but also of its collaboration in other sectors. But it is important to underline that in the view of President Xi Jinping, the chief architect of BRI, human resource exchange and development are one of just four major connectivities: "enhanced infrastructure connectivity, increased trade connectivity, expanded financial connectivity, and strengthened people-to-people connectivity." The latter covers cooperation in education, health, culture, and science. It is best captured in Xi's own words, from the opening ceremony of the BRI in May 2017:

> These four years have seen strengthened people-to-people connectivity. Friendship, which derives

from close contact between the people, holds the key to sound state-to-state relations. Guided by the Silk Road spirit, we the Belt and Road Initiative participating countries have pulled [sic] our efforts to build the educational Silk Road and the health Silk Road, and carried out cooperation in science, education, culture, health and people-to-people exchange. Such cooperation has helped lay a solid popular and social foundation for pursuing the Belt and Road Initiative. (Xi, 2017a, p. 3)

In the "vision for cooperation" of the *Education Action Plan*, it is perhaps significant that promoting closer people-to-people ties is the first element, followed by cultivating talent, and achieving common development. This emphasis on mutuality and sharing knowledge was evident across FOCAC texts. But they are also critical to the BRI education vision:

The countries along the routes will work together to deepen mutual understanding, expand openness, strengthen cooperation, learn from each other, to pursue common interests, face our shared future, shoulder common responsibilities, and work concertedly to build a Belt and Road educational community. (MOE, 2016, p. 1)

> The *Action Plan* has four "principles for cooperation." These follow the vision in stressing the nurturing of the people, but very much through sharing, learning from each other, and encouraging dialogue between different civilizations. The emphasis is particularly on building bridges for people-to-people exchange across the entire BRI region. (MOE, 2016, pp. 2–3)

These principles are then fleshed out in three priority areas for educational cooperation, with each of these containing several components (MOE, 2016, pp. 3–8). Many of these dimensions go far further than FOCAC commitments, as they seek to build and coordinate policy across a vast and highly differentiated set of countries. On the one hand, this suggests mechanisms for mutual recognition and joint degrees. But it also speaks to the need for joint laboratories, research centers, and technology transfer centers. "Cooperation" is the core theme across the tightly argued 11 pages, occurring no less than 77 times (MOE, 2016).

Only a few examples of such cooperation can be illustrated here, but one of the more suggestive of these is concerned with "breaking the language barriers between the Belt and Road countries" (MOE, 2016, pp. 4–5). The main focus is on encouraging the use of each other's languages, and the implications of this for foreign language training in the BRI universities. There is a strong appeal "to institutions from the Belt and Road countries to work in partnership with Chinese institutions to establish programmes that teach their own languages in China" (MOE, 2016, p. 4). Alongside this, there is a call for more social actors to consider establishing Confucius Institutes and Classrooms. But in this regard, it is worth underlining that the BRI is not concerned solely with the promotion of Mandarin.

While there is a very strong promotion of education for international understanding into the curricula of BRI countries, and for introducing what is termed "Silk Road cultural heritage protection" into curricula along the routes, there is also a forceful promotion for the mutual recognition of qualifications in the region.

This "Silk Road" brand in respect of heritage is also extended to several other dimensions of education in the BRI countries. One of these is the "Silk Road Teacher Training Enhancement Programme" which aims to ensure that the best practice in teacher education is shared around the region. It is worth noting that though China is ready to support this, it does not assume that all good practice derives from China. Quite the opposite. China states that they will facilitate the export of equipment, courseware, and teaching solutions "from countries along the routes" (MOE, 2016, p. 7).

A further example of the Silk Road brand in the service of shared development is covered by the *Silk Road Joint Education and Training Enhancement Programme*. This is a powerful call to universities to carry out joint training projects, and not just in a few areas such as those previously linked to the Millennium Development Goals. Rather, they could be "in fields such as languages, transportation, architecture, medicalscience, energy, environmental engineering, hydraulic engineering, bio-sciences, marine sciences, ecological preservation, and cultural heritage protection" (MOE, 2016, p. 7).

In the FOCAC Action Plans, as was noted above, a crucial element was always the paragraph giving the numbers of scholarships for Africans to learn in China, as well as short-term training awards for African professionals to go there. In the *Education Action Plan*, while there is space given to the Silk Road Scholarship, aimed at students and technicians along the routes, there is strong encouragement for more Chinese students to study in the Belt and Road countries. At the present moment, very large numbers of privately funded Chinese students go to some five main Anglophone countries (Canada, U.S., U.K., NZ, and Australia), but the *Action Plan* would like to redirect some of this mobility toward the BRI countries and would see some alterations of student mobility priorities beyond students coming to China:

> China will place equal importance on sending students overseas and receiving international students, equal importance on funding students to study overseas and encouraging self-sponsored overseas studies,

equal importance on increasing the number of international students and improving the quality of education offered to them, equal importance on law-based management of the students and improving services to them, as well as equal importance on cultivating the talent and giving full play to their roles. (MOE, 2016, p. 6)

But the *Action Plan* is not just about university students and short-term professional training. Technical vocational education and training (TVET) is perceived as an equally important priority, and not least because of the association of TVET with the crucial role of infrastructure development across BRI countries. The talk is of "multi-layered cooperation in vocational and technical education and training" developing talent for the BRI regions. There is, in addition, a challenge to China's top vocational and technical institutions to consider an overseas branch presence, through links with industry (MOE, 2016, p. 6).

Although the majority of the *Action Plan* text is concerned with joint actions and shared programs, there is still a role for "Silk Road Education Assistance." This will be delivered in the usual form of SSC and will target the least developed countries along the routes. This is not just seen as government to government, but ideally, it should involve nongovernmental resources. Such diversified funding, from state and non-state actors, is also encouraged for each country along the new Silk Roads:

> By combining government funding, private financing, and public donations, we aim to broaden the funding sources for education, enlarge the scope of education assistance, and achieve shared development in education. (MOE, 2016, p. 8)

Belt and Road: From education ambitions to action

The last section of the *Education Action Plan* acknowledges that there has to be a pooling of resources across the education communities in the BRI countries, but recognizes that China can play "a proactive and exemplary role" (MOE, 2016, p. 9). China perceives the challenge as involving not just central government but also provinces and major cities. Following a very long-standing tradition of provinces partnering with particular African countries, it is suggested that China's provinces and cities should identify "friendship provinces" and "sister cities" across the BRI regions (MOE, 2016, p. 9). It is recognized that these measures will help the internationalization of all the different partners.

In concluding the ambitions of the *Education Action Plan*, the text chooses the moral high ground. It argues for an ethical international education policy that works with and for others and recognizes that this means learning from and benefiting from educational cooperation. This quotation captures the core values of the *Action Plan*:

> Guided by the old Chinese motto that "He who craves for success empathizes with others and helps them to be successful," Chinese schools and universities should steadily expand cooperation and exchange with their counterparts in the Belt and Road countries. They should take their best educational resources with them as they engage in cooperation and exchange outside China, and select the most valuable educational resources to bring home from other countries, being inclusive and tolerant, and both learning from and teaching others. In this way together we can make our education more internationalized and strengthen our ability to act in service of the common development of the Belt and Road Initiative. (MOE, 2016, p. 10)

To parallel the Chinese adage about cooperation being the road to success, an African saying is also drawn upon: "He who travels alone travels faster, yet he who travels in company travels farther" (MOE, 2016, p. 11). In this cooperative spirit, the *Action Plan* ends with a major emphasis upon mutuality, and even with an aspiration to usher in an era of beauty:

> Based on principles of mutual understanding, mutual trust, mutual assistance and mutual learning, we shall join hands to promote the development of education and closer people-to-people ties. With these efforts, we will build an educational community among the Belt and Road countries together and create a new chapter of beautiful life for all humanity. (MOE, 2016, p. 12)

Three years later, in April 2019, there was a chance for the BRI to report on "Progress, contributions and prospects" just before the second BRI conclave in Beijing from April 27, 2019 (BRI, 2019). As usual, in the FOCAC and BRI reports, there was a section on HRD, "Closer people-to-people ties." Despite all the coverage given to the networking of roads, ports, railways, energy, and air transport, it was claimed in the report that these people-to-people ties were "the cultural foundation for building the Belt and Road" (BRI, 2019, section 5.1). According to the report, there have been, in the two years since the first BRI forum in April 2017, a welter of Silk Road events, covering theaters, museums, arts festivals, libraries, and NGOs. But apart from the cultural dimension, there have been achievements claimed in the sphere of formal education and training. Already in 2017, no less than 66% of all Chinese government scholarships were going to students in the BRI countries. It was noted, in addition, that there were 153 Confucius Institutes operating in 54 BRI countries. This figure illustrates just one way of describing the coverage of the BRI. But, as noted earlier, it is the connectedness rather than the China-centeredness that is at the heart of BRI vision. So instead of promoting the idea of all roads leading to Beijing, the "road of connected civilizations" is projected on the shared BRI map:

> In pursuing the Belt and Road Initiative, we should ensure that with regard to different civilizations, exchange will replace estrangement, mutual learning will replace clashes, and coexistence will replace a sense of superiority. This will boost mutual understanding, mutual respect and mutual trust between different countries. (BRI, 2019, para. 6)

From FOCAC to Belt and Road—On the ground

This article has analyzed and compared some of the discourse of FOCAC Action Plans VI and VII with the *Education Action Plan* of BRI. Textual analysis and comparison of the language of goals, plans, and pledges, of course, are very different from tracing the implementation on the ground, or from talking to African students in China, or discussing capacity cooperation with Chinese investors in Ethiopia or Kenya. Some of these realities of studying in China or investing in Africa were discussed in *China's Aid and Soft Power in Africa* (King, 2013),[1] and were discussed further in Tanzania in the November 2018 conference on Sino-Africa Education Policy Reform and Institution Innovation.[2]

It is also possible to compare the language and discourse of major schemes such as the AAGC with the overall *Action Plan on the Belt and Road Initiative* or with the sector-specific *Education Action Plan* (King, 2018). Very substantial differences in approach can be detected between the AAGC and the BRI, and not least in the fact that the authorship of AAGC was solely carried out by three Asian think tanks, with no substantial involvement by Africa. By contrast, it can be seen that the FOCAC plans are widely endorsed by "the two sides," though the *Education Action Plan* remains the ambition and aspiration of China's MOE, and not yet of the very substantial number of countries along the routes, in Asia, Africa, and Europe.

Nevertheless, it is undeniable that the text of key discourses remains powerful in its own right. This could be as true now of the "Eight principles of economic aid and technical assistance to

---

[1] For African students in China, see also King (2019a).
[2] This conference took place in the University of Dar Es Salaam, Tanzania on November 26, 2018.

other countries" enunciated by Zhou Enlai in January 1964 in Ghana, as it is of the 14 principles of "Xi Jinping thought." It is crucial that these latter contain the conviction that social welfare is central to development: "Improving people's livelihood and well-being is the primary goal of development" (Xi, 2017b).

Words do, however, make a difference—even before they are translated into reality. Hence the contrast by Frankopan between a US administration that seeks to reshape the world to its own interests, using the stick, rather than the carrot; on the other, a Chinese government that talks of mutual benefits, of enhancing cooperation and of using incentives to weave together peoples, countries and cultures in a "win-win" scenario (Frankopan, 2018, p. 242).

References

Alden, C., & Large, D. (Eds.). (2019). *New directions in Africa-China studies*. Routledge.

Belt and Road Initiative. (2018). *Elaboration on the eight major initiatives of the FOCAC Beijing Summit*. https://eng.yidaiyilu.gov.cn/wcm.files/upload/CMSydylyw/201809/201809201101028.pdf

Belt and Road Initiative. (2019). *The Belt and Road Initiative: Progress, contributions and progress*. https://eng.yidaiyilu.gov.cn/zchj/qwfb/86739.htm

Forum on China-Africa Cooperation. (2015). *The Forum on China-Africa Cooperation Johannesburg action plan (2016 - 2018)*. https://www.focac.org/eng/zywx_1/zywj/t1327961.htm

Forum on China-Africa Cooperation. (2018a). *Forum on China-Africa Cooperation Beijing action plan (2019 - 2021)*. https://www.focac.org/eng/zywx_1/zywj/t1594297.htm

Forum on China-Africa Cooperation. (2018b). *Beijing Declaration: China and Africa: Toward an even stronger community with a shared future through win-win cooperation*. https://www.focac.org/eng/zywx_1/zywj/t1594324.htm

Frankopan, P. (2018). *The new Silk Roads: The present and future of the world*. Bloomsbury.

King, K. (2013). *China's aid and soft power in Africa: The case of education and training*. James Currey.

King, K. (2015). *China's new pledges with Africa: 2016 - 2018: Multi-dimensional support to human resource development?* http://theasiadialogue.com/2015/12/15/chinas-new-pledges-with-africa-2016-2018-multi-dimensional-support-to-human-resource-development/

King, K. (2018). Japan, India and China on Africa: Global ambitions and human resource development. In J. Panda & T. Basu (Eds.), *China, India and Japan in the Indo-Pacific: Ideas, interests and infrastructure*. Pentagon Press.

King, K. (2019a). *Education, skills and international cooperation: Comparative and historical perspectives* (Comparative Education Research Center Monograph Series, No 36). The University of Hong Kong and Springer.

King, K. (2019b). *India-Africa cooperation in human resource development: Education, training and skills* (Occasional Paper No. 51). Institute for Defence Studies and Analyses (IDSA).

Kragelund, P. (2019). *South-South development*. Routledge.

Mawdsley, E., & McCann, G. (Eds.). (2011). *India in Africa: Changing geographies of power*. Pambazuka Press.

Ministry of Education. (2016, July). *Education action plan for the Belt and Road Initiative issued by the Ministry of Education of the People's Republic of China.* https://eng.yidaiyilu.gov.cn/zchj/qwfb/30277.htm

Taylor, I. (2011). *The Forum on China-Africa Cooperation (FOCAC).* Routledge.

Xi, J. (2017a, May 12). *Speech at the opening ceremony of the Belt and Road Forum for International Cooperation.* http://news.xinhuanet.com/english/2017-05/14/c_136282982.htm

Xi, J. (2017b). *His own words: The 14 principles of "Xi Jinping Thought".* https://monitoring.bbc.co.uk/product/c1dmwn4r#section8

Yang, C. (2019, April 18). 10 Luban workshops to provide training in Africa. *China Daily.* http://www.exploringtianjin.com/2019-04/18/c_356532.htm

By reviewing policies on higher education for international students, this article aims to investigate the change of social-historical context, policy issue, and policy solution and provide implications for policymaking. It used qualitative text analysis to analyze 112 policy papers collected from PKULAW database and Ministry of Education official website. Four stages have emerged from the text analysis. The policy focus witnessed a shift from openness to expansion and then to quality. The policies made by central government changed a lot accordingly. China is increasingly active in higher education internationalization and eager to make the education for international students an attractive brand with high quality. To realize this target, policies should be made based on different types of international students and provide detailed guidance and accelerate capacity building in all majors. This study contributes to existing knowledge of higher education for international students in China and the relating insights may also be of assistance to the policymaking in the future.

Higher Education for International Students in China: A Review of Policy From 1978 to 2020 [1]

Yuting Zhang and Yu Liao

Overview of the problem

With the increase of international student mobility as a global phenomenon, a considerable amount of literature has been published in this field to investigate the policy in individual country or compare the policies between countries. Knight (2004) defined four rationales driving internationalization: social/cultural, political, academic, and economic rationales. Stier (2004) identified idealism, instrumentalism, and educationalism as the ideologies in higher education internationalization. Stein and de Oliveira Andreotti (2016) categorized the instrumentalist discourses into cash, competition, and charity. Although reducing international student issues to a category of internationalization has been viewed as unsatisfied, there is a strong consensus among researchers with regards the rationale of related policies in major recruiting countries, like U.S.,

---

1 This article was funded by the 2019 Key Project of Educational Science Program in Zhejiang Province (2019SB114). It was published on *ECNU Review of Education*, March 17, 2021.

U.K., Australia, and Canada. As indicated by the term "great brain race" (Wildavsky, 2012), attraction and retention of international students were recognized as the main policy issue in these countries. International students have been viewed as a solution to national skills and funding shortfalls (Sá & Sabzalieva, 2018) because of their possible contribution to human capital and revenue sources (Zheng, 2010). Overall, economic rationale and instrumentalism ideology, especially in the form of cash and competition (Chan & Wu, 2019), played a leading role in the literature studying policies in these common destination countries. On July 6, 2020, the Trump administration announced the policy that would bar international college students if their school's classes are all online. In contrast, U.K., Australia, and Canada issued more friendly and open policy to support and keep international students affected by COVID-19 pandemic. New visa policy in America was viewed as serving political aims and making international students "pawns in a political drama" (Columbia Broadcasting System [CBS], 2020). This policy has sparked controversy considering the fact that many American colleges depend on international student tuition (Stimson, 2020) and the destination countries including America need more immigrants with college degrees to avoid shrinking economy introduced by dropping fertility rate (The Roanoke Times, 2020). Facing eight federal lawsuits and opposition from universities, the Trump administration rescinded the restrictions for international students on July 14, 2020 (Bierman et al., 2020). It's fair to argue that economic rationale is still the mainstream for policymaking in traditional recruiting countries even if there was temporary political consideration during a pandemic.

As a traditional large exporter of international students, China is becoming a competitor with leading host countries in this market during recent years. It is now one of the biggest study abroad destinations with a total number of 492,185 international students in 2018 (Ministry of Education of the People's Republic of China [MOE], 2019). There are a large number of published studies (e.g., Guo & Wang, 2008; Liu & Zhang, 2018; Wang & Xie, 2017; Zhang, 2014) that describe the policies in China generally and reflect on these policies by listing various challenges China is facing. However, few of them have been able to draw on any policy study based on empirical evidence. Considering the changing role of China in international student mobility, different reviews and explanations emerged from existing empirical policy studies. Kuroda (2014) held the view that policies in China have been implemented primarily for political reasons but the education for international students had also been viewed as providing economic benefits for China during 1990s. Chen (2016) found that political rationales are dominant across different periods and economic rationales were only highlighted after 1980s. Apart from a strong instrumental agenda, idealism is also in play, at least rhetorically, by emphasizing the platform for mutual understanding between China and international students' home country. Chan and Wu (2019) argued that policies in China fit in the discourse of charity before the turn of the century. However, more attention should be paid to the role of charity discourse in cultural diplomacy with the influence of political factors in new century, especially after 2010. The evidence reviewed here seems to suggest a dominant role for political rationale. Nevertheless, much uncertainty still exists about the role of other types of rationale and ideology. As a result, the authors seek to address these gaps in this study by investigating the change of social-historical context, policy issues, and policy solution with the policy papers published after 1978 as evidence.

Method

Public policy study became an independent field since the 1950s. Policy-oriented education research mentioned by Ball (1997) is one of the applications of public policy study. It can be categorized into three types. They are research on alternative policy plans, research on proposing alternative plans, and research on policy process (Lu & Ke, 2007). The third type aims to understand education from social, political, economic, and cultural perspectives, which is represented by Stephen Ball. Around 1960s to 1970s, empirical-technical approach was dominating in policy research, which views policy as a kind of fact and aims for optimal solution. However, policy was more inclined to be studied as text or discourse after 1970s, which is called discursive-critical approach (Tsang, 2007). This discursive-critical approach advocates understanding policy text against the context they were embedded in.

Following this discursive-critical approach, qualitative text analysis was used in this study in order to gain insights into the social-historical context, policy text, and the relation between them. Different from classical content analysis which limits to "manifest content," qualitative text analysis is a form of analysis in which understanding and interpretation of the text play a far larger role (Kuckartz, 2014, pp. 31–33).

Policies were searched from 1978 until June 2020 in the PKULAW database developed by

Peking University Yinghua Company and Peking University Center for Legal Information [1] and archive stored on MOE official website. [2] Policies were only included in the analysis if they were issued by central government and if they were related to any of the following key words. The key words cover international student, foreign student, overseas student, scholarship, and international education. Since this study only aims to investigate policies related to international students in college, [3] those policies not relevant to higher education were excluded from this study. After eliminating irrelevant policies, 112 policy papers were selected for this study finally.

Sixty-one percent of the 112 policies were issued by MOE independently, while 21% of them were issued in cooperation with other ministries. The three most usual cooperators were the Ministry of Finance (MOF), Ministry of Public Security (MOPS), and Ministry of Foreign Affairs (MOFA). More than half of the policies (58%) were published as notification, which is strong in terms of binding force but lacks specific guidance. In Table 1, there are basic descriptions of policies mentioned in this review. The policies will be named after their number in the following paragraphs for convenience.

Table 1. Selected policies addressing higher education for international students.

No.	Year	Policy name
2	1979	Report of Conference on Foreign Student Affairs
15	1985	Regulations on the Administration of Foreign Students
16	1986	Regulations on Foreign Student's Learning in China
17	1987	Notification of Enhancing and Improving the Administration of Foreign Students
22	1989	Regulations on Enrollment of Self-financed Foreign Students
27	1991	Trial Measures of Awarding Degree for International Students in Chinese Higher Education Institutions
33	1992	Measures of Expenditure Standard and Administration Regulations Related to Foreign Students
34	1992	Trial Measures of Accepting Foreign Students into Postgraduate Programs

1 See https://www.pkulaw.com/.
2 See http://www.moe.gov.cn/.
3 According to the latest definition given by *Regulations on the Enrollment and Education for International Students*, international students refer to all students studying in China without Chinese nationality. Since the number of international students in Chinese kindergarten, primary school, and secondary school is still very small, most of the policies and researches only pay attention to international students in higher education. As a result, international students in this study mean junior college students, undergraduate students, and graduate students in degree programs and preparing students, advanced visiting students, and visiting scholars in nondegree programs.

Continued

No.	Year	Policy name
35	1992	Measures of Chinese Proficiency Test (HSK)
46	1995	Measures on Funds Management for International Students
48	1995	Regulations on International Student Registering with Certificate of Chinese Proficiency (HSK)
51	1997	Measures on Annual Review of Scholarship for International Students
55	2000	Regulations on the Administration of Foreign Students in Higher Education Institutions
62	2003	Notification of Training Program on Integrated Service Related to International Student Affairs (2003)
63	2004	Notification of Enabling National Management Information System for International Students
64	2004	Notification of Establishing National Training System for Leaders in Charge of International Student Affairs (Notification of Training Program)
68	2005	Notification of National Training Program for Leaders in Charge of International Student Affairs
72	2006	Notification of Training Program on Integrated Service Related to International Student Affairs (2006)
74	2007	Provisional Regulations on Quality Control Standard of Medical Undergraduate English-Taught Program for International Students
75	2007	Notification of Seminar for Directors in Charge of International Student Affairs
83	2010	Regulations on International Student Registering with New Certificate of Chinese Proficiency (New HSK)
84	2010	Project of Study in China
90	2013	Notification of Selection of Branded Curriculum in English-Taught Program
92	2014	Notification of the Statistics of International Students
95	2015	Visions and Actions on Jointly Building Silk Road Economic Belt and 21st-Century Maritime Silk Road
97	2015	Notification of Improving the Chinese Government Scholarship System and Increasing the Funding Standard
100	2016	Opinions on the Work of the Opening-up of Education in the New Era
101	2016	Education Action Plan for Jointly Building the Belt and Road
104	2017	Regulations on the Enrollment and Education for International Students
107	2018	Quality Regulations of Higher Education for International Students (on Trial)
110	2020	Notification of Learning and Implementing President Xi's Response to Pakistani Students in University of Science and Technology Beijing
111	2020	Notification of Normalizing the Work of Accepting International Students into Chinese Higher Education Institutions
112	2020	Opinions on Accelerating and Expanding Opening-up of Education in the New Era

All of the 112 policies were analyzed to build thematic categories in light of the topics they are addressing. Deductive category construction was used to find code segments of the text under themes like social-historical context, policy issue, and policy solution separately following the research objective. Four stages emerged from the analysis based on the change of context and policy issue. The first three stages show us how and why the policies changed in the past. The last stage indicates the focus of recent policies and the possible direction for future.

Evolution of policy issue and solution: From cautious opening-up to integrated management

Cautious opening-up and quality priority

After 10 years of the "Cultural Revolution", the education system in China has been damaged seriously. In order to build basic frames of education for international students, the policies after 1978 mainly focused on synthetic issues, which referred to various aspects related to international students' learning and life. The number of international students at this stage is relatively small and increased very slowly. In 1978, only 1,236 international students were studying in China. The number increased to 5,835 until 1988 (Yu, 2009, p. 284). The policies at this stage proposed enrollment of self-financed students and local government autonomy in decision-making. According to Policy 15, a complete higher education system, including technical secondary school, junior college, undergraduate program, postgraduate program, and visiting program, has been established in 1985.

The policy response at this stage was opening the education system to the world cautiously and quality was given priority. This finding emerged from the policy text analysis in terms of the target group, their status, and the treatment they got in China. In Policy 2, accepting and educating foreign students were defined as China's internationalism duty. It is expected to cultivate talents for friendly countries, improve mutual understanding between China and countries of origin, and unite more power against hegemony. As mentioned by Policy 15, international students should be required strictly with honest help in learning, be affected actively without coercion in political attitude, and be treated considerately with strict management in daily life. Policy 16 stated that students from those countries having intergovernmental agreement with

China are most welcome. Policy 17 mentioned that cooperation with developing countries is the base for China's foreign policy and quality assurance is the precondition of multilevel and multichannel development in terms of recruiting students from developing countries. As for foreign students' learning, Policy 17 defined strict requirement and enthusiastic help as the basic principle. As for foreign students' living, Policy 17 defined moderate preference and strict management as the basic principle. Based on these policies, we can conclude that the international students at this stage mainly came from developing and friendly countries. They are viewed as foreigners with political status as much as learners. As a result, selection was very cautious with clear criteria. Once they were enrolled in Chinese colleges, they were expected to be treated seriously and strictly to make sure the quality of academic learning and the stability of political alliance with friendly countries.

Standard establishment and resource guarantee

As a result of social and political changes in Eastern Europe and Soviet Union countries around 1990, the world system had changed so much and exchange between China and other economies became more intensive. Policy 22 set up regulations helpful for increasing self-financed international students, including the power of decision-making at college level in terms of enrollment. This policy indicated government's active attitude toward expansion of education and involvement of more universities. The number of international students at this stage increased fast and the percentage of self-financed students went up and kept at a high level until now. In 1990, there were 7,494 international students studying in China and half of them were self-sponsored (Yu, 2009, p. 284). In 2000, the number of international students jumped to 52,150 and almost 90% were self-sponsored (MOE, 2005). However, the existing policies failed to provide detailed education standards and adequate resource for the rapid expansion. As a result, the policies at the second stage paid much attention to establishing standards and guaranteeing resource.

Policy 27 defined the requirement and procedure that international students being conferred bachelor's, master's, and doctoral degrees in China. According to Policy 33, the lump sum appropriation of scholarship was transferred from central government to college and the college can keep the balance. However, the college was also responsible for the excessive expenditure. Under this general regulation, the way of spending money by the college was also clarified in the policy in detail. As the revised version of Policy 33, Policy 46 additionally defined the appropriation as earmarking, which provides the further financial guarantee for international students. According to Policy 51, a student awarded scholarship was required to be evaluated on their performance and achievement every year in order to make sure the scholarship was used properly. Policy 34 formulated the qualification and procedure of international students applying for postgraduate programs in China. Policy 35 introduced details of Chinese Proficiency Test (HSK) and Policy 48 defined HSK certificate as one of the requirements for international students applying for undergraduate and postgraduate program in China. This review of policy solutions shows that a package of standards, from enrollment to graduation, has been set up. Additionally, financial support with strict supervision from central government is the main strategy to make sure these standards are realized at college level.

Integrated management and leadership development

After two decades of reform and opening-up, China has witnessed rapid economic development. Under the background of higher education internationalization, the number of international students in China increased more rapidly, especially after China joined the World Trade Organization (WTO) in 2001 and the central government removed limitation on the number of international students according to Policy 55 issued in 2000. Facing the challenges introduced by rapid expansion, the policies issued before 2000 was not enough to deal with various problems in international students' learning and daily life. Colleges needed more support apart from the standard and financial support mentioned in the last section, especially for colleges with little experience in accepting international students. As a result, the policies at this stage attempted to enhance the integrated management and leadership development.

Compared with policies on synthetic issues published at the first stage, Policy 55 was legislation on college behavior. This policy aimed to realize legalization and standardization in management at the college level by requiring that all leaders and teachers related to education for international students should learn and obey the policy. Management Information System (MIS) was created and demanded to be used by colleges who are accepting international students according to Policy 63. With the increasing number of international students living in China, various aspects of the society were expected to set up clear rules. In order to respond to the social need, policies on banking, public health, and insurance affairs related to international students were issued as well.

Apart from learning policy, leaders in charge of international student affairs were also required to participate in a training program hosted by the MOE from 2003 to 2007 according to Policies 62, 64, 68, 72, and 75. The content of training program held in 2003 included international relations, challenges in the education for international students, administration skills, and experience exchange between trainees. From 2004, training program has been divided into three parts emphasizing general management skill, special project management skill, and overseas investigation respectively. Until 2007, more than 1,500 leaders have been trained according to the data published by Policy 75.

Education quality began to be mentioned as an agenda by Policy 74 and a series of policies on enrollment plan for undergraduate English-taught programs in medicine were issued every year accordingly. Different from the focus on helping students' learning at the first stage, these policies covered all elements of education quality including enrollment, curriculum, teaching, and graduation with detailed regulation. However, the attention was only paid to undergraduate English-taught programs in medicine at this stage.

By establishing integrated management at college and social level and developing leadership by training program, the policies at this stage aimed to provide solutions for issues introduced by rapidly increasing number of international students from more countries of origin.

Policy solution in the new era: Brand building and quality assurance

Since China surpassed Japan and became the second largest economy in 2010, it engaged in global governance more actively and attempted to push forward major country diplomacy with Chinese characteristics. Education for international students has been viewed as part of national strategy and national image in the new era. However, the education quality for international students is questioned by public, especially when the public have the misunderstanding that Chinese government has sponsored most of the international students by scholarship. In addition to continuous policy based on those issues that had been discussed before 2010, like enrollment plans and teacher training in medicine majors, the theme of policies published at this stage mainly focused on brand building and quality assurance in order to show China's active engagement in higher education internationalization.

As one of the education history milestones, the *Outline of China's National Plan for Medium-*

and Long-Term Education Reform and Development (2010 - 2020) proposed further expansion of education for international students and the idea of Project of Study in China. As response to this outline, Policy 84 formulated in 2010 set the China 2020 targets of 500,000 person-times for the international students studying in all education sectors and 150,000 international students in tertiary degree programs. It indicated that China is expecting to "construct education and service system for international students which is compatible with China's international status" and "cultivate large quantities of graduate who know China well and treat China friendly" (MOE, 2010). By keeping balance between quantity, structure, quality, and effectiveness, China is more confident to build the study in China as an international brand. Policy 95 explaining Belt and Road Initiative defined student exchange as one of the strategies to enhance "people-to-people bond" (National Development and Reform Commission [NDRC], 2015) and improve cooperation between countries. Ten thousand government scholarship opportunities have been promised to the countries along the Belt and Road every year according to this policy. Policy 100 and Policy 101 provided more educational solutions under the general framework established by Policy 95. Policy 100 reaffirmed the target of branding the study in China by making branded majors and curricula. The policymaker expected that Chinese experience can be understood better through international students. Policy 101 explained the branding as making China the most attractive destination for international students along the Belt and Road and started several special projects to support the branding.

As for the theme of quality assurance, the policies at this stage aimed to go beyond English-taught program in medicine. Policy 84 first proposed quality assurance as an independent section in policy paper. Specific policy solutions for quality assurance included reform of HSK (Policy 83), selection of branded curriculum in English-taught program for all majors (Policy 90), regulation on the use of MIS and publication of the data collected (Policy 92), and raising funding standard of scholarship (Policy 97).

The transfer of policy solution to brand building and quality assurance broadly supports the work of previous studies on international student mobility. "Push-Pull" theory which was originally developed to explain the migration (Lee, 1966) has since become common in researches on international students' motivation for studying abroad. A great deal of research has attempted to investigate push (outbound) and pull (inbound) factors influencing international students' decisions (Mazzarol & Soutar, 2002; McMahon, 1992). The quality and reputation of education in host country, students' knowledge and awareness of the host country, recommendations from friends and relatives are among the most frequently mentioned pull factors. Obviously, the policy solutions of brand building and quality assurance help Chinese government to enhance the pull factors attracting more international students.

Even considering the possible trend of deglobalization and the statements of decoupling from China made by some developed countries recently, Chinese government does not plan to change its policy solution in 2020. In Policy 110, humanity was defined as the basic principle for dealing with international student affairs under COVID-19 pandemic. Improving education quality to attract international students and insisting on opening-up by building internationally renowned study centers was claimed as the long-term strategy. Policy 112 reconfirmed the role of opening-up of education in the new era. More active and broader opening is expected by the policymakers. Again, branding the study in China was mentioned as strategy to realize high quality of education for international students.

Among the policies aimed at brand building and quality assurance, two policies issued recently are worthy of further analysis to decode the current policy concern and direction in the near future. They are Policy 104 and Policy 107. Policy 104 has been defined to deactivate Policy 55 and Policy 107 followed Policy 104 to provide more detailed regulations on quality assurance. Recent Policy 110 discouraging the expansion at the expense of quality referred Policy 104 and Policy 107 as basis. This citation confirms the significance of Policy 104 and Policy 107 in current policy system. As a result, the authors analyze Policy 104 and Policy 107 by comparison with Policy 55. Three themes emerged from the comparison of policy text.

Shift of Chinese government's standpoint from passive involvement to active engagement

The word "accepting" used in Policy 55 was replaced by the word "enrolling" in Policy 104. International students had to leave China after graduation within the limited time according to Policy 55. Such kind of regulation was not mentioned in Policy 104. On the contrary, the colleges were required to establish contact with international alumni. More detailed guidance about how to facilitate international alumni network can be found in Policy 107.

Other specific articles in Policy 107 also showed that the Chinese government is holding a standpoint of complying with international norms and building confidence in its own culture as well during the transition from access expansion to quality improvement. For example, one of the education targets is cross-cultural communication and global competence for participation in international affairs. Curriculum structure is required to be internationally compatible and comparable, especially for majors like science, engineering, agriculture, and medicine. International students' rights including security, privacy, and so on are also guaranteed. Meanwhile, the international students are expected to understand China better by taking compulsory courses like Chinese language and Chinese culture. Passing level III or above in HSK has been listed as one of the requirements for graduation according to the type of program. Level III in HSK requires that students know 600 words and can communicate in Chinese at a basic level in daily, academic, and professional lives.

Decentralized management helping to establish quality assurance system with multiple subjects

Before Policy 55, there was another policy on education for foreign students in kindergarten, primary school, and secondary school issued in 1999. The publication of Policy 104 deactivated the two policies together and Policy 104 is suitable for international students of all ages. According to Policy 104, the decision-making authority related to international students in basic education was totally moved to provincial government. For higher education, there was no national planning for international student enrollment anymore and the decision-making authority was moved to colleges in most cases. However, the enrollment of students sponsored by central government scholarship was still mainly decided by government. As defined by Policy 107, colleges were asked to establish internal supervision mechanism and were supposed to take principal responsibility in quality assurance.

Multi-participation and external quality assurance were also defined clearly. Different from Policy 55 which defined university as the only organization in charge of foreign student affairs, Policy 104 allowed non-university organization and industry association to provide management and service for international students. Public and private enterprise, social group, and individual were allowed to set up scholarship after approval by higher education institution and provincial government according to Policy 55. In Policy 104, they were encouraged to set up scholarship without any regulation of approval. The authority of scientific research institution providing masters program and education organization providing nondegree program were also recognized by Policy 104. Meanwhile, central and provincial government's responsibilities to supervise international students and colleges enrolling them were emphasized as an independent chapter in Policy 104.

Converged management helping to set up comprehensive quality standard

Teaching plan and curriculum structure were allowed to be adjusted according to foreign students' background in Policy 55. However, they are required to be integrated into the general planning under converged management. Like assistant for political and ideological work in class of local students, assistant for class of international students was also required by Policy 104 to deal with students' daily affairs and help them to communicate with administrative offices. These changed policies have been defined more clearly by Policy 107 as converged teaching, management, and service for local and international students with same target, procedure, and criteria. The government aimed to set up comprehensive quality standard by realizing converged management and Policy 107 can be viewed as the initial step of the effort.

Taken together, policy text analysis in the new era shows that China is increasingly active in higher education internationalization. Although she has become the third biggest around the world and the most popular in Asia as destination country for international students, China is eager to make the education for international students an attractive brand with high quality. Additionally, the three specific themes emerged from recent policies suggest that management improvement has been viewed as the leading strategy for education quality.

Conclusion and implication

This study reviewed policies related to higher education for international students in China after 1978. It has identified that policy issues changed according to context at home and abroad. Policies published by central government tried to provide solutions as response to the changing issues. Four stages have emerged from qualitative text analysis.

Around 10 years after 1978, a basic framework was required for a career starting from scratch. As an opportunity mainly opened to friendly countries, the education for international students was advanced cautiously by targeting at quality of academic learning and political alliance.

With the great change of world system happening around 1990, education opening-up in China became more aggressive. Clear standard and sufficient resource were needed to motivate students and higher education institutions. Overall standards from entrance requirement to degree granting were set up by policies. Scholarship with strict supervision of winners and colleges was viewed as resource guaranteed by central government.

Facing the challenges introduced by rapid expansion of international students after 2000, part of the policy issues have been transferred from campus management to the society management and from government responsibility to college responsibility. As response to this transformation, integrated management at college and social level was established and training programs for college leaders were defined as routine by policies.

After 30 years of reform and opening-up, year 2010 was viewed as a new starting point for education development in China. Education for international students is expected to be compatible with China's rising international status. Therefore, policies published in the recent 10 years put emphasis on brand building through quality assurance.

Generally speaking, the policy focus witnesses a shift from openness to expansion and then to quality. The policies made by central government have changed a lot accordingly. The authors argue that the policies before 2010 were relatively independent from the "brain race" (Wildavsky, 2012) discourse. Although political concern was mentioned as motivation in policy papers, educationalism also played as a major rationale since most of the policy solutions were aiming at the improvement of education for international students. After 2010, pervasive instrumentalism seems to play a rising role in policymaking when China joined the global competition more actively and deeply. However, the concern is not what international students contribute to Chinese economic development but what cultural and political ideas they understand and introduce to their own countries. This concern can be understood as political or idealism agenda. Nonetheless, the meanings of these terms need to be reinterpreted in Chinese context. By emphasizing education quality in recent policies, it seems a rolling-back of educationalism. However, the current policy system does not provide sufficient solutions for building an international brand under instrumentalism, nor does it meet the requirement of improving education quality under educationalism. Therefore, the authors provide several insights for the future policymaking to realize expansion with high quality.

First, this study suggests that policies should be made based on different types of international students. According to the latest statistics of international students, degree students account for 52.44% and graduate students only account for 17.28% in 2018 (MOE, 2019). Compared with the statistics in 2000,[1] the structure of education levels has changed quickly. However, the percentage of degree students is still lower than the numbers in many traditional recruiting countries.[2] There are differences between degree students and nondegree students in terms of their learning motivation, education experience, and expecting outcome. Nonetheless, most of the policies are general or particular for students holding Chinese government scholarship. These policies failed to provide specific solutions for education related to different types of international students. Insufficient attention was paid to the education issues exclusively related to self-financed students who have been accounting for around 90%[3] after 1994. For degree students, a strict standard of enrollment is the precondition for education quality. It is suggested to make policy giving college full autonomy to select degree students based on their academic performance. For nondegree students, they are mainly self-financing and strict academic qualification for entrance does not make much sense, but quality assurance of the education process is still vital. It is suggested to make policy encouraging market competition and guaranteeing supervision by college and government as well. Considering the controversy over the quality of education for international students, raising the percentage of degree students is a helpful strategy to realize expansion with high quality, especially the percentage of graduate students. Apart from annual statistics, quality evaluation of education for all types of international students needs to be published every year as a response to public concern.

Second, this study raises the necessity that policies provide detailed guidance and accelerate capacity building in all majors. Based on 40 years' policy evolution, mechanism of resource input and general quality regulation has been set up. However, colleges, who are supposed to take the principal responsibility in more decentralized system, are facing various challenges in quality

---

1 In 2000, degree students accounted for 26.28% and graduate students accounted for 6.23% (MOE, 2005).
2 Take U.S., U.K., Australia, and Canada as examples, the enrollment of international students at bachelor level accounted for 4%, 14%, 14%, and 11%, respectively, while the enrollment of international students at graduate level accounted for 39%, 76%, 80%, and 49%, respectively, in 2017 (OECD, 2019, p. 242). In the MOE statistics for Chinese higher education, degree students include international students in junior colleges, undergraduate programs, and graduate programs. Other types of international students in long-term programs and trainees in short-term programs are counted as nondegree students. This standard of classification is different from OECD indicator system. Meanwhile, the numbers of international students in long-term programs, in junior colleges, or in undergraduate programs are not always available in MOE statistics. As a result, it is hard to compare the percentage of degree students between China and OECD countries directly. However, the reader can estimate that the percentage of degree students in China is relatively lower. It could be attributed to the fact that a large number of international students are studying Chinese in nondegree programs.
3 The percentage is summarized from the data in the *Educational Statistics Yearbook of China* (1978–1997), *Educational Yearbook of China* (1998–1999), and *MOE Statistics of Education for International Students* (2000–2018). The specific percentage for each year is not listed here because of the space limitation.

assurance. Considering the existing difference between international students and local students in terms of political and cultural background, the policy solution of converged management is too vague to direct teaching and administrative practice. Policies are expected to set up more specific quality indicator system for teaching and learning in all kinds of majors. The *National Standard on the Teaching Quality of Higher Education Institutions* (2018) covering 587 undergraduate majors and the *Provisional Regulation on Quality Control Standard of Undergraduate English-Taught Program in Medicine* (2007) may provide reference to the construction of indicator system. In order to implement these policies well, teachers in all majors and administrative staff at basic level are suggested to participate in training programs regularly. The routine training programs for leaders and teachers in medicine already established by policies may provide reference to the construction of full-scale capacity-building system.

References

Ball, S. J. (1997). Policy sociology and critical social research: A personal review of recent education policy and policy research. *British Educational Research Journal*, 23(3), 257–274. https://doi.org/10.1080/0141192970230302

Bierman, N., Wailoo, E., & Watanabe, T. (2020, July 14). Trump administration does about-face, drops rule that threatened foreign students. *Los Angeles Times*. https://www.latimes.com/world-nation/story/2020-07-14/trump-administration-rescinds-rule-on-foreign-students

Chan, W., & Wu, X. (2019). Promoting governance model through international higher education: Examining international student mobility in China between 2003 and 2016. *Higher Education Policy*. https://doi.org/10.1057/s41307-019-00158-w

Chen, K. (2016). *International student mobility in higher education in China: Tensions between policies and practices* [Master's thesis, Western University]. Electronic Thesis and Dissertation Repository. https://ir.lib.uwo.ca/etd/3985

Columbia Broadcasting System. (2020, July 10). "Pawns in a political drama": International students studying in SoCal sue Trump administration over new visa rule. *CBSLA*. https://www.msn.com/en-us/news/us/pawns-in-a-political-drama-international-students-studying-in-socal-sue-trump-administration-over-new-visa-rule/ar-BB16BsT1

Guo, X., & Wang, J. (2008). The policy analysis and system transition of Chinese higher education for international students [in Chinese]. *Journal of University of Science and Technology Beijing (Social Sciences Edition)*, 24(4), 141–145.

Knight, J. (2004). Internationalization remodeled: Definition, approaches, and rationales. *Journal of Studies in International Education*, 8(1), 5–31. https://doi.org/10.1177/1028315303260832

Kuckartz, U. (2014). *Qualitative text analysis: A guide to methods, practice, and using software*. SAGE.

Kuroda, C. (2014). The new sphere of international student education in Chinese higher education: A focus on English-medium degree programs. *Journal of Studies in International Education*, 18(5), 445–462. https://doi.org/10.1177/1028315313519824

Lee, E. S. (1966). A theory of migration. *Demography*, 3(1), 47–57.

Liu, B., & Zhang, J. (2018). The development of international students education policies in the forty years of reform and opening-up in China [in Chinese]. *Journal of Northwest Normal University (Social Sciences)*, 55(6), 91–97.

Lu, N., & Ke, Z. (2007). Classification, characteristics, and inspiration of education policy studies [in Chinese]. *Comparative Education Review*, (2), 27–31.

Mazzarol, T., & Soutar, G. N. (2002). "Push-pull" factors influencing international student destination choice. *International Journal of Educational Management*, 16(2), 82–90.

McMahon, M. E. (1992). Higher education in a world market. An historical look at the global context of international study. *Higher Education*, 24(4), 465–482.

Ministry of Education of the People's Republic of China. (2005, June 29). *Statistics of education for international students in 2000* [in Chinese]. http://www.moe.gov.cn/s78/A20/gjs_left/moe_850/tnull_8292.html

Ministry of Education of the People's Republic of China. (2010, September 21). *Notification of publishing the project of study in China* [in Chinese]. http://www.moe.gov.cn/srcsite/A20/moe_850/201009/t20100921_108815.html

Ministry of Education of the People's Republic of China. (2019, April 12). *Statistics of education for international students in 2018* [in Chinese]. http://www.moe.gov.cn/jyb_xwfb/gzdt_gzdt/s5987/201904/t20190412_377692.html

National Development and Reform Commission of the People's Republic of China. (2015, March 28). *Vision and actions on jointly building Silk Road Economic Belt and 21st-Century Maritime Silk Road*. https://en.ndrc.gov.cn/newsrelease_8232/201503/t20150330_1193900.html

OECD. (2019). *Education at a glance 2019: OECD indicators*. OECD Publishing.

Sá, C. M., & Sabzalieva, E. (2018). The politics of the great brain race: Public policy and international student recruitment in Australia, Canada, England and the USA. *Higher Education*, 75(2), 231–253. https://doi.org/10.1007/s10734-017-0133-1

Stein, S., & de Oliveira Andreotti, V. (2016). Cash, competition, or charity: International students and the global imaginary. *Higher Education*, 72(2), 225–239. https://doi.org/10.1007/s10734-015-9949-8

Stier, J. (2004). Taking a critical stance toward internationalization ideologies in higher education: Idealism, instrumentalism and educationalism. *Globalisation, Societies and Education*, 2(1), 1–28. https://doi.org/10.1080/14767724042000177069

Stimson, B. (2020, July 10). California first state to sue Trump administration over new international student visa rules. *Fox News*. https://www.foxnews.com/politics/california-first-state-to-sue-trump-administration-over-new-international-student-visa-rules

The Roanoke Times. (2020, July 11). Editorial: Why Trump's move to expel international students hurts rural areas. *The Roanoke Times*. https://roanoke.com/opinion/editorial/editorial-why-trumps-move-to-expel-international-students-hurts-rural-areas/article_e38755a4-a190-5136-8265-604c7bc0f110.html

Tsang, W. (2007). Policy studies in education: Discursive-critical perspective [in Chinese]. *Peking University Education Review*, 5(4), 2–30.

Wang, X., & Xie, S. (2017). Reflection on the policy of education for international student [in Chinese]. *Higher Education Exploration*, (3), 102–106.

Wildavsky, B. (2012). *The great brain race: How global universities are reshaping the world*. Princeton University Press.

Yu, F. (2009). *The education for international students in China during the 30 years (1978–2008)* [in Chinese]. Beijing Language and Culture University Press.

Zhang, J. (2014). The text analysis of policy of education for international students after 1949 [in Chinese]. *Xueyuan*, (12), 188–190.

Zheng, J. (2010). *Exploring international student mobility: Neoliberal globalization, higher education policies and Chinese graduate student perspectives on pursuing higher education in Canada* [Master's thesis, University of Alberta]. ProQuest Dissertations Publishing.

Comparison of Female Teachers in Primary, Secondary, and Tertiary Education: China and the World[1]

William Anderson

This report is based on statistics published yearly in the World Bank and the Education Statistics Yearbook by the Ministry of Education of the People's Republic of China. Using these freely available statistics, *ECNU Review of Education* aims to provide a basic comparative overview of representation of female teachers in all levels of basic education—both in China and the world. While this report articulates the aforementioned data in a comparative way, no absolute or final conclusions are meant to be drawn from these comparisons. Rather, we hope the following serves as a method of drawing attention to educational issues such as gender equality. Furthermore, we also hope that this report will serve to encourage follow-up research related to this topic.

Before comparing China's percentage of female educators across all level of basic education to that of the world average, certain distinctions are necessary. Following a law passed in 1986, the People's Republic of China solidified the country's compulsory education standard of 6 years of primary education and 3 years of secondary education. Secondary education is divided into two parts: junior secondary education and senior secondary education. Both parts include vocational schools in supplied statistics, and as such any conclusions reflect all students participating in secondary education—vocational or otherwise. Despite this, the statistics given by the Ministry of Education separate the two parts of secondary education, whereas the World Bank does not. In order to offer an easier-to-follow comparison, China's percentage of female teachers at the secondary level of education was found by averaging the percentages of both junior and senior secondary education. It is therefore worth noting that the annual percentage of female teachers was higher in junior secondary education than that of the senior secondary level. This difference usually took the form of being within three percentage points—the smallest being a 2.53% difference in 2013 and the largest a 3.3% difference in 2017. In addition, data are taken only from the years 2013–2017

---

1 This article was published on *ECNU Review of Education*, 2(2), 246–250.

solely for the reason that the Ministry of Education has only published data for these years.

Primary education

Primary education sees the highest percentage of female educators both in China and worldwide. These values represent the highest across the three levels of education. Both China and the world show a positive trend in annual percentages. In addition, the primary level of education sees the fastest growth in the 5 years of published statistics, represented by China's 6.53% jump from 2013 to 2017. China saw an annual average growth of 1.63% in female educators, with the greatest annual growth of 1.84% taking place between 2016 and 2017. Despite initially starting nearly three percentage points lower than the worldwide average, China's most recent statistics from 2017 now represent a 1.42% lead over the world. Given the increasing annual growth in China's percentage of female educators, it would be sound to assume that this trend will continue with future statistics (see Figure 1).

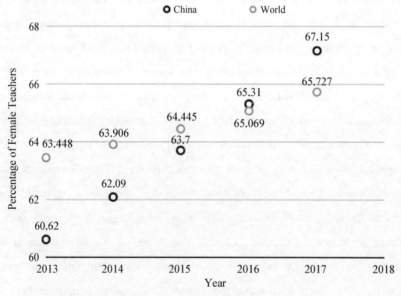

Figure 1. Comparison of percentage of female teachers in primary education.

Secondary education

Figure 2 shows the compared percentages of female educators in secondary education in both the world (World Bank, 2017) and China during the years 2013 (Ministry of Education, 2014), 2014 (Ministry of Education, 2015), 2015 (Ministry of Education, 2016), 2016 (Ministry of Education, 2017) and 2017 (Ministry of Education, 2018). While both China and the world see a positive trend in percentages of female educators in secondary education, the worldwide average sees an occasional decrease. During the same period of time, China maintains consistent annual growth. While this growth starts at a mere 0.46%, it quickly doubles in all subsequent years. China's percentages start below that of the world—a deficit of 2.73%, similar to that of the China-world primary education deficit of the same year—and end 0.41% higher than that of the world. While China's primary education percentage overtook the world's in 2016, the secondary level of education doesn't see China overtake the world until 2017. Similar to the primary education level, it would be sound to assume continued positive growth (see Figure 2).

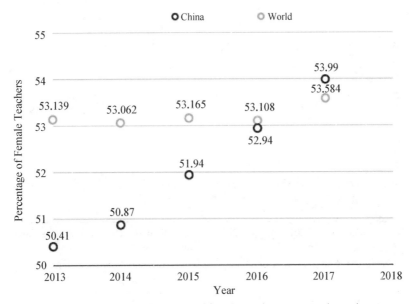

Figure 2. Comparison of percentage of female teachers in secondary education.

Tertiary education

Figure 3 shows the compared percentages of female educators in tertiary education in both the world (World Bank, 2017) and China during the years 2013 (Ministry of Education, 2014), 2014 (Ministry of Education, 2015), 2015 (Ministry of Education, 2016), 2016 (Ministry of Education, 2017) and 2017 (Ministry of Education, 2018). While other levels of education see

China starting below the worldwide average, China's tertiary education level sees far higher percentages of female teachers. Starting in 2013 at a six percentage point lead, China's annual growth only increases. The world average sees growth until a dip in 2016, before making its greatest leap in 2017. The World Bank defines equal female employment in all levels of education as being greater than or equal to 50%. All previous levels of education met this standard, and tertiary education is the first and only level to have this standard not apply. While neither China nor the world on average has achieved this result, China is far closer. Based on the trend of continuous annual growth, China would be well within the equality threshold in the next year (see Figure 3).

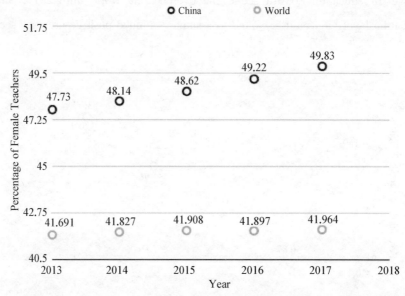

Figure 3. Comparison of percentage of female teachers in tertiary education.

Data sources

China:

Ministry of Education. (2014, December 12). *Number of female educational personnel and full-time teachers of schools by type and level*. http://en.moe.gov.cn/documents/statistics/2013/national/201412/t20141216_181717.html

Ministry of Education. (2015, August 21). *Number of female educational personnel and full-time teachers of schools by type and level*. http://en.moe.gov.cn/documents/statistics/2014/national/

Ministry of Education. (2016, October 17). *Number of female educational personnel and full-time teachers of schools by type and level*. http://en.moe.gov.cn/documents/statistics/2015/national/

Ministry of Education. (2017, August 24). *Number of female educational personnel and full-time teachers of schools by type and level.* http://en.moe.gov.cn/documents/statistics/2016/national/

Ministry of Education. (2018, August 8). *Number of female educational personnel and full-time teachers of schools by type and level.* http://en.moe.gov.cn/documents/statistics/2017/national/

Worldwide:

World Bank, UNESCO Institute for Statistics. (2017). *Primary Education, Teachers (% Female).* https://data.worldbank.org/indicator/SE.PRM.TCHR.FE.ZS

World Bank, UNESCO Institute for Statistics. (2017). *Secondary Education, Teachers (% Female).* https://data.worldbank.org/indicator/SE.SEC.TCHR.FE

World Bank, UNESCO Institute for Statistics. (2017). *Tertiary Education, Teachers (% Female).* https://data.worldbank.org/indicator/SE.TER.TCHR.FE.ZS

Basic Education

This piece of policy review explores a new landmark teacher policy titled *Opinions on Comprehensively Deepening the Reform of the Teaching Force Development in the New Era*, which was endorsed at the highest decision-making level since the establishment of the People's Republic of China. The study discovers three distinct characteristics of this reform program and also reveals the potential difficulties and challenges faced by the relating reforms and innovations. Looking forward to 2035, the Chinese government has proposed the goal of cultivating highly qualified, professional, and innovative teachers, in addition to proposing a thorough series of related programs. However, it must be recognized that China has several practical problems to overcome in order to achieve this goal.

Making Teaching an Enviable Profession: New Epoch-Making Teacher Policy in China and Challenges[1]

Tingzhou Li

In early 2018, China promulgated the *Opinions on Comprehensively Deepening the Reform of the Teaching Force Development in the New Era*. This was a new landmark teacher policy endorsed at the highest decision-making level since the establishment of the People's Republic of China. The policy established ambitious objectives: by 2035, it aims to increase the quality of teachers greatly, to modernize governance systems, and to make teaching an enviable profession. At the same time, it proposes a series of policy programs that include 23 policy measures.

Over the past decades, China's education policies have valued the construction of basic educational infrastructure over the teacher development. Some reviews have noted that this new policy is a milestone in Chinese education (Zhang, 2018b), and signifies a shift in the strategic focus of China's education policy away from hardware inputs and towards the teacher development (Li, 2018). It is certain that this policy will have profound effects on the construction of the teacher resources in China, and will serve as an important authoritative reference for educational reforms, public financial investment, and the development of the teaching profession in the

---

[1] This article was funded by the Key Project, Beijing Educational Science Planning Program during the 13th Five-Year Plan (project No. AEGA17007). It was published on *ECNU Review of Education*, 1(2), 145–152.

coming future.

Policy characteristics and innovations

Opinions on Comprehensively Deepening the Reform of the Teaching Force Development in the New Era is an anticipated policy that has been developed over a long period. It has some distinct characteristics and proposes constructive programs.

This policy is featured by its authoritativeness since it was determined at a high level of decision-making and published by a high-ranking body. The policy was decided upon by the Central Leading Group for Comprehensively Deepening Reforms of Chinese Communist Party and was issued under the Central Committee of the Communist Party of China and the State Council of the People's Republic of China. The Central Leading Group for Comprehensively Deepening Reforms is one of the four key top-level decision-making and coordination bodies established after the 18th National Congress of the Communist Party of China and is responsible for designing and implementing reforms. The other three groups are the National Security Commission of the Communist Party of China, the Central Cyberspace Affairs Commission, and the Central Leading Group for Military Reform. This is the first time since the establishment of the PRC that a teacher policy has been executed at such a high decision-making level and published by such a prominent body. This gives the policy a high degree of authority, and is an important reason why the policy has received extensive attention.

A second distinct characteristic of this reform program is that it is related to a variety of teacher policy fields and has strong comprehensive and systematic characteristics. A World Bank study argues that teacher policy can be divided into ten elements (SABER, 2012). The reform programs proposed in this new policy cover each of these ten elements of teacher policy.

- With regard to initial teacher preparation, the new policy proposes an increase in the per-student funding allocation to normal schools, colleges, and universities, incentivizing early student recruitment by normal schools, colleges, and universities, establishing a college assessment with teaching characteristics, and supporting high-level and comprehensive universities in the development of teacher training.
- With regard to qualifications for the employment and retention of teachers, the new policy proposes "gradual participation in ongoing education programs for teachers and participation in practical

teaching as an essential condition for determining teaching ability and obtaining teacher qualifications." In addition, the policy proposes gradually upgrading the educational qualifications for teachers by "upgrading the preschool teachers' qualifications to an associate's degree, the elementary school teachers' qualifications to an associate's degree in teaching or a bachelor's degree in non-teaching, the junior high school teachers' qualifications to a bachelor's degree, and the senior high school teachers' qualifications to graduate experience in some locations."

- With regard to recruitment and employment, the policy proposes the "selection of people with superior ability who are passionate about teaching and are suited to the teaching profession."
- With regard to workload and professional autonomy, the policy proposes that teachers should be able to select their own courses in teacher training, and that the formalist assessment should be prevented from interfering with the normal teaching.
- With regard to professional development, the policy proposes measures to strengthen teacher training and improve the teaching and research system.
- With regard to remuneration and benefits, the policy proposes that the average salary level of elementary and secondary school teachers should not be lower than that of local civil servants, and that institutional measures should be used to protect the social status of teachers.
- With regard to retirement rules and benefits, the policy proposes that rural teachers who have worked for 30 years or more should be honored at retirement.
- With regard to monitoring and evaluation of teacher quality, the policy emphasizes the dual necessity for morality and teaching performance, and the avoidance to use students' test scores and enrollment rates to assess teachers.
- With regard to the representation and participation of teachers, the policy proposes the establishment of a completely representative assembly for teaching staff in order to guarantee the democratic rights of teachers to participate in school decision making.
- With regard to school leadership, the policy proposes a reform of the ranking system for the principals of elementary and junior high schools, expanding the space available for career development, and promoting professionalization of school principals.

These policy measures are coordinated with one another and come together as a strongly systemic body. In addition, the policy also proposes reforms with distinct Chinese characteristics. For example, by strengthening the leadership of the Communist Party of China (CPC), the policy states the need to "strengthen leadership and implement a Yibashou (literally as first hand, meaning head leader) responsibility system (i.e., a head leader is held directly responsible and accountable for implementation and supervision)" and "prioritize teachers and teaching in the educational agenda." Additionally, the policy specifically emphasizes teacher morality. China has traditionally viewed teachers as having significant ethical importance, rather than being just a profession. The Chinese language has idiomatic expressions such as "a teacher for a day is a father for a lifetime." As such, the policy proposes to improve the ideological and political quality of teachers and to implement programs for improving teacher's morality and professionalism.

A third distinct characteristic of this policy is that it clarifies that policies aimed at the teacher development are granted preferential development status within the field of education. This is apparent particularly in the prioritized allocation of political resources and the preferential investment of public finances.

With regard to the preferential allocation of political resources, it is noteworthy that the phrase "Yibashou responsibility system" is used. Here, "Yibashou" refers to the CPC branch secretaries as head leaders of public organizations of every level and type. It is widely known that the CPC has a unique status in China, and "party leadership of government" and the "mutual embedding of the party and state" are characteristics specific to China's political ecology (He & Kong, 2011). The adoption of the "Yibashou responsibility system" implies that questions related to the construction of the teacher resources will be given high priority over policy issues.

With regard to investment of public finance, the policy proposes that each level of government will be required to give priority to the construction of the teacher resources as a focus of educational investment. Chinese financial investment in education in the past has emphasized investment in the hardware and infrastructure. Public investment in teachers' salaries is insufficient, especially on the county level. The new teacher policy proactively addresses these issues (Zhang, 2018a, pp. 5-8).

Difficulties and challenges

The policy looks forward to 2035, and the Chinese government has proposed the goal of cultivating highly qualified, professional, and innovative teachers, in addition to proposing a thorough series of related programs. However, it must be recognized that China has several practical problems to overcome in order to achieve this goal.

First, teacher education has suffered marginalization within the overall system of higher education. China adopted a relatively closed and elitist system for teacher training prior to the

1990s. This teacher education system comprised three tiers: secondary normal schools for training primary school teachers, higher normal schools for training primary school and junior high school teachers, and normal universities for training junior high school and senior high school teachers. This system allocated teacher resources according to the logic embedded in the era of the planned economy. Guided by the government and separate from other non-teaching professions, it conducted early recruitment and employment distribution and adopted individual training models (Zhu, 2005).

As China's higher education system became more available to the wider public, this independent teacher education system dissolved over time, and previous normal universities gradually transformed into comprehensive universities, junior and senior high normal schools were gradually integrated, and secondary normal schools were merged. At present, the teacher education system is significantly weakened, and public finances have not provided adequate support for normal schools and teaching profession. In addition, the proportion of student teachers recruited by normal schools has declined steadily (Wang, 2018). The overall result of these changes has been that teacher education has been gradually marginalized within the overall higher education system (Zhang, 2018a).

Second, China's high-level universities participate limitedly in teacher education. China's modern teacher education system has adopted a joint model that includes normal schools and universities, and comprehensive universities. However, participation of high-level universities is constrained. For example, China's high-level universities, such as Peking University, Tsinghua University, Fudan University, Shanghai Jiao Tong University, and Renmin University of China, do not provide teacher education. In terms of total numbers, more than 3,000 Chinese higher education institutions provide teacher education; although this is a large number, more than 2,000 of these institutions are at or below the junior college level and are at the lowest tier of China's higher education system. The system for establishing China's top-tier universities and academic disciplines emphasizes cutting-edge scientific and academic contributions (Liu, 2018). Given this type of policy guidance, it is difficult to reverse the tendency of high-level universities to avoid providing teacher education quickly. Without the participation of high-level universities, it is difficult for Chinese higher education development to improve the overall quality of Chinese teacher education, which poses significant challenges for training high-quality teachers.

Third, China's county-level teacher training system is weak. Prior to the 1990s, China's county-level teacher training institutions experienced rapid development, and contributed significantly to improving the professional development and academic backgrounds of primary school and junior high school teachers, especially those rural teachers. Subsequently, county-level teacher training institutions gradually weakened and the quality of training declined, due to the indistinct nature of these institutions and a lack of funding guarantees. Currently, county-level teacher training institutions are incapable of performing the function of teacher training. There are about 11 million teachers at the basic education level in China, and nearly 80% of these are concentrated in schools at or below the county level (county, township, or village). The fact that county-level teacher training institutions are largely incapable of playing an effective role implies that more than eight million Chinese teachers have no opportunity to receive adequate in-service training. At present, China's county-level teacher training institutions are attempting to restructure and integrate, although they still face significant challenges.

Fourth, there are still obvious shortcomings in the construction of the teaching force in poor rural regions of China. China is undergoing a process of rapid urbanization at present, which has maintained an average annual growth rate of about 1%. Urbanization creates a continuous outflow of rural school-aged populations, leading to a deterioration of rural schools. The work environment of rural teachers tends to be poor with their long work hours and their lack of professional development support; these factors make rural teaching positions very unattractive, making it impossible to attract young teachers to work in rural areas (Li, 2015). An increasing number of rural teachers reside in cities and towns, and commute between the city and countryside to teach, sometimes spending long periods away from their families; therefore, teachers exhibit a strong trend towards urban relocation. There are about 3.3 million teachers working in rural schools at present, and they constitute a weak point in China's efforts to build the highly qualified and professional teacher resources. China continues to face the problem of how to guarantee the quality of rural teachers while attracting new teachers to work in rural areas.

References

He, D., & Kong, F. (2011). China's experience in public policy implementation. *Social Sciences in China*, (5), 61–79.

Li, T. (2015, April 2). How do rural teachers get rid of the island dilemma [in Chinese]. *China Teacher Paper*.

Li, T. (2018, February 13). The development of education has entered the age of "software" [in Chinese]. *China Education Newspaper*.

Liu. X. (2018). The "Double First Class" initiative under top-level design. *ECNU Review of Education*, *1*(1), 147–152.

SABER (Systems Approach for Better Education Results). (2012). *What matters most in teacher policies? A framework for building a more effective teaching profession.* Human Development Network, The World Bank.

Wang, D. (2018). The situation and tasks of the construction of teaching staff in the New Era. *Educational Research*, (3), 4–11.

Zhang, Z. (2018a). Teachers as the primary resources of education [in Chinese]. *Journal of the Chinese Society of Education*, (4), 5–8.

Zhang, Z. (2018b, February 13). To profoundly understand the strategic connotation of strengthening the construction of teaching staff [in Chinese]. *China Education Newspaper*.

Zhu, X. (2005). Reconstruction of the teacher education system in the post-era of the Shifan. *Journal of Educational Studies*, (2), 76–81.

In August 2018, the Chinese State Council issued a document on regulating private tutoring institutions, which was the first central level regulation on private tutoring. Against this backdrop, this piece of policy review mainly focuses on the development of regulatory policies on private supplementary tutoring, which is widely called *Xiaowai Peixun* (校外培训) in China, and their possible negative results. According to the author, the years development of private tutoring in China has brought about some possible negative results, such as heavy study burden on students, reducing students' interests and energy in school classes, anxieties among parents and students, and the heavy financial burden on some families. That is why the private tutoring should be regulated. Based on the information collected during the Nationwide Special Inspection in 2018, the establishment of a long-term mechanism of private tutoring institutions to promote healthy and orderly development is on the way, but the current policies may also cause some negative results in the short run, which should be given due attention. At last, two suggestions to complement regulations are proposed by this article, which could contribute to the policymaking in the future.

Review of Regulatory Policies on Private Supplementary Tutoring in China[1]

Junyan Liu

The present paper focuses on the regulations on private supplementary tutoring, which in China is widely called *Xiaowai Peixun* (校外培训). Although much previous international literature has mostly focused on tutoring in academic subjects, tutoring in non-academic ones such as piano and painting has become popular in China and is also seen as educational investment by families. To fit this context, the present paper adopts a definition of private tutoring covering tutoring in both academic and non-academic subjects.

The present paper first elaborates on the development of private tutoring in China and why it should be regulated. And then it depicts a general picture about how governments have regulated private tutoring institutions and identifies the elements in regulatory framework. At last, it discusses the possible negative results and proposes two suggestions to complement

---

1 This article was published on *ECNU Review of Education*, *1*(3), 143–153.

regulations.

Development of private tutoring in China and its negative impacts

Private tutoring has expanded to be a worldwide phenomenon alongside school education (e.g., Aurini, Davies, & Dierkes, 2013; Bray, 2017; Liu & Bray, 2017; Park, Buchmann, Choi, & Merry, 2016). Development of private tutoring in China is more recent than elsewhere, but it has become widely visible over the last decade (Lei, 2005; Tsang, Ding, & Shen, 2010; Xue, 2015; Zhang & Bray, 2016). Nationwide representative data from the 2017 iteration of the China Household Finance Survey (CHFS) indicated that 48% of students in primary and secondary schools received private tutoring with an average cost of 2,697 CNY per year, and that the market volume of the tutoring industry was over 0.49 trillion CNY (Huang & Wei, 2018, p. 101). The booming demand for private tutoring has stimulated the supply—and vice versa. Huge numbers of tutoring institutions have been set up in last decade, and many individual tutors have entered the marketplace.

The considerable growth of private tutoring in China has brought attention from both the public and scholars. One element arousing wide concern relates to the heavy study burden on students. According to the CHFS data, primary and secondary students spent 5.9 hours per week on private tutoring during the ordinary term-time, and 15.0 hours per week during vacation periods (Huang & Wei, 2018, p. 109). Another element widely criticized concerns the backwash on regular schooling. This backwash may occur in several ways, such as reducing students' interests and energy in school classes, making the teaching in school class of students with and without private tutoring more challenging, distracting teachers who provide private tutoring from their regular duties, and encouraging misconduct among teachers like deliberately withholding content in school class to push students to private tutoring (Bray & Kwo, 2014; Kobakhidze, 2018; Zhang & Bray, 2017). Tutoring-school partnership in admissions, which may distort the officially-advocated procedures, have been another issue of concern (Liu, 2017; Zhang & Bray, 2017; Zhao, 2014). Other negative influences of private tutoring include (but not limited to) the anxieties among parents and students, the social inequality due to unequal probabilities of taking tutoring, and the heavy financial burden on some families. These negative impacts call for regulations on private tutoring.

Regulatory policies on private tutoring

Previous policies

Around the world, the private tutoring sector is still under-regulated compared to the formal schools (Bray & Kwo, 2014, p. 66). It is the same in China. Government previously paid little attention to private tutoring. Policy, if any, usually focused on a specific problem of private tutoring. For example, the Ningbo government introduced a guideline on the charges and refunds by tutoring institutions in 2009. The Ministry of Education (MoE) issued a policy in 2015 to prohibit in-service school teachers from organizing or providing private tutoring; and in 2017 the Chengdu Education Bureau stated that tutoring institutions should not organize academic contests among students in compulsory education. Only a few local governments have designed policies to regulate private tutoring institutions regarding various aspects including setting up and operation. The Hangzhou authorities did so in 2008, and the Chongqing counterparts in 2011.

The nationwide special inspection in 2018

The negative impacts, especially the study burden on students got worse as private tutoring further intensified and expanded in China, which have been under the attention of Central Government since late 2017. The Central Government raised the necessity of easing students' workload from private tutoring at the Central Economic Work Conference in Dec. 2017 for the first time. Premier Li Keqiang emphasized "[t]he government will spare no effort to resolve the heavy workloads of primary and secondary school students" when he delivered the Government Work Report in March 2018.

The MoE and three other ministries jointly issued a guideline to inspect private tutoring institutions in February 2018. Subsequently, all the 31 provinces/municipalities/autonomous regions released their guidelines in April 2018. [1] Under these guidelines, inspections and checks had been made on 382,000 tutoring institutions across the country by 20 August 2018, among which 259,000 were found to have problems and were ordered to rectify and improve (Wang,

---

1 Shanghai was ahead of other places in terms of inspecting private tutoring institutions. Shanghai launched the inspection in February 2017 as a pilot for the nationwide inspections, and then issued three documents on the registration standard of tutoring institutions and monitoring measures in December 2017. Shanghai also joined the nationwide inspections in 2018.

2018). To fit the aim of reducing study workload and promoting the healthy development of primary and secondary school students, besides the major focus of tutoring institutions, this nationwide inspection also touched school education.

The elements of tutoring institutions which were inspected in 2018 are presented in Table 1. This inspection mainly focused on four aspects as follows:

(1) Safety issues: Tutoring institutions with safety hazards would be ordered to stop their businesses to make rectification within the prescribed time limit.

(2) Licenses: A school license and a business license are required to set up and operate a private tutoring institution. However, because of the demanding requirements for license like a site of more than 300 square meters, it has been a common practice for tutoring institutions to operate without a license (Hu, 2018). For example, among the 7,000 tutoring institutions in Shanghai which were checked in 2017, more than 1,300 had no licenses, only one quarter held both school license and business license, and the others only had business license (Wu, 2017).

Under this regulation, the tutoring institutions without license would be guided to apply for the school license from local education authority and the business license from the local industry and commerce authority if satisfying the requirements, or would be ordered to close down if not. Tutoring institutions only holding a business license would be guided to apply for the school license if satisfying the requirements, or would be ordered to stop providing tutoring services to primary and secondary school students if not.

(3) Teaching in tutoring class: Government has been concerned a lot about the teaching in tutoring classes, the academic tutoring class in particular. Private tutoring institutions of problems like teaching beyond the national syllabus, teaching ahead of school schedule, and exam-oriented teaching would be ordered to rectify strictly. Institutions should report the information of tutoring content, targeted students, class organization and tutoring hours to local education authorities for recording and make the information public.

(4) Contest organization and the tutoring-school partnership in admissions: The contest or ranking test in academic subjects organized by tutoring institutions was criticized as causing anxieties among students and their parents (Liu, 2017). And its result may be used by formal schools to enroll high-performing students. This tutoring-school partnership in admissions undermined governments' efforts in promoting balanced development of education (Zhang & Bray, 2017). Therefore, this contest and partnership in admissions would be strictly prohibited.

Table 1. The elements of private tutoring institutions under inspection in 2018.

	Safety	License	Tutoring Progress	Tutoring Content	Targeted Students	Class Organization	Tutoring Hours	Qualifications of Tutors	Contest Organization	Partnership in Admissions	Fee Charging	Advertising
MoE	✓	✓	✓	✓	✓	✓	✓		✓	✓		
Anhui	✓	✓	✓	✓	✓	✓	✓		✓	✓		
Beijing	✓	✓	✓	✓	✓	✓	✓		✓	✓	✓	✓
Chongqing	✓	✓	✓	✓	✓	✓	✓	✓	✓	✓		
Fujian	✓	✓	✓	✓	✓	✓	✓			✓		
Gansu	✓	✓	✓	✓	✓	✓	✓		✓	✓		
Guangdong	✓	✓	✓	✓	✓	✓	✓	✓	✓	✓		✓
Guangxi	✓	✓	✓	✓	✓	✓			✓	✓		
Guizhou	✓	✓	✓	✓	✓	✓	✓	✓	✓	✓		
Hainan	✓	✓	✓	✓	✓	✓	✓		✓	✓		
Hebei	✓	✓	✓						✓	✓		
Heilongjiang	✓	✓	✓	✓	✓	✓	✓		✓	✓		
Henan	✓	✓	✓	✓	✓	✓			✓	✓		
Hubei	✓	✓	✓	✓	✓	✓	✓		✓	✓		
Hunan	✓	✓	✓	✓	✓	✓	✓	✓	✓	✓	✓	✓
Inner Mongolia	✓	✓	✓	✓	✓	✓	✓		✓	✓		
Jiangsu	✓	✓	✓	✓	✓	✓	✓	✓	✓	✓		✓
Jiangxi	✓	✓	✓	✓	✓	✓	✓		✓	✓		
Jilin	✓	✓	✓	✓	✓	✓	✓		✓	✓		
Liaoning	✓	✓	✓	✓	✓	✓	✓		✓	✓		

Continued

	Safety	License	Tutoring Progress	Tutoring Content	Targeted Students	Class Organization	Tutoring Hours	Qualifications of Tutors	Contest Organization	Partnership in Admissions	Fee Charging	Advertising
Ningxia	✓	✓	✓	✓	✓	✓	✓	✓	✓	✓		
Qinghai	✓	✓	✓	✓	✓	✓	✓		✓	✓		
Shandong	✓	✓	✓	✓	✓	✓	✓		✓			
Shanghai	✓	✓	✓	✓	✓		✓		✓	✓	✓	✓
Shanxi	✓	✓	✓	✓	✓	✓	✓		✓	✓		
Shaanxi	✓	✓	✓						✓	✓	✓	✓
Sichuan	✓	✓	✓	✓	✓	✓	✓	✓	✓	✓		✓
Tianjin	✓	✓	✓	✓	✓	✓	✓		✓	✓		
Tibet	✓	✓	✓	✓	✓	✓	✓		✓	✓		✓
Xinjiang	✓	✓	✓	✓	✓	✓	✓		✓	✓		
Yunnan	✓	✓	✓	✓	✓	✓	✓		✓	✓		
Zhejiang	✓	✓	✓	✓	✓	✓	✓	✓	✓	✓		

Note. The author coded the regulatory guidelines of MoE and the 31 provinces/municipalities/autonomous regions to identify the elements of private tutoring institutions under inspections.

Tutoring institutions organizing contest or seeking partnership with schools in admissions shall be pursued according to law.

In addition to the four common elements under inspection, provincial authorities in Chongqing and Hunan also checked the qualifications of tutors. Besides the prohibition of hiring in-service school teachers, these governments paid attention to the teacher certificate and teaching experiences of tutors. Beijing, Shanghai, Hunan and Shaanxi also inspected and regulated the fee-charging of tutoring institutions. Beijing, Guangdong and Jiangsu checked the advertising practices and identified the unacceptable ones for regulation.

As the major sector to educate students, schools were also inspected. The major foci include the teaching and teachers. Because of the availability of private tutoring, some teachers might assume that their students have already learnt or have opportunities to learn in tutoring class, and they would put less efforts in teaching (Bray & Kwo, 2014, p. 30). And then the problem of teaching not according to syllabus and teaching plan was noticed in some schools. Under this regulation, schools of this problem would be penalized.

In-service school teachers were investigated in terms of their involvement in private tutoring. In-service teachers are not allowed to organize or participate in the provision of private tutoring. Teachers who persuade or coerce students to attend private tutoring would be dealt with severely or even stripped of their teacher certificates.

The regulations issued in August 2018

Following the work of special inspection, based on the information collected during inspection, the State Council issued a document on regulating private tutoring institutions in August 2018, which was the first central level regulation on private tutoring. It aims to establish a long-term mechanism of regulating private tutoring institutions to promote healthy and orderly development, which will be beneficial for maintaining a good education environment and reducing the extracurricular workload on primary and middle school students.

This document proposed four fundamental principles. First, the regulating work must be in accordance with education laws. Second, institution of academic tutoring is the major focus of regulating work, while institution of non-academic tutoring promoting students' more-rounded development and cultivating students' innovation spirit and practice ability will be encouraged. Third, school will be reformed to improve its education quality at the same time when regulating tutoring institutions. Fourth, regulating work calls for the collaboration of governments of different level, and the coordination of different departments.

This document stipulated further regulations on private tutoring institutions based on the guidelines released in Feb. 2018.

On setting up: It requires the education department at provincial-levels to set specific standards according to local contexts in coordination with other departments regarding the setting up of tutoring institutions. Some basic requirements are applied to institutions across the country. For example, the area shall be more than 3 square meters per student during any tutoring period. Tutors in academic subjects must hold teaching credentials.

On registration and approval: Besides the requirement of school license and business license before providing tutoring service, this newly released document requires the approval from local education authorities when the tutoring institution sets up branches in other county or district.

On operation: In addition to the requirements stated in the aforementioned guidelines, tutoring institutions have to abide by some new ones. For example, all tutoring classes shall finish before 8:30 pm. The tutoring fees shall not be charged for more than three months at a time.

Besides, certificates and licenses shall be reviewed by local education authorities every year. Local governments shall publish lists on their websites of both the qualified institutions and those failing to meet the standards.

Regarding mainstream schools, besides the regulations on in-service teachers and on class teaching in the aforementioned guidelines, this document prohibits schools to enroll students in collaboration with private tutoring institutions. To reduce the demand for certain types of private tutoring, schools shall provide after-school-hours services to their students with no lessons but activities which can cultivate students' interests, broaden their horizons and strengthen their practice abilities.

To cooperate with the efforts in regulations at central level, some local governments have issued documents to regulate private tutoring institutions within their jurisdictions, like Shanghai (in 2017), Wuhan (in 2018), Xian (in 2018), Hangzhou (in 2018) and Jinhua (in 2018).

Discussions

Governments are responsible for monitoring and regulating private tutoring, although it is a form of privatized education service (Bray & Kwo, 2014; Fielden & LaRocque, 2008). As Fielden and LaRocque (2008, p. 13) remarked, "[g]overnments have an obligation to ensure that their citizens receive a good education from whatever source it is provided ... In the case of private sector provision the same principles apply, with the necessity of developing instruments of monitoring and control to ensure that provision of both public and private sectors are of the highest quality possible." The regulating task will be more challenging as private tutoring gets more deeply rooted in society and becomes more widespread. As private tutoring expands rapidly in China, it is wise and necessary for governments at different levels to monitor and regulate it.

The current regulatory policies will promote the sound and sustainable development of private tutoring sector in the long run. But it may cause some negative results in the short run, which should be given due attention. Some institutions, small ones in particular, which have difficulties to satisfy the demanding requirements may close down without prior notifications and the owners may skip off with money, as reported on newspapers (Ren, 2018). Some unqualified institutions may choose to provide tutoring services secretly and then the cost of private tutoring may increase because of the growing risks, as what happened in Korea (Lee, Lee, & Hyo-Min, 2010, p. 104). The large-scale institutions have advantages in rectification with stronger capital and more resources and are more likely to expand and develop sustainably than small ones. As more small institutions close down under regulation, their tutees may move to large-scale ones gradually, which then occupy a larger market share and get more influence on pricing (Zhao, 2018). Then families have to pay more money for private tutoring.

Besides the major provider of tutoring institutions, some private tutoring in China is offered by university students, in-service or retired school teachers, and self-employed persons on an informal basis. Although the object of current regulation is the tutoring institution, tutoring offered by other providers also needs to be regulated. However, much of the informal private tutoring is beyond the reach of governments, and it is impossible for governments to regulate the whole private tutoring industry by themselves (Bray & Kwo, 2014). Many governments in other societies have placed weight on consumer awareness and tried to educate consumers, since well-informed consumers are "an important building block in a more liberalized regulatory framework for education" (Fielden & LaRocque, 2008, p. 22). For students in primary and secondary schools, their parents act as consumers to choose and purchase private tutoring (Devi et al., 2011; Jokić, 2013; Liu, 2017). Well-informed parents can help to monitor the private tutoring industry. Among the current guidelines, only those of Fujian, Guangxi and Jiangxi proposed to guide parents to choose private tutoring institutions rationally. Educating parents to make informed choices regarding private tutoring and empowering parents to monitor tutoring shall be introduced as a useful strategy into the current and future regulatory works.

Implementation of regulations is highly demanding in both personnel and finance, and governments have many other, even more crucial responsibilities. A balance between regulatory control and self-regulation must be found. For tutoring institutions, it is wise to be proactive in self-regulation, which is considered as a way not only to preserve their autonomy but also to enhance consumer confidence in their services (Bray & Kwo, 2014). For example, 16 tutoring institutions in Hefei signed a document of self-regulation in September 2018 to promote sound development under regulations (Chen, 2018). Such efforts shall be encouraged by governments.

References

Aurini, J., Davies, S., & Dierkes, J. (2013). Out of the shadows? An introduction to worldwide supplementary education. In J. Aurini, J. Dierkes, & S. Davies (Eds.), *Out of the shadows: The global intensification of supplementary education* (pp. xv – xxiv). Emerald Group Publishing.

Bray, M. (2017). Schooling and its supplements: Changing global patterns and implications for comparative education. *Comparative Education Review*, 62(3), 469–491.

Bray, M., & Kwo, O. (2014). *Regulating private tutoring for public good: Policy options for supplementary education in Asia*. Comparative Education Research Centre (CERC), The University of Hong Kong, and UNESCO.

Chen, J. (2018). *Hefei made good efforts in regulating private tutoring* [in Chinese]. http://news.hefei.cc/2018/0905/028208528.shtml

Devi, R. et al. (2011). A study of perception of parents, students and teachers towards private tuitions: A case study of Kathua Town. *International Journal of Educational Administration*, 3(1), 1–8.

Fielden, J., & LaRocque, N. (2008). *The evolving regulatory context for private education in emerging economies*. The World Bank and International Finance Corporation.

Hu, Y. (2018, July 3). Extracurricular tutoring under the spotlight with tough checks. *China Daily*. http://www.chinadaily.com.cn/a/201807/03/WS5b3ac855a3103349141e049b.html

Huang, X., & Wei, Y. (2018). The private supplementary tutoring system in China: Findings from a national survey [in Chinese]. In R. Wang (Ed.), *Annual report on new types of education suppliers (2017)*. Social Sciences Academic Press.

Jokić, B. (2013). *Emerging from the shadow: A comparative qualitative exploration of private tutoring in Eurasia*. Network of Education Policy Centres.

Kobakhidze, M. N. (2018). *Teachers as tutors: Shadow education market dynamics in Georgia*. Comparative Education Research Centre (CERC), The University of Hong Kong, and Springer.

Lee, C. J., Lee, H., & Hyo-Min, J. (2010). The history of policy responses to shadow education in South Korea. *Asia Pacific*

Education Review, 11(1), 97 – 108.

Lei, W. (2005). Expenditure on private tutoring for upper secondary students: Determinants and policy implications [in Chinese]. *Education and Economy*, 1, 39 – 42.

Liu, J. (2017). *Parents as consumers in a marketised educational environment: The demand for private supplementary tutoring at primary and lower secondary levels in China* [Doctoral dissertation, The University of Hong Kong].

Liu, J., & Bray, M. (2017). Understanding shadow education from the perspective of economics of education. In G. Johnes, J. Johnes, T. Agasisti, & L. López-Torres (Eds.), *Handbook of contemporary education economics* (pp. 398 – 415). Edward Elgar.

Park, H., Buchmann, C., Choi, J., & Merry, J. J. (2016). Learning beyond the school walls: Trends and implications. *Annual Review of Sociology*, 42, 231 – 252.

Ren, Z. (2018). *The high risk of skipping away with money among private tutoring centers* [in Chinese]. http://www.cqn.com.cn/ms/content/2018 – 04/28/content_5718180.htm

Tsang, M. C., Ding, X., & Shen, H. (2010). Urban-rural disparities in private tutoring of lower-secondary students [in Chinese]. *Education and Economics*, (2), 7 – 11.

Wang, J. (2018). *259,000 private tutoring insitutions were found to have problems in the nationwide inspection* [in Chinese]. http://education.news.cn/2018 – 08/23/c_129938881.htm

Wu, Z. (2017). *502 private tutoring instituions without licenses in Shanghai will be closed* [in Chinese]. http://www.xinhuanet.com/city/2017 – 07/24/c_129661830.htm

Xue, H. (2015). From school education to shadow education: Education competition and social reproduction [in Chinese]. *Peking University Education Review*, 13(3), 47 – 69.

Zhang, W., & Bray, M. (2016). Shadow education: The rise and implications of private supplementary tutoring. In S. Guo & Y. Guo (Eds.), *Spotlight on China: Changes in education under China's market economy* (pp. 85 – 99). Sense Publishers.

Zhang, W., & Bray, M. (2017). Micro-neoliberalism in China: Public-private interactions at the confluence of mainstream and shadow education. *Journal of Education Policy*, 32(1), 63 – 81.

Zhao, Y. (2014). *China's determination to end school choice and testing: New development* [in Chinese]. http://zhaolearning.com/

Zhao, Y. (2018). *Only 14% of private tutoring insitutions are qualified* [in Chinese]. http://news.ifeng.com/a/20180728/59473373_0.shtml

Focusing on the hot-debating issue of school choice in China, this article aims to present a narrative of the policy interventions, especially promulgated by the Chinese central government during the past 20 years, and to discuss those challenges facing the governments and the society as a whole in the new era. It conceptually approaches the topic based on policy texts analysis and literature review. According to the study, school choice governing in China experienced three stages since the middle of the 1990s, namely controlling "choice fees," promoting equalization and equity as well as comprehensive governance toward greater quality and equity. The effective implementation of the policy measures is gradually cooling down the "choice fever" in urban areas and restoring order for student enrollment in compulsory education, but significant challenges are still lying ahead since the problem of school choice turns to be "wicked" in nature and cannot be simply solved within the education sector.

School Choice in China: Past, Present, and Future[1]

Hui Dong and Lulu Li

Over the past two decades, school choice policies remain a popular and controversial reform option internationally. There already exists a sizable body of research on the topic, one that is constantly growing. In recent years, certain English-language articles have been published addressing the topic of school choice in China (see, e.g., Wu, 2008, 2011, 2014). These articles have provided valuable insight into the international academic community regarding school choice policies and practices in the world's most populous country. Prior studies, however, generally fail to reflect the most recent trends affecting school choice in China. This article strives to provide an up-to-date reference for the international academic community. We cover the Chinese government's core policies affecting school choice and describe the general pattern of their evolution over the past 20 years. We conclude by presenting the challenges China faces today with respect to the issue of school choice.

1　This article was funded by the Peak Discipline Construction Project of Education at East China Normal University (2017). It was published on *ECNU Review of Education*, 2(1), 95 – 103.

The past: School choice and policy intervention in an era of "chaos"

As a global social movement, school choice reforms assume a wide variety of incarnations from country to country (Forsey, Davies, & Walford, 2008). In China, the phenomenon particularly known as "school choice fever" at the primary—and secondary—school first appeared in the late 1980s and began to take shape in the early 1990s. It is undeniable that the winners of this positional competition have always been those professional middle- and upper-class parents who possess a certain degree of economic, political, social, and cultural capital (much similar to what has taken place in many Western countries). But obviously, the choice phenomenon and policies in China are deeply rooted in somewhat unique economic, political, social, and cultural contexts and naturally turn out to be a different tale from the West (Wu, 2014). The striking features may go as following: (1) School choice in China has generally been a "bottom-up" phenomenon, primarily driven by parents competing (through various channels) for a limited number of slots at the so-called key schools or demonstrative schools (Wu, 2008). The widespread existence of school choice throughout China coexists with a long-standing lack of formal recognition of its legitimacy. This is one of the prominent features of the phenomenon of school choice with Chinese characteristics. (2) Chinese parents choose schools for their children through a variety of channels and means, including money (school fees, sponsorship fees), power, *guanxi*, and academic achievements (test scores, various competition certificates, and honorary awards). (3) School choice has brought about a series of negative influences in education and society; the public maintains complex attitudes toward parents' school choice strategies. Parents feel the pressure to find the best school for their children even though they are not always happy about the means they choose, especially when it comes to the use of unconventional methods such as wealth and power. School choice has led to vicious and ever-intensifying educational competition. These are sensitive issues that often offend the public's concept of social justice and evoke widespread social dissatisfaction and anxiety. (4) The government's attitude toward school choice seems to be ambiguous. The government has simultaneously banned school choice while turning a blind eye toward its prevalence. This subtle politics of "not seeing" has become another unique manifestation of school choice in China (Kipnis, 2008; Liu & Apple, 2016; Wu, 2014).

In fact, since the chaotic phenomenon of school choice emerged, a series of policy interventions from the central government have never been absent. Starting in the mid-1990s through to the beginning of the 21st century, the Chinese government's policy on school choice has gone through two stages: prohibition of choice fees and a focus on educational equalization (Dong, 2014; Wu & Shen, 2006).

Controlling "choice fees"

One of the toughest problems of school choice for the policymakers was the involvement of choice fees, referring to the additional money paid by parents to the school of their choice which is not in their catchment area. Subsequently, the State Education Commission sought to address the issue of school choice by calling off the misconduct of schools receiving different kinds of "choice fees." From 1993 to 1998, the government promulgated a series policies and commands aimed at addressing those fees-related choice behavior (see Table 1, for specific policy texts). Besides, the government also recognized that the choice fees controversy had complex social and educational roots, one of which was the uneven development in compulsory education and the striking inequality that lay in different schools. Therefore, the government also proposed implementing policies like adopting proximity-based compulsory education admissions, downplaying the "key school/class" system, providing additional support to underperforming schools, reforming the overall enrollment model, promoting the balanced distribution of students, encouraging the development of private schools, and offering assistance to help guide parents through the school-selection process. However, due to the policy climate putting "efficiency" ahead of "equity," many measures were difficult to be enacted, and the "choice fever" continued more or less unabated.

Table 1. Representative policies addressing "unreasonable fees" in the context of school choice.

Year	Agency	Policy name
1993	SEC	Notice of the State Education Commission on resolutely correcting unreasonable fees in primary and secondary schools
1995	SEC	Implementation opinion on governing unreasonable fees in primary and secondary schools
1996	General Office of the State Council of the People's Republic of China; SEC	1996 Notice concerning the implementation opinion on governing unreasonable fees in primary and secondary schools

Continued

Year	Agency	Policy name
1996	SEC; State Council Office for Rectification of the People's Republic of China	1996 Implementation opinion on governing unreasonable fees in primary and secondary schools
1997	SEC	1997 Opinion on governing unreasonable fees in primary and secondary schools
1997	SEC	Principles and suggestions regarding the standardization of contemporary school administration in compulsory education
1998	Ministry of Education of the People's Republic of China	Opinions on the experimental work of the reform of the school system at the compulsory education stage

Note. SEC = State Education Commission of the People's Republic of China.

Shifting toward equity and equality in education

By the beginning of the 21st century, the government had become increasingly aware that the gap among different schools has been enlarged. This quality gap, in turn, fueled a series of social conflicts (including those related to school choice). As a result, "reducing the gap," "balanced development," and "educational equity" became the dominant values of education policy during this period. School choice governance was thus incorporated into the framework of "educational equalization" (Wu & Shen, 2006). In 2006, the newly revised *Compulsory Education Law* reaffirmed the legal status of "educational equality," emphasizing that public schools implement test-free, proximity-based admissions while ceasing the practice of keeping a key school system. Since then, the Ministry of Education has also published various guidance and orders, requiring local education administrative departments at all levels to increase the rational allocation of educational resources. These efforts include the following: encouraging movement among principals and teachers, improving enrollment policies, sharing quality education resources, accelerating the transformation of lower-preforming schools, reducing class size, standardizing the practice of school administration, and improving the overall school performance. The goals of these efforts were to promote equality among compulsory education schools, to ensure each student's admission to the appropriate nearest school and to alleviate the problem of school choice in urban settings (Ministry of Education of the People's Republic of China, 2010). It can be said that the basic orientation of China's school choice governance policies was established in the first decade of this century.

The present: Comprehensive governance to achieve "quality and equity"

The abovementioned policies attempted to solve the problem of school choice by reducing the performance gap among schools. However, school choice is a complex matter, and the policy results were not ideal. Parents still often feel forced to resort to "underground" methods to secure admission for their children at desirable schools. The public's dissatisfaction with the school admission system has grown. In recent years, ideas such as "education that satisfies the people," "achieving a higher level of quality and equity in compulsory education," and "building a modernized educational governing system" have gradually become a national focus. The governance of school choice has entered a new phase featuring comprehension, legalization, districtization, and standardization.

Integration of school choice governance

In 2010, *The National Medium- and Long-Term Education Reform and Development Plan* (2010 – 2020) initiated the process of "comprehensive reform" in the field of education. On the issue of school choice, the Ministry of Education proposed 10 policy measures including "balanced resource allocation," "standardized enrollment procedures," "improvement of lower-performing schools," "expansion of quality resources," "increasing supervision and accountability," "guiding social opinion," and so on. These 10 measures marked the arrival of a more comprehensive stage in the governance of school choice (Xinhua Net, 2010). At this time, the coordination between the central and the local governments (including the Ministry of Education and its provincial and city counterparts) has increased to focus on the overall design of the national education system while still encouraging active local experimentation. Through this approach, school choice governance tools have become increasingly diverse and integrated (Dong, 2014).

Implementing a test-free, proximity-based admission system in accordance with law

Compared with the past, the legal status of test-free, proximity-based admission in compulsory education has been strengthened. In particular, in 2013, the Third Plenary Session of the 18th Central Committee of the CPC passed the *Decision of the Central Committee of the Communist*

Party of China on Comprehensively Deepening Reform on Certain Major Issues, reemphasizing the fundamental importance of this policy. Since 2014, the Ministry of Education has issued annual guidance on how to implement test-free, proximity-based admissions and has promulgated a series of regulations regarding appropriate school enrollment practices. With these measures, the legal status of school choice issues has been greatly clarified.

Promotion of school "districtization" and "grouping"

Following the Third Plenary Session of the 18th Central Committee of the CPC, the government has embarked on implementing a "school district management" system and a "student matching" system in primary and secondary schools (Ministry of Education of the People's Republic of China, 2014a). Specifically, according to the principles of geographic proximity and balanced school performance, primary schools and middle schools are now grouped for overall management. By optimizing the location of schools, the arrangement of school districts and certain other technical measures (such as lotteries), the government hopes to achieve its test-free, proximity-based admissions policy. In terms of school administration, the government seeks to promote the establishment of school alliances and groups, collaboration among schools, the balanced distribution of teachers and administrators within school districts, and the sharing of teaching resources. Additionally, the government has emphasized the need to improve teaching management, teacher training, teacher assessments, and the quality of classroom instruction and extracurricular activities. By allocating students to primary, middle, and high schools on the basis of geographic proximity, the number of students enrolled in "hot" schools will be roughly equal in each district, which will promote the relative balance of students (Ministry of Education of the People's Republic of China, 2014b, 2015).

Standardizing the private tutoring market

China's school choice problems are inextricably linked to the market for private tutoring. The strong demand among parents to enroll their children in the best schools coupled with the government's suppression of school choice has driven the demand for private tutoring (especially English and mathematics tutoring, which can help students secure admission to high-quality schools). In 2017, the government increased its regulation of private tutoring centers in Shanghai. In early 2018, the Ministry of Education and three other departments issued the *Notice on Effectively Reducing the Extracurricular Burden of Primary and Secondary School Students and the Implementation of Government Action Regarding Private Tutoring Agencies.* This policy seeks to standardize the regulation of the market for private tutoring services across the country in three stages: first, by investigating the safety, access qualifications, and subject-based training content of tutoring organizations; second, by punishing those who organize illegal subject-based academic competitions; and third, by curtailing the illegal involvement of schools and teachers in private tutoring organizations (including the practice of collusion between schools and tutoring organizations in the admissions process; Ministry of Education of the People's Republic of China, 2018a). At the same time, the Ministry of Education also issued an announcement stating that "in principle, competitions for compulsory education should not be held; and—without the approval of the Ministry of Education—activities such as competitions, listings, naming, and recognition should not be labeled as 'National'" (Ministry of Education of the People's Republic of China, 2018b). The increased regulation of private tutoring organizations and academic competitions has further reduced room for school choice.

The future: New policy challenges under the "new format" of education

Over the past two decades, the Chinese government's rejection of school choice and respect for balanced development have remained consistent policy themes. However, the 19th National Congress of the Communist Party of China made it clear that one of the main conflicts in current Chinese society is the conflict between the people's growing need for a better life and unbalanced economic development. In education, this conflict is manifested in the conflict between people's demand for high-quality, personalized education services and the limited availability of such services (particularly in the light of their uneven distribution across the country). At the same time, Chinese education is taking on a "new format" that is different from the past: Training institutions and educational technology enterprises are beginning to play a key role in the supply of education services. The methods and forms of education supported by new technologies are constantly evolving, and the organization of the entire education industry is also quietly changing (Wang, 2018). Under these circumstances, the increasing demand for school choice has become a fundamental policy issue that cannot be ignored (Wang & Tian, 2018).

Regarding school choice, the Chinese academic community has long supported the approach of "guiding" instead of "blocking" (Zeng, 2010). In the light of the new format of education in China, it is necessary to address the current rationality of school choice as a policy goal (Wang, 2018). This raises the question: What is the future direction of China's policies on school choice? The author believes that the following conflicts need to be addressed in the decision-making process.

First, how to balance fairness and quality? For a long time, the balanced development of China's basic education system and the governance of school choice have been based on the policy consensus of achieving education and social equity. With the concept of "fairness and quality" education development, fairness is important, but quality is even more indispensable. In particular, after achieving a basic balance, localities have generally begun to move toward the goal of "quality and balance." Although people's understanding of what constitutes quality is not the same, school choice has gradually become an important parameter to measure the quality of a country's and region's education systems. The paradox is that if school choice is permitted under the current policy framework, it will add legitimacy to the educational advantages currently enjoyed by certain privileged groups within Chinese society. A lack of equity in the education system will damage the public's acceptance of the system. China may not be able to provide an education system that is acceptable to the public if the country continues to ignore the growing demand for school choice. In the long run, ignoring the demand for school choice will not promote competitiveness and quality, and it may further intensify educational anxiety and exacerbate the outflow of talent.

Second, how to balance the needs of the country with the needs of the individual? Undoubtedly, education in China develops a clear "nationalism" approach since the beginning of its modernization journey. After reform and opening-up, China gave priority to the development of education, and education also serves the state (Yuan, 2018). However, an education system driven by a strong nationalistic ideology is always limited in its tolerance for freedom of choice. Given the continued influence of nationalism and collectivism and the historic absence of school choice in Chinese compulsory education laws and cultural traditions, a wholesale cultural update is necessary to give the concept of school choice legitimacy within the framework of compulsory education admissions policies.

Third, how can the government and the market work together? China once embarked on a short-term attempt to reform the market for basic education. Private schools and public-to-private school transformations expanded aggressively. The policy of "No choice in state schools, choices allowed in *minban* schools ('people-run schools'), and famous school (usually those 'hot' state schools) encouraged to run *minban* schools" (Ding, 2004) provided an opportunity for parents to choose schools for their children the italics emphasis is originally given because this word "minban" is presented in Chinese spelling. However, this policy was suspended because it contributed to "chaos" in the school-choice process and worsened the ecology within the compulsory education system (Ministry of Education of the People's Republic of China, 2006). The overall pattern of state-dominated compulsory schooling system was further solidified.[1] In contrast, the popularity of the private tutoring market shows that while the market mechanism has a limited role in the supply of formal education, it satisfies the needs of parents in certain educational contexts (Wang, 2018). At the same time, the phenomenon of parents paying a premium to buy houses in high-quality school districts (thereby making it difficult, if not impossible, for lower-income families to live in such districts) has emerged in recent years and has presented new challenges to the government's proximity-based admissions system. Looking to the future, we must face the needs of parents to choose schools for their children. Obviously, these needs cannot be fully satisfied by the government or the market alone. It is necessary to reconstruct the relationship between the two on the supply side. The key is how to best integrate government- and market-based initiatives.

Fourth, how to coordinate higher- and basic-education policies? Certain researchers have pointed out that the main conflict between China's educational supply and demand underlying the school choice problem in the conflict between the "equality" orientation of basic education and the "elite" orientation of higher education. The key policies supporting the renovation of higher education in China (e.g., "211," "985," and "double first-class") have reduced competitive pressure at the top of the education system and, correspondingly, at the bottom, but—at the same time—have fueled the desire among parents to have additional options with respect to school choice (Wang, 2018). School choice is not only an issue driven by policies at the compulsory education stage, it must also be considered while designing policies for the overall education system. This level of coordination represents a unique challenge.

---

1 In some areas, such as Shanghai, there is still a relatively high proportion of *minban* schools at the compulsory education stage. However, at the national level, the proportion of *minban* schools at the compulsory education stage is low (only 12.31% for junior high schools and 7.63% for primary schools; Wang, 2018).

Finally, how to meld local with global? In the context of globalization, the diversity of educational choices cannot evade the impact and challenges of internationalization. The well-known new media writer, Li (2016), vividly described the process of school choice from elementary to middle school in Shanghai. Li likened the process to five "spectral routes" from "East" to "West," revealing the complex ecology of "international" and "local" cultural forces that shape parents' thoughts about school choice. At present, China's education reform embraces both international and traditional culture. This compound policy orientation is reflected in the issue of school choice governance. It is especially apparent in the context of school administration when attempting to integrate international and local elements to form different types of schools to meet the evolving needs of parents and students. In tackling this challenge, breakthroughs are needed in both theory and practice.

The issue of school choice in China has complex economic, political, and cultural roots. Therefore, governance must be a systematic project. There is no doubt that China's researchers and policymakers face a monumental task in shaping China's school choice policies to meet the challenges presented by the new era. It might be somewhat difficult to accurately predict the specific direction of policymaking on the choice matter, but it is undeniable that the parents' rational demand for more choices for their kids' education needs to be addressed in the future. In designing policy, it is important to abandon the dualistic thinking of "either/or" and replace it with a more nuanced approach to policymaking that treats different stakeholders from a holistic perspective and takes into account the impact individual policies may have on other entities and the educational ecosystem as a whole (Wang, 2018). This is clearly the proper way to dealing with those "wicked" social problems in the complex era.

References

Ding, W. (2004, March 26). Zhou Ji: No choice students for public schools; parental choice for *minban* schools; reputable schools run *minban* schools [in Chinese]. *People's Daily*, 11.

Dong, H. (2014). *Policy research on the choice of compulsory education in China* [in Chinese]. Education Science Press.

Forsey, M., Davies, S., & Walford, G. (2008). The globalization of school choice? An introduction to key issues and concerns. In M. Forsey, S. Davies, & G. Walford (Eds.), *The globalization of school choice?* (pp. 9–25). Symposium Books.

Kipnis, A. (2008). Competition, audits, scientism and school non-choice in rural China. In M. Forsey, S. Davies, & G. Walford (Eds.), *The globalization of school choice?* (pp. 165–184). Symposium Books.

Li, Z. (2016). *Commencing from the absolute public to the international route: How these five roads touched the pain of middle-class parents in Shanghai* [in Chinese]. http://learning.sohu.com/20161227/n477027224.shtml

Liu, S., & Apple, M. W. (2016). Parental choice of school, class strategies, and educational inequality: An essay review of "School choice in China: A different tale?". *Education Policy*, 30, 940–955.

Ministry of Education of the People's Republic of China. (2006). *Some opinions on implementing the compulsory education law to further standardize the behavior of running a school for compulsory education* [in Chinese]. http://www.moe.gov.cn/srcsite/A06/s3321/200608/t20060824_81811.html

Ministry of Education of the People's Republic of China. (2010). *Opinions of the Ministry of Education on implementing the scientific outlook on development and further promoting the balanced development of compulsory education* [in Chinese]. http://www.moe.gov.cn/srcsite/A06/s3321/201001/t20100119_87759.html

Ministry of Education of the People's Republic of China. (2014a). *Notice on further implementation of major cities education to exempt nearby enrollment* [in Chinese]. http://www.moe.gov.cn/srcsite/A06/s3321/201401/t20140129_164088.html

Ministry of Education of the People's Republic of China. (2014b). *Suggestions on how to further improve the elementary school into the junior high school which exempt from examination nearby enrollment implementation* [in Chinese]. http://www.moe.gov.cn/srcsite/A06/s3321/201401/t20140126_163246.html

Ministry of Education of the People's Republic of China. (2015). *Notice on how to enroll students for compulsory education in cities in 2015* [in Chinese]. http://www.moe.gov.cn/srcsite/A06/s3321/201503/t20150324_189380.html

Ministry of Education of the People's Republic of China. (2018a). *Measures on the administration of national competition activities for primary and middle school students (for trial implementation)* [in Chinese]. http://www.moe.gov.cn/srcsite/A06/s3321/201809/t20180920_349550.html

Ministry of Education of the People's Republic of China. (2018b). *Notice on the effective reduction of the extracurricular burden of primary and secondary school students and the launching of special administrative actions for off-campus training institutions* [in Chinese]. http://www.moe.gov.cn/srcsite/A06/s3321/201802/t20180226_327752.html

Wang, R. (2018). *Annual report on new types of education suppliers (2017)* [in Chinese]. Social Sciences Academic Press.

Wang, R., & Tian, Z. (2018). Welcoming the era of education finance 3.0 [in Chinese]. *China Economics of Education Review*, (3), 26–46.

Wu, X. (2008). The power of positional competition and market mechanism: A case study of recent parental choice development in China. *Journal of Education Policy*, 23(6), 595–614.

Wu, X. (2011). The power of positional competition and market mechanism: An empirical study of parental choice of junior middle school in Nanning, P. R. China. *Research Papers in Education*, 26(1), 79–104.

Wu, X. (2014). *School choice in China: A different tale?* Routledge.

Wu, Z., & Shen, J. (2006). School choice and education equity [in Chinese]. *Tsinghua Journal of Education*, 27, 111–118.

Xinhua Net. (2010). *Ministry of Education adopting "ten measures" to deal with arbitrary fees in school choice* [in Chinese]. http://www.gov.cn/fwxx/wy/2010-11/02/content_1735834.htm

Yuan, Z. (2018). Dual priority agenda: China's model for modernizing education. *ECNU Review of Education*, 1(1), 5–33.

Zeng, X. (2010). On the policy's sub-optimal choice: Based on analysis on public school-choosing preference [in Chinese]. *Research in Education Development*, (2), 18–22.

This piece of policy review might facilitate the understanding of the current high school curriculum in China, especially on its features, changes, contexts, and history. In January 2018, the new national curriculum program and standards for high school education was announced by the Ministry of Education of the People's Republic of China (MOE). Applying textual analysis, this article interprets the significant changes in the national curriculum program and standards and further discusses these changes based on literature and research on curriculum. According to the study, corresponding to the international trends on core competencies, China takes a further step and designs subject core competencies to narrow the gap between theories, policy, and practice. The new national curriculum highlights the coherent design in curriculum, textbooks, teaching, and assessment. Yet there are still puzzles and challenges in high stakes examination, diverse contexts, and curriculum implementation.

Competence for Students' Future: Curriculum Change and Policy Redesign in China [1]

Tao Wang

Changing the curriculum has been viewed and used as an effective way to change classroom practice and to influence student learning to meet the needs of the ever-changing world (Cai & Ni, 2011). Curriculum programs and standards in China serve as both professional and administrative guidelines for the design of textbooks and learning materials and for teaching, learning, and assessment. On a rolling basis, the Ministry of Education of the People's Republic of China (MOE) revised the national curriculum to meet contemporary and future needs. This article aims to provide a policy review of the new curriculum program and standards for high school education announced in January 2018 and their systematic design and interpret with some subject examples. Initiated in 2013, the new curriculum program and standards, signing a move from a *suzhi*（素质）-based (quality-based) to a *suyang*（素养）-based (competency-based) curriculum, will involve more than 20 million high school students via their school education and

---

[1] This article was funded by the Major Program at the Key Research Institute of Humanities and Social Sciences affiliated with the Ministry of Education, China (16JJD880021). It was published on *ECNU Review of Education*, 2(2), 234–245.

the *Gaokao* (高考, National Higher Education Entrance Examination). This is a whole redesign and reframing of China's high school curriculum. In short, fewer credits are needed to graduate, and there are now more course categories and elective courses and refined subject goals and contents (see Table 1).

Table 1. Credits and subjects of general high school education in China.

Subjects	Required credits	Required elective credits	Elective credits
Chinese	8	0-6	0-6
Mathematics	8	0-6	0-6
Foreign language	6	0-8	0-6
Ideology and politics	6	0-6	0-4
History	4	0-6	0-4
Geography	4	0-6	0-4
Physics	6	0-6	0-4
Chemistry	4	0-6	0-4
Biology	4	0-6	0-4
(Information and general) technology	6	0-18	0-4
Arts (music/fine arts)	6	0-18	0-4
Physical education and health	12	0-18	0-4
Comprehensive practical activities	14		
School-based curriculum			≥8
Total	88	≥42	≥14

Continuing the compulsory education at the primary and middle school levels, high school education is defined as "basic education that serves to and improves the quality of the public" (MOE, 2018a, p. 1). General high schools usually have an attendance duration of 3 years, each of which has 40 weeks for instruction, 1 week for practicum, and 11 weeks for vacation. In a regular week, students have 35 classes (45 min per class) and every 18 classes count together as one credit. To serve for various graduation and admission purposes, the 14 high school curricula are categorized as required, required elective, and elective courses. These categories, respectively, address the requirements of graduation, *Gaokao*, and independent recruitment from top universities. As indicated in Table 1, students need to take at least 144 credits of required and required elective courses to graduate and (or) attend the *Gaokao*. Students may also take elective courses to apply for universities that allow autonomous admission.

The idea of core competencies

The key strategy to redesign the curriculum is the idea of core competencies. Joining the global trends of competencies in education such as used by the Organisation for Economic Co-operation and Development and countries such as Finland, Australia, and the U.S., China's ambition is to educate and prepare individuals for future and probably unknown life and work. There has been an evolution of educational goals in the last 20 years from *shuangji* (双基, "double fundamentals," that is, fundamental knowledge and skills) to *suzhi* (qualities), and then to the current goal of *suyang* (competencies). The curriculum goal was framed as a *suzhi* education (often translated as "quality" education, Dello-Iacovo, 2009) in the last round of curriculum reform. This term was intended to incorporate students' moral, intellectual, physical, and aesthetic education (MOE, 2001; Wang, 2012). It was an upgrade from *shuangji* ("double fundamentals"). Specific changes included adding the goals of helping students learn how to learn; cultivating information processing, knowledge acquisition, problem-solving, and cooperative learning abilities; and developing essential knowledge and skills in relation to lifelong learning (Cui, 2001; Feng, 2006; Guo, 2012).

The new idea of *suyang* (competencies) reorients the learning from content to outcome and textbooks and standards to the ultimate function of education (Zhong & Cui, 2018). China defines *suyang* as the key competencies, characters, and values that individuals show when they apply knowledge and skills to deal with complex situations. Cui (2016a) illustrated this idea using a metaphor of good drivers: to be a good driver, one needs knowledge of traffic laws and road signs, the skills of driving, turning, and stopping, and most importantly, characters and values to instill in the individual respect for rules and for life. As the artificial intelligence replaces human in many areas, education needs to rethink what kind of competencies human should possess. For the self-driving car to eventually remove humans from the agency of regular driving, the most crucial challenge automated driving systems face is to deal with complicated driving incidents and conflicts. What keeps human necessary in driving is not just driving knowledge or skills but conscience and humanity.

China's core competencies framework includes three "dimensions," six "modules," and 18 "items." As indicated in Figure 1, to develop a whole person, we have three dimensions of autonomous development, civic participation, and cultural foundation, and six modules: learning to learn, healthy living, assuming responsibility, innovation and practice, humanistic understanding, and scientific spirit. The module of humanistic understanding, for instance, consists of "human culture, human passions, and human aesthetics."

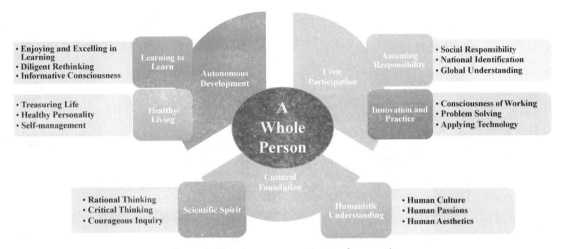

Figure 1. China's core competencies framework.

A further step: Subject core competencies

To answer the question of how to educate to achieve these overarching goals, a further step is to design more operational subject core competencies. This step also aims to narrow the enduring gap between educational goals and enacted curriculum in practice, a gap which occurs not just in China but also in many other countries in the world. China's use of subject core competencies tends to lead to further exploration and implementation than in many other countries designing only the overarching core competencies. Subject core competencies, by definition, are the positive values, crucial characters, and key skills that students acquire in learning each subject (Zhong & Cui, 2018). The core competencies of each subject vary according to its nature from three to six. The subject of Chinese, for example, has four core competencies: language construction and application, cultural inheritance and understanding, aesthetic appreciation and creation, and development and advancement of thoughts (see Figure 2). Mathematics has six subject-based core competencies: mathematical calculation, mathematical abstraction, logical reasoning, intuitive imagination, mathematical modeling, and data analysis (see Figure 3). Note that subject core competencies and overarching core competencies are connected and coherent so that different subjects can be integrated and used together to cultivate the common core competencies.

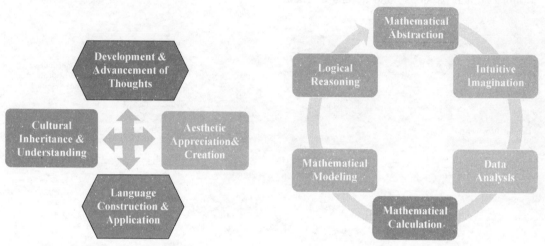

Figure 2. Core competencies for Chinese.   Figure 3. Core competencies for Mathematics.

Subject core competencies further clarify the direction and goal of subject teaching and assessment and guide teaching practice. The latest round of curriculum reform legitimates the "three-dimensional goals" (knowledge and skills, process and method, and affection, attitudes, and values) and brings decisive change in the quality and nature of classroom practice in China (Jin, 2012; Ni & Cai, 2011; Ni et al., 2011). The subject core competencies are considered a cognitive upgrade from the three-dimensional goals with further integration and improvement (Zhong & Cui, 2018). Defining the goal of each subject identifies and clarifies the value and role of each subject. These identifications and clarifications allow teachers and researchers to legitimate and professionalize their subject discourse. In return, educational administrations and departments can develop more reliable and responsive accountability systems for each subject.

Coherent design in textbooks, teaching, and assessment

As Fullan (2016) noted, a whole-system plan is required for successful and sustained educational change. Ambitious as it was to cover the centralized national educational system of the largest school population, a systematic plan and coordinated support programs were set in place when the last round of curriculum reform in China started (Gao & Wang, 2014; Marton, 2006; Tan, 2015). Besides new curriculum standards, textbooks, and teaching materials, rounds of training at the national and local levels were arranged (Paine & Fang, 2006; Qian, Walker, & Li, 2017). Following the same tradition, the big idea of core competencies guides the systematic design of curriculum goal, textbooks, teaching, and assessment (see Figure 4).

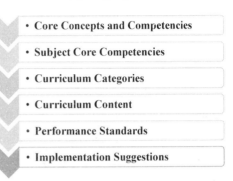

Figure 4. Coherent design in core competencies, teaching, learning, and assessment.

An area of ongoing work is the perpetuation of subject core competencies in the country's textbooks and learning materials. Textbooks, as the dominant source of the national curriculum in China, will be subject to reframing and reorganization according to subject core competencies in the next few years. Since September of 2017, the textbooks for Chinese, history, and ideological and political education (names vary in different grades) in compulsory education are designed, edited, and reviewed by the National Commission of School Textbooks (affiliated with MOE). The same mechanism will be applied to textbooks of these three subjects in high school education. For other subjects, too, both national and local publication agencies in different provinces will need to redesign their textbooks to ensure coherence with the overarching and subject core competencies.

Curriculum standards for each subject list the curriculum content as required, required elective, or elective. Learning themes and units are suggested. For instance, through all course categories in mathematics, students learn content themes including functions, geometry and algebra, probability and statistics, and mathematical modeling and inquiry activities (MOE, 2018d, p. 9). Each theme has detailed learning units, such as units of "concept and features of functions," "powers, exponents, and logarithmic functions," "trigonometric functions," and "the application of functions" within the "functions" theme. Each unit then has a brief introduction and interpretations of the learning content. Within the required course category, the subject of Chinese includes learning themes of "reading and discussing the whole book," "participating in the discussion of contemporary culture," "multimedia reading and communication," "language accumulation, arrangement, and inquiry," "literature reading and writing," "critical reading and expression," and "practical reading and communication" (MOE, 2018b, p. 10). Chinese traditions and the concepts of revolution and socialism are also infused into these themes. Learning themes in the categories of required elective and elective courses may vary slightly yet still center on these themes.

A new section in the curriculum standard is the learning performance levels that comprehensively reflect students' subject core competencies and performance after learning each subject. This provides guidance for autonomous learning and self-assessment, teaching and assessment, and textbook and exam design (MOE, 2018d). Each subject has specific definitions and performance level descriptions. The subject of mathematics describes three levels of performance via the constructs of "context and questions," "knowledge and skills," "minds and expression," and "communication and reflection" (MOE, 2018d). In comparison, the subject of Chinese defines five levels in learning performance via four constructs corresponding to the four subject core competencies for mathematics. Standards and descriptions of learning performance are intended to be coherent and be supported by the core competencies framework and curriculum content. Teaching suggestions are also given. These sections together form a linear and coherent system of core concepts and competencies, subject-based core competencies, curriculum categories, curriculum content, performance standards, and implementation suggestions.

Prior experience and remaining puzzles and challenges

Although dawn is just breaking in this new round of curriculum reform, there remains a need to look back to the last round of curriculum reform for experience and lessons. After two decades of changes in curriculum and instruction, China's schooling evolved in a systematic yet discursive fashion in aspects of discourse, best practice, and assessment system. China's education system as measured by recent PISA tests has also become the subject of attention and praise. As evidenced by longitudinal and individual studies (Jin, 2012; Ni & Cai, 2011; Ni et al., 2011), the last round of curriculum reform has already had positive effects on the quality and nature of classroom practice in China. Analyzing official policies and previous curriculum standards, there were changes, attempted at the policy level, in advancing human capital through education and allowing more autonomy in local control (Law, 2014). Along with the policy regulations, new and diversified discourse systems emerged around *suzhi*, with key concepts such as student-centered, autonomy, collaboration, innovation (Kipnis, 2007; Murphy, 2004). New changes in policies also brought more standard definitions of teacher quality and common forms of accountability (Paine & Fang, 2006). Institutional effort has also been made to ascertain the accountability of teachers by developing a national system to evaluate students' academic achievement (Xin, 2016) and the quality of curriculum implementation (Cui, 2017). On the other side, it is also true that there are still challenges and practices unchanged by the reforms. These challenges will likely remain while new challenges are slowly revealed.

Coherent and reciprocal relations with the Gaokao. One of the major barriers identified to thwart changes is China's high-stakes examinations (Jin, 2012). Assessments and exams in the schools, graduation exams, and National Higher Education Entrance Examination (*Gaokao*) are all required to refer to curriculum programs, curriculum standards, and related policies on teaching (MOE, 2018a). The wording of the policies makes clear that these curriculum and performance standards are meant to assist with teaching, learning, and assessment. Nevertheless, specific measurable items, variables, and related metrics are missing for students and teachers to understand how well students learned and where they are regarding each competency. This type of clear assessment metric is particularly important in countries with high-stakes examinations. Both teachers and students want to make sure these competencies are applicable in teaching and eventually measurable in the exams. Yet it is often the case that exam design is not coherent with school learning, particularly for high-stakes examinations like the *Gaokao*.

When the examination is so important, it is short-term interests rather than long-term benefit which competencies-based curricular promotes. Shanghai and Zhejiang province started to pilot a new *Gaokao* in 2017. One salient feature of this new *Gaokao* is greater flexibility and options offered to the students by allowing them to freely choose two or three from six subjects as exam subjects, besides the three required subjects of Chinese, mathematics, and English. That is different from the dominant model of "3+X" in which students choose either a social science package of history, geography, and politics or a natural science package of physics, chemistry, and biology. That is to say, students may choose their own combination such as history plus chemistry so that they might be admitted to related majors in the universities. However, this well-intentioned freedom has led to huge controversies in the examination. It was found that the number of students choosing Physics in the *Gaokao* dropped from 160,000 in 2011 to 90,000 in

2017 in Zhejiang province (Zhu, 2017). A major reason students cited was the difficulty of learning and taking exams in physics. In another word, students or their parents tend to choose the most profitable package when the stakes are high. As for students and parents, there seems to be a dilemma between competencies-based education and exam-preparation education. Parents, students, and even some educators think students could wait until university education to develop the more vague and long-term competencies, as if it is a zero-sum mechanism in which effort and time spent on competencies-based education compromise students' potential academic performance. The competencies-based curriculum still has a long way to go before it can solve this dilemma in both theory and practice.

Core competencies in a huge country with unbalanced resources. China's massive and ambitious curriculum reform has indeed brought significant and decisive changes. Yet the traditional curriculum, doctrinal teaching practice, and huge performance gaps remain in school districts and classrooms across the vast country. A large-scale survey on curriculum and instruction (Cui, 2016b) showed that rural middle schools have poorer performance than urban ones in almost every schooling index, including school curriculum leadership, curriculum planning, teacher engagement, student learning quality, opportunities for learning, social relationships, family support and intervention, and learning outcomes. These differences exist not only among different schools in rural or urban areas but also among different classes within the same school. This survey also corroborates empirical studies that show unequal distribution of teaching expertise, professional support, and training opportunities contributes to further scaling-up, especially for weaker schools, schools in less developed areas, and schools for disadvantaged students (Jin, 2012; Peng et al., 2014). Balancing the tensions between urban and rural schools or among classrooms within a school with respect to resource allocation, teacher capacity, opportunities for learning, classroom teaching, teacher-student relationships, and family-school relationships with equity and no loss of quality is the major challenge that China's governmental entities at various levels face in curriculum reforms and development in K-12 education.

The challenges of core values implementation. The preface of the curriculum program notes that the fundamental mission of Education is to *Lide Shuren* (立德树人, "develop morality and cultivate humanity"). The connotation of this phrase carries both traditional and contemporary expectations of nobility in China. The underlying principle is the key role of values that transcend knowledge, skills, capabilities, and affections within the greater overarching idea of core competencies (Cui, 2016a). That is to say, the key role of education is to cultivate human beings who value family, community, society, and the nation. In the context of China, this is framed as

> Forming positive worldview, outlook on life, and values; loving the motherland and supporting the Chinese Communist Party; fostering the fine traditional Chinese culture, inheriting the revolutionary culture, and developing the advanced socialist culture; cultivating and practicing the core socialist values. (MOE, 2018a, p. 2)

This statement corresponds to the characteristics of the Chinese socialist system but also parallels ongoing puzzles of citizenship education in many other countries. In an era of neoliberalism and globalism, cultivating citizens for society is a hard job. Citizens often have weak national allegiance and infrequent civic participation (Banks, 2017). To address this issue, the *Ideological and Political Education* curriculum standard proposes activities- and issues-based civic education along with practice (MOE, 2018c), providing as examples issues such as "The Value of School Mottoes," "Rational Choices in the Era of Internet+," and "Assessment and Suggestions for Solving Traffic Congestion." Yet the challenge of the implementation of core socialist values is getting harder as China promulgates civic values via Marxist/socialist ideological management (Wang & Longoria, 2016). Some of the challenges of traditional citizenship education systems are common issues of democracy, equality, and human rights and also conversations with other countries.

Summary

The Chinese government periodically changes its curricula to meet current and anticipated future needs as the world is becoming more globalized and diverse, and information and technology will probably soon replace human beings in many jobs. As the Ministry of Education announced the curriculum programs and standards in early 2018, work for compulsory education was initiated in early 2019. This new round of curriculum changes is based on core competencies and aims to prepare students to deal with authentic problems. The core feature of China's experience is coherent design and linear implementation. The bigger idea of core competencies and more focused subject-based core competencies are China's attempt to implement its standards in all aspects of teaching, learning, and assessment in daily practice.

As China did in its last round of massive curriculum reform, China tends to bring promised changes in intentional, coordinated, responsive, and systematic "Chinese" ways. Curriculum reform opens up a new institutional context to welcome, reward, and support changes. An accelerated framework to bring on changes and diversified teaching practice are being imposed on teachers. It is tempting to view the new environment and imperatives as having provided opportunities to change, but these are usually fragmented and perfunctory changes. Meanwhile, the top-down system and coordination, in the Chinese case, are a double-edged sword (Yuan, 2017). Disruptive changes and challenges in curriculum, learning, and schooling remain to be initiated, questioned, emerged, and scaled up in China.

Acknowledgements

The author would like to thank Professors Yunhuo Cui and Shuangye Chen for their inputs and comments on this policy review.

References

Banks, J. A. (2017). Failed citizenship and transformative civic education. *Educational Researcher*, 46, 366-377.

Cai, J., & Ni, Y. (2011). Investigating curricular effect on the teaching and learning of mathematics in a cultural context: Theoretical and methodological considerations. *International Journal of Educational Research*, 50, 65-70.

Cui, Y. (2001). What's the "new" for the new curriculum? An analysis of the basic education curriculum reform outline (Trial) [in Chinese]. *Exploring Education Development*, 9, 5-10.

Cui, Y. (2016a). Further probing of core competencies [in Chinese]. *Global Education*, 45, 3-11.

Cui, Y. (2016b). *Opening the "black box": The equity and quality of education process in schools* [in Chinese]. Manuscript submitted for publication.

Cui, Y. (2017). *Evaluation of curriculum implementation quality* [in Chinese]. East China Normal University Press.

Dello-Iacovo, B. (2009). Curriculum reform and "quality education" in China: An overview. *International Journal of Educational Development*, 29, 241-249.

Feng, D. (2006). China's recent curriculum reform: Progress and problems. *Planning and Changing*, 37, 131-144.

Fullan, M. (2016). *The new meaning of educational change* (5th ed.). Teachers College Press.

Gao, S., & Wang, J. (2014). Teaching transformation under centralized curriculum and teacher learning community: Two Chinese chemistry teachers' experiences in developing inquiry-based instruction. *Teaching and Teacher Education*, 44, 1-11.

Guo, L. (2012). New curriculum reform in China and its impact on teachers. *Education Canadian and International Education*, 41, 87-105.

Jin, Y. (2012). *Transformation of teaching in new curriculum* [in Chinese]. Southwest Normal University Press.

Kipnis, A. (2007). Neoliberalism reified: Suzhi discourse and tropes of neoliberalism in the People's Republic of China. *Journal of the Royal Anthropological Institute*, *13*, 383–400.

Law, W. W. (2014). Understanding China's curriculum reform for the 21st century. *Journal of Curriculum Studies*, *46*, 332–360.

Marton, A. M. (2006). The cultural politics of curricular reform in China: A case study of geographical education in Shanghai. *Journal of Contemporary China*, *15*, 233–254.

Ministry of Education of the People's Republic of China (MOE). (2001). *Outline of basic education curriculum reform* [in Chinese]. http://old.moe.gov.cn/publicfiles/business/htmlfiles/moe/moe_309/200412/4672.html

Ministry of Education of the People's Republic of China (MOE). (2018a). *Curriculum program of high school education* [in Chinese]. People's Education Press.

Ministry of Education of the People's Republic of China (MOE). (2018b). *Curriculum standard of high school Chinese* [in Chinese]. People's Education Press.

Ministry of Education of the People's Republic of China (MOE). (2018c). *Curriculum standard of high school ideology and politics* [in Chinese]. People's Education Press.

Ministry of Education of the People's Republic of China (MOE). (2018d). *Curriculum standard of high school mathematics* [in Chinese]. People's Education Press.

Murphy, R. (2004). Turning peasants into modern Chinese citizens: "Population quality" discourse, demographic transition and primary education. *The China Quarterly*, *177*, 1–20.

Ni, Y., & Cai, J. (2011). Searching for evidence of curricular effect on the teaching and learning of mathematics: Lessons learned from the two projects. *International Journal of Educational Research*, *50*, 137–143.

Ni, Y., Li, X., Li, Q., & Zhang, Z. (2011). Influence of curriculum reform: An analysis of student mathematics achievement in mainland China. *International Journal of Educational Research*, *50*, 100–116.

Paine, L. W., & Fang, Y. (2006). Reform as hybrid model of teaching and teacher development in China. *International Journal of Educational Research*, *45*, 279–289.

Peng, W., McNess, E. M., Thomas, S. M., Wu, X., Zhang, C., Li, J., & Tian, H. (2014). Emerging perceptions of teacher quality and teacher development in China. *International Journal of Educational Development*, *34*, 77–89.

Qian, H., Walker, A., & Li, X. (2017). The west wind vs. the east wind: Instructional leadership model in China. *Journal of Educational Administration*, *55*, 186–206.

Tan, C. (2015). Education policy borrowing and cultural scripts for teaching in China. *Comparative Education*, *51*, 196–211.

Wang, J. (2012). Curriculum reform in mainland China, 1978–2008: Change, maintenance, and conflicts. *Chinese Education & Society*, *45*, 59–68.

Wang, T., & Longoria, A. (2016). Civic values in curriculum standards of China and the United States: A comparative study on citizenship education within different social systems. In K. H. Shin (Ed.), *Multicultural education in global era* (pp. 73–96). Nova Science Publisher.

Xin, T. (2016). Standards of learning achievement: Bridges between core competencies and curriculum standard, exams, and assessment [in Chinese]. *People's Education*, *19*, 17–18.

Yuan, R. (2017). Appropriating national curriculum standards in classroom teaching: Experiences of novice language teachers in China. *International Journal of Educational Research*, *83*, 55–64.

Zhong, Q., & Cui, Y. (2018). *Research on core competencies* [in Chinese]. East China Normal University Press.

Zhu, B. (2017). *Why the dramatic drop in the number of students electing the physics exam in Zhejiang is a concern* [in Chinese]. http://cul.qq.com/a/20171024/013215.htm

> The Chinese experience of teacher education reform is the main focus of this article. The author firstly examines the history of China's teacher education policies based on a detailed analysis of the relevant policies implemented by China since 1978. The actual practice of Chinese teacher education reform is also explored by examining how such reforms have contributed to the overall reform of China's basic education system. The findings about the Chinese experience of teacher education reform read: Chinese teacher education places emphasis on the cultivation of teachers' devotion to education and the importance of improving the teaching skills of normal college students; an effective teacher governance mechanism is the institutional guarantee for the positive role of teachers. In addition, this review demonstrates that the absence of comprehensive universities in the open teacher education system and a lack of autonomy for teachers in the performance management system are major challenges facing teacher education in China.

From Scale to Quality: Experiences and Challenges in Teacher Education in China [1]

Bin Zhou

China is a country with a vast educational system. As of December 2017, there were 513,800 schools of various educational levels and types in China, with a total of 270 million enrolled students and 16.27 million full-time teachers. Maintaining such an enormous education system demands not only sufficient funds but also—more importantly—consistent support from highly committed teachers. In 2017, the national education expenditure in China amounted to 3,420.4 billion CNY, accounting for 4.14% of the country's total gross domestic product (GDP). 2017 was the first year in which China's education expenditure exceeded 4% of its total GDP. However, during the same year, the world average was 7%, with developed countries averaging around 9% and developing countries averaging 4.1%. Viewed from this perspective, China's enormously large education system is supported financially at a level consistent with the world's less developed countries. The relative strength of China's education system lies not with rich

---

[1] This article was funded by the research project of the Humanities and Social Sciences Youth Interdisciplinary Innovation Team, East China Normal University and the Fundamental Research Funds for the Central Universities Project (No. 2018ECNU-QKT003). It was published on *ECNU Review of Education*, 2(2), 196–204.

educational resources but with its dedicated and hardworking corps of teachers.

However, the question of how to create a large and, at the same time, stable team of teachers remains. How can such an already "enlarged" team of teachers be "strengthened?" In January 2018, the Central Committee of the Communist Party of China and the State Council issued *Opinions on comprehensively deepening the reform of the teaching staff construction in the new era*, thereby raising the development of the nation's teaching profession to be a paramount national strategic issue. Thereafter, in February 2018, the Ministry of Education and four other departments jointly issued the *Action plan for the revitalization of teacher education (2018 – 2022)*. By November 2018, 25 provinces, municipalities, and autonomous regions in China issued local teacher team construction programs to implement this plan. Continuous and timely reforms for teacher education is not only a challenge facing China but also a common strategic issue for teacher education all over the world.

Selecting a teacher education model to serve the needs of teachers in basic education

At the beginning of its establishment, China's teacher education system was borrowed extensively from the European model, especially that of France (Xu & Li, 2009). The French teacher education system was relatively independent of the then-existing higher education system. The French teacher education system pursued the large-scale training of teachers from the very beginning; this approach differed from that of the elite training modes of higher education. "At the same time, these schools maintained a strong sense of professional responsibility. State control and regulation were seen as essential because the vast majority of teachers were expected to serve at emerging public schools" (Xu & Li, 2009, p. 55). The French model played an important role in demonstrating the establishment of a comprehensive teacher education system.

After the founding of the People's Republic of China, Chinese education planners also studied the teacher education system of the Soviet Union, and subsequently formed relatively independent pre-service and in-service teacher training systems. The pre-service system included secondary normal schools for primary school teachers; junior teachers' colleges for junior secondary school teachers; and provincial or subordinate normal universities for senior secondary school teachers, secondary normal school teachers, and college and university teachers (Xu & Li, 2009, pp. 54 –

62). This educational model, with its clearly defined levels and functions, closely resembled a planned economy model. Achieving this result was based on two important prerequisites: first, secondary normal school enrollment took priority over that of ordinary senior middle schools; second, subordinate normal university enrollment took priority over other universities due to the "zero-voluntary" recruitment method.

With the massification of higher education and basic education in China, it has become a dominant trend for teacher education to be conducted through higher education. On this stage, Chinese education planners began to learn from the American teacher education model. They used the integration of the two systems as an opportunity to improve the overall standards of the teacher education system and to prevent the closure of the system. The teacher education system was opened up to the entire higher education system, with the hope of recruiting more high-quality academic resources and creating additional educational opportunities for students in teacher schools. From the 1990s onward, teachers' colleges and universities were either elevated to the comprehensive university level or merged into comprehensive university-run teacher education colleges. The adaptation of the traditional American model was popularized in China, with the goal of establishing a more open teacher education system. At the same time, the old three-level teacher education model of "secondary normal school, junior teachers' college, normal university" was replaced with a new three-level model of "teachers' college, normal university, Master of Education."

In practice, the massification of higher education in China facilitated the transformation of the original teachers' colleges and universities into comprehensive universities; however, the initiative to establish teachers' colleges within comprehensive universities was not met with much enthusiasm, and certain of these colleges have been closed down. Moreover, most of the integrated teachers' colleges and universities were dissolved by the comprehensive universities, and the functionality of the former was improved by the academic quality of the latter in only a few cases. As Zhu et al. (2016) state:

> At the institutional level, among the '985' and '211' educational institutions, the number of colleges and universities participating in teacher education decreased annually. In contrast, the number of colleges and universities outside of the '985' and '211' institutions that participated in teacher education increased annually. This indicates that high-level institutions are still not keen to participate in teacher education. (p. 27)

While opening up the teacher education system had the potential to reinvigorate it and improve the quality of teacher education, openness and marketization have proven insufficient to maintain and replenish China's ranks of teachers or to ensure that the demand for qualified basic education teachers is fulfilled. China's more recent policies regarding teacher team construction have once again emphasized the independence and irreplaceability of its normal education system and have stipulated that teachers' colleges and universities should no longer be renamed. Moreover, the Chinese government has further expanded publicly funded teacher education, which was originally implemented in the subordinate normal universities, demonstrating again that "teacher education requires a relatively stable system and that, for a long time to come, teachers' colleges and normal universities should be at the core of this system" (Guan, 2009, p. 8). The *Action plan for the revitalization of teacher education (2018–2022)* states that:

> the main role of teachers' colleges and universities should be brought into play, and the construction of the teacher education system should be strengthened. The support for teachers' colleges should be increased, and the structure of the teacher education layout should be continuously optimized, forming an open, coordinated, and interactive modern teacher education system with the national teacher education base as the guide, the teacher's college as the main body, participation by high-level comprehensive universities and teacher development institutions as the link, and high-quality primary and secondary schools as the practice base.

Nurturing teachers' passion for education is the prerequisite for creating vast and stable teacher ranks

The *Teacher's Law of the People's Republic of China* defines teachers as "professionals who engage in education and teaching." However, as a professional group, teachers have certain unique characteristics. Because the educational service provided by teachers falls under the public goods category, there is a spillover effect related to its value, which results in teachers' earnings being disproportionate to their professional efforts. As a result, only those teachers who derive intrinsic enjoyment from the educational process or gain a sense of achievement from their students' progress are willing to persist in the profession. In other words, the uniqueness of the teaching profession lies not only in the requirement for teachers to have specialized knowledge and skills but also in the distinctive requirement that they have a passion for their profession.

However, the American teacher education model holds that there is no essential difference between teachers and other professions, so a good command of the relevant subject coupled with verbal communication skills are all that is required to make one a qualified teacher. This kind of understanding has led to the practice of teachers leaving the education profession once they find a better position within the same academic discipline. The high turnover rate of teachers has had a negative impact on the long-term process of teaching and educating.

For this reason, in the *Teacher education curriculum standards (Trial)* developed by China's Ministry of Education, the professional growth of teachers is divided into three areas: educational beliefs and responsibilities, educational knowledge and abilities, and educational practice and experience. This arrangement not only assigns one third of the total weight to the area of educational beliefs and responsibilities but also places it ahead of the other two areas. The *Opinions on comprehensively deepening the reform of the teaching staff construction in the new era* listed "stress on professional ethics" as one of the five major principles for constructing new-era teacher ranks. Moreover, "striving to enhance the ideological and political quality and strengthening the professional ethics and morality of teachers" was mentioned first in the section regarding reform initiatives. The *Action plan for the revitalization of teacher education (2018 – 2022)* proposed five major goals and tasks for plan implementation. Among them, "implementing the new requirements of teacher ethics education and enhancing its effectiveness" was listed as the first of the five major goals and tasks, once again demonstrating the seriousness with which Chinese administrative education departments treat the professional ethics of teachers.

In fact, the requirement to cultivate a passion for teaching and high professional ethics not only helps to alleviate the urgent need for teachers in basic education but also stabilizes the entire teaching profession. More importantly, it promotes a deep understanding of the intrinsic value of education among teachers. It also allows the teaching process to rise above merely imparting knowledge; thus, this requirement allows teachers to fully demonstrate the fundamental function of education. As a result, teachers develop a profound sense of responsibility, which allows them to persevere as educators and gain a deep sense of achievement while doing so. Furthermore, it is crucial for teachers themselves to view their profession as a career and to transform the external requirements based on their own educational beliefs. Thus, the requirement to cultivate a passion for their profession can enable teachers to delve into the problems and issues in education and teaching and continually improve their professional level; this, in turn, will enhance their value as educators. Emphasizing teachers' education and ethics can help support the stability and peace of mind among basic education teachers.

Emphasis on practical teaching skills is conducive to developing the professional value of teachers

Chinese teacher education policies emphasize the importance of subject matter knowledge. However, due to the uniqueness of the evaluation criteria for knowledge in different disciplines, the requirements related to educational and teaching skills are more widely emphasized. In practice, this means that teacher education in China assigns a high value to teaching skills, even leading to the "criticism of the teacher education model of the traditional normal universities, especially for overemphasizing specialized training while neglecting general education courses" (Song & Zhong, 2011, p. 66). In the *Measures for the implementation of teachers' professional certification in general colleges and universities (Provisional)*, the Ministry of Education stipulated that, for aspiring teachers, academic credits for the humanities and social sciences, as well as scientific literacy, should not be less than 10% of the total credits taken, whereas discipline-specific course credits should be no less than 50% of the total credits taken. On the other hand, [teacher education programs] must comply with the requirements of the *Teacher education curriculum standards (Trial)*, which stipulates that [teaching skills] courses should account for no less than 14 credits, excluding the full-semester teaching practice. If calculated based on a total of 160 credits over 8 semesters, it follows that [education students'] discipline-specific courses should include no less than 80 credits, and that [teaching skills] courses should include no less than 34 credits. There were previously specific stipulations and guidelines regarding the objectives, categories, and evaluation criteria for teacher education courses. However, the current policies seem to have no corresponding guidelines or normative provisions for such courses due to the overabundance of discipline-specific courses and the difficulty of setting proper guidelines.

From the perspective of improving the professional level of teachers, intentionally emphasizing the teacher education curriculum—in particular, emphasizing teaching skills and educational practice—demonstrates a certain bias. Discipline-specific courses occupy 50% of the total curriculum, thus rendering the teaching-major graduates inferior to the nonteaching-major graduates at the discipline-specific level; thus, it is not surprising that elite secondary schools are not interested in the former type of graduates. However, this kind of curriculum is very beneficial for the improvement of overall teaching efficiency and the stability of large teacher teams. Emphasizing discipline-specific courses is indeed conducive to the professional improvement of teachers. Emphasizing teaching skills and educational practice helps teachers to impart knowledge more effectively and guides them to become better educators. Moreover, it allows them to solidify their professional quality and subject knowledge in the field of education and teaching. This, in turn, allows them to perceive education and teaching as their "field," thus reducing the flow of teachers into other professions within the same discipline and increasing the likelihood of teachers remaining in education and teaching positions.

A systematic governance mechanism to assure the development and maintenance of a national teaching corps

The development and maintenance of a stable corps of teachers who are highly professional and have a passion for education requires both a high-quality teacher education system and a nationwide governance mechanism. The construction of a nation's teaching profession can enter a virtuous cycle only if teachers' colleges and universities train excellent teachers while the state provides an effective teacher management system. If there is no effective governance mechanism for teachers, outstanding students will not be attracted to apply for admission to teachers' colleges and universities; moreover, even those students who are admitted will not be motivated to strive for excellence. Ensuring the stability of the teaching profession in China requires a unique and systematic governance mechanism.

The *Teacher's Law of the People's Republic of China*, which came into effect on January 1, 1994, defines teachers as "professionals who perform educational and teaching responsibilities." It was with this clear positioning that a series of follow-up governance tools were launched. For example, the teaching qualification system has been clearly defined, and at the same time, the academic requirements for obtaining teaching qualifications at different stages have been stipulated; the implementation of a teacher appointment system and teacher position system has been proposed, thus establishing a professional title system. A clear rule that the "average salary of teachers should not be lower than the average salary of national civil servants and that it will gradually increase" has been formulated. This series of governance tools has enabled the teaching profession in China to form a self-contained system, in which (1) professionals set the direction, (2) the teaching qualification system is the first-level threshold, (3) the teacher post and professional title systems are the development steps, (4) the teacher appointment system is a second-level threshold, and (5) the teacher salary standard is a fundamental guarantee. Moreover, with the abundant teacher reserves of today, education planners changed the tenure system for teaching qualifications to a periodical registration system, thus ensuring that the entire teaching team would have up-to-date teaching knowledge and qualifications.

If the teacher education system trains highly qualified teachers, but the teaching profession fails to offer sufficient professional self-fulfillment opportunities, occupational rewards, and advancement opportunities worth pursuing, qualified teachers will leave the profession—or remain without any motivation to work hard. When the teacher governance mechanism is inadequate, the most likely phenomenon is not the departure of excellent teachers or their work burnout but the failure of the entire education system to recruit outstanding talents. However, the teaching profession needs to recruit suitable—not outstanding—talents because not all outstanding talents are suitable. However, if more outstanding and talented individuals are willing to teach, perhaps more of the suitable talents can become outstanding. In order to enable teachers with high performance to receive high incomes, from January 2009 onward, the teacher performance salary system was introduced among the teachers in the compulsory education stage, and then, the teacher performance salary system was introduced to high school teachers, thus covering all teachers within the basic education system. Of course, the implementation of the teacher performance salary system is not necessarily satisfactory in terms of producing specific results, but the concept of this preferential treatment has penetrated into the teacher governance mechanism. At present, new components are being added to the performance pay to further adjust the previous relatively solid teacher performance pay system in order to make it more suitable for the actual situation of teacher management in basic education.

In order to satisfy the urgent need for teachers in basic education, it is essential to form a relatively closed teacher education system and a relatively systematic teacher governance mechanism. The former system can guarantee the supply of teachers that China requires now and in the future, whereas the latter can ensure the stability of the teaching profession in China. However, given the guaranteed supply and ensured stability of this enormous team of teachers, the teacher supply system needs to remain open to strengthen it further (e.g., by becoming open to comprehensive universities). Moreover, the teacher governance system should remain competitive (e.g., by introducing a merit-based salary system). However, when the teacher education system was actually opened up to comprehensive universities, it did not attract the attention of high-quality comprehensive universities. Instead, the teachers' colleges and universities were transformed or integrated into the comprehensive university education system. In addition, after the introduction of the merit-based salary system, rather than highly efficient education work spurred on by the competition mechanism, we observed more conflicts in the school administration, which, in turn, dampened teachers' passion for teaching. In short, China has obtained remarkable results on the "scale" aspect of its national team of teachers. However, there remains a long way ahead on the path of enhancing its "quality."

References

Guan, P. (2009). The course, achievements, and basic experiences of teacher education reform and opening-up in China in the past thirty years [in Chinese]. *China Higher Education Research*, (2), 3–11.

Ministry of Education of the People's Republic of China. (2011). *Teacher education curriculum standards (Trial)* [in Chinese]. http://old.moe.gov.cn//publicfiles/business/htmlfiles/moe/s6136/201110/125722.html

Ministry of Education of the People's Republic of China. (2017). *Measures for the implementation of teachers' professional certification in general colleges and universities (Provisional)* [in Chinese]. http://www.moe.edu.cn/srcsite/A10/s7011/201711/t20171106_318535.html

Ministry of Education of the People's Republic of China. (2018a). *Action plan for the revitalization of teacher education (2018–2022)* [in Chinese]. http://www.gov.cn/xinwen/2018-03/28/content_5278034.htm

Ministry of Education of the People's Republic of China. (2018b). *Opinions on comprehensively deepening the reform of the teaching staff construction in the new era* [in Chinese]. http://www.moe.gov.cn/jyb_xwfb/moe_1946/fj_2018/201801/t20180131_326148.html

Song, H., & Zhong, B. (2011). Towards practice and the risk of vocational training: A study of Sino-American teacher education model reform [in Chinese]. *Journal of Higher Education*, (9), 64–69.

Xu, M., & Li, J. (2009). A historical comparison of teacher education development in the world [in Chinese]. *Education Research*, (6), 54–62.

Zhu, X., et al. (2016). *A research of China's teacher preparation institute development* [in Chinese]. Beijing Normal University Press.

This interesting piece of policy review concerning AI Education in China leverages the author's experience as a key member of national information technology curriculum development. It mainly summarizes recent developments in the use of artificial intelligence (AI) in Chinese education, paying particular attention to the different applications of AI at a number of different levels: AI implementation is at its early stage in elementary education; more prevalent in higher education, and even more common in the field of civic education. As a result, in multiple dimensions, Chinese students are becoming better trained to face an age of AI and working together to create an informatized education environment. The whole article describes how China is searching for the point where top-down system design meets bottom-up applications to chart its own course for the use of AI in education.

Accelerated Move for AI Education in China [1]

Xiaozhe Yang

Recent developments in artificial intelligence (AI) have garnered worldwide attention. Pressure from business and industry to transform has made every nation start paying attention to the changes AI technologies can bring to different fields. AI is becoming a new focus of international competition, and at the same time a new development opportunity, and even for humanity itself. As a developing country at a juncture such as this, China is taking another look at its resources—whether human, natural, data, or intelligence—and the relationships between them.

In July 2017, the State Council published the *Next generation artificial intelligence development plan* (State Council of China, 2017). This important state-level document expressed China's need to take every advantage of the great strategic opportunity presented by the development of AI, build upon the first-mover advantage China already has in the field, and accelerate its growth into a technological powerhouse of innovation. The report also made clear

---

1 This article was an interim report on the research achievements of the Shanghai Information Technology Education and Pedagogy Research Base, one of the key research bases of humanity and social sciences under the Shanghai Lide Shuren Program for Higher Education Institutions [Project No. 3000 - 412221 - 16054]. It was published on *ECNU Review of Education*, 2(3), 347 - 352.

that AI should be broadly applied in basic education, higher education, vocational education, and civic education, and that China must train a new generation of talent skilled with AI. In October of the same year, the Communist Party of China (CCP) held its 19th National Congress. AI was the most representative technology field discussed at the meeting and was written into Xi Jinping's Report, confirming the elevation of AI to a field of highly strategic national import.

As a new age of AI approaches, China is looking at a variety of new strategies and new approaches for the field of education, with its sights on both the long-term and the immediate, basic education, and higher education, laying out a comprehensive AI strategy for a skilled workforce and for civic education. The country also has a large number of hi-tech enterprises actively participating in exploring how the use of AI can change education.

Beginning at the Beginning: AI Education in Primary and Secondary Schools

Elementary education is central to the question of what kind of people society wants to create, and AI has a fundamental impact. Training people who will not be replaceable by AI is a crucial problem that needs to be addressed.

As early as 2013, the Ministry of Education (MOE) kicked off a new round of revisions to the standard high school curriculum, putting more than 260 experts on the job for 4 years. Revision of the country's curriculum, standards, and textbooks was managed by the MOE, revealing the great significance of these revisions.

Among the revised standards is clear reference to "core competencies (*hexin suyang*)." This educational goal has been set under an environment of reflection on the relationship between AI and human intelligence, the collaboration between man and machine, and shared development of the future. Education in China is beginning to realize a transformation from the traditional systemic emphasis on the completeness of academic knowledge and the structure of that knowledge with an understatement of skill training to an equal weighting of raising students' abilities and the quality of their thinking to promote well-rounded development (Wang, 2019).

More directly relevant to the field of AI, the revised standards for the secondary education information technology curriculum include specific pedagogical content for AI. The revised high school IT curriculum no longer centers on computers and the Internet, instead focusing on data, algorithms, information systems, and the information society. The IT curriculum is not merely intended to eliminate computer illiteracy but rather to be a pathway for students to get acquainted with the world, to understand it, and to change it.

The high school IT curriculum has added an "AI" course worth two credits of 18 classroom hours each, for a total of 36 class hours. Through studying the AI course module, students learn about the concept and historical development of AI and can describe the process of realization of common AI algorithms. Through a module in which they develop their own simple intelligent technology applications, they gain hands-on experience with techniques and the basic process of designing and creating a simple intelligent system, strengthening their sense of responsibility in using intelligent technologies to serve human development. Through Science, Technology, Engineering and Mathematics (STEM) education, combining AI and the exploration of other courses to give students a thorough grounding in interdisciplinary thinking, the basic mode of thinking behind AI can permeate students' studies and everyday life. At present, new high school course materials are being developed based on the revised national curriculum standards. The new textbooks and methods are scheduled to go into use across the nation in several batches beginning in September 2019. The next step in curriculum reform to include AI will be the secondary education level, currently under consideration.

Extending AI education at the higher education level

At the higher education level, China is right now building an AI course environment and working to improve its execution, making course majors in AI available, and promoting the development of a top-level course of study in the field of AI. At pilot postsecondary institutions, colleges of AI are being set up and universities are working to increase enrollments in AI-related master's and doctoral programs. Up through May 2018, China had already established 32 colleges of AI. Universities research institutions are strengthening cooperation among academics, research, and production, and among AI courses, enterprises, and other institutions. China encourages those colleges and universities with existing AI programs to expand their scope to establish "AI + x" compound majors and stress the cross-disciplinary integration of AI with mathematics, computer science, physics, biology, psychology, sociology, law, and other fields.

As the age of AI unfolds, higher education must both train professionals specializing in AI and help professionals in other disciplines to also understand, utilize, and integrate AI. Higher education sector in China is training multitalented professionals, both longitudinally versed in AI theory, methods, techniques, products, and applications and laterally knowledgeable of the use of AI in economics, sociology, management, law, education, and other fields.

Popularization of AI education

In the campaign to strengthen basic science education, China is broadly developing a variety of AI education activities to encourage technology professionals nationwide to participate in the effort to popularize AI education and increase the public's overall knowledge of AI, building, and improving all aspects of basic infrastructure for AI science education. The usefulness of all types of platforms for AI innovation is fully realized in science education displays and science museums.

In 2017, the Ministry of Science and Technology announced the first national platforms for the innovation and development of New Generation Chinese AI. These are the National Platform for Autonomous Driving (with Baidu), the National Platform for Medical Imaging (with Tencent), the National Platform for City Brain (with Alibaba), and the National Platform for Voice Recognition (with iFlytek). The setting up of development platforms by AI corporations and scientific research institutions is intended to open AI R&D up to the public sector and facilitate production. With these platforms, China can have AI competitions and all manner of scientific innovation and increase the participation of scientists in the spreading of AI education. China hopes to make education available to all its people to foster the gradual spread of programming and AI education and encourage the participation of all areas of society.

Future education to prepare for the age of AI

Looking at education from the perspective of AI development, the system in China is proactively adapting and preparing for challenges. Through elementary education, higher education, and civic education, the country is training a population to have the core skills, professional abilities, and intellectual consensus necessary to be prepared for an age of AI, and it is setting up the lifelong learning and employment apparatus necessary for an intelligent society of the future.

From another angle, AI is bringing an opportunity for individualization to the entire educational system. Many Chinese tech corporations are increasing the use of intelligent technologies to construct an educational system. A great variety of educational technology enterprises are actively exploring and broadly utilizing AI and other technologies to commence the building of "smart campus" schools, develop online learning and education platforms that use Big Data intelligence, and promote the application of AI in mathematics, management, resource construction, and other areas. In April 2018, MOE published *Education informatization 2.0 action plan* (MOE, 2018). The Plan clearly noted the need to bring about shifts from dedicated resources to shared resources, from raising students' skill in IT applications to raising general IT attainment, and from integrated application to integrated innovation, and also to build a learner-centered education environment, provide precisely targeted educational services, and create "school credit bank" systems using innovative blockchain technologies, to make continuing education more flexible and customized.

Meanwhile, with the development of AI, continued advancements in voice recognition, gesture recognition, facial expression recognition, and brain wave recognition are providing new tools for educational research. Explorations of the application of these technologies in educational environments, their manner of application and their effectiveness are becoming the new direction of educational research. In 2017, National Natural Science Foundation of China added a new code (F0701) for educational research to encourage collaboration and integration between the natural sciences and the social sciences and to encourage the establishment of a new mode of interdisciplinary educational research.

There remain many areas of uncertainty. Imagined scenarios of machine intelligence persist. It is too easy for us to overemphasize potential short-term effects and discount longer-term import. Objectively, the basic technologies for AI have not yet produced any breakthrough advances in the past few years, but as computational power increases and integration in all facets of society drives a consolidation with production, popular knowledge, and application of AI is growing.

Education prepares people to face the future. What AI education really is and where it belongs remain questions to be explored. Ensuring that the interaction between AI and education is a beneficial relationship is especially important. Should either AI or education get too far ahead of or too far behind the other, the forces of production and relations of production fall out of step and become unable to take us to a new era.

Rome wasn't built in a day, and we cannot train a whole crop of AI professionals in one fell swoop. Reaching this goal will take long-term planning and several stages. In China, AI education has been planned out for different stages of schooling with the system being actively adjusted through a forcible, top-down approach. Proclaiming at the government level the importance of AI education makes it easier for China to grasp the important strategic opportunity presented by the field's development, and China's Internet companies are at the same time working to push and innovate to apply AI technologies in the educational system. The power of fields outside education, exemplified by corporations, with the help of AI technologies can more strongly force changes in the school system, putting the focus more squarely on users to build a new educational system. But at the same time, we need to be wary lest the surge in popularity of AI education leads to a new mechanized form of the old rote system, or AI education becomes a device for competitive education and selective hiring.

Education will change with scientific and technological progress and developments in industry. As AI and education come to intersect, China is looking for a way to combine its top-down education system design with bottom-up teaching applications so that society as a whole might be fully prepared as it steps into the age of AI, to support every instance of personal development as we enter an age of intelligent systems, and to both create and nurture all those who will help build new-generation AI.

References

Ministry of Education of China (MOE). (2018). *Education informatization 2.0 action plan* [in Chinese]. Retrieved April 18, 2018, from http://www.moe.gov.cn/srcsite/A16/s3342/201804/t20180425_334188.html

State Council of China. (2017). *Next generation artificial intelligence development plan* [in Chinese]. Retrieved July 8, 2017, from http://www.gov.cn/zhengce/content/2017-07/20/content_5211996.htm

Wang, T. (2019). Competence for students' future: Curriculum change and policy redesign in China. *ECNU Review of Education*, 2(2), 234–245.

This article reviews China's labor education theories and policies to reveal the main objectives, contents, and methods of the new era, as well as analyzes future development in labor education. Marxist and traditional approaches to labor education, as well as the historical development of education in China provide the macroscopic backdrop of this study. By reviewing the relevant labor education theories and examining the relating labor education policies, authors find that China's labor education policy has placed labor education on the same level as that in morality, intellect, sports, and aesthetics, thereby endowing labor education with new meaning, that is the cultivation of workers with all-round physical and mental development and the adoption of systematic approaches and methods including formal programs and teaching, education in daily life at home and school, and practical activities outside of school. This study provides a useful reference for the implementation of labor education in elementary and middle schools.

Refreshing China's Labor Education in the New Era: Policy Review on Education Through Physical Labor [1]

Guorui Fan and Jiaxin Zou

Introduction

Labor education has long been an important component of the Chinese education system—especially basic education—since the founding of the People's Republic of China (PRC) in 1949. This type of education serves to enhance human development while promoting productive labor and social development. Labor education has accrued various connotations over time. In the initial stage of the country's founding, education was intended "to serve the workers and peasants, and for production and construction" (Qian, 1950). During 1966 – 1976, education was combined with productive labor in service to proletarian politics (Lu, 1958; The Central Committee of CPC & The State Council of PRC, 1958). By the 1990s, "education served the socialist cause, and was integrated with social practices" (Jiang, 2000). Since the turn of the 21st century, the National People's Congress of PRC (2016) has argued that "education must

---

1 This article was published on *ECNU Review of Education*, 3(1), 169 – 178.

serve the modernization of socialism and the people, and must be combined with productive labor and social practices." At a national education conference held in 2018, Xi Jinping announced the need to place labor education on par with education in the other four life domains, namely morality, intellect, sports, and aesthetics. This was the first time that labor education was given such importance. Xi Jinping emphasized the need to strengthen labor education and invest further efforts in building an education system that comprehensively "Educating Five Domains Simultaneously" (五育并举) to cultivate citizens capable of enhancing and developing socialist China (Xinhua News Agency, 2018). Promulgating *China's Education Modernization 2035*, in 2019, the Chinese government began advancing education policies centered on themes of "methods to reform general high school education" and "intensifying reforms in education and teaching to comprehensively improve the quality of compulsory education" (General Office of the State Council of PRC, 2019; The Central Committee of CPC & The State Council of PRC, 2019; Xinhua News Agency, 2019a). These directions have provided new ways in which to interpret the meaning of labor education in the new era while advancing new requirements and deployments for the reform and development of labor education in China. Indeed, the "novelty" of labor education in the new era is fully reflected in its objectives, methods, and contents.

Objectives: Education "for the workers"

The primary question of education is "What types of people are to be cultivated?" In terms of educational goals, labor education is designed to cultivate workers. Its motives are to nurture the comprehensive and harmonious development of human physical and mental capabilities. According to Marx, the essence of humans is the ensemble of all social relations (Marx, 1845). Humans form and develop social relationships through the course of productive labor and social practices. In the 1950s, there was a huge demand for production and construction talent in China to help establish socialism. Mao Zedong argued that "our educational policies should enable the students to achieve development in moral and intellectual education, sports, and other aspects, and become cultural workers who are conscious of socialism" (1957, p. 226).

Following the country's reform and opening-up, and in response to the development of the times, this idea was elevated to "cultivating the builders and successors of socialism" (Jiang, 1990; The Eighth National People's Congress of the PRC, 1995). The fundamental task in the development of a contemporary Chinese society is the building of a modern country that is prosperous, powerful, democratic, civilized, and harmonious. To achieve social development, there is an urgent need to strengthen labor education and cultivate high-quality workers who are knowledge-based, technically competent, and innovative.

In regard to school education, labor education constitutes an important component of education for students' comprehensive development. It has irreplaceable and unique educational importance in cultivating the core values of and abilities in labor, as well as improving labor literacy. Marx believed that future education should combine productive labor with instruction and gymnastics, arguing that this was "not only one of the methods of adding to the efficiency of production, but the only method of producing fully developed human beings" (1867, p. 317). The integration of labor, moral, intellectual, sports, and aesthetic education will strengthen students' education in life practices, labor techniques, and vocational experiences (The Central Committee of CPC & The State Council of PRC, 2019).

According to the policy paper, labor education is believed to enhance social relations and develop students' moral qualities. It can also cultivate passion among youths regarding labor and production, temper their wills, and improve their abilities to pursue truth and creativity, thereby enhancing their intellects. Students are also encouraged to produce and shape beautiful works to hone their aesthetic abilities, thus enabling them to experience the values and strengths of life through aesthetics. Labor education in the new era must "enhance the spirit of labor, and strengthen the cultivation of practical, hands-on, collaborative, and innovative capabilities" (Xinhua News Agency, 2019a). Labor is the means through which to develop an individual's morality, increase their wisdom, strengthen their body, cultivate their sense of aesthetics, and enhance their innovativeness (Ministry of Education et al., 2015). Labor education instills the habit of and passion for labor, while providing the necessary skills (General Office of the State Council of PRC, 2019). Accordingly, labor education ensures comprehensive physical and mental development.

Contents: Education "about labor"

Labor is the most basic and important means of human existence and possesses its own unique educational values (Qu & Liu, 2019). In contemporary society, growing demands for productive labor have resulted in the need to improve the quality of workers. This has led to an increasingly close relationship between education and labor. The connotations of labor education have changed in accordance with the evolution of productive labor, as well as scientific and technological developments.

Labor skills and technologies education

Arguing that the division of labor would hinder artisans from acquiring full knowledge of their professions, Marx (1867) advocated the implementation of technological training (the German text refers to this as "polytechnical training"). According to Marx (1866), such training imparts the general principles of all processes of production while initiating youths in the practical use of the elementary instruments of all trades. With the increasing demand for technological innovation in social production, recent exploratory directions for labor education in the new era include a focus on technology, emphasis on practice, and pursuit of innovation (Li & Qu, 2018). As a component of general education, labor education is linked to productive labor. However, it differs from the education provided by vocational and technical schools, which is the singular form of technical education or vocational and technical education. Rather, labor education involves technological education that allows and helps students to (i) understand the general scientific principles behind modern production; (ii) acquire modern skills and knowledge regarding processes, organization of production, and management; as well as (iii) master the skills and techniques required to use work tools and equipment. With such an extensive foundation in technological training, students can achieve complete and harmonious development.

Developing creative thinking and capabilities

Labor is a receptacle for humans' practical and creative activities. Accordingly, labor education is essentially innovative education (Xu, 2018). Rapid developments in mobile communication and artificial intelligence technologies have had significant impacts on labor. Indeed, just as machine production replaced manual labor in the industrial revolution, so procedural labor in production processes is increasingly being replaced by robots with artificial intelligence. This has resulted in an increasing need for technological and innovative talent. To a large extent, STEAM and Maker education—markedly popular among youths and students—reflect the requisite innovative features of labor in the new era. Originating in the U.S. in the 1980s, STEAM education has developed into a comprehensive approach integrating education in science, technology, engineering, art, and mathematics (National Science Board, 1986). STEAM emphasizes the relationship between knowledge and innovative practice and aims to cultivate students' creative, hands-on, and practical abilities. Meanwhile, Maker education is oriented toward the development of creativity, design, and manufacturing in youths. This approach discovers problems and needs through creative actions and practices and strives to find solutions to practical activities. In the process, students excel in creativity to become creators, inventors, and designers.

Ideologies of labor

The fundamental task of education is to develop and cultivate people's abilities, thus elevating them. Labor education guides students' entrance into the labor market, helping them develop a positive attitude toward the reality of labor. Accordingly, labor education in the new era centers on the cultivation of labor values (Tan, 2019), while emphasis is placed on its inherent pedagogic value. Labor education promotes the spirit of labor and labor morality, thus contributing to social construction (Qu, 2019). Labor education promotes students' respect for labor, resulting in the formation of a labor consciousness that views labor as honorable, majestic, mighty, and beautiful. Students also develop an appreciation for labor quality—that is, the virtue of working hard, honestly, and creatively (Xi, 2016). Labor education also serves to hone and temper students' personalities, encouraging the desire and willpower to work hard, overcome difficulties, and dare to struggle—thus helping them develop healthy personalities. Furthermore, labor itself has aesthetic value. In this regard, labor education stimulates students' aesthetic experiences and cultivates their emotional connection to labor, guiding them to enjoy the fruits and pleasures of labor. In doing so, they experience the beauty of labor.

Method: Education "through labor"

Education is a social activity unique to human society. Human education originated from labor and the needs generated by labor practices and was conditional upon the development of human language and consciousness (Kaiipob, 1950). Since its creation, the function of education has been transmitting the production and life-related experiences formed during the labor process.

Using "experience" to illustrate the relationship between education and labor, Dewey (1916) defined education as "the continual reorganization, reconstruction, and transformation of experience" (p. 50). In doing so, he advocated "learning by doing," establishing "creative workshops" involving the use of various woodworking tools across various grades at the University of Chicago Laboratory School (Mayhew & Edwards, 1965). In the new era, the connotations of "combining education with productive labor" have become even more plentiful, while the means and formats of labor education have become more diversified (He, 2003, pp. 119, 314). These include various types of labor that are production-, service-, and creativity-based (General Office of the State Council of PRC, 2019).

Labor education curriculum and teaching

Specialized courses in labor education should constitute the main means of implementing this type of education. So, it is necessary to design the objectives and contents of the labor education curriculum scientifically based on the physical and mental developmental characteristics of elementary and middle school students. The scientific and technical knowledge and skills of the relevant disciplines required for the cultivation of labor skills and literacy in students of different ages should be systematically designed and developed according to their respective grades. Teaching resources and tools that are compatible with the relevant scientific and technical knowledge and skills should be developed and introduced. Strengthening the curriculumization and systematization of labor education will enhance its purpose and direction. When developing the curriculum resources of labor education in the new era, attention should be paid to the application of new technologies, techniques, and methods. Moreover, it is necessary to ensure effective correlation between the curriculum and local conditions in terms of natural resources so that a diverse range of choices are provided for students' individualized development based on their personal compatibility with the industrial, agricultural, or commercial sectors.

Life at home and in school

Labor is an important component of life and production. The implementation of the labor education curriculum requires coordination in terms of combining activities in and outside of school as well as a consideration of the diverse forms of labor education applicable to daily life, services, and production. Students' daily lives encompass the two aspects of family and school.

Schools must provide parents with some advice on labor education in the family, and parents should arrange for their children to participate in housework that corresponds with their abilities. Schools must insist on the day-duty system for students and have them conduct various tasks in the school compounds (The Central Committee of CPC & The State Council of PRC, 2019). For instance, elementary and middle school students can sweep and clean the classrooms, perform rostered day duties, assist teachers in preparing the laboratories for lessons, and participate in public welfare activities. Schools should also encourage students to pay attention to the labor opportunities around them so that they make good use of the available labor education resources. This includes attending to their own basic tasks in daily life, such as cleaning their rooms, as well as tidying their classroom and schoolyard environments. As such, labor education must be established in everyday life in the school environment, home life, and normal social activities. In this regard, varied forms of practical activities can be organized according to local conditions, such as housework, labor tasks in and outside of school, and voluntary services.

Practical activities outside of school

The implementation of labor education in general elementary and middle schools will inevitably face limitations in terms of the available technology, equipment, environment, and number of professional teachers. To ensure the effective implementation of labor education, schools need to rely on external resources and encourage students to actively participate in practical activities outside of school. In the U.S., STEM education has developed several such implementation approaches, including those related to practice communities, activity design, educational experiences, learning spaces and measurements, and sociocultural environments. These spaces ensure that learners of all ages and types are able to enjoy quality STEM learning experiences (The U.S. Department of Education et al., 2016). In the process of implementing labor education, it is necessary to optimize the curriculum structure for comprehensive practical activities and "ensure that classes related to labor education do not comprise less than half of the total" (The Central Committee of CPC & The State Council of PRC, 2019).

General elementary and middle schools can establish joint cooperation with various external institutions in developing a cluster of experimental zones for labor education, thereby creating a comprehensive mechanism for the sharing of labor education resources. For instance, schools can cooperate with vocational and technical schools to integrate general education with vocational and technical education. Collaborations with relevant organizations in various industries—such as research institutions, colleges, commercial organizations, manufacturing enterprises, farms, creative spaces, and social institutions—will also be beneficial. In addition to breaking through organizational and institutional barriers, such collaborative ventures can aid the establishment of practice bases for labor education outside of schools.

Moreover, positive interactions between labor education and community building can be facilitated by providing students with labor education resources for various professions (Spencer, 2007). The specialized resources and technical strengths of the various organizations can provide students with the appropriate conditions in which to participate in exploratory, comprehensive, and project-based labor. Similarly, arrangements can be made for the pastures, fields, forests, and mountains in the rural areas to become practice bases for learning about agriculture. In this regard, schools in cities and towns should ensure that their students are given opportunities to participate in agricultural production and gain experiences in the industrial, commercial, and service sectors (The Central Committee of CPC & The State Council of PRC, 2019).

Future of labor education in China

In November 2019, the No. 11 meeting of the CPC Committee on Comprehensively Deepening Reform approved *Opinions on Comprehensively Reinforcing New-Era Labor Education in Primary, Secondary and Higher Education*, which stipulates again that labor education is essential to China's characteristic socialism education, and it should be integrated into the whole process of students' cultivation, spanning across different educational levels and through families, schools, and societies (Xinhua News Agency, 2019b). In constructing a comprehensive labor education system for the new era, close attention must be paid to the impact of intelligent technologies on productive labor and social development. It is essential that society develop its adaptability to new technical labor based on artificial intelligence by cultivating a workforce for the artificial intelligence era, while providing the preparatory workforce with educational opportunities in relevant fields. This will allow all workers to rapidly switch roles in the artificial intelligence era (National Science and Technology Council & Networking and Information Technology Research and Development Subcommittee, 2016).

Meanwhile, the Education Law of the PRC needs to be revised so that "labor education" is incorporated into China's education policies, thus strengthening the legality and rationality of labor education. To meet economic and societal needs in the intelligent era, a system must be established to cultivate the knowledge, abilities, and literacy of workers. In addition to creating a corresponding target system for labor education in schools, guidelines should be formulated for labor education (General Office of the State Council of PRC, 2019; The Central Committee of CPC & The State Council of PRC, 2019). The formulation and implementation of standards for labor education, as well as the corresponding curriculum and instructional documents for teaching, will result in the development of a comprehensive policy system for implementing labor education.

The system through which curriculum content for labor education is developed should integrate multiple disciplines, including science, mathematics, engineering, and art. This should be supported by a resource system for labor education. Students' participation in practical labor activities should be incorporated into the relevant courses in elementary and middle schools and serve as an evaluation criterion of their overall character development. This will create an evaluation system for labor education that is both scientific and rational. Moreover, the education and training of teachers in labor education needs to be improved. This involves revising the structures of their knowledge and abilities to enhance their educational and teaching capabilities. In turn, they can better adapt to the needs of labor education in the new era. Finally, the integrated development of education in and outside of schools should be promoted. Indeed, the educational forces of society as a whole should be mobilized in establishing an open system for labor education with mutual support between schools and society.

References

Dewey, J. (1916). *Democracy and education: An introduction to the philosophy of education.* The Free Press.

General Office of the State Council of PRC. (2019, June 11). *Guiding opinions on promoting the reform of education mode in senior high schools in the new era* [in Chinese]. http://www.gov.cn/zhengce/content/2019-06/19/content_5401568.htm

He, D. (2003). *Important educational documents of the People's Republic of China (1998-2002)* [in Chinese]. Hainan Press.

Jiang, Z. (1990). "We should adhere to the correct direction of running schools and train socialist builders and successors." On June 26, 1990, Jiang Zemin, then general secretary of the CPC Central Committee, wrote an inscription for the middle school affiliated to South China Normal University [in Chinese].

Jiang, Z. (2000, March 1). Speech on education [in Chinese]. *People's Daily*, 1.

Kaiipob, N. A. (1950). *Pedagogy* (Y. Shen, et al., Trans.) [in Chinese]. People's Education Press.

Li, K., & Qu, X. (2018). The historical evolution and reflection of labor education in the Party's educational policy since 1949 [in Chinese]. *Journal of Educational Studies*, (5), 63 – 72.

Lu, D. (1958). Education must be combined with productive labor [in Chinese]. *Red Flag*, (7), 9.

Mao, Z. (1957). On the correct handling of contradictions among the people. In Party Documents Research Office of the CPC Central Committee (Ed.), *Works of Mao Zedong* (Vol. 7) [in Chinese]. People's Press.

Marx, K. (1845). *Theses on Feuerbach*. https://www.marxists.org/archive/marx/works/1845/theses/theses.htm

Marx, K. (1866). 4. Juvenile and Children's Labor (both sexes). *Instructions for the delegates of the provisional general council: The different questions*. https://www.marxists.org/history/international/iwma/documents/1866/instructions.htm

Marx, K. (1867). *Capital* (Vol. 1) (F. Engels, Ed.; S. Moore & E. Aveling, Trans.). Progress Publishers. https://www.marxists.org/archive/marx/works/download/pdf/Capital-Volume-I.pdf

Mayhew, K. C., & Edwards, A. C. (1965). *The Dewey school: The Laboratory School of the University of Chicago 1896 – 1903*. Transaction Publishers.

Ministry of Education, Central Committee of the Communist Youth League, & National Committee for the Work of the Youth League of PRC. (2015). *Opinions of the Ministry of Education, the Central Committee of the Communist Youth League and the National Committee for the Work of the Youth League on strengthening labor education in primary and secondary schools* [in Chinese]. http://www.moe.gov.cn/srcsite/A06/s3325/201507/t20150731_197068.html

National People's Congress of PRC. (2016). *Education Law of the People's Republic of China* [in Chinese]. *Gazette of the Standing Committee of the National People's Congress of the People's Republic of China*, 46 – 53.

National Science Board. (1986). *Undergraduate science, math, and engineering education*. https://www.nsf.gov/nsb/publications/1986/nsb0386.pdf

National Science and Technology Council, & Networking and Information Technology Research and Development Subcommittee. (2016). *The national artificial intelligence research and development strategic plan*. Executive Office of the President of the United States.

Qian, J. (1950). The current policy of education construction [in Chinese]. *People's Education*, (2), 10 – 16.

Qu, B. (2019, May 6). The ideological and practical significance of labor education in the new era [in Chinese]. *Guangming Daily*, 6.

Qu, X., & Liu, X. (2019). Connotation analysis and system construction of labor education in colleges and universities in the new era [in Chinese]. *China Higher Education Research*, (2), 73 – 77.

Spencer, B. (2007). The present and future challenges of labor education in the global economy. International Labour Organization (ILO). *Strengthening the trade unions: The key role of labor education* (Labor Education 2007/1 – 2, No. 146 – 147). https://library.fes.de/pdf-files/gurn/00346.pdf

Tan, C. (2019). Understanding the concept of labor education—How to understand the basic connotation and characteristics of the concept of labor education [in Chinese]. *Journal of the Chinese Society of Education*, (2), 82 – 84.

The Central Committee of CPC, & The State Council of PRC. (1958, September 20). Instruction on education [in Chinese]. *People's Daily*, 1.

The Central Committee of CPC, & The State Council of PRC. (2019, June 23). *On deepening the reform of education and teaching and improving the quality of compulsory education in an all-round way* [in Chinese]. http://www.gov.cn/zhengce/2019 – 07/08/content_5407361.htm

The Eighth National People's Congress of the PRC. (1995). *Education Law of the People's Republic of China* [in Chinese]. http://www.npc.gov.cn/wxzl/gongbao/1995 – 03/18/content_1481296.htm

The U. S. Department of Education, et al. (2016). *STEM 2026: A vision for innovation in STEM education*. The U. S.

Department of Education. https://www.air.org/system/files/downloads/report/STEM-2026-Vision-for-Innovation-September-2016.pdf

Xi, J. (2016, April 30). Speech at the symposium of intellectuals, model workers and youth representatives [in Chinese]. *People's Daily*, 2.

Xinhua News Agency. (2018). *Xi Jinping attended the National Education Conference and delivered an important speech* [in Chinese]. http://www.gov.cn/xinwen/2018-09/10/content_5320835.htm

Xinhua News Agency. (2019a). *The Central Committee of the Communist Party of China and the State Council printed and distributed China's Education Modernization 2035* [in Chinese]. http://www.gov.cn/xinwen/2019-02/23/content_5367987.htm

Xinhua News Agency. (2019b). *Xi Jinping: Important measures to ascertain the Fourth Plenary Session of the 19th Central Committee of the Communist Party of China, continuation of comprehensively deepening reform to realize organic transition and integration* [in Chinese]. http://www.gov.cn/xinwen/2019-11/26/content_5455918.htm

Xu, C. (2018). The logic of the redevelopment of labor education in the new era [in Chinese]. *Educational Research*, (11), 12–17.

China has a long history of private school education, which is also widely called nongovernmental education or *Minban* Education (民办教育). Since the founding of the People's Republic of China, nongovernmental education once disappeared from Chinese society until its revival following the 3rd Plenary Session of the 11th Central Committee of the Communist Party of China. With its development of more than four decades, nongovernmental education has become an important part of China's educational system and is vigorously promoting the modernization progress of Chinese education. Against this historical backdrop, this study reviews the policies on nongovernmental education (private school education) since the founding of the People's Republic of China and finds that being different from its counterparts in Western countries, China's nongovernmental education sector has operated based on private capital investments and contributions, with the organizers (contributors) typically expecting economic returns. Marked by the introduction of regulations and policies for nongovernmental education around the year of 2016, China's nongovernmental education sector officially entered a new era of registration, support, and regulation by category and the implementing of the relevant new policies on nongovernmental education shall have significant impact on the development and reform of China's nongovernmental education in the future.

China's New Laws and Policies on Nongovernmental Education: Background, Characteristics, and Impact Analysis [1]

Shengzu Dong

China has a long history of private school education. Incorporated into the state-owned or publicly run education system after the founding of the People's Republic of China (PRC), nongovernmental education disappeared from Chinese society until its revival following the 3rd Plenary Session of the 11th Central Committee of the Communist Party of China (CPC) in 1978. Nongovernmental education has since undergone vigorous development facilitated by market promotion and policies. As of 2018, China had around 183,500 private schools of various types and levels—a figure accounting for approximately 35.35% of the total number of schools. Private schools had a total enrollment of 53.7821 million students in 2018, comprising 19.51% of the national total (Ministry of Education of PRC, 2019). In addition to increasing the supply of and

---

1 This article was published on *ECNU Review of Education*, *3*(2), 346–356.

options for education, the rise and development of nongovernmental education in China has promoted education reform, stimulated the sector's vitality, and made a significant contribution to popularizing basic and higher education in China.

The evolution of China's policies on nongovernmental education

The proliferation of nongovernmental education in China is the results of socioeconomic development and systemic reform. As early as 1982, the *Constitution of the PRC* clearly stated that "the state encourages collective economic organizations, state enterprises and institutions, and other social forces to organize various educational undertakings in accordance with the law." When the Central Committee of the CPC issued *Guidelines for Reform and Development of Education in China* in 1993, it reiterated that the government should not be responsible for operating all schools in the country. Accordingly, the CPC announced its goal to gradually establish an education system in which government-run schools would remain the mainstay but with all sectors of society cooperating to run schools. These regulations served as the basis for the laws and policies that facilitated the rise of nongovernmental education in China. Unlike other countries—where such education is predominantly funded and organized by public welfare funds or social forces—China's nongovernmental education sector has operated on the basis of private capital investments and contributions, with the organizers (contributors) typically expecting economic returns. This situation has contributed to the particularity and complexity of designing and reforming China's nongovernmental education system.

In the mid- to late-1990s, the Chinese government actively encouraged and vigorously advocated that all sectors of society make donations toward the operating of schools. This was intended to effectively alleviate the discord between the supply of and demand for degree holders as a result of the state's insufficient investment in education. The state also made reference to and learned from the field of economics. More specifically, the CPC explored means of introducing a corresponding market mechanism for developing nongovernmental education based on the premises that the nonprofit legal status of private schools would remain unchanged, and that education provision as a public interest would not be compromised in any way. In doing so, the state sought to mobilize social forces to become more proactive in the operating of schools.

The provisions for such explorations were made through two sets of laws and regulations.

The first, *Regulations on Schools Operated by Social Forces*, was issued by the State Council in 1997.[1] These administrative regulations clarified the state's basic policies toward schools being operated by social forces, namely, "active encouragement, strong support, correct guidance, and strengthening of management." The regulations further stipulated that upon the liquidation of educational institutions, the remaining assets could be used to reimburse the organizer(s) for their investments, either in part or in full. The second regulation, the *Law of the PRC to Promote Non-Governmental Education*, was promulgated by the Standing Committee of the National People's Congress (NPC) in 2002. This law formally established the equal legal status of private and government-run schools. It also stipulated that funders could obtain reasonable returns from the operating surpluses of private schools after deducting operating costs, reserving funds for development, and covering any other necessary expenses in accordance with the relevant state regulations. Containing distinctive Chinese characteristics, this top-level policy was designed to adapt to the state's specific conditions at that time. The law was able to mobilize people's enthusiasm for running schools and effectively promoted the growth of nongovernmental education.

However, there were inconsistencies in the provisions of the various laws and regulations under the old institutional framework. Consequently, when private schools tried to register themselves as legal entities with the Ministry of Civil Affairs, the vast majority were required to do so in accordance with the administrative regulations promulgated by the State Council in 1998, namely, the *Provisional Regulations on the Registration and Management of Private Non-Enterprise Units*. As their status was that of a "private non-enterprise unit (legal entity),"[2] which belonged to the nonprofit category, the distribution of surpluses from school operations was not permitted. This situation is clearly inconsistent with the actual development of nongovernmental education in China, which was characterized by the investment in the operating of schools for returns. In practice, this inconsistency significantly hampered the healthy development of nongovernmental education. As the attributes of a legal entity were unclear, actual nonprofit private schools (NPPS) could not benefit from the legal preferential policies, while for-profit private schools (FPPS) were unable to operate autonomously based on the market mechanism.

---

1 This administrative regulation was revoked when the *Law of the PRC to Promote Non-Governmental Education* was promulgated on December 28, 2002.
2 According to the *Provisional Regulations on the Registration and Management of Private Non-Enterprise Units* issued by the State Council of the PRC in 1998, "a private non-enterprise unit is organized by an enterprise, institution, social organization, other social forces, or individual citizens using non-state assets and is engaged in non-profit social service activities."

This also caused the property rights system and reward mechanism to be incomplete or inadequate, thereby restricting the conversion of social resources into educational resources (Dong, 2019).

To address these bottlenecks and restrictions, in December 2015, the Standing Committee of the NPC reviewed and approved amendments to the *Law of the PRC on Education* and *Law of the PRC on Higher Education*, effectively removing all prohibitive provisions imposed on the operation of FPPS. In November 2016, the Standing Committee of the NPC passed the *Decision to Revise the Law of the PRC on the Promotion of Non-Governmental Education* (hereinafter the *New Law on Non-Governmental Education*). This further clarified the standards for categorizing NPPS and FPPS, as well as the policy system applicable to each category.

The State Council later issued *Opinions on Encouraging Social Forces to Set Up Schools and Promoting the Healthy Development of Non-Governmental Education* (hereinafter the *State Council's 30 Articles*) to further promote the reform of managing private schools by category. The Ministry of Education and other relevant departments also jointly promulgated *Regulations on the Registration of Private Schools by Categories and Regulations on the Supervision and Management of FPPS* (hereinafter the *Two State Regulations*). Subsequently, the various provincial people's governments successively introduced local support systems in accordance with the state's authorization and requirements. This facilitated the implementation of upper-level regulations, refinement of related policies, as well as further promotion of reform and development in nongovernmental education at the regional level.

The main characteristics of China's new policies on nongovernmental education

With the introduction and implementation of the aforementioned laws and policies on nongovernmental education, the macroscopic governance system of China's nongovernmental education sector officially entered a new era of registration, support, and regulation by category. China's current macroscopic policies on nongovernmental education present new departures and characteristics.

Emphasizing education provision as a public interest and comprehensively strengthening private school leadership

From the relevant laws and policies—including the *New Law on Non-Governmental Education*,

State Council's 30 Articles, and *Two State Regulations*—to various provincial supporting documents, the state has consistently emphasized that nongovernmental education is a socialist undertaking with Chinese characteristics in service of the public interest. Regardless of whether it is provided by the state, education must serve to educate and cultivate the population, with social benefits the primary consideration. Educational institutions must fully implement the CPC's educational policies and adhere to socialist approaches to their operation. They must also accept moral education and the cultivation of people as their fundamental task and be committed to grooming the builders and successors of socialism through their all-round development in morality, intelligence, physique, aesthetics, and labor skills.

In order to ensure that nongovernmental education continues to cater to public interests and that the approach to school operations is correct, the relevant documents emphasize that party building should be a major focus of private schools. Party leadership must be upheld and strengthened to ensure that private schools operate and educate people according to the party's requirements, and that the core values of socialism are practiced throughout the entire school education process. This was determined by the fundamental characteristics of a socialist system with Chinese characteristics. It is also a concrete manifestation of the political superiority of socialism with Chinese characteristics in regard to the control of nongovernmental education.

Managing negative lists and broadening the means by which social forces participate in operating schools

The state introduced several policies and directives to encourage the participation of social forces in the operation of schools. First, the *New Law on Non-Governmental Education* forbid the setting up of FPPS for the provision of compulsory education. Additionally, schools and other educational institutions established with financial funding and donated assets (including if these resources were involved in the setting up process) cannot be registered as for-profit organizations. However, organizers can independently decide whether their private schools are NPPS or FPPS. Second, the *State Council's 30 Articles* relaxed the criteria for the operation of schools by social forces, who were encouraged to enter the educational field to operate schools or invest in related construction projects through donations, capital contributions, investments, cooperation, and other methods. Third, financial institutions were encouraged to provide diversified financial services and pledge loans for the establishment of private schools. Fourth, the public-private partnership model was promoted to encourage the directing of social capital toward the construction, operation, and management of educational infrastructure, as well as the provision of professional services. Finally, government-run and private schools were encouraged to purchase services from one another and even explore establishing vocational colleges and schools with mixed ownership (Dong, 2017).

Implementing preferential policies for private schools through categories based on the principle of being fair but different

The new laws and policies provided better policy support for NPPS in a number of aspects, including tax collection, use of campus land, and financial assistance. Meanwhile, many of the policies and regulations applicable to FPPS meet market characteristics (Dong, 2018a). These were manifested in the following ways:

i. Corresponding tax deductions were given for charitable donations to education by corporations and individuals, while enterprises operating NPPS were exempted from income tax according to the regulations. Additionally, government-run and private schools were charged similar rates for electricity, water, gas, and heating.

ii. Land for the setting up NPPS and FPPS was supplied by means of allocation and according to the corresponding state policies, respectively.

iii. FPPS were exempted from fee control by the state, while NPPS could gradually implement market-adjusted fees through pilot points for market-oriented reform.

iv. Governments at all levels were instructed to support the development of private schools by adopting various measures, including the purchasing of services, provision of student loans and scholarships, as well as the leasing or transfer of unused state-owned assets. They were also directed to support NPPS by providing government subsidies and incentives for raising funds and donations.

Supporting the development of private schools with the goal of improving education quality

The state also introduced policy measures intended to guide and support the development of private schools and their essential properties as part of a broader objective of improving education quality. These policy measures included the following three aspects.

First, guidance was provided so that all types of private schools could position themselves correctly. Schools were encouraged to run inclusive private kindergartens, as well as support the high-quality development and operation of elementary and middle schools based on their respective characteristics. Vocational colleges were directed to promote further integration between production and teaching, as well as cooperation between schools and enterprises. The state also emphasized the need for private sector support for training and education in order to play an active role in the building of a learning society.

Second, private schools were urged to strengthen their teaching teams. This task was incorporated into the overall plan to establish the faculty of private schools, which were encouraged to set up supplementary endowment insurance for working faculty and staff, as well as improve the treatment of retired faculty and staff. Private schools were also allowed to independently recruit and hire teachers and other staff, as well as assess their teachers' professional and technical duties.

Third, private schools were given the authority to operate independently. Private colleges and vocational schools could establish their own specializations and courses, and select teaching materials. Private high schools and schools under the compulsory education program could also set up special courses and implement innovation in education and teaching. Finally, private schools could independently determine the scope, standards, and methods of enrollment providing they were within the schools' approved scale of operations.

Standardizing private schools' operating practices in order to promote healthy and orderly development

The state has also sought to standardize the operating practices of private schools in an effort to promote stable development. The *New Law on Non-Governmental Education* and related new policies have imposed strict regulations on the operating practices of private schools. First, the state sought to improve the corporate governance system of private schools with a focus on perfecting the charter. In addition to improving the decision-making mechanisms, the state encouraged the development of supervision mechanisms to ensure that school principals could independently exercise the right to manage their schools in accordance with the law. However, the law stipulates that family members and relatives of a school principal cannot be appointed to the school's key management positions.

Second, the state has encouraged the refinement of asset management and financial accounting systems. Legal property rights were granted to private schools in accordance with the law. The state has also directed that school fees are to be primarily used for education and teaching activities, improving the school's operating conditions, as well as ensuring the proper treatment of faculty and staff. Moreover, school operating funds cannot be transferred to other fund accounts except for those belonging to the school.

Third, the state has sought to improve the risk warning and intervention mechanism. This includes the establishment of a system for the public display of information and documenting cases involving a breach of faith so that illegally operated schools, their organizers, and the individuals responsible can be duly blacklisted. Additionally, a comprehensive supervision mechanism linking multiple departments is being developed to enhance the ability to investigate and take action against illegally operated schools.

In addition to the aforementioned legal and policy provisions, the General Office of the State Council of the PRC printed and distributed *Opinions on Regulating the Development of After-school Training Organizations* in August 2018. In doing so, the state sought to reiterate that the defining attribute of education is that it serves the public interest, as well as enhance the stability of school operations. Related proposals include promoting a long-term mechanism for developing social training institutions catering to elementary and middle schools, exploring the establishment of negative lists and a joint supervision mechanism, and effectively addressing the issues posed by extracurricular burdens on elementary and middle school students.

In November 2018, the State Council of the PRC and the Central Committee of the CPC jointly issue *Several Opinions on Further Reforming the Development of Regulations for Preschool Education*. This document reflects several concerns, including the need to implement the management of private preschools by category within a stipulated deadline, curb excessive profit-seeking behaviors, manage preschools operating without license by category, and regulate the development of private preschools.

Moreover, *Regulations on Implementing the Law to Promote Non-Governmental Education*—which is currently being revised—was intended to introduce new provisions to specifically deal with several emergent issues. These include the control of domestic compulsory education by foreign capital under disguise, public schools participating in the operation of private schools, the implementation of enterprise-based school operations by multiple agents, as well as related transactional behaviors by various parties.

Predicting the impact of the new nongovernmental education policies on the development of industries

Looking ahead to 2035 or even 2050, several actions must be taken to ensure the successful realization of the ambitious goals envisioned in the policy document, *Chinese Education Modernization 2035*. These include increasing investments in fiscal education, accelerating the popularization of quality education at all levels and in all types, furthering the comprehensive reform of the school system, as well as encouraging and attracting more social forces to participate in operating schools (Dong, 2018b). The introduction and implementation of new laws and policies on nongovernmental education is predicted to have an extensive and far-reaching impact on the future development of such education in China. This section discusses these potential outcomes in greater detail.

The rapid development of NPPS due to government support

Various analyses have shown that further reform in the management of NPPS and FPPS by category can facilitate their development, particularly under the policy guidance of prioritizing the development of NPPS. Even faster development will be achieved once the various preferential policies—including government subsidies, purchasing of services by government, student loans, and incentives for raising funds and donations—are fully implemented. With the strong promotion of the new policies, all types of NPPS will be better equipped to realize their respective positioning and complementary developments.

In reality, a batch of private colleges—including West Lake University, Jilin International Studies University, Shanghai Sanda University, and Zhejiang Shuren University—have rapidly risen to prominence as a result of the support of their respective local governments. Founded through society's donations or contributors that did not seek returns, these colleges are the examples and benchmarks leading the development of China's nonprofit private colleges into the new era. With the continuous improvement of the legal system and regulations for nongovernmental education, any attempt to profit under the guise of being nonprofit will be subject to increasingly stringent regulations and face greater legal risks.

FPPS may face polarization in a fiercely competitive market environment

According to the relevant revised education laws, there is no longer any legal barrier to the provision of for-profit education in China beyond the compulsory education stage. Theoretically, and based on the premise of upholding the attribute of education provision as in the public's interest, FPPS can levy their own fees according to the law, have greater operational autonomy, and be able to operate flexibly and independently in order to achieve diversified investments and development with their own characteristics. However, given the fact that NPPS have received significantly more policy support, the government clearly has not prioritized the development of FPPS.

This lack of prioritization is compounded by the fact that FPPS are required to pay taxes in accordance with regulations and encounter fierce market competition. In the course of development, FPPS are likely to face further unfavorable circumstances, including higher operating costs, lower public recognition, and greater operational risks. Both theory and practice show that only those FPPS with strong characteristics, comparative advantages, and the ability to accurately meet the needs of the market (customers) will survive and develop. Meanwhile, homogenized for-profit educational institutions that are of low quality with high operating costs will eventually be eliminated from the market. In the short term, no breakthrough is expected for the development of FPPS in China due to various degrees of conceptual discrimination and institutional exclusion.

Heavy burden of categorizing and transferring existing stock of schools due to various historical and realistic constraints

Under the new laws and policies, each private school is granted a transition period (usually 3 to 5 years) by the local government, after which they must decide whether to categorize themselves as FPPS or NPPS. While the future development of nongovernmental education in China will not and cannot permit a "third path,"[1] this state of affairs will prove a very thorny situation for local governments and the organizers of existing schools. First, there are currently

---

1 Pan et al. (2012) have proposed a third path for the development of private colleges. The first and second paths refer to those private colleges established through donations and for-profit private colleges, respectively. The third path refers to private colleges established: (i) through investments, but for which returns are not expected; or (ii) with reasonable returns expected, but which remain nonprofit.

more than 180,000 private schools, and implementing management by category will be an extremely huge undertaking. Indeed, this will involve a series of complicated tasks—including financial settlement, confirmation of rights over assets, tax payment, constitutional amendments, and changes of legal entities—which cannot possibly be completed over a short period of time.

To assuage the concerns of private school organizers, local governments must adopt a standardized approach in accordance with the state's requirements, simplify the categorization and transfer process as much as possible, reduce related regulation fees, and lower various institutional transaction costs. At the same time, policy administration must be done according to the law, with private schools of different legal statuses treated fairly. There must also be full implementation of the various preferential policies under the law, as well as efforts to improve positive expectations for social forces to operate schools. It is only through such measures that the reform of managing private schools by category can be successfully implemented, realizing the sound and rapid development of nongovernmental education in China.

References

Dong, S. (2017, January 25). Learning and using the "new policies" to promote reform and development of nongovernmental education [in Chinese]. *People's Political Consultative Daily* (10th ed.).

Dong, S. (2018a). Mission and responsibilities of private schools under the new laws and policies, and the coping strategies [in Chinese]. *Journal of National Academy of Education Administration*, 249(9), 36–42.

Dong, S. (2018b). Promising future for nongovernmental education with the modernization of education [in Chinese]. *China Education Daily*, 2018b-4-2, 12.

Dong, S. (2019). Encouraging and supporting the development of for-profit private schools according to the law [in Chinese]. *Exploring Education Development*, 39(9), 3.

Ministry of Education of the People's Republic of China. (2019). *Understanding the state's basic situation in education development in 2018 through numbers* [in Chinese]. http://www.moe.gov.cn/fbh/live/2019/50340/mtbd/201902/t20190227_371426.html

NPC Homepage. (2002). *Law of the PRC to promote nongovernmental education* (passed at the 31st Meeting of the Standing Committee of the 9th NPC on December 28) [in Chinese]. http://www.npc.gov.cn/wxzl/wxzl/2002-12/30/content_304804.htm

Pan, M., Wu, D., & Bie, D. (2012). A third path for developing private higher education in China [in Chinese]. *Journal of Higher Education*, 33(4), 1–8.

State Council of the PRC. (1997). *Regulations on schools operated by social forces* (Order No. 226 dated July 31) [in Chinese]. http://www.people.com.cn/zgrdxw/faguiku/jy/F44-1010.html

This article will be helpful for learning and understanding the current background, stage, and future path of China's education informatization. On April 18, 2018, *Education Informatization 2.0 Action Plan*, the latest education informatization policy blueprint in China, was promulgated by the Ministry of Education. According to the study, this new Chinese education informatization policy was driven by three factors and the framework for action can be summarized as "One Goal, Three Tasks, and Eight Actions." The main features and future vision of the education informatization 2.0 are also expounded by the article.

Education Informatization 2.0 in China: Motivation, Framework, and Vision [1]

Shouxuan Yan and Yun Yang

Released on April 18, 2018, the *Education Informatization 2.0 Action Plan* proposed clearly that "the education informatization has entered the 2.0 era from the 1.0 era," marking that China's education informatization has entered a new historical stage. The education informatization 2.0 in China is believed to need to take the road of innovation-driven development and "to improve the development level of education informatization comprehensively, resulting in China's education informatization entering the advanced ranks in the world, promoting education modernization comprehensively through education informatization, and starting the new journey of education in intelligent era" (Du, 2018a). During the period of 12th Five-Year Plan, China has completed the education informatization 1.0 based on application-driven development. Breakthrough progress had been made in various tasks, including the basic universalization of conditions for informatization, the initial sharing of quality educational resources, the significant improvement of teachers' application ability, and the increasingly prominent role of technology in education. At present, China has entered education informatization 2.0 era originated from innovation-driven development, which is no longer limited to the supporting role of information

---

1 This article was funded by the General Project of the National Social Science Foundation (Pedagogy) in 2016 "Research on Countermeasures for Undergraduate Teaching Development Oriented to Innovation" (No. BIA160123). It was published on *ECNU Review of Education*, 4(2), 410–428.

technology in the education system. The role of information technology needs to be shifted from exogenous variables to endogenous variables. The rapid development of artificial intelligence, 5G network, and big data profoundly changes the demands for talents, which promotes the talents cultivation, education services, and education governance in the education informatization 2.0 era in China.

Motivation of the education informatization 2.0 in China

The education informatization 2.0 in China is the achievement of China's education informatization development in the past 40 years. It is the urgent requirements of China's education modernization strategy. Moreover, it is also the response to the education revolution in artificial intelligence era.

The promotion of the education informatization 1.0 in China

During early stages of reform and opening-up, China has formally taken the initial step in building educational informatization. At the national conference on education in April 1978, Deng Xiaoping pointed out:

> measure should be formulated to accelerate the development of modern educational means such as television and radio, which is the essential approach to develop education by the principle of achieving greater, faster, better and more economical results, and must be given full attention. (Deng, 2001, p. 108)

The combination of modern educational technology and education first appeared in China in the form of "audio-visual education." "Audio-visual education" is "the precursor of education informatization in the new stage of reform and opening-up" (Ministry of Education of the People's Republic of China [MOE], 2012a). In the following 30 years, China's education informatization has achieved remarkable achievements. They include:

> the initial formation of a nationwide education information infrastructure system, the construction and connection of campus networks in the schools of all levels and types in cities and economically developed areas, the continuous enrichment of digital educational resources, the effective expansion of information teaching, the initial improvement of education informatization management, and the steady development of online distance education. (MOE, 2012b)

These achievements show that the level of education informatization in China has been greatly improved. They have played a crucial role in promoting educational fairness, realizing the sharing of quality educational resources, building a learning society, and cultivating innovative talents with international competitiveness.

On the basis of the well-round development of China's education informatization in the past 30 years, the *Ten-Year Plan for Education Informatization (2011 – 2020)* was issued by the Ministry of Education of China in 2012. It established a "two-step" strategy for the development of China's education informatization. The first step involves focusing on construction and application. The second step entails achieving integration and innovation. By 2017, the first step had been completed, which means the goal of China's education informatization 1.0 has been accomplished. The education informatization 1.0 has achieved "Five Major Advances" and "Three Major Breakthroughs." Specifically, "Five Major Advances" include the construction and application of "three links and two platforms," the significant improvement of teachers' application ability of information technology, the substantial improvement in the level of information technology, the great promotion of informatization to education reform, and the significantly enhanced international influence of education informatization. "Three Major Breakthroughs" involve achieving the application mode of educational informatization, the promotion mechanism of social participation, and the exploration of education informatization with Chinese characteristics (Du, 2017a). After the first step is completed, the second step begins. Thereby China has successfully entered the education informatization 2.0 phase, which places significant emphasis on integration and innovation.

The requirement of education modernization toward 2035

The realization of the education informatization 1.0 in China is enough to prove that China has made remarkable achievements in the development of the Internet and informatization. The network has entered thousands of households. The number of netizens is the largest in the world. China has become a major network country in the world. However, it must be admitted that, at present, China is still relatively backward in independent innovation of core technologies, resulting in a large gap with the international advanced level, thus is still difficult to be called a powerful network country. Information technology determines the level of informatization. The low level of informatization not only limits the country's soft power and competitiveness but also hinders the construction of socialist modernization. China proposed early in its constitution that "the fundamental task of China is to concentrate on building socialist modernization" (National People's Congress, 1954). In different historical periods, socialist modernization has diverse connotations. In the 21st century, with the rapid development of information technology, China's socialist modernization involves improving the innovation ability of core technology, providing excellent information technology facilities and services, creating healthy, civilized, and safe network culture, fostering a team of professional and innovative teachers, and building a nation with powerful network. "There is no modernization without informatization" (Xi, 2014). Therefore, informatization is an indispensable way to modernization.

In February of 2019, the central government of China issued *China's Education Modernization 2035*. The eighth strategic task, "accelerating education reform in the information age," pointed out the development direction of education informatization in 2035 from a policy perspective. The reform includes upgrading the level of campus intelligence, exploring new teaching forms, innovating educational service format, and promoting education governance. This means that to achieve the changes in the four aspects in the new era, the education modernization toward 2035 requires higher level education informatization. Specifically, the education modernization toward 2035 requires China's education informatization 2.0. In China's education informatization 1.0 era,

> the main indicators of China's education informatization have doubled. The Internet access rate in primary and secondary schools nationwide has increased from 25% to 90%, the proportion of multimedia classrooms has increased from less than 40% to 83%, and the number of online learning space for teachers and students has soared from 600,000 to more than 63 million. (Du, 2017b)

Although China's education informatization has developed rapidly and achieved remarkable results, on the whole, information technology mainly remains simple application at the tool level. The revolutionary impact of information technology on education modernization has not been fully demonstrated. The low level of education informatization is difficult to realize the education modernization toward 2035. In the next 15 years, the education information 2.0 in China will definitely become a new national initiative to achieve the education modernization toward 2035. "We must attribute priority to education, speed its modernization, and develop education that people are satisfied with" (Yuan, 2018, p. 33). As a vital content of prioritizing education development in China, the education informatization 2.0 is an inevitable requirement of the education modernization toward 2035.

The response to Wisdom Education

"Wisdom Education" is no longer a new concept. In the 1990s, Xuesen Qian put forward "*Dacheng* Wisdom (Theory of Metasynthetic Wisdom)." According to Qian, human intelligence is the unity of quantitative intelligence and qualitative intelligence, and the talents cultivation with intelligence and innovative ability is the hot topic and important task of education in the world today (Qian, 2012, p. 23). It is actually a kind of knowledge that integrates intelligence into education to cultivate talents, which can be considered as a philosophical concept of "Wisdom Education." From the perspective of educational technology, intelligent education is a new form of education based on the deep integration of modern information technology and education. This kind of integration has improved the efficiency and intelligence of traditional education, thereby giving birth to a new form of education informatization that promotes individualized teaching and learning. "Information technology means helping to realize the intellectualization, informatization and individuation of classroom teaching, to build a classroom teaching environment with wisdom, and to promote the transformation from traditional knowledge classroom to modern wisdom classroom" (Chen & Li, 2020, p. 106). In the past, due to the slow development of information technology, it is mainly used as a tool in the field of education, playing a role of "icing on the cake" not yet a revolutionary impact on education. Therefore, "Wisdom Education" is only a kind of expectation within this context, the pursuit of education for wisdom in an intelligent way is just a vision, and the embedding of information technology has not really promoted the internal unity of educational purpose and educational method.

With the rapid development of big data and artificial intelligence, "Wisdom Education" becomes a reality. Du Zhanyuan, Vice Minister of Education believes that "artificial intelligence will accelerate the profound changes in education in the future" (Du, 2018b). To seize the great strategic opportunity of artificial intelligence that involves building China into an innovative country and a powerful country in science and technology in the world, in 2017, the State Council issued the *Development Plan for New Generation of Artificial Intelligence*, which marked "the development of artificial intelligence has entered a new stage." Big data-driven knowledge learning is characterized by deep learning. Human-computer cooperation is conducive to enhancing intelligence. Teachers with wisdom can effectively promote the wisdom development of students. "Wisdom Education" based on deep integration of big data, artificial intelligence, and education has emerged. In January of 2019, the Ministry of Education launched the construction project of "Wisdom Education Demonstration Zone," which opened the practice exploration of the new form of "Wisdom Education" (Wang et al., 2019, p. 27). "Wisdom Education" once considered to be far away has come and thrives on China's land. "Wisdom Education" urgently needs education informatization 2.0 in China. The education informatization 2.0 in China is the response to the emergence of "Wisdom Education" in the new era. Through the embedding of modern information technology, the pursuit of wisdom in intelligent way has become the motivation of the education informatization 2.0 in China.

Framework for action and its characteristics of the education informatization 2.0 in China

To speed up the education modernization, promote the development of education informatization in the new era, and foster a new engine of innovation-driven development, in 2018, the Ministry of Education issued the *Education Informatization 2.0 Action Plan* in combination with the tasks related to the major strategies of national "internet+," big data, and the new generation of artificial intelligence. It thus proposed the framework for action, thereby resulting in China entering the education informatization 2.0 era.

Framework for action

A goal and its essence. The *Education Informatization 2.0 Action Plan* proclaiming an objective to basically achieve that, by 2022, teaching application covers all teachers, learning application covers all school-age students, digital campus construction covers all schools, the application level of informatization and the information literacy of teachers and students are generally improved, and the platform of "internet+education" will be built up (MOE, 2018).

Compared with the education informatization 1.0 in China, the goal of the education informatization 2.0 in China has essential differences. The goal of the education informatization 1.0 in China emphasizes that each school's accesses to the broadband network, each class's accesses to quality resource, each person's accesses to network learning space, and the public service platforms of education resource and management are constructed and applied. However,

In the 2.0 phase, education informatization needs to exceed the 'application drive' of the 1.0 phase and devote itself to 'innovation guidance.' That is, information technology supports the innovation of teaching and learning methods to lead the transformation and upgrading of educational production methods in the information age. (Yang et al., 2018, p. 18)

The goal of the education informatization 2.0 in China has transcended the goal of the education informatization 1.0 in China. The essence of transcendence is the transformation from a focus on "things" to caring for "human," from a focus on quantitative expansion to emphasizing on quality improvement, and from connectivity rate to efficiency.

Three major tasks and the connotation. Three major tasks are outlined by the *Education Informatization 2.0 Action Plan*, including continuously advancing "three links and two platforms," further promoting the deep integration of information technology and education, and building an integrated platform of "Internet + Education."

It is worth noting that the three major tasks have special connotation. The education informatization 2.0 in China is the inheritance and development of the education informatization 1.0 in China. The initial intention of education informatization to serve the reform of education is the same, but the education informatization 2.0 in China upholds the core concept of deep integration of information technology and education.

At present, the Internet access rate of primary and secondary schools in China has reached 93%. The proportion of multimedia classrooms has also reached 86%. The number of online learning spaces for teachers and students is 71 million. For a country hosting the largest education in the world, such achievements should be acknowledged. However, when entering the 2.0 phase, we may not be able to evaluate education informatization with such a 1.0 perspective. (Ren, 2018b, p. 3)

Important as it is to continue to strengthen the construction and application of "three links and two platforms," the concept of innovation-driven development is followed fundamentally by the education informatization 2.0 in China. From the perspective of education informatization promoting education modernization, the education informatization 2.0 in China seeks to realize the transformation from application-driven development to innovation-driven development and from exogenous variables to endogenous variables.

Eight actions and the levels. The *Education Informatization 2.0 Action Plan* propounds eight actions including the universalization of digital resources services, the coverage of network learning space, the storming of network fostering wisdom, the optimization of educational governance capability, the guidance of hundreds of districts, thousands of schools, and millions of courses, the standardized construction of digital campus, the innovative development of "Wisdom Education," and the comprehensive improvement of information literacy.

As a whole, "eight actions" can be divided into three levels of "guaranteeing bottom line, well-round development and guidance innovation" (Wu et al., 2018, p. 33) (see Figure 1).

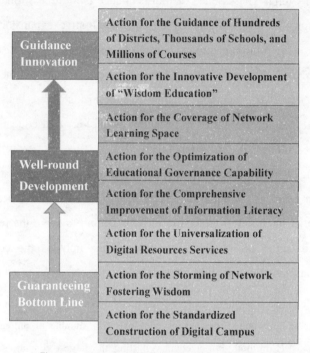

Figure 1. Three-level distribution of eight actions.

Specifically, first, the action for the universalization of digital resources services is intended to build a national public service system for educational resources, to connect the national hub, the national public service platform for educational resources and 32 provincial systems, and to fully form the mechanism for the development and utilization of educational resources. The action for the storming of network fostering wisdom aims to strongly support the development of educational informatization in deep poverty-stricken areas with the focus on "three regions and three states," to promote educational equity, and to effectively improve educational quality. The action for standardized construction of digital campus aims at exploring effective ways to achieve Internet access in remote schools through broadband satellites and to expand the coverage of quality educational resources by means of informatization means in the pilot.

Based on the practical case analysis of 71 pilot schools of wisdom schools in Guangzhou, at present, the innovative application of wisdom campus is mainly reflected in five aspects: creating ecological environment, reconstructing digital resources, integrating innovative teaching, reshaping the teaching team, and innovating governance services. (Xie et al., 2019, p. 66)

The "three actions" are all for "guaranteeing the bottom line."

Second, the action for the coverage of network learning space is meant to standardize the construction and application of network learning space, to ensure that all teachers and school-age students "have space for all," and to popularize the application of network learning space. The action for the optimization of educational governance capability aims at improving the top-level design of educational management and comprehensively improving the ability of educational management, decision, and public services with big data. The action for the comprehensive improvement of information literacy is designed to fully understand the important role of promoting information literacy in the implementation of the moral cultivation and innovative talents cultivation and to establish an evaluation index system of information literacy. The "three actions" place significant emphasis on "all-round development."

Third, the action for the guidance of hundreds of districts, thousands of schools, and millions of courses aims at identifying hundreds of typical regions, thousands of benchmark schools, and millions of demonstration courses, thus gathering excellent cases and promoting typical experience. The action for the innovative development of "Wisdom Education" seeks to actively carry out innovative research and demonstration of "Wisdom Education" based on the emerging technologies such as artificial intelligence and big data, to further promote the ecological reconstruction of education. Thus, the "two actions" further emphasize "guidance innovation."

Main features

Originating from innovation-driven development rather than technology-driven development. What problem will be brought about by the rapid development of artificial intelligence is the theme faced by the education informatization 2.0 in China. People generally pay attention to such problems: Will artificial intelligence bring about the second machine revolution or the fourth industrial revolution? Will artificial intelligence replace teachers? What impact does artificial intelligence have on learning mode? The key to answering these questions lies in how to view information technology, which determines the relationship between technology and education.

Can information technology solve all the problems facing mankind? Some scientists have proposed the "singularity" hypothesis brought about by science and technology. They believe that all the problems faced by human beings can be solved by the utilization of ever-increasing intelligent computing power (Kurzweil, 2011, p. 96). However, there is one thing that cannot be denied. Technology cannot be free from defects. The defect of technology lies in that it cannot have the self-consciousness, reflective ability, emotion, creativity, critical thinking, and creative thinking as human beings. Thereby it is impossible to solve all related problems. Technology is not everything. Its imperfection will be made up by the way of human beings using and thinking technology. The essence of artificial intelligence technology should not be regarded as an external tool applied to education but rather to be regarded as an internal concept that guides artificial intelligence technology to reconstruct educational ecology based on human self-consciousness, reflective ability, emotion, creativity, critical thinking, creative thinking, and so on.

The education informatization 2.0 in China is driven by innovative ideas to further coordinate the relationship between artificial intelligence technology and education. Compared with the education informatization 1.0 in China, the education informatization 2.0 in China is obviously not an upgrade of technology, but an upgrade of concept. The fundamental reason is that the revolution in science and technology has triggered profound reforms in politics, economy, and culture. This kind of change has created new requirements for talents cultivation, which can be fulfilled only when the development of education is driven by innovation instead of technology application. "Innovation-driven" has special connotation. It means "reconstructing the concept, theory, mechanism and system of education informatization, innovating the way of education informatization supporting educational reform, and cultivating innovative and creative talents" (Chen et al., 2018, p. 18). The education informatization 1.0 in China is mainly committed to the construction of information technology infrastructure and environment, as well as the normal application of information technology in education and teaching, which is determined by the national conditions that informatization is at the primary level. In the new era, it is the national strategic deployment to build a nation with strong network and powerful education. The education informatization 2.0 in China shoulders the new mission of the new era.

It completely gets rid of the developing idea based on technology application, takes the education innovation as the starting point and end result, effectively demonstrates the power of technology in education reform, and continuously creates a new form of education in the future through the innovative application of information technology. (Yang et al., 2018, p. 17)

Committing to the expansion of digital educational resources rather than the digital presentation of textbooks. Educational resources are the essential elements of education, which determine the form of education. For a long time, educational resources based on paper textbooks have shaped modern schools and modern education. Entering the 21st century, information technology has penetrated into all aspects of economic development and social life. Profound changes are occurring in educational methods. For example, the emergence of digital educational resources represented by network resources has made education for all, quality education, personalized learning, and lifelong learning the crucial features of education information. In China's education informatization 1.0 era, the digital education resources mainly focused on paper textbooks. Thereby the offline education resources are presented online in digital form through information technology, showing strong dependence and specificity. It inevitably brings about the problem that classrooms and textbooks are moved online, which severely limits the broad space that digital education resources can exert.

In China's education informatization 2.0 era, the connotation and function of digital educational resources have undergone tremendous changes that involve shifting from dependence and specificity to openness and universality, which provide infinite possibilities for the reconstruction of the information education. First of all, the openness of digital educational resources break through the limitations of textbooks, giving new meaning to digital educational resources. Secondly, digital educational resources provide advantages for breaking the isolation of disciplines. When the function of digital educational resources is regarded as the digital presentation of textbooks, it only means the change of the carrier form of educational content. However, when the openness and universality of digital educational resources are emphasized, there are new opportunities to disintegrate the separation of knowledge among various disciplines. Finally, when students study online, they will generate a lot of behavioral data that can reflect learning progress and thinking characteristics.

Aiming at improving teachers' and students' information literacy rather than the applied skills of information technology. The education informatization 1.0 in China emphasizes how information technology is applied to education to realize the initial combination of information technology and education. The requirement for teachers is to pay attention to the operational skills of information technology in the teaching process, aiming at urging teachers to skillfully apply information technology to education. With the rapid development of 5G network and artificial intelligence, we are entering a highly developed information society. In this society, it is a great challenge for people to become qualified digital citizens only by mastering the application skills of information technology. The education informatization 2.0 in China is in such a highly developed information society. The requirements for teachers have shifted from the application of information technology to teaching innovation based on information technology, enabling teachers to realize the transformation from the application skills to the information literacy. Information literacy is the essential key competency for teachers in the intelligent era, which includes computational thinking, programming ability, and the corresponding "moral literacy, emotional literacy, innovative literacy based on critical thinking, philosophy and aesthetic literacy" (Xiang, 2018, p. 79). The computational thinking is an increasingly important key competency in the future. In the newly revised *Information Technology Curriculum Standard for Ordinary Senior High Schools (2017 Edition)*, the "information awareness," "computational thinking," "digital learning and innovation," and "information society responsibility" are taken as the core competencies in senior high school (Li et al., 2017, p. 28).

The education informatization 2.0 in China not only requires "significant improvement of teachers' information literacy" but also emphasizes "strengthening the cultivation of students' information literacy" (MOE, 2018). The cultivation of students' information literacy is not simply to impart information technology knowledge but rather to emphasize improving digital competence. The cultivation of digital competence cannot ignore students' critical consciousness and reflective ability. They are the important guarantee for students to have digital competence. Critical thinking is helpful for students to analyze and judge network information, thus to identify and screen complicated information according to correct value. Reflective ability enables students to understand the subjective responsibility and communicative ethics they should bear when studying in the virtual world. The education informatization 2.0 pays attention to cultivating students' essential character of using information technology in a reasonable and legal way, which involves understanding and respecting intellectual property rights, abiding by network ethics, protecting personal privacy, and maintaining network security (Yang et al., 2016, p. 10). In a highly developed information society, the bottom-line character is the vital guarantee for students to become qualified digital citizens.

Vision of the education informatization 2.0 in china

The *Education Informatization 2.0 Action Plan* clearly identifies three requirements for striving to construct new mode of talents cultivation under the condition of "Internet+," developing new mode of education service based on the Internet, and exploring new mode of education governance in the information age so as to achieve its goal (MOE, 2018). The education informatization 2.0 in China insists on innovating talents cultivation mode, education service mode, and education governance mode, which become the vision in the future. Richard Mayer believes that "whenever a new technology is introduced into educational practice, great expectations are often placed" (Mayer, 2014, p. 89). What matters is that "the fundamental purpose of educational reform is to promote the all-round development of human beings, and the application of technology is to liberate human beings" (Chen, 2018, p. 6). Therefore, the vision of the education informatization 2.0 in China follows the educational concept of "people-oriented."

Striving to build new models on talents cultivation under the support of "artificial intelligence+"

The education informatization 2.0 in China is relative to the development of the education informatization over the past 40 years. The education informatization in the first 40 years focused on the construction and application of "things" (Ren, 2018a, p. 1). The *Education Informatization 2.0 Action Plan* shows its concern for "people," which involves "focusing on the new demand for talents cultivation in the new era and strengthening the talents cultivation concept of putting ability first." At present, "artificial intelligence+" provides unlimited opportunities and possibilities for the kind of talents cultivation in the new era.

Establishing "Wisdom Teaching" mode under the artificial intelligence technology. In the artificial intelligence era, "Wisdom Education" has become a hot topic. "Wisdom Education" cannot be separated from "Wisdom Teaching," which is an important teaching mode of the education informatization 2.0 in China. First of all, exploring teaching modes such as synchronous classroom, flip classroom, MOOC, online learning to enhance the innovative ability of teachers integrating information technology and teaching. Since 2019, the Science and Technology Department of MOE has set up 20 projects to support network learning space, online open courses, interdisciplinary learning (STEAM education), and intelligent education. The National Center for Educational Technology has carried out 38 teaching and research activities to promote the level of informatization in Wei County of Hebei Province, Pingyuan County of Shandong Province, Pizhou City of Jiangsu Province, and so on (Science and Technology Department of the Ministry of Education of the People's Republic of China, 2020). This has promoted the innovation of teaching mode based on information technology in the practical development. Secondly, each student's network behavior will leave traces in the system. Teachers can efficiently acquire students' learning habits, learning interests, and problems existing in the learning process according to the big data. They can thus adjust and design teaching mode to achieve personalization and synergy of "Wisdom Teaching." At present, many places in China have implemented "Wisdom Teaching." Seven schools in Xixia District of Yinchuan City, capital of Ningxia Hui Autonomous Region, including No. 10 Primary School and Zhongguancun Middle School, have carried out the national pilot work to boost the construction of teaching staff with artificial intelligence. WISROOM classroom, big data application and analysis platform, artificial intelligence laboratory, VR classroom, and other informatization teaching forms have been effectively implemented, which has played a major role in "Wisdom Teaching" (Ningxia Education TV Station, 2019).

Building learning mode supported by "artificial intelligence +." "Artificial intelligence technology can support inclusive and ubiquitous learning visits, help ensure fair and inclusive educational opportunities, promote personalized learning, and enhance learning outcomes" (Ren et al., 2019, p. 4). Personalized learning is the learning mode that conforms to human nature. Confucius, China's most famous teacher and a great educator, was the first to propose "teaching students according to their aptitudes" so that everyone can receive a matching education according to their abilities and characteristics. Artificial intelligence technology provides advantages for "teaching students according to their aptitude." China's earliest massive open online course platform "Xuetang Online" has an AI "Xiao Mu." When a learner chooses a course, "Xiao Mu" will prompt whether it is necessary to make a learning plan and make different prompts at different learning stages. After the course, it will also recommend some courses and papers for the learners according to their preferences. The distinctive feature of personalized learning mode brought by artificial intelligence is that "everyone can learn, everywhere can learn, and always can learn," which is conducive to students to establish the concept of lifelong learning, thereby to cope with changes in work, learning, and life in the artificial intelligence era. Its advantage is the accurate and fast analysis of students' online learning. Artificial intelligence technology "encourages personalized analysis of students based on big data, formulates personalized nurturing programs that meet the development needs of students, and organically combines large-scale education with personalized fostering in the form of intelligent collaboration and virtual teaching" (Sun et al., 2019, p. 4).

Constructing intelligent learning environment. Intelligent learning environment includes online and offline learning places, platforms, and environments, such as intelligent machines, intelligent classrooms, intelligent education cloud platforms, intelligent mobile terminal devices, and App services. In the artificial intelligence era, "educational robot" has attracted much attention because it will become the key point in constructing an intelligent learning environment. "Educational robot" is the representatives of robots applied in the field of education. It is the typical applications of artificial intelligence, speech recognition, and bionic technology in education. Its goal is to foster students' analytical ability, creative ability, and practical ability. It is worth noting that VR/AR technology can help build an immersive learning environment. Learning in the immersive learning environment is conducive to the development of space thinking and creativity, thereby is helpful for achieving deep learning.

Developing new education service models based on the Internet

The education informatization 2.0 in China escorts education services through the latest network and emerging technologies. First, it constructs the co-construction and shares mechanism of quality education resources based on National Network for Education to further realize education fairness. The year of 2020 is an extraordinary year. Under the new crown pneumonia epidemic situation, telecommuting and online teaching through the network have become the main working methods in a special period. CERNET, the special education network, adheres to the aim of network service education and shoulders the important mission of supporting and serving the national education system. "China has achieved breakthroughs in key technologies of IPv6, leading China's education and research network to the forefront of the world's Internet construction; CERNET has become the world's largest academic network" (Shen et al., 2020, p. 6). At present, CERNET is building the "China's Supercomputing Internet System." The next step will complete 100G network interconnection of several national high-speed supercomputing centers (Wu & Bi, 2008, p. 10). Obviously, improvement of National Network for Education will effectively escort education service. The National Network for Education can provide safe and high-speed network support for education resource service platforms at all levels. The education department can use the National Network for Education to obtain independent jurisdiction, to ensure that quality teaching resources can be accurately pushed to the "three Western regions and three Western prefectures," and to further promote the coordinated development of education in the East and West, thus promoting education fairness.

Second, it establishes the public service platform and system for educational resources by means of the cloud computing and artificial intelligence to promote personalized learning. Cloud computing technology has inherent advantages in the construction of cloud platforms. By the end of March 2020, China's public service platform for educational resources has opened 13.46 million teacher space, 6.49 million student space, 5.92 million parent space, and 410,000 school space. China's public service system for digital education resources has been connected to one provincial, one municipal, and one county-level platform, respectively. The total number of system space logins has reached 9.656 million (Science and Technology Department of the Ministry of Education of the People's Republic of China, 2020). China's public service platform and system for digital education resources have expanded their coverage to more schools, teachers, students, and parents. In recent years, artificial intelligence technology has attracted much attention. The learning environment created by the man-machine symbiotic intelligent learning system will no longer be confined to the traditional classroom but will expand the network learning space and provide students with resources and space for autonomous learning anytime and anywhere. Digital learning resources will break discipline barriers and be pushed accurately based on learners' behavior data analysis. Personalized learning based on information technology will be truly guaranteed.

Exploring new educational governance models in the information age

Educational governance is a process in which the governance subjects openly manage educational affairs with the help of external technologies. It pursues "good governance" to maximize the protection of public educational benefits (Wang, 2017, p. 46). In China's education informatization 2.0 era, 5G network, artificial intelligence, and big data have provided conditions and possibilities for innovative education governance models. First, precise education governance is to be explored. Education management platform supported by 5G and artificial intelligence will be useful to register and record students' information to provide accurate and comprehensive data. Each student's electronic portfolio supported by big data technology can continuously record the details of students' growth, which is conducive to the evaluation of students' comprehensive quality and the personalization of education governance. Intelligent solutions generated on the basis of artificial intelligence technology are conducive to the elimination of personal emotions and prejudices, thus improving the scientific decision-making in education. The Second Experimental Primary School in Dehua County, Quanzhou City, Fujian Province, has implemented intelligent management mode. Supervision and evaluation, teacher management, and student management realize intelligent management through one intelligent platform (Cheng et al., 2019). In the process of intelligent management, the principals, directors, teachers, students, and parents have realized mutual communication in time, thereby improving the coordination and accuracy of education governance between schools and families.

Second, flat education governance is to be achieved. For a long time, verticalization and stratification have been the main features of education governance. In China's education informatization 2.0 era, "artificial intelligence processing problems is integrated and cross-border, which indicates that the stratified and hierarchical model of educational governance in industrial society has not adapted to or even hindered the efficiency and effect of education governance" (Sun et al., 2019, p. 5). The main problems of hierarchical education governance are the low efficiency of governance caused by hierarchical forms and operational processes only completed by people. The greatest advantages of artificial intelligence technology are intelligence, convenience, and efficiency, which provide opportunities to weaken the hierarchical educational governance. Therefore, it is necessary to establish the artificial intelligence management system and form an education management and monitoring system covering all schools and learners. It is helpful to directly link various departments and subjects, enhance the ability of communication and cooperation at different levels, and improve the efficiency of education governance, thereby achieving flat education governance.

Third, humanized education governance is to be explored. The role of human cannot disappear in the process of education governance supported by artificial intelligence technology. The important feature of education governance supported by artificial intelligence is rationalization and de-emotionalization. In order that the role of human is not neglected, the humanization of education governance supported by artificial intelligence must be highlighted. Therefore, it is necessary to confirm the premise that artificial intelligence technology serves human beings, which should be agreed upon when formulating education governance systems and norms supported by artificial intelligence. Moreover, it is worth guarding against the leakage of information between teachers and students in the process of education governance by artificial intelligence. Education governance "should construct strict anti-theft system, monitoring system and safety guarantee system to avoid more advanced and more dangerous situations" (Sun et al., 2019, p. 5). In the process of humanized education governance, human should be the main body of education governance, while artificial intelligence is only the auxiliary of education governance. Artificial intelligence does not possess self-awareness, emotion, reflective ability and creativity, and so on. If artificial intelligence is taken as the main body of decision-making, it is inevitable to ignore humanized factors. The education governance mode with human as the main body and artificial intelligence as the auxiliary is conducive to the combination of rationality and humanity.

References

Chen, K., & Li, J. (2020). Wisdom education boosts individualized development of students [in Chinese]. *Journal of The Chinese Society of Education*, (3), 106.

Chen, L. (2018). Education informatization 2.0: Trends and directions of internet promoting education reform [in Chinese]. *Distance Education in China*, (9), 6–8.

Chen, L., Liu, X., Feng, X., & Chen, L. (2018). Transformation and upgrading of educational informatization: Motivation, characteristic direction and essential connotation [in Chinese]. *e-Education Research*, (8), 15–20.

Cheng, Z., Li, H., & Xu, H. (2019). Management communication, teacher-student interaction and home-school interconnection are easily realized on a smart platform [in Chinese]. *Fujian Daily*.

Deng, X. (2001). *Selected works of Deng Xiaoping* [in Chinese]. People's Education Press.

Du, Z. (2017a). *Breakthrough progress in China's educational informatization* [in Chinese]. http://www.chinamde.com/?p=1478

Du, Z. (2017b). *Promote the modernization of education in an all-round way with education informatization* [in Chinese]. http://edu.china.com.cn/2017-10/24/content_41782598.htm

Du, Z. (2018a). Accelerating the development of integration and innovation to make education informatization 2.0 reality [in Chinese]. *China Education News*, 4–25.

Du, Z. (2018b). *Deputy Minister of Education Du Zhanyuan: Artificial intelligence and future educational reform* [in Chinese]. http://www.360doc.com/content/18/0527/10/30898787_757374036.shtml

Kurzweil, R. (2011). *The singularity is near: When humans transcend biology* (Z. Dong & Q. Li, Trans.) [in Chinese].

Mechanical Industry Press.

Li, F., Xiong, Z., & Ren, Y. (2017). Focusing on digital competitiveness and developing students' core competency-viewing information technology education in primary and secondary schools in Shanghai from international and domestic curriculum reform [in Chinese]. *e-Education Research*, (7), 26–31.

Mayer, R. E. (2014). *The Cambridge handbook of multimedia learning*. Cambridge University Press.

Ministry of Education of the People's Republic of China. (2012a). *Seize the opportunity to accelerate and create a newsituation in education informatization work-speech by Vice Premier Liu Yandong at the National Video Conference on Education Informatization Work* [in Chinese]. http://www.ict.edu.cn/laws/jianghua/liuyandong/n20121120_4805.shtml

Ministry of Education of the People's Republic of China. (2012b). *Ten-year development plan for education informatization (2011–2020)* [in Chinese]. http://old.moe.gov.cn/publicfiles/business/htmlfiles/moe/s5892/201203/133322.html

Ministry of Education of the People's Republic of China. (2018). *Education Informatization 2.0 Action Plan* [in Chinese]. http://wwwmoe.gov.cn/srcsite/A16/s3342/201804/t20180425_334188.html

National People's Congress. (1954). *The Constitution of the People's Republic of China* [in Chinese]. http://www.npc.gov.cn/wxzl/wxzl/2000-12/26/content_4264.htm

Ningxia Education TV Station. (2019). *Artificial intelligence to build wisdom education highlands* [in Chinese]. https://www.nxnews.net/nxrbzk/jsmlxnx/201905/t20190510_6285781.html

Qian, X. (2012). Qian Xuesen's exploration of "Dacheng wisdom science"—Commemorating Qian Xuesen's centennial birthday [in Chinese]. *Studies in Science of Science*, (1), 14–27.

Ren, Y. (2018a). Entering the new era of China's education informatization—One of the interpretations of education informatization 2.0 action plan [in Chinese]. *e-Education Research*, (6), 1–2.

Ren, Y. (2018b). How should we discuss "Education Informatization 2.0" [in Chinese]. *Journal of Distance Education*, (4), 3.

Ren, Y., Wan, K., & Feng, Y. (2019). Promoting the sustainable development of artificial intelligence education-interpretation and enlightenment of UN's "artificial intelligence in education: Challenges and opportunities for sustainable development" [in Chinese]. *Modern Distance Education Research*, (5), 3–10.

Science and Technology Department of the Ministry of Education of the People's Republic of China. (2020, April 22). *March 2020 monthly report on education informatization and network security* [in Chinese]. http://www.moe.gov.cn/s78/A16/s5886/s6381/202004/t20200422_445508.html

Shen, Y., Tian, Y., & Zeng, H. (2020). Education private network: Helping China's education informatization to a new stage-interview with Professor Wu Jianping, academician of the Chinese Academy of Engineering [in Chinese]. *e-Education Research*, (3), 5–9.

Sun, L., Liu, S., & Li, M. (2019). Prospect of China's educational informatization development for 2035—Based on description of *China's Educational Modernization 2035* [in Chinese]. *China Educational Technology*, (8), 1–8.

Wang, Y. (2017). Construction and path selection of modernization of educational governance ability in big data era [in Chinese]. *e-Education Research*, (8), 44–49.

Wang, Y., Li, Y., & Li, D. (2019). Current situation, contents and countermeasures of construction of wisdom education demonstration zone [in Chinese]. *Modern Educational Technology*, (11), 26–32.

Wu, D., Xing, C., & Jiang, L. (2018). Taking the road of education informatization with Chinese characteristics—Interpretation III of *Education Informatization 2.0 Action Plan* [in Chinese]. *Shanxi e-Education*, (4), 32–34.

Wu, J., & Bi, J. (2008). Trusted next generation internet and its development [in Chinese]. *ZTE Technology Journal*, (1), 8–12.

Xi, J. (2014). *No modernization without informatization* [in Chinese]. http://it.people.com.cn/n/2014/0228/c1009 - 24495308.html

Xiang, X. (2018). How to learn to be a teacher in the age of artificial intelligence [in Chinese]. *Journal of the Chinese Society of Education*, (3), 76 - 80.

Xie, Y., Li, J., Qiu, Y., & Huang, Y. (2019). Construction and new development of wisdom campus in the era of education informatization 2.0 [in Chinese]. *China Educational Technology*, (5), 6 - 69.

Yang, H., Xu, J., & Zheng, X. (2016). Digital citizenship education in the information age [in Chinese]. *China Educational Technology*, (1), 9 - 16.

Yang, Z., Wu, D., & Zheng, X. (2018). Education informatization 2.0: Key historical transition of education in the new era of information technology transformation [in Chinese]. *Educational Research*, (4), 16 - 22.

Yuan, Z. (2018). Dual priority agenda: China's model for modernizing education. *ECNU Review of Education*, *1*(1), 5 - 33.

This article intends to introduce the recent Chinese compulsory education quality assessment. It examines the development of Chinese education quality assessment in the context of the nation's pursuit of holistic education which bore the three recent relevant reports: *The Chinese Compulsory Education Quality Monitoring Report*, *The Chinese Compulsory Education Quality Monitoring Report on Mathematical Learning*, and *The Chinese Compulsory Education Quality Monitoring Report on Physical Education and Health*. Findings and frameworks of the assessment are also clearly demonstrated by the author, with the extended discussion of the significance, limitations, and special issues of the assessment.

Education Quality Assessment in China: What We Learned From Official Reports Released in 2018 and 2019 [1]

Danqing Yin

The Chinese Compulsory Education Quality Monitoring Report was first published in July 2018 by the National Assessment Center for Education Quality in China, under the supervision of the Ministry of Education, People's Republic of China (hereinafter referred to as "Chinese MOE" or "MOE"). Two additional subject reports, *The Chinese Compulsory Education Quality Monitoring Report on Mathematical Learning* and *The Chinese Compulsory Education Quality Monitoring Report on Physical Education and Health*, were later released in 2019. These reports presented the assessment results from the 2015 – 2017 assessment cycle in a recent large-scale assessment in Chinese compulsory education.

This article aims to examine the development of Chinese education quality assessment in the context of prevailing international large-scale assessments and the nation's pursuit of holistic education. It first reviewed a brief history of the education quality monitoring work in China that bore the fruits of the above three reports. The general information of Chinese compulsory education, the guiding law, and the policy for the assessment are introduced in this section. Second, findings from the reports are presented by individual report with a comparative analysis

---

[1] This article was published on *ECNU Review of Education*, 4(2), 396 – 409.

on results of available subjects: One is mathematics, and the other is physical education and health. The framework of the assessment is also demonstrated. Finally, I discuss the significance and limitations of the compulsory education quality monitoring in China. Special attention is placed on the common issues that international large-scale assessments have shared and the unique issues of Chinese assessment.

There has not been a consistent English translation for the Chinese names of reports and assessment work. Chinese MOE translated the 2018 report as the "China Compulsory Education Quality Oversight Report" and the 2019 subject reports as the "National Assessment of Education Quality—Mathematics" and the "National Assessment of Education Quality—PE and Health" (The National Assessment Center for Education Quality, 2018, 2019a, 2019b). Some researchers referred the assessment work as the "National Assessment of Education Quality" and the subject report as the "China National Assessment of Education Quality—Physical Education & Health"; some used "education monitoring" or "educational surveillance" to represent education quality assessment (Jiang et al., 2019; Tian & Sun, 2018; Wu et al., 2019).

To speak with a larger and broader audience who come from different countries, and to indicate the stage of the education that was originally included in the names of Chinese reports, the author avoided ambiguous adjectives like the "national" and applied following names, which reflected the assessment work and content of the reports more accurately and consistently:

1. *The Chinese Compulsory Education Quality Monitoring Report*,
2. *The Chinese Compulsory Education Quality Monitoring Report on Mathematical Learning*, and
3. *The Chinese Compulsory Education Quality Monitoring Report on Physical Education and Health.*

This policy review uses education assessment and education monitoring interchangeably to identify the related work since 2015 that generated the recent reports for clarification purposes. Subject and subdisciplinary are also used interchangeably in this review.

Background of the *Chinese Compulsory Education Quality Monitoring Work*

According to China's Ministry of Education, as of 2015, China has more than 260,000 compulsory schools (covering Grade 1 through Grade 9), more than 9 million full-time teachers, and nearly 140 million students (MOE, 2015a, 2015b). Policy documents showed that the major purpose of monitoring the quality of compulsory education is to scientifically assess the overall quality of compulsory education in China, objectively unfold the basic situation of relevant factors that affect the quality of compulsory education, and systematically monitor the implementation of national curriculum standards, eventually providing reference to educational improvements. (MOE, 2015a, 2015b)

The overall assessment work related to these reports is guided by *The Compulsory Education Law of the People's Republic of China* and *The National Compulsory Education Quality Monitoring Policy*, with a view to assessing the progress of the compulsory education and improving the quality of education with effective policies. Both of these legal instruments, first initiated in 1980s and 2010s, respectively, rooted in *The Constitution of the People's Republic of China* and intended to protect the rights to receive basic education for children of school age. As *The Compulsory Education Law of the People's Republic of China* in 1986 articulated, a 9-year compulsory education should be implemented by Chinese governments at different levels (6- to 15-year-olds, Grades 1 – 9), mainly serving primary school students and middle school (also called junior high school) students.

Before officially launching the recent compulsory education quality assessment, China had already possessed a few conducive conditions for it (Jiang et al., 2019; MOE, 2015a, 2015b; Wu et al., 2019).

Regarding the leading organization, the National Assessment Center for Education Quality (hereinafter referred to as "the Center") was formally established and housed in Beijing Normal University, a public and prestigious research university located in Beijing, China, with a 118-year history so far (BNU History). Since the establishment in November 2007, the Center has been responsible for performing daily work of assessment.

Led by the Center, approximately 300 domestic experts, international scholars, special personnel of leading departments, principals of primary and secondary schools, and schoolteachers—a capable group of representatives—participated in the assessment work and supervised the assessment.

The experts developed multiple research tools for the assessment in different subject areas and disciplines. For example, paper test tools and field test tools were designed to measure the performance of six subjects including moral education, Chinese reading, mathematics, science, art, and physical education.

Furthermore, a pilot study for the quality assessment had been conducted in those six subject areas for eight consecutive years, five of which were nationwide large-scale tests with the sample from 32 Chinese provinces, municipalities, autonomous regions, and other equivalent units. In total, more than 460,000 students, 110,000 teachers, and principals from 695 sample counties (cities and districts) participated in the pilot study.

In a nutshell, a top-down administrative approach had been tested and moderated by trials and errors, with the Chinese MOE supervising the assessment, the Center organizing the assessment, the participated provinces coordinating the assessment, and counties further operating the assessment. Specific methods designed included sampling, testing, data analysis, and so forth. All of these work provided basic conditions and practical experience for the Ministry of Education to carry out a larger scale of compulsory education quality monitoring throughout China.

Findings from *The Chinese Compulsory Education Quality Monitoring Report*

The nationwide project that generated *The Chinese Compulsory Education Quality Monitoring Report* (hereinafter referred to as "the 2018 Report") officially started in 2015. Evaluations were conducted in mid-June each year from 2015 to 2017. During this first cycle of quality assessment, a total of 572,314 fourth-grade and eighth-grade students from 32 Chinese provinces, municipalities, autonomous regions, and other equivalent units have participated in the assessment, where a broad range of knowledge and skills, processes and methods, emotional attitudes and values were measured. In addition, 19,346 primary and middle school principals and 147,610 schoolteachers completed the questionnaire survey.

According to the 2018 Report, the large-scale education quality monitoring produced the following sample results.

For moral education, the questions were mostly around cultural, artistic, social, and historical achievements of the country. The result showed that a majority of Chinese students had a positive life value orientation and had a good understanding of their traditional culture. To be specific, when asked whether they are proud of being a Chinese citizen, 96.2% of fourth graders and 97.9% of eighth graders said yes. The rate that sampled students answered cultural questions accurately and correctly was relatively high, with 66.1% among fourth graders and 74.5% among eighth graders.

As for Chinese reading, mathematics, and science subjects, for which learning usually happens inside a school building and for which higher stakes are frequently attached (Popham, 1987), sampled students did well. The typical monitoring questions categorized student academic performance into four levels, which include "to be improved," "medium," "good," and "excellent." As for reading performance, the proportion of students in the fourth and eighth grades reached and above "medium" were 81.8% and 79.6%, respectively; about 21.0% fourth graders and 22.7% eighth graders reached the "excellent" level. As for mathematics performance, the proportions of students in the fourth and eighth grades reached and above "medium" were 84.6% and 78.9%, respectively; about 23.8% fourth graders and 26.7% eighth graders reached the "excellent" level. As for science, 76.8% of fourth graders and 83.6% of eighth graders achieved the "medium" or higher level; those who reached the "excellent" level in science were 16.0% for fourth graders and 12.0% for eighth graders.

As for art and music, and physical education, where learning not always happens inside a classroom and for which lower stakes are attached as most are not included in Chinese National College Entrance Examination (*Gaokao*), the assessment results left much space for students to improve.

For health, the classification from Chinese *National Student Physical Health Standard* (revised in 2014) put student weight into four scales: normal weight, low weight, overweight, and obesity. The results from the 2018 Report showed that the proportions of normal weight were 74.2% for male students and 79.2% for female students in fourth grade; 78.2% and 80.6% for male and female students, respectively, in eighth grade. As for low weight scale, the numbers for male and female students were 8.4% and 7.0% in fourth grade, 5.1% and 2.1% in eighth grade, respectively. Regarding the overweight rate, 8.9% of male and 8.6% of female fourth graders and 8.2% of male and 11.1% of female eighth graders fell into this scale. In addition, the obesity scale included 8.5% of male fourth graders and 5.1% for female ones; and the numbers were 8.5% and 6.2% for male and female eighth graders, respectively. For some regions, the obesity problems were more prominent, with a rate over 15%. However, the specific information about those regions was not disclosed in this report.

Besides the student weight condition, the 2018 Report also summarized a number of other aspects of health issues, such as the cardiopulmonary function, vision, and sleep quality, among sampled students. For example, the data showed that the detected rates of poor vision in Grades 4 and 8 were 36.5% and 65.3%, respectively. For some regions, the numbers could reach as high as 60% for fourth graders and 80% for eighth graders. Detailed information was not given in this report.

For music and art, the monitoring assessed student performance in singing and listening, as well as knowledge and appreciation of art. Tested students are required to sing two songs, one required, the other elective chosen from a pool of 10 different songs, which all came from student music textbooks at school (Hu, 2018). The following figures (Figures 1 and 2) showed the percentage of fourth graders and eighth graders reached the "medium" benchmark and landed above it (including "medium," "good," and "excellent") in five different categories that the assessment tested.

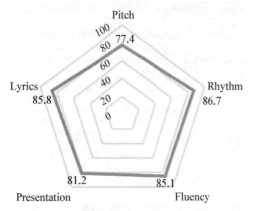

Figure 1. Percentage of the fourth graders who reached certain benchmark in music.

Source. The Chinese Compulsory Education Quality Monitoring Report, p. 14.

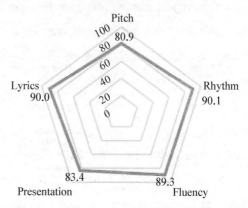

Figure 2. Percentage of the eighth graders who reached certain benchmark in music.

Source. The Chinese Compulsory Education Quality Monitoring Report, p. 14.

In addition, the assessment result showed correlations and suggestions. For instance, sampled students had a relatively high degree of interest in their curriculum, but the arrangements of course hours and course content could be more reasonable. Students generally spent too much time on homework, with a high percentage of off-campus tutoring classes and high learning pressure. Most teachers were liked by their students, but some teachers could be more responsible and professional. Plenty of schools have had positive cultural atmosphere and good environment, equipped with sufficient teaching facilities, which can be utilized more efficiently though. Parents generally cared about their children's learning and there was still room for improvement in parent-child communication and parenting type.

Results of the first subdisciplinary reports on the Chinese compulsory education quality assessment

The education quality monitoring in China has planned a 3-year cycle and a focus on two disciplines each year. By doing this, the assessment team intend to ensure the systematicity and consistency of the monitoring, to track changes of the quality of Chinese compulsory education, and to maximize the monitoring effectiveness. Specific arrangements have included the following: monitoring mathematics and physical education for the first year, language and art education for the second year, and science and moral education for the third year.

Based on *The Chinese Compulsory Education Quality Monitoring Report* released in July 2018, two monitoring disciplines, mathematics and physical education, were officially completed with subdisciplinary reports published, respectively, in the following year.

On November 20, 2019, the Center released two subdisciplinary results: *The Chinese Compulsory Education Quality Monitoring—Subject Report on Mathematical Learning* (2019a) and *The Chinese Compulsory Education Quality Monitoring—Subject Report on Physical Education* (2019b). These two subdisciplinary reports focused on presenting student learning achievement in mathematics and physical education with health condition and demonstrated takeaways from teachers working on related disciplines at school to further analyze factors that affect the quality of education.

The mathematics and the physical education subjects have been monitored in 32 Chinese provincial level units. A total of 6,680 primary and secondary schools got selected, with nearly 200,000 fourth graders and eighth graders being assessed (MOE, 2019). In addition, questionnaire surveys were conducted among more than 6,000 primary and secondary school principals and more than 30,000 mathematics and physical education teachers (MOE, 2019). The two reports used data to reveal the development of student performance in mathematics and physical education. As the fruit of the second-cycle monitoring, the two subdisciplinary reports released in 2019 not only summarized the specific monitoring results but also compared the results with those from the previous assessment cycle, displaying the yearly progress.

Following are details of the two subject reports that include the preparation of the related assessment, examples of specific assessment tools, general results from the assessment aligned by key questions, and some comparative results among different student groups.

Subdisciplinary report 1: The Chinese Compulsory Education Quality Monitoring on Mathematical Learning

Before the assessment of mathematics performance, more than 1,000 researchers and practitioners had engaged in the pilot discussions to develop the tools for the education quality assessment. For example, experts from the field of mathematics and pedagogy, education measurement and evaluation, education policy, and education leadership and management worked on finding valid tools for measurement; frontline teachers, principals, and researchers from Chinese primary and secondary schools participated in testing those tools and making improvement of the measurement (example of tools shown in Table 1). All the questionnaires put to use in real assessment process had already undergone multiple rounds of pretests, and each indicator was supposed to meet the requirement of metrology, with good reliability and validity.

Table 1. Assessment tools designed for mathematical learning assessment.

Assessment Categories	Assessment Indicators	Assessment Tools
Academic Performance	Arithmetic, Geometry, Data Analysis, Reasoning, Problem Solving	Mathematics Test (Paper and Pen)
Academic Attitudes and Emotions	Motivation of Mathematics Learning, Confidence of Mathematics Learning, Anxiety of Mathematics Learning	Student Survey (Paper and Pen)
Education and Teaching Condition	Popularity of Teachers, Education Degree of Teachers, Training Experience of Teachers, Internet Usage of Classes, Library Resources Equipment and Utilization, Multi-media Equipment, etc.	Student Survey (Paper and Pen), Teacher Survey (Online), and Principal Survey (Online)

Source. The Chinese Compulsory Education Quality Monitoring on Mathematical Learning, 2019a, p. 2.

As for the mathematics subject assessment, 116,529 fourth graders and 79,057 eighth graders participated. Among those responses, 115,804 effective ones from fourth graders and 77,949 ones from eighth graders were collected. The response rates were 99.4% and 98.6%, respectively. In addition, 12,505 fourth-grade math teachers, 12,438 eighth-grade math teachers, 4,139 primary school principals, and 2,538 junior high school principals participated effectively in the questionnaire survey, with a 100% response rate.

The results from this subject report in 2019 showed that students' mathematics performance made some progress, compared to the 2018 Report. For example, according to the subject report, the average mathematics score of the fourth graders was 502 points, which was 2 points higher than that from the previous report, while the latest monitoring result of the eighth graders showed an average mathematics score of 505 points, 5 points higher than the previous one.

While the overall performance of students in mathematics achieved a slightly better position, the proportions of students in Grades 4 and 8 that reached "medium" and higher levels in the measurement scale were 84.8% and 78.8% in 2018, respectively, which remained stable compared with their counterparts of 84.6% and 78.9%, respectively, in 2015.

As for motivation of learning mathematics, the proportion of students who indicated large interests in mathematics learning among fourth graders was 88.1%, and 67.9% for eighth graders in 2018. The fourth graders seemed having more confidence and less anxiety in mathematics: As 72.9% of them indicated having a "high" or "very high" level of self-confidence in mathematics learning, while the number was 58.8% among eighth graders in the same monitoring cycle on the one hand; on the other hand, the proportion of students indicating "low" or "very low" anxiety level of learning mathematics was 75.2% among fourth graders and 59.1% among eighth graders of sampled students.

The 2019 subject report for mathematics also showed student satisfaction with their teachers, or teachers' popularity among their own students, as the percentage of fourth graders who adored their mathematics teachers was 92.2%, while that number of eighth graders was 85.6%. As for the percentage of mathematics teachers who met national basic degree qualification of teaching mathematics, the number was 97.1% for fourth grade and 99.4% for eighth grade, which remained steady since 2015 (with the numbers of 97.1% for fourth grade and 99.0% for eighth grade then).

According to the subject report in mathematics, the proportions of the fourth-grade mathematics teachers participating in various levels of professional development were between 41.0% and 93.7%, with more than 99% of mathematics teachers holding the belief that professional training is helpful, while the proportion of the eighth-grade mathematics teachers participating in professional development ranged from 40.4% to 91.4%, more than 97% of whom found the professional training helpful.

Subdisciplinary report 2: The Chinese Compulsory Education Quality Monitoring on Physical Education

To write *The Chinese National Compulsory Education Quality Monitoring—Subject Report on*

Physical Education, the team assessed 116,631 fourth graders and 79,078 eighth graders from 4,141 primary schools and 2,539 junior high schools.

Furthermore, a total of 6,854 fourth-grade physical education teachers, 5,750 eighth-grade physical education teachers, 4,139 primary school principals, and 2,538 junior high school principals participated in the monitoring questionnaire surveys. The response rate was 100%. Results were presented in the subject report about physical education and health.

Results from the physical education subject report showed that the overall health condition of the students in the fourth and eighth grades was relatively good, as the rate of students reaching overall national physical fitness standards exceeded 93.0% and 85.0% for fourth graders and eighth graders, respectively. However, there were increasingly high obesity and poor-vision issues among students. For instance, the obesity rates of fourth graders were 8.8% and 9.7% for eighth graders, which were 1.9 and 2.2 percentage points higher than numbers from those student groups in 2015. The detected rates of poor vision in fourth graders and eighth graders were 38.5% and 68.8%, which were 2.0 and 3.5 percentage points higher than that in 2015.

In addition, as for sleep time, the 2019 report showed that 22.2% of students in the fourth grade could sleep 10 hr or more, the proportion of which decreased 8.5 percentage points from the 2018 report. The proportion of students in the eighth grade who spent 9 hr or more in sleep time was 19.4%, which was 2.8 percentage points higher than previous result. As for minimum requirement for class time of physical education, 69.2% of the fourth graders and 51.9% of the eighth graders had certain classes that met the national requirement of three sessions per week. These numbers had the rises of 13.5 percentage points and 12.7 percentage points, respectively, from that of previous result.

From the analysis of key factors on student physical performance, the subject report found that good physical exercise habits, healthy lifestyles, parents' appreciation and support for physical exercises, and proper implementation of physical education curriculum and teaching at school were all factors related to positive results on students' physical fitness.

The significance of the compulsory education quality assessment in China

China has a long history of holistic education that dated to the Confucius thinking and its philosophical product. Three thousand years ago, Chinese people in Zhou Dynasty highly valued "six arts" (*liuyi*): "rites, music, archery, charioteering, literature, and mathematics" for talent cultivation in Confucian aristocracy (Jiang et al., 2019). That was the early expression of a holistic education, the essence of which remained today for basic education in China.

With the hope to ensure students to receive quality education and grow holistically, the monitoring work added nontraditional subjects into assessment process, such as the art and music, physical education and health (Jiang et al., 2019; Tan, 2018). The embrace of those subjects in addition to reading and mathematics might not be an absolutely new attempt, regarding what an education assessment can cover. Decades earlier than the recent assessment, there have been a number of subject areas covered for compulsory level education assessment in China of a smaller scale. For example, the Beijing Municipality Compulsory Education Quality Assessment Project in 1990s tested subject areas including Chinese, mathematics, arts, civics, handiwork, and common knowledge in natural science for primary schools (generally Grade 1 through Grade 6 or Grade 5); and for junior middle schools (Grade 7 or 6 through Grade 9), Chinese, mathematics, English, music, fine arts, humanities, natural sciences, hands-on skills, and behaviors have been covered in the education quality assessment (Tian & Sun, 2018, p. 187). However, it was adventurous and uncommon, considering the inclusiveness and the scopes of assessment are not seen in other countries, or international large-scale assessments, which only focus on few subjects.

Consequently, innovative methods were sought, applied, and invented. As examples, the stratified probability proportionate to size (PPS) sampling, systematic PPS sampling, and stratification were adopted in student sampling; partial balanced incomplete block design was employed for item development in assessment booklets; unidimensional item response theory models, the Rasch model, and the partial credit model were used for scaling and scoring assessment results. The experience from coordinating the complex quantitative and qualitative process of the assessment was valuable and transferable.

Moreover, assessment results offer empirical evidence for policy changes and social discussions. For example, based on specific and comprehensive profile of students living in high poverty regions, the results have been incentivizing policy suggestions on more financial assistance, such as improved meal plans, extra fundings, and boarding fee subsidies (Tan et al., 2018). Applying policy changes helps the country to allocate educational resources based on real needs and to ensure more educational equity. Another example from the mathematics subject assessment, the report presented a statistical analysis of student learning attitude and their academic performance, arguing that students with more positive mathematical learning attitudes were correlated with higher academic performance in mathematics, which stimulated questions among Chinese society, such as "how to improve mathematical learning attitudes in China," "who has more positive mathematics learning attitudes," "who has better mathematics performance," "are there causal relations between these," and so forth.

Additional significance of the assessment lies in its dynamic application of new technology for assessment per se and for results display. The compulsory education quality monitoring work has relied on a range of new media and online platform to inform the public about the whole process. It uses both websites and mobile applications to monitor process and results, helping both the participants and the public understand it. The monitoring center has also launched a special network platform called "the National Compulsory Education Quality Monitoring Platform" (https://eachina.changyan.cn/), which displays the information from the monitoring center, for provincial level units and sample schools. The website also provides a variety of guiding documents for downloads, such as operating methods and contact information for additional information of the monitoring. Furthermore, the team has also established a Chinese WeChat account called "Quality Monitoring and Big Data" that has regularly published articles on assessment topics.

To sum up, including broad subjects, applying advanced method, informing critical policy discussions, and engaging the public with new media helped the latest assessment stand out from traditional ones and become a significant Chinese national topic in education.

The limitation and caveats of Chinese compulsory education quality assessment

As large-scale assessments have exerted power over education policy research around the world to use it more responsibly, one should also be aware of the caveats of using monitoring results to inform policy. There are a few remained concerns regarding the assessment, including the limitation of large-scale assessment per se, the danger of using results for accountability purposes, and the lack of detailed evidence on real effects on policy, and the need of data disclosure.

There are inherent limitations of what large-scale assessment like this could measure. According to the researchers who work at the assessment Center, the designs and instruments of the recent education quality assessment could be learned from the experience of other advanced large-scale assessment programs like international assessment PISA and quality assessment from other advanced economies, such as the National Assessment of Educational Progress (NAEP) in the United States.

A number of policy researchers shared key insights of what large-scale assessment cannot measure. For example, these assessments cannot measure unknown constructs, thus cannot fully predict success of individuals and societies; they cannot measure "exceptionality" and ignored the real frontiers and exceptional talents among top performers, thus stifling innovation; they cannot measure inconclusive, dynamic, and context-dependent human abilities, such as effective communication skills in different cultural contexts; assessments do not represent the qualities that different individual needs merely using the same standards to measure every child (Pons, 2017; Yuan & Zhao, 2019; Zhao et al., 2019).

As for reflecting the real purposes of education, previous critique argues that what large-scale assessments tried to represent is still too simplified that it ignored other meaningful educational purposes such as "citizenship, solidarity, equity, curiosity and engagement, compassion, empathy, curiosity, cultural values, physical health," and so on (Zhao, 2019). These are just a few examples of assessment concerns. Without fully addressing concerns like this, using the same standards to measure individuals' ability and make policy changes can be improper and prejudiced.

Furthermore, it can be dangerous to make hasty comparison and hold any provincial unit accountable. Researchers worldwide cast doubts on making simple comparison merely using rankings in assessment results to judge the education quality. Looking inside of a nation's education systems could be proper and helpful, compared to looking outside from other countries due to different cultural and social backgrounds (Carnoy et al., 2015). However, policymakers should also be careful about how much variance actually happened within different economic, cultural, and social backgrounds of these units.

Next, unlike NAEP in the United States that published open data for the public and researchers to use and examine (see https://nces.ed.gov/nationsreportcard/data/), the data from the Chinese compulsory education assessment collected from provinces and counties have been kept exclusively and confidentially. There is no way for researchers outside of the Center and for researchers at Beijing Normal University to reach the data, conduct statistical analysis, or examine the national analysis published in national reports.

In addition to the inherent limitation of quality assessments and dangerous comparison using those results, there are lack of direct research on the positive impact of such quality assessment on making education policy, neither are any detailed data open to researchers to use and examine. So far, what we really know about the effect and significance of the Chinese compulsory education quality monitoring work are still fairly limited.

References

Beijing Normal University (BNU). (2020). *BNU history*. https://english.bnu.edu.cn/about/bnuhistory/index.htm

Carnoy, M., Garcia, E., & Khavenson, T. (2015). *Bringing it back home: Why state comparisons are more useful than international comparisons for improving US education policy*. Economic Policy Institute. https://www.epi.org/publication/bringing-it-back-home-why-state-comparisons-are-more-useful-than-international-comparisons-for-improving-u-s-education-policy/

Compulsory Education Law of the People's Republic of China. (2014). *Laws (and) regulations*. The State Council, People's Republic of China. http://english.www.gov.cn/archive/laws_regulations/2014/08/23/content_281474983042154.htm

Hu, Y. (2018). Analysis on the way of singing and music assessment in the first round of Chinese compulsory education quality monitoring [in Chinese]. *Teacher Doctrines*, (8), 256−257. http://m.fx361.com/news/2018/0719/3861833.html

Jiang, Y., Zhang, J., & Xin, T. (2019). Toward education quality improvement in China: A brief overview of the national assessment of education quality. *Journal of Educational and Behavioral Statistics*, 44(6), 733−751.

Ministry of Education of the People's Republic of China. (2015a). *MOE Official Press Conference Material Part I. Establishing a national monitoring system to promote the quality of compulsory education* [in Chinese]. http://www.moe.gov.cn/jyb_xwfb/xw_fbh/moe_2069/xwfbh_2015n/xwfb_150415/150415_sfcl/201504/t20150415_187149.html

Ministry of Education of the People's Republic of China. (2015b). *MOE Official Press Conference Material Part II. Spokesperson from Chinese Ministry of Education answering reporters' questions on the National Compulsory Education Quality Monitoring Program* [in Chinese]. http://old.moe.gov.cn/publicfiles/business/htmlfiles/moe/s8677/201504/185888.html

Ministry of Education of the People's Republic of China. (2018). *Release of China's first oversight report on quality of compulsory education*. http://en.moe.gov.cn/News/Top_News/201808/t20180801_344002.html

Ministry of Education of the People's Republic of China. (2019). *Release of China's national compulsory education quality monitoring subject reports on mathematics and PE* [in Chinese]. http://www.moe.gov.cn/jyb_xwfb/gzdt_gzdt/s5987/201911/t20191120_409046.html

Pons, X. (2017). Fifteen years of research on PISA effects on education governance: A critical review. *European Journal of Education*, 52(2), 131−144.

Popham, W. J. (1987). Preparing policymakers for standard setting on high-stakes tests. *Educational Evaluation and Policy Analysis*, 9(1), 77−82.

Tan, H. (2018). On changes of quality monitoring of basic education in the new era [in Chinese]. *Educational Research*, 461(6), 98−104.

Tan, H., Li, W., & Luo, L. (2018). Considerations on using quality assessment to promote targeted poverty alleviation in basic education [in Chinese]. *Educational Research*, *456*(1), 99−107.

The National Assessment Center for Education Quality. (2018). *The China compulsory education quality oversight report* [in Chinese]. http://www.moe.gov.cn/jyb_xwfb/moe_1946/fj_2018/201807/P020180724685827455405.pdf

The National Assessment Center for Education Quality. (2019a). *The Chinese national compulsory education quality monitoring—Subject report on mathematical learning* [in Chinese]. http://www.moe.gov.cn/s78/A11/moe_767/201911/W020191120537554536852.pdf

The National Assessment Center for Education Quality. (2019b). *The Chinese national compulsory education quality monitoring—Subject report on physical education* [in Chinese]. http://www.moe.gov.cn/s78/A11/moe_767/201911/W020191120537554570333.pdf

Tian, H., & Sun, Z. (2018). *Academic achievement assessment: Principles and methodology*. Springer.

Wu, L., Ma, X., Shi, Y., Tao, S., Yu, Y., Wang, S., Luo, L., Xin, T., & Li, Y. (2019). China national assessment of education quality—Physical education & health (CNAEQ-PEH) 2015: An introduction. *Research Quarterly for Exercise and Sport*, *90*(2), 105−112.

Yuan, Z., & Zhao, Y. (2019). Respect the power of large-scale assessments: What they cannot measure. *ECNU Review of Education*, *2*(3), 253−261.

Zhao, Y., Wehmeyer, M., Basham, J., & Hansen, D. (2019). Tackling the wicked problem of measuring what matters: Framing the questions. *ECNU Review of Education*, *2*(3), 262−278.

Zhao, Y. (2019). *Yong Zhao: The PISA illusion*. National Education Policy Center. https://nepc.colorado.edu/blog/pisa-illusion

This article provides a historical overview of the progress made in the moral education curriculum (MEC) reform of China's elementary and middle schools in the 21st century and also discusses its prospects. The main methods used were textual and policy analysis. According to the study, while China's MEC reform is characterized by an openness and modernity achieved through international dialogue, it remains distinctively Chinese. The continued development and improvement of MEC reform can only occur through the careful handling of the various relationships between China and the international community, traditionality and modernity, central and local authorities, as well as theory and practice. In addition to providing greater insights into and understanding of China's new MEC reform, this article mainly contributes to suggest several ideas for the further development of the relevant educational reform.

Moral Education Curriculum Reform for China's Elementary and Middle Schools in the Twenty-First Century: Past Progress and Future Prospects[1]

Hanwei Tang and Yang Wang

Introduction

In China, elementary and middle schools follow a specialized moral education curriculum (MEC) similar to social studies curriculum provided in countries like the U.S. and Australia. Moral education is intended to provide students with guidance on morality and values, improve their social understanding and capacity for social mobility, and thus ensure their development as responsible citizens. Given such objectives, moral curricula are invariably constrained by a country's sociopolitical and economic context, as well as its historical development.

Known as the new curriculum reform, China's eighth wave of national curriculum reform for basic education (1999 – present) is its most ambitious attempt since the founding of the People's

---

1 This article was funded by the project titled "A Study on the Civilization Gene by Integrating Morality in Data and Reason: A New Model of Moral Education" (Project No.: 16AWTJ12), a key project under Shandong Province's Philosophy and Social Science Planning Division. It was published on *ECNU Review of Education*, May 7, 2020.

Republic of China (PRC) in 1949. This new curriculum reform champions moral and values education. Borrowing and learning from the social studies taught in the West, the MEC seeks to fully embody modernity, openness, and cosmopolitanism, while retaining distinctive Chinese characteristics. Providing an overview of China's MEC reform, this article elucidates both its cosmopolitan and Chinese characteristics. In doing so, this article addresses the future of MEC reform, emphasizing the importance of various relationships—including that between China and the world, traditionality and modernity, central and local authorities, as well as theory and practice—being deftly handled. Such relationships are crucial for the MEC to be effective in guiding China's progress toward social and educational modernity while better serving the growth of the young people.

China's new MEC reform

Historical overview of the new MEC reform

Since the founding of the PRC in 1949, the MEC has been a specialized curriculum for elementary and middle schools. Indeed, the name itself embodies China's traditional emphasis on moral education over the past millennia. Unlike Western countries, China has no religious traditions. As such, Confucianism lies at the core of China's moral education—the philosophy playing a role akin to that of religion in the growth of individuals' lives and the maintenance of social order. Moral education can also be understood as civic education centered on the teaching of morality and values, but including other historical, geographical, political, economic, cultural, and psychological content. In this sense, the MEC is similar to the social studies curriculum provided in Western countries. This article understands the MEC in terms of this broader definition of moral education.

In June 2001, the Ministry of Education of the PRC (MOE) issued *Guidelines for Curriculum Reform of Basic Education (Trial Implementation)* in officially launching the new curriculum reform for elementary and middle schools. This reform covered the entire K12 curriculum, with the original "Ideology and Morality" curriculum for the elementary school stage (Grades 1–6) separated into two courses: (i) "Morality and Life" for Grades 1–2, and (ii) "Morality and Society" for Grades 3–6. A course entitled "Ideology and Morality" (or "History and Society") formed part of the middle school curriculum, while "Ideology and Politics" was integrated to the high school curriculum. The management model for the courses at the state, local, and school levels was established at the same time. In June 2002, the MOE officially published *Standards for the "Morality and Life" Course in Full-Time Compulsory Education (Experimental Draft) and Standards for the "Morality and Society" Course in Full-Time Compulsory Education (Experimental Draft)*. These were followed by the release of *Standards for the "Ideology and Morality" Course in Full-Time Compulsory Education (Experimental Draft)* in middle schools in 2003, and *Standards for the "Ideology and Politics" Course in General High Schools (Experimental Draft)* in 2004.

Following the introduction of these new curriculum standards, new textbooks were prepared based on the approach of "having multiple versions for one guiding principle." Essentially, while curriculum standards were standardized at the state level, individual localities had the option of selecting which versions of the textbooks to use. Teams comprising moral education theorists, frontline teachers, as well as teaching and research staff cooperated closely in writing the textbooks—thus elevating the level of professionalism in textbook writing. At the same time, the Chinese government launched a large-scale training program for teachers so that they could adapt to the needs of the new curriculum reform.

In 2011, after the curriculum standards had been in place for nearly a decade, the MOE revised the standards for the MEC during the compulsory education stage, resulting in *Standards for the "Morality and Life" Course in Compulsory Education (2011 Edition)* and *Standards for the "Morality and Society" Course in Compulsory Education (2011 Edition)*. The new curriculum standards were more detailed and had stronger operability. In 2016, the courses for compulsory education—namely, "Morality and Life" and "Ideology and Morality"—were combined into "Morality and the Rule of Law." Meanwhile, the approach to developing textbooks was changed from "multiple versions for one guiding principle" to "one version for one guiding principle," with all textbooks standardized and prepared by the state.

The MOE initiated revisions of the standards for the general high school curriculum in 2013. This was followed by the release of *Standards for the "Ideology and Politics" Course in General High Schools (2017 Edition)* in January 2018. On the basis of retaining the original course name, the course structure was further optimized and the contents adjusted. The curriculum comprised compulsory, elective, and selective compulsory courses. There were four compulsory courses: namely, "Economic Life," "Political Life," "Cultural Life," and "Life and Philosophy." These were later modified to "Socialism with Chinese Characteristics," "Economy and Society," "Politics and the Rule of Law," and "Philosophy and Culture." There were originally six elective courses: "General Knowledge on Scientific Socialism," "General Knowledge on Economics," "General Knowledge on State and International Organizations," "General Knowledge on Scientific Thought," "General Knowledge on Laws in Daily Living," and "General Knowledge on Civic Morality and Ethics." These were later modified to three modules: "Finance and Daily Living," "Judges and Lawyers," and "Philosophers in History." In addition to the original compulsory and elective courses, a third category of selective compulsory courses was introduced in 2013. Three modules were offered: namely, "Modern International Politics and Economics," "Law and Life," and "Logic and Thought."

As noted, the approach to high school textbooks has changed to "one version for one guiding principle." In general, the problem with China's nine-year compulsory education program is that the teaching materials were prepared prior to the issue of the curriculum standards. In other words, the teaching materials on "Morality and the Rule of Law" were already in use before the relevant curriculum standards were announced. As such, the MOE is currently organizing the writing and editing of standard ideological and political textbooks for high schools.

Reflecting on the new MEC reform

Overall, the new curriculum reform reflects an unprecedented modernity and openness through international dialogue, while retaining distinctive Chinese characteristics. The former is characterized by the cultivation of modern civic awareness as an important training goal. In this regard, curriculum content is more comprehensive and course implementation has emphasized proactive student participation and the practical application of lessons in their daily lives. In regard to the maintenance of an educational curriculum with distinct Chinese characteristics, new curriculum reform has continued to focus on the status and role of moral education. Indeed, these aspects have been elevated to the primary goal and fundamental task of education in China. As such, while the MEC content emphasizes modern values, greater attention has been placed on traditional Chinese culture and virtues. State standards for and control over the MEC management model have also been strengthened. This section explores these developments in greater detail.

Modernity and cosmopolitanism of the new MEC reform

Cultivating civic awareness as an important goal of the new MEC. The cultivation of civic awareness constitutes a historic shift in the development of China's moral education. Certainly, there is no concept of "citizenship" in traditional Chinese society and education. However, with the acceleration of political democratization, economic marketization, and cultural pluralism since the country's reform and opening-up, the cultivation of civic awareness had gradually become an important goal of Chinese education. The new MEC standards and textbooks clearly advance the objective of cultivating modern civic awareness. For example, Standards for the "Ideology and Morality" *Course in Full-Time Compulsory Education* (*Experimental Draft*) notes that,

> [T]he task of this course is to guide students to come to realize the meaning of life and to gradually form the correct outlook on the world, life, and values, as well as know what is fundamentally good and evil and right and wrong, thereby learning to be responsible citizens and leading positive and healthy lives. (MOE, 2003)

Moreover, published by People's Education Publishing House, the *Morality and Society* textbook describes the course as helping students "understand the forms of expression and the general procedure of democratic life in schools and classes"; "be able to exercise one's own rights in accordance with the principles of fairness, openness, democracy and equality"; and "actively participate in the democratic life in schools" (Li, 2012, p. 24).

In short, the course should instill in students a basic awareness of their rights, care for and knowledge of the state and society, civic responsibility, as well as global awareness and understanding of multiculturalism. These objectives reflect the modernity of China's curriculum reform and its integration into the global mainstream. China's education system also reflects the country's core values of freedom, equality, justice, and rule of law (Du & Cao, 2015, p. 34). Such core values reflect the spirit of modernity and highlight a more open attitude in the country's MEC reform.

However, contemporary China differs from countries that overemphasize the rights, individuality, and confrontational spirit of their citizens. Although the civic awareness advocated by the state respects and promotes civil rights, it also emphasizes civic responsibility, a sense of dedication, and national identification. Solving problems through consultation and dialogue is also advocated. These qualities are directly reflected in the MEC reform. For example, *Standards for the "Ideology and Morality" Course in Full-Time Compulsory Education* (*Experimental Draft*) claims that the course is intended "to promote the ethnic spirit and establish shared ideals of socialism with Chinese characteristics"; help students "feel the connections between personal emotions and the ethnic culture and the state's destiny, and enhance one's cultural identity"; as well as "promote and cultivate the ethnic spirit, understand the social responsibilities of contemporary youths, establish shared ideals of socialism with Chinese characteristics, and aspire to serve the motherland" (MOE, 2003). These qualities are communicated through particular modules or lessons. For instance, in *Morality and Society* for Grade 5 (Volume II), the theme for Lesson 6 of Module 2 is "I am a citizen of the Republic." It comprises four sections: "We are citizens," "What are my basic rights?" "Unavoidable obligations of citizenship," and "Valuing rights and fulfilling obligations."

As such, the goal of China's MEC reform is to cultivate cooperative and responsible citizens willing to enter dialogue, instead of people who expect rights but refuse to undertake responsibilities or who care only for themselves and not others. These choices are in line with both China's historical traditions and its actual state-level conditions.

Making MEC content more comprehensive. Prior to the introduction of the new curriculum reform, moral education had a focus, namely ideological education and the teaching of moral qualities. Reform thus saw the expansion of MEC content. This is indicative of the ideology of the ruling Communist Party of China (CPC) and the desire to cultivate individual morality; the basic social common sense, skills, and attitudes that individuals need for socialization; as well as the spirit of civic mindedness, criticism, and innovation. In this respect, the MEC has become more similar to social studies taught in the Western countries. Indeed, the course names— "Morality and Life" and "Morality and Society" for elementary schools, and "Ideology and Morality" (or "History and Society") for middle schools—all refer to social development centered on moral values. They are also comprehensive; for example, "Morality and Life" integrates moral, life, social and cultural, as well as scientific education, while "Morality and Society" integrates morality, behavioral norms, the legal system, patriotism, collectivism, socialism, conditions of the state, history and culture, and the geographical environment (Zou, 2011).

Indeed, the "Morality and Society" course is not merely a combination of classes on morality and society, but a course encompassing society, life, geography, history, ethics, law, politics, economy, culture, environment, as well as the various knowledge and skills necessary for the cultivation of civic mindedness (Gao & Zhao, 2003). The course covers three elements of students' social lives: namely, the social environment, social activities, and social relations. The social environment comprises spatiotemporal aspects of life, as well as the human and natural environments; social activities cover student's daily lives, as well as culture, economics, and politics; while social relations include interpersonal relationships, social norms, laws, and social systems. Moral education courses are comprehensive. For example, "Loving the Environment" teaches children about time and space, as well as the human and ecological environments.

As noted, the coursework has also been adapted so that the information and skills are relevant to students' lives. Meanwhile, the Grade 4 "Morality and Society" textbook contains a module entitled "Communication" that incorporates content on history, communication, security, and law, while conferring civilized communication behaviors and the skills necessary for gathering and processing information (Du, 2009, p. 143). Taught at middle school, "Ideology and Morality" was similarly revised: The lives of middle school students—rather than the knowledge system—form the course's foundation. While the students' cognitive levels and real lives constituted the course's starting points, the course centered on their expanding scope of life to integrate politics, ethics, law, conditions of the state, and mental health education. As such, the students were presented with comprehensive curriculum content similar to the social studies taught in the U.S.

In 2016, the names of the elementary and middle school courses under China's compulsory education system were revised and unified; that is, "Morality and Life," "Morality and Society," and "Ideology and Morality" were integrated into a single course: "Morality and the Rule of Law." This does not mean that the MEC content in elementary and middle school were simplified. Rather, this change sought to strengthen education on the rule of law and promote the idea of state governance according to the law. Although the curriculum is currently being revised, the comprehensive approach is not expected to change significantly.

Linking implementation to student's daily lives. Since the 21st century, the concept at the very core of China's MEC reform has been "a return to life." Prior to this, the country's MEC followed the subject logic—that is, focus was placed on the integrity of the subject knowledge system and the differentiation, analysis, and memorization of related moral knowledge. The connection between knowledge and the students' daily lives was largely ignored, as was the significant role of moral experiences in their moral growth (Ban & Tan, 2008). Such was

China's "intellectual moral education" prior to the MEC reform, the main characteristic of which was the disconnection between the course content and forms, and students' cognitive characteristics and life experiences. Following the new reform, the MEC became more closely linked to students' lives in terms of the implementation method, reflecting a respect for life and student experiences. Indeed, according to the curriculum standards for "Morality and Life,"

> [T]he "Morality and Life" course is based on children's lives and emphasizes the existence of morality in their lives. The formation of children's morality stems from their experiences, understanding, and perception of life. Only educational activities that originate from their real lives can trigger their inner (rather than superficial) moral emotions, and their real (rather than false) moral experiences and cognition. (Department of Basic Education, MOE, 2003, p. 3)

In terms of curriculum development, the MEC closely related course content with students' living experiences and morality. For instance, "Morality and Life" specifically selected materials from the pursuit of four values: to live healthily and safely, happily and actively, responsibly and caringly, as well as intelligently and creatively. As such, students learn about morality through a process that is healthy, safe, active, enjoyable, intelligent, and creative. In revising "Morality and Society," content and materials were first organized according to students' ever-expanding living domains: family, school, hometown or community, the motherland, and the world. Efforts were made to ensure that the curriculum was based on the students' own life experiences (Gao, 2004). The presentation and layout of the new textbooks were also more in line with the students' cognitive and aesthetic characteristics. In this regard, where previous versions only contained text, the new textbooks incorporated many of their favorite animations and cartoon characters. China also adopted a new source of teaching contents by generating educational topics and examples using problems that children frequently encounter in their daily lives. These were presented in the form of "life events" in the textbooks.

Next, China's new MEC has replaced its indoctrination-based model for its implementation and teaching methods with a more activity-based approach. The goal was to meet student needs in terms of practicing a moral life. Various and diverse forms of activities leading to both direct and indirect learning—including role-playing, tracking and observation, storytelling, singing, games, visits, interviews, information checking, arts and craft, production, as well as discussions—were incorporated in a particular version of moral education textbooks. For younger children (Grades 1 −2), at least one activity was included for practically every topic in the moral education textbooks. These included packing one's school bag, introducing oneself, coloring the national flag, and talking about one's home (Du & Lu, 2009, p. 141). These activities are familiar and close to the children's experiences, thus providing a space in which they can practice and reflect upon morality.

Traditional and Chinese characteristics of the new MEC reform

Elevating moral education. China has emphasized moral education for several millennia through Confucianism. Contemporary moral education remains centered on Confucian ethics. Family, school, and social education form a complete system that regards moral education as an important means for improving individuals' cultivation and maintenance of social order. Moral education was still considered important following the founding of the PRC in 1949, and moral courses have been taught in primary schools and high schools. It was not until 1997 that the State Education Commission promulgated moral education in *Standards for the "Ideology and Morality" Course for Elementary Schools and "Ideology and Politics" Course for Middle Schools Under the Nine-Year Compulsory Education Program (Trial Implementation)*. Indeed, this was the first set of curriculum standards issued since the founding of the PRC. However, the formulation of these standards lacked professionalism and scientific basis, and the standards failed to address a series of critical issues related to the development of teaching materials and reform. As a result, this set of curriculum standards did not play any substantial role in subsequent curriculum reform.

Initiated at the beginning of the 21st century, the country's new curriculum reform paid unprecedented attention to the MEC. The status and role of moral education in overall educational reform became more prominent. For instance, the teaching of morality to cultivate better people became the fundamental task of education. Indeed, at the Peking University Teacher-Student Forum held on May 2, 2018, President Xi Jinping even emphasized that "fostering integrity and promoting rounded development of people should be adopted as the fundamental standard for evaluating all work done by schools" (Xi, 2018a).

The state invested substantial amounts of people, power, and material resources in the formulation, revision, and improvement of the curriculum standards, preparation of teaching materials, supervision of teaching quality, and teacher training. In the process of doing so, the MOE established a specialized bureau responsible for the development and management of textbooks, while colleges set up research institutions on the MEC and related textbooks.

Additionally, a professional MEC research team was formed during this round of curriculum reform. Its members comprised moral education teachers from elementary and middle schools, as well as professional researchers from colleges and research institutions. The team was dedicated to assessing the effectiveness and scientific basis of Chinese curriculum reform (Chen & Du, 2012).

Emphasizing traditional values and culture in modernity. Over the past century, the attitude of Chinese society toward its own historical traditions was generally derogatory. At one time, traditionality was even regarded as an obstacle to China's modernization, and the mentality of the majority was to learn from modern, developed, and civilized Western countries. However, China has achieved enormous economic development since the beginning of the 21st century. Having gained a better understanding of the West and modernity, China's attitude toward traditionality changed, particularly with the belief that certain aspects of traditionality can be positive forces for modernization. Certainly, the need for a renewed recognition of the significance of traditional virtues and the value of traditional Chinese culture, as well as the need to establish cultural self-confidence, were clearly emphasized in the new MEC reform. In 2014, the MOE published the *Guidelines for Improving Education in the Excellent Traditional Chinese Culture*, which stated its intention to integrate traditional Chinese culture into the curriculum and teaching materials of the education system. According to these guidelines, the proportion of content on traditional Chinese culture was to be increased when revising the curriculum standards for moral education, Chinese, history, art, and sports in elementary and middle schools. Moreover, schools across the country were encouraged to fully exploit and utilize local educational resources on traditional Chinese culture to offer specialized local and school-based courses (MOE, 2014).

Issued by the General Office of the State Council in 2017, *Opinions on Implementing the Project to Pass Down and Develop the Excellent Traditional Chinese Culture* expressed the state's intention to integrate traditional Chinese culture into all aspects of education. This was to be implemented in various areas of education across all levels, with a particular "focus on textbooks for preschoolers and students in elementary and middle schools, while establishing a system of courses and teaching materials on Chinese culture" (Meng & Wu, 2017, p. 27). The new moral education textbook, *Morality and the Rule of Law*, also emphasizes the incorporation of content on traditional Chinese culture at each stage of learning and in each textbook module. This constitutes a new trend in the reform of Chinese moral education textbooks.

Against this backdrop, some schools have been more proactive. For example, the Qufu

Experimental Elementary School in Shandong developed a school-based textbook titled *Spirit of the Almond Platform* (*Xingtan Hun*). In an effort to transmit traditional Chinese culture, the school also held activities such as reading competitions that enhanced students' moral education (Wang & Zhang, 2016). Meanwhile, tapping community resources, the Yaohua Elementary School in Guangzhou's Liwan District used jade culture as a means of transmitting Chinese tradition. The school established the ideals of moral education and the goals of running the school through the following lines: "Jade symbolizes the cultivation of morality. The forging and tempering of one's will is akin to finely polishing and delicately carving a piece of jade, with its eventual luster reflecting the glories of one's life." They also developed a school-based moral education course entitled "Knowing Jade, Appreciating Jade" (Lu, 2016, pp. 66 – 67).

Enhancing state control. Issued in 2001, the *State Council's Decision on the Reform and Development of Basic Education* proposed the "implementation of curriculum management at the state, local, and school levels." The Ministry of Education is responsible for the formulation of the overall plan for the curriculum development of elementary and middle schools, determining the categories of and class hours for the state curriculum, setting of the state curriculum standards, and provision of guidance at the macroscopic level for the implementation of elementary and middle school curricula. In addition to ensuring the implementation of the state curriculum, local regions are encouraged to develop courses adapted to their local contexts, as well as develop or select courses that match their respective characteristics (The State Council of the People's Republic of China, 2001). This system was elaborated upon in *Guidelines for Curriculum Reform of Basic Education* (*Trial Implementation*) as follows,

> [W]hen schools implement the state and local courses, they should develop or select the curriculum after taking into consideration the actual situation in terms of the local socioeconomic development, their own school traditions and advantages, and their students' interests and needs. The educational administrative departments at the various levels should guide and supervise implementation and development of the curriculum. Schools have the authority and responsibility to provide feedback on the problems encountered when implementing the state and local courses. (MOE, 2001)

As such, the new curriculum reform propelled the redesign of China's curriculum management system, leading to the establishment of the current three-tier management model at the state, local, and school levels. However, local authorities and schools only have partial autonomy for decision-making related to the MEC. The state (i.e., the central government) retains overall authority over curriculum management, including the formulation of curriculum standards and professional standards for teachers, as well as the development of teaching materials. This is especially true for the MEC due to its relation to ideology and the transmission of mainstream culture. Although the new curriculum reform gave local authorities and schools a certain amount of autonomy in comparison to the past—including textbook development, teacher training, the formation of local and school-based curricula, and curriculum evaluation—the state's control is authoritative and dominant. From 2016, the MEC textbooks are compiled and published by the state, while curriculum standards are standardized across the whole country. Consequently, the development of the MEC at the local and school levels, as well as that of local and school-based textbooks, are strictly controlled and can only serve to supplement the state curriculum and textbooks. For all schools, the main priority is fully implementing the state-prescribed curriculum and utilizing state-published textbooks.

Future prospects

From a historical perspective, the new MEC reform has introduced numerous changes and is unquestionably progressive. Nevertheless, several deep-seated issues need to be addressed going forward, particularly in regard to the approach to managing the relationships between traditionality and modernity, China and the world, central and local authorities, as well as theory and practice. These have long been controversial issues in China, emerging in the country's rapid transformation and modernization. Issues were either completely ignored or met with an approach too extreme, restrictive, or lacking in understanding. Moreover, these issues have been compounded by biases, which have always existed in one form or another. In contrast, the new MEC reform reflects a more rational, open, and steady spirit and attempts to transcend the traditional mode of thinking in which only binary opposites and a case of either/or are considered. Instead, the requisite tension and balance between opposing categories have been maintained. In the future, the balancing of the relationships between these mutually opposing categories must be further addressed to ensure that a suitable path for the modernization of China's education system is identified through practice and experimentation. This section discusses these relationships in greater detail, focusing on the approach to and management of these relationships going forward.

The relationship between traditionality and modernity

With a history and culture spanning several millennia, China has always been proud of its traditions. However, during the evolution of tradition into modernism, traditionality and modernity were once opposed to each other. At the time, many believed that traditionality would encumber modernization and must thus be abandoned if modernity was to be achieved. Since 1978, China has followed a policy of reform and opening-up, with various social experiments conducted in the process. Consequently, the attitude toward traditionality had changed by the turn of the 21st century. China has realized that traditionality and modernity are not necessarily antithetical but can coexist harmoniously. Indeed, some elements of traditional culture can even make up for the shortcomings of modernity. Traditions need not be completely abandoned to achieve modernity and modernization. As such, it is more effective to constantly discover beneficial aspects of traditionality and make use of and integrate traditions going forward. Moreover, the significance of traditional culture and values—as represented by Confucian culture—to both China's modernity and cosmopolitanism has also been recognized. The traditions, ways of thinking, and values that originated in China several millennia ago have given China what it requires to hold international dialogues. Therefore, the positive aspects of traditional virtues and culture should be rediscovered on the premise of advocating modern values. In this respect, the MEC has the important task of developing new interpretations of traditionality.

The relationship between China and the world

China once considered itself the center of the world, and at the apex of the hierarchy of global cultures and values. However, following contact with Western countries since the latter half of the 19th century, China realized that it lagged behind developed industrial countries and recognized the scope of cultural differences that existed. This produced a sense of ethnic inferiority and led to the Chinese revering the cultures and values of developed Western countries, resulting in a conviction that anything from the West was naturally the best. Over the course of the 20th century, officials and academics began reevaluating their understanding of the relationship between China and the wider world, although none examined Western culture and values with objectivity or the desire to enter a dialogue as equals. It was either a case of resolute opposition, ethnic arrogance, or ethnic inferiority. Most of the time, it was the case of looking at the world from China's perspective and examining ways for it to manage its relationship with the West from its own standpoint and situation.

In the wake of tremendous sociopolitical, economic, environmental, and technological changes, both China and the rest of the global community must reevaluate and adjust their relationship accordingly. In regard to China's reform of its education and the MEC, its relationship with the rest of the world must be viewed from a broader, more rational, and future-oriented perspective. First, China is a member of the global community and plays an important role in globalization. It should participate in dialogues with other countries, work together to build a global community of shared human destiny, assume global responsibility, and cultivate global awareness and international vision in its students. Second, there should be communication with Western countries in all aspects of curriculum development. This should be done from the position of holding dialogues as equals, and in the spirit of learning from and referencing one another. In doing so, China will cultivate both a consciousness of Chinese culture and international understanding, as well as a desire for national and international collaboration, in its citizens. Third, innovative and responsible talents must be cultivated for the future. Such talents can promote the creation and development of a new future based on mutual integration and intercommunication between China and the rest of the world.

The relationship between the central and local authorities

A topic that must be addressed in China's curriculum reform is the relationship between the central and local authorities. On the one hand, as a centralized state, there are uniform standards and requirements in terms of the formulation of standards, development of teaching materials, teacher training, education evaluation, and education investments. The government-led, top-down promotion of curriculum reform facilitates efficient improvements to the curriculum and is conducive to both the implementation of the state's will and balanced educational development. On the other hand, there are significant regional differences across China, and over-standardization will lead to the neglect of diverse local needs. This is especially true for the MEC, for which it is necessary to incorporate the cultural diversity of different regions and actual characteristics of students' values.

Generally, top-down administrative promotion is not good at mobilizing enthusiasm at the grass-roots level of schools. This has been addressed in the new curriculum reform model through the introduction of state, local, and school levels, with local authorities and schools allowed a certain degree of flexibility and autonomy in some aspects, such as course development, teaching materials, teaching, and teacher training. This is an attempt to combine top-down and bottom-up methods, as well as the state's need for standardization and local needs for diversity. Overall, this approach has achieved concrete results. However, the advantages of this three-tier curriculum management system should be further developed and related experiences should be investigated. This will allow the MEC reform to fully mobilize schools at the grassroots level, while ensuring attention to the cultural differences of various regions. While strengthening state standards, local governments and schools should be empowered with greater autonomy, motivation, vitality, and diversity. Ultimately, the deciding factors are participation and creation at the school and teacher level.

The relationship between theory and practice

Current curriculum reform differs from that of the past in having a certain degree of theoretical consciousness. This has been achieved in two ways. First, new curriculum reform has involved the academic community, which had held detailed discussions of the various issues involved in reform. Professional and specific viewpoints were also advanced based on curriculum reform experiences in Western countries. Second, new curriculum reform has directly involved educational theorists in policy formulation and the actual process of curriculum reform. For example, college professors and researchers have played an important role in the formulation of curriculum standards, preparation of teaching materials, teacher training, and even classroom teaching instruction. Such efforts have greatly improved the quality and professionalism of basic education curriculum reform.

However, a gap between theory and practice persists, with the effectiveness envisioned by theorists not fully realized in practice. First, the progress of implementing curriculum reform in elementary and middle schools has varied substantially across different regions. There are significant gaps between the urban and rural areas, developed and undeveloped regions, as well as eastern and western regions, and southern and northern regions. Curriculum reform in some of the more remote, undeveloped, and poor regions is far from ideal. Second, many teachers have continued using the original traditional concepts and methods, which means that classroom teaching and implementation at the school level has not undergone any substantial change. As such, the ideas, models, methods, and goals advocated by the new curriculum reform existed only in text, policy, and verbal statements and were not put into practice.

There are several reasons for this. One of the most direct factors is that the educational evaluation mechanism did not make fundamental adjustments to adapt to the new curriculum. For instance, the policy on college entrance examinations is predominantly based on the student scores. Consequently, teachers have ignored the comprehensive quality, moral development, and key abilities advocated by the new curriculum. As such, the Chinese government is currently pushing for a reform of the educational evaluation system. Indeed, President Xi Jinping has clearly advocated the need to further reform the education system, improve the MEC implementation mechanism, reverse unscientific aspects of education evaluation, and resolutely overcome the stubborn and recalcitrant views that good scores and entering a higher school are education's only objectives (Xi, 2018b). The education system reform represented by the evaluation mechanism has become the bottleneck blocking the further development of China's educational reform, including that of the curriculum. It also constitutes a significant obstacle for the effective communication between theory and practice.

Discussion

Scholars have reached different conclusions regarding China's MEC. For instance, Lee and Ho (2005, p. 413) argue that, in the wake of its reform and opening-up, China's MEC reform has been more concerned with personal well-being and civic literacy. However, as this article has shown, although China's MEC reform emphasizes modern values, it retains distinctive Chinese characteristics and focuses on the teaching of traditional virtues and culture. While paying attention to individual and civil rights, the MEC also emphasizes individual responsibilities, obligations, and loyalty to the state. Meanwhile, Reed (1995, p. 99) has argued that the content of China's political/moral education primarily centered on core Confucian virtues. However, as observed in this article, modern Chinese society and its education system—especially following the founding of the PRC—actually held a derogatory attitude toward China's history and traditions. It was only after China entered the 21st century and gained a deeper understanding of the West and modernity that its attitude toward and treatment of traditionality changed, resulting in China making a decisive statement of cultural self-confidence.

As Tan and Reyes (2016, p. 43) have shown, China's curriculum reform has not involved the wholesale copying of policies introduced by foreign countries. Rather, reform has involved the integration of Western ideas and practices with Chinese traditions and values, as well as localized transformations. In this regard, this article has provided a more in-depth discussion, concluding that China must not view the world through the narrow lens of its own development, but understand the way the rest of the world views it. China must adopt a broader, more rational, and future-oriented perspective when examining its relationship with the world. China must also assume the responsibility of cultivating cosmopolitan citizens with a global consciousness. Finally, this article agrees with Law (2014, p. 332) in noting that China's curriculum reform may not meet the state's expectations because of the influence of the curriculum itself, as well as other external factors. Nonetheless, further developments can still be made in China's curriculum and education reforms by means of internal adjustments within education and system reforms at the institutional level.

References

Ban, J., & Tan, C. (2008). Change and development of moral education curriculum in primary and secondary schools in China during 30 years of reform and opening-up [in Chinese]. *Ideological & Theoretical Education*, (24), 14–19.

Chen, G., & Du, S. (2012). Reflection and prospects of moral education reform in the last ten years. *Curriculum, Teaching Material and Method*, 32(5), 84–90.

Department of Basic Education, Ministry of Education of the People's Republic of China. (2003). *Standards for the "Morality and Life" course in full-time compulsory education (Experimental draft)* [in Chinese]. Beijing Normal University Publishing Group.

Du, S., & Cao, S. (2015). How do the core values of socialism guide moral education textbooks? [in Chinese]. *Educational Research*, 36(9), 34–39.

Du, S., & Lu, X. (2009). *Moral education curriculum construction under the background of diversity* [in Chinese]. Jiangsu Education Publishing House.

Gao, D. (2004). Moral curriculum: Returning to life [in Chinese]. *Curriculum, Teaching Material and Method*, 24(11), 39–43, 73.

Gao, X., & Zhao, Y. (2003). Exploring new ideas in the "Morality and Society" course in primary schools [in Chinese]. *Journal of the Chinese Society of Education*, 24(4), 31–33.

Law, W. W. (2014). Understanding China's curriculum reform for the 21st century. *Journal of Curriculum Studies*, 46(3), 332–360.

Lee, W. O., & Ho, C. H. (2005). Ideopolitical shifts and changes in moral education policies in China. *Journal of Moral Education*, 34(4), 413–431.

Li, L. (2012). Comparison of "Morality and Society" textbooks from the perspective of civic education [in Chinese].

Ideological & Theoretical Education, 28(4), 23–27, 143.

Lu, Y. (2016). Inheriting fine traditional culture and developing the school-based curriculum of moral education: On the development and implementation of the school-based moral education course "Jade Appreciation" [in Chinese]. *Primary School Teaching Reference*, 55(5), 66–67.

Meng, Y., & Wu, L. (2017). Review of the research on Chinese traditional culture and primary school moral education [in Chinese]. *Theory and Practice of Education*, 37(32), 27–30.

Ministry of Education of the People's Republic of China. (2001). *Guidelines for curriculum reform of basic education (Trial implementation)* [in Chinese]. http://www.gov.cn/gongbao/content/2002/content_61386.htm

Ministry of Education of the People's Republic of China. (2003). *Standards for the "Ideology and Morality" course in full-time compulsory education (Experimental draft)* [in Chinese]. http://www.moe.gov.cn/srcsite/A26/s8001/200305/t20030513_167351.html

Ministry of Education of the People's Republic of China. (2014). *Guidelines for improving education in the excellent traditional Chinese culture* [in Chinese]. http://www.moe.gov.cn/srcsite/A13/s7061/201403/t20140328_166543.html

Reed, G. G. (1995). Moral/political education in the People's Republic of China: Learning through role models. *Journal of Moral Education*, 24(2), 99–111.

Tan, C., & Reyes, V. (2016). Curriculum reform and education policy borrowing in China: Towards a hybrid model of teaching. In C. P. Chou & J. Spangler (Eds.), *Chinese education models in a global age* (pp. 37–49). Springer.

The State Council of the People's Republic of China. (2001). *State Council's decision on the reform and development of basic education* [in Chinese]. http://www.gov.cn/gongbao/content/2001/content_60920.htm

Wang, L., & Zhang, J. (2016). A journey with classics: Exploration on practice of promoting the fine traditional culture in experimental primary schools in Qufu City [in Chinese]. *Journal of Shanghai Educational Research*, 32(9), 17–19.

Xi, J. (2018a). *Talks with students and faculty at Peking University* [in Chinese]. http://www.moe.gov.cn/jyb_xwfb/moe_176/201805/t20180503_334882.html

Xi, J. (2018b). *Persist with the developmental path of socialist education with Chinese characteristics; Cultivate builders and successors of socialism with all-round development in morality, intelligence, physique, aesthetics, and labor skills* [in Chinese]. http://edu.people.com.cn/n1/2018/0911/c1053-30286253.html

Zou, Q. (2011). Retrospect and prospect of the moral education curriculum reform in primary schools [in Chinese]. *The Party Building and Ideological Education in Schools*, 29(3), 39–41.

Higher Education

In 2017, Chinese government launched a massive higher education initiative targeting at developing selected universities and disciplines into the world first-class universities as well as first-class disciplines in the world (abbreviated as the "Double First Class" initiative). The initiative was interpreted as an ambitious higher education project following the previous "985" and "211" key projects. By scrutinizing the list of the selected universities, selection criteria, and administrative measures in use, this study identifies five policy features of this initiative and three possible challenges to the "Double First Class" initiative under top-level design. This article can contribute to the understanding of the significant initiative and the relevant policymaking in the future.

The "Double First Class" Initiative Under Top-Level Design[1]

Xiao Liu

In 2017, Chinese government launched a massive higher education initiative targeting at developing selected universities and disciplines into the world first-class universities as well as first-class disciplines in the world (abbreviated as the "Double First Class" initiative). The initiative was an ambitious higher education project following the existing "985" and "211" key projects.

After two years of wide discussions and deliberations, in January 2017, the Ministry of Education, Ministry of Finance, and National Development and Reform Commission jointly released a document titled as *Implementation measures to coordinate development of world first-class universities and first-class disciplines construction (tentative)*. The document specifies the goals of future development, and details selection criteria, procedures, supporting schemes, and strategies of management and implementation.

By 2020, a number of universities and a group of disciplines will meet the world-class standards, and a number of disciplines will be in leading positions. By 2030, more universities and disciplines will be enlisted in the world-class category, and a number of universities will be among the best worldwide and China will be in the leading position in more disciplines. The overall strength of higher education will be

---

1 This article was published on *ECNU Review of Education*, *1*(1), 147–152.

substantially increased. By the middle of the century, the number and strength of the first-class universities and disciplines will be in the leading position in the world. This solid foundation will transform China into a strong power in higher education. (Ministry of Education, Ministry of Finance, & National Development and Reform Commission, 2017a)

In September 2017, a list of the universities and disciplines was released [1]. A total number of 42 universities were selected as in the world first-class universities initiatives; among them, 36 were in the category A and 6 in the category B. A total of 95 universities were identified under the first-class disciplines initiative (Ministry of Education, Ministry of Finance, & National Development and Reform Commission, 2017b). In total, 137 universities met the criteria of the "Double First Class" initiative, accounting for 4.7% of 2,914 universities in China. Among the 42 nominated universities under the world-class initiative, 33 are affiliated to the Ministry of Education, four to the Ministry of Industry and Information Technology, and one to the Chinese Academy of Sciences. There is only one military university and three provincial universities included in the initiative.

Policy features of the "Double First Class" initiative

By scrutinizing the list of the selected universities, selection criteria, and administrative measures in use, policy features of the initiative are identified as follows:

Cumulative effects of previous projects

The selected first-class universities are characterized by their undergoing long-term construction, advanced education philosophy, substantial academic strength, and high level of social recognition. The chosen universities must own a number of nationally and internationally leading disciplines, and have highly visible performance in education reform, innovation and building modern universities. Despite of the favorable regional layout consideration for Zhengzhou University in the central China, Yunnan University and Xinjiang University in the west, the enlisted universities under the initiative are virtually those bearing cumulative advantages from the previous "985" project.

1　The list of the world-class universities and the first-class disciplines can be retrieved from http://www.moe.edu.cn/srcsite/A22/moe_843/201709/t20170921_314942.html.

Call for meeting the national strategic needs and advancing the international cutting-edge science and technology

The selection criteria aiming at serving the key national strategies emphasized close connections with industrial development, social needs, and the cutting-edge science and technology. As a result, Engineering and Natural Sciences are the most benefited research fields under the initiative. Material Science and Engineering, Chemistry, and Biology were the top three favored disciplines with 30, 25, and 16 universities enlisted respectively under the first-class disciplines initiative. Mathematics and Computer Science and Technology were the next two blessed disciplines, each with 14 selected universities.

Favorable consideration towards certain disciplines with Chinese characteristics

From the perspective of the national strategy, development of the "Double First Class" initiative adheres to Chinese characteristics, supporting strong disciplines while nurturing those of special needs, e.g., Marxism Studies and Chinese Traditional Medicine. These two disciplines are of outstanding features, irreplaceable, and urgently needed in the national development. They were not suitable for international comparison through the third-party evaluations. There are six universities with Marxism Studies and six with Chinese Traditional Medicine included in the initiative.

Uneven regional distribution of selected universities and disciplines

The selection criteria of the initiative were based on merits rather than on bottom-line qualifications, prioritizing efficiency while taking fairness into account. In Beijing, Shanghai, and Jiangsu, 153, 57, and 43 disciplines were selected respectively. Such regional distribution is similar to the distribution in previous key initiatives. Beijing and the Eastern area retain their clear advantage; universities in regions such as Hebei and Shanxi were less favored. Some universities in the Western area were favored because of the designated and biased support of the policy.

Guiding administrative principles of total quantity limit, open competition, and dynamic adjustment

Running on a 5-year cycle, the initiative aims to break labelling effect, and objectively formulate reasonable criteria of selection and performance evaluation. Assessments are implemented in the early, middle, and final terms of the project. Dynamic adjustment is employed to regulate the funding and the number of the selected disciplines. Therefore, the selected universities and disciplines are subject to funding reduction or even elimination in the next round if their performance is evaluated poor. Conversely, those unselected in the first round will have opportunities to become enrolled in the initiative if they improve.

The "Double First Class" initiative as part of the national strategy

For the past 20 years, global competition in higher education has been extraordinarily fierce. Higher education is an essential driving force of a nation's economy; therefore, governments worldwide have concentrated unprecedented attention on higher education, pouring tremendous resources into Bioengineering, Information Technology, and several other fundamental areas of research, hoping that the contribution of higher education to the economy could be increased (Altbach, Reisberg, & Rumbley, 2010). This tactic is particularly crucial for developing countries, which display their economic competence through the number of world-class universities they have. Therefore, establishing world-class research universities is regarded as an investment to the future of the nation (Rhoads, Li, & Ilano, 2014). Many countries in Asia and Latin America have formulated policies to elevate their universities to the world-class status. However, for universities in the developing countries, establishing a high-quality education system of world-class universities in a short period of time is highly challenging (Lee, 2013). To address this challenging task, Chinese government adopted a frequently applied strategy, i.e., to drive systemic development of higher education through a top-down plan.

A master development plan for higher education is a comprehensive configuration to incorporate higher education in the overall national development strategy, driven by a series of resource allocation policies. Therefore, the "Double First Class" initiative does not only consider the development of higher education itself, but also coheres with the overall strategy of national development, and dynamically adjusts to the strategies implemented in the economic and social sectors.

Possible challenges to the "Double First Class" initiative

In order to synchronize educational and social development, Chinese government proposed to push a group of high quality universities to enter the world first-class group by driving institutional reforms and leveraging performance. However, there is an inconvenient reality lying behind the blueprint of the initiative.

Ambiguous definition under ambitious goals

How world-class universities and disciplines should be defined is unclear. To the general public, various rankings help identify "the first-class" ones. But every ranking system has its own limitations. Some researchers suggested several essential indicators such as concentrated academic research, visible international reputation, solid financial foundation, and attraction to talents (Salmi, 2009; Rodriguez-Pomeda, & Casani, 2016). However, these measures still cannot precisely define "the first-class." Furthermore, "the first class" is a nebulous label; an ambiguous concept that can be arbitrarily elaborated.

Excessive resource concentration in competition

The foundation of the initiative is discipline, which means that the selection and evaluation criteria are based on academic development of disciplines. Only 12 of the 42 selected as the potential first-class universities have more than 10 disciplines enlisted as the first-class disciplines. Some nominated universities only have one or two outstanding disciplines. In order to increase their competitive advantages, universities would strategically concentrate the limited resources on the existing outstanding disciplines. This may induce fluctuations and the constant adjustment of academic structures in universities, which will cause the instability of disciplinary structures. Such adjustment is virtually a costly survival game of the fittest among the disciplines within a university, but also may lead to unbalanced academic structure impairing training high quality personnel.

Tensions between academic autonomy and performance evaluation

Academic autonomy is the core principle of higher education; this is particularly true for the world-leading research universities. The balance between institutional autonomy and accountability is a complicated issue in the developing countries (Altbach, 2013). The strategic goals, selection criteria, and selection procedures of the initiative have revealed the core values of nationalism. Although the selected universities have begun to announce their construction plans, they are still subject to the achievement expectations of the government.

The "Double First Class" initiative has just begun to be implemented. The problems and challenges discussed herein can only be overcome in the future implementation. The universities and disciplines selected in the first round should exercise more of their academic autonomy, to deepen the reforms of the institutions and mechanisms, and to lead development of a clustered and extended disciplines around their core outstanding disciplines. For those unselected, their key strategies might involve amplifying their advantages and increasing their competitiveness.

References

Altbach, P. G. (2013). Advancing the national and global knowledge economy: The role of research universities in developing countries. *Studies in Higher Education*, *38*(3), 316–330.

Altbach, P. G., Reisberg, L., & Rumbley, L. E. (2010). Tracking a global academic revolution. *Change: The Magazine of Higher Learning*, *42*(2), 30–39.

Lee, J. (2013). Creating world-class universities: Implications for developing countries. *Prospects*, *43*(2), 233–249.

Ministry of Education, Ministry of Finance, & National Development and Reform Commission of China. (2017a). *Implementation measures to coordinate development of world-class universities and first-class disciplines construction (tentative)* [in Chinese]. http://www.gov.cn/xinwen/2017-01/27/content_5163903

Ministry of Education, Ministry of Finance, & National Development and Reform Commission of China. (2017b). *List of the world-class universities and first-class disciplines* [in Chinese]. http://www.moe.gov.cn/srcsite/A22/moe_843/201709/t20170921_314942.html

Rhoads, R. A., Li, S., & Ilano, L. (2014). The global quest to build world-class universities: Toward a social justice agenda. *New Directions for Higher Education*, (168), 27–39.

Rodriguez-Pomeda, J., & Casani, F. (2016). Legitimating the world-class university concept through the discourse of elite universities' presidents. *Higher Education Research & Development*, *35*(6), 1269–1283.

Salmi, J. (2009). *The challenge of establishing world-class universities*. The World Bank.

This article provides an overview of the composition and evolution of China's high-level talent programs in higher education. It reviews key talent policies adopted by the Chinese government since the 1990s, using content analysis methods to identify policy characteristics and reform trends. According to the study, talent programs in China operate at four levels: the national level, provincial level, city level, and institutional level. The main objectives of China's high-level talent programs are to support and promote the development of young talent and encourage overseas scholars to return to China. China's high-level talent programs have undergone various changes since 1993, characterized by five major aspects: individual program optimization; replacement, integration, and separation; preventing overlapping funding; mitigating the unbalanced impact the programs have on higher education institutions across regions; and strengthening risk assessment for programs focused on attracting overseas talent. This article helps to offer a comprehensive assessment of the talent programs implemented by Chinese universities and explores the key trends and content of recent policy changes.

The Composition and Evolution of China's High-Level Talent Programs in Higher Education[1]

Junwen Zhu

In 1995, the Chinese government proposed the strategy of "Reinvigorating China Through Science and Education." The aim of the strategy was to facilitate the transition from extensive to intensive economic growth by promoting technological advancement and improvements in labor quality. In connection with this initiative, the government launched two main projects designed to accelerate the development of the nation's higher education system. Project 211, initiated in 1995, targeted construction of approximately 100 key higher education institutions and a number of key disciplines for the 21st century. In 1998, Project 985 was put into action with the aim of enhancing the competitiveness of China's top universities toward world-class-level institutions. Project 211 and Project 985 each emphasized the need for faculty training and development, as a first-class teaching faculty was considered the foundation for any high-level university. Since the

---

1 This article was funded by the National Education Science Foundation of China (No. BIA160116). It was published on *ECNU Review of Education*, 2(1), 104–110.

1990s, the Chinese government has launched a series of high-level talent programs. These programs have exerted a widespread and profound influence on the construction of teaching faculties in China's institutions of higher education.

Composition of China's high-level talent programs in higher education

Talent programs geared toward the development of teaching faculties in China's higher education institutions operate at four levels: the national level, provincial level (including autonomous regions and direct-controlled municipalities), city level, and institutional level. On the national level, the high-level talent system mainly consists of programs focused on the development, introduction, and utilization of high-level talent across domestic institutions of higher education. These programs, launched by national ministries and commissions, not only serve an important macro-level role in the overall design of talent policies in higher education but also help shape the formation of talent policies on a more local level. That is, local governments typically refer to the national programs in formulating their own talent recruitment initiative, especially with respect to programs targeting overseas talent (Zhu & Shen, 2013). At the institutional level, colleges and universities establish individual programs designed to accommodate their own orientations and objectives; such programs are marked by significant cross-institutional differences.

Table 1 shows the composition of China's high-level talent programs in higher education. In the early 1990s, as the strategy of Reinvigorating China Through Science and Education and Project 211 were taking shape, the government launched a series of talent programs as part of its overall strategy package.

The high-level talent programs in the 1990s were mainly formulated by the former State Education Commission of the People's Republic of China,[1] the National Natural Science Foundation of China, and the former Personnel Department of the People's Republic of China. Coordination among the different talent programs has strengthened over the last decade or so, especially following the establishment of the Central Coordination Group for Talent Work in 2003.

The main objectives of the high-level talent programs are to support and promote the development of young talent, to encourage overseas scholars to return to China to work, and to

---

[1] The State Education Commission of the People's Republic of China was replaced by the Ministry of Education in 1998.

Table 1. Composition of China's high-level talent programs in higher education.

Year of initiation	Name of program	Leading department(s)	Objective
1993	Trans-Century Training Program Foundation for the Talents	State Education Commission of the People's Republic of China	To cultivate and foster young academic leaders
1994	The National Science Fund for Distinguished Young Scholars	National Natural Science Foundation of China	To promote the development of young talent in science and technology and encourage overseas scholars to return to China to work
1995	The Hundred-Thousand-Ten Thousand Talents Project	Seven departments including the former Personnel Department of China, the State Science and Technology Commission, the State Education Commission, the Ministry of Finance, the State Planning Committee, the China Association for Science and Technology, and the National Natural Science Foundation of China	To cultivate outstanding young "cross-century talent"
1998	Changjiang Scholars Program	Ministry of Education of the People's Republic of China	To cultivate and foster world-class academic leaders
2004	Program for New Century Excellent Talents in University	Ministry of Education of the People's Republic of China	To strengthen teams of young academic leaders in higher education institutions and cultivate and foster innovative elites
2008	Overseas High-Level Talents Introduction Plan (the Thousand Talents Plan)	Eleven ministries and commissions including the Organization Department of the Central Committee of the Communist Party of China and the Ministry of Human Resources and Social Security	To attract high-level talent from overseas
2010	Young Overseas High-Level Talents Introduction Plan (the Thousand Young Talents Plan)	Eleven ministries and commissions including the Organization Department of the Central Committee of the Communist Party of China and the Ministry of Human Resources and Social Security	To attract high-level talent (under 40 years of age) from overseas to work in China on a full-time basis
2012	National Special Support Program for High-Level Talents (the Ten Thousand Talents Plan)	Eleven ministries and commissions including the Organization Department of the Central Committee of the Communist Party of China and the Ministry of Human Resources and Social Security	To support the cultivation of high-level domestic talent
2012	Science Foundation for Excellent Young Scholars	National Natural Science Foundation of China	To cultivate young "innovative talent" (males aged under 38 and females aged under 40)

Source. Talent program documents from the respective government departments listed above.

cultivate world-class academic leaders. These programs mainly target young professionals in fields of science and technology and leading academics under the age of 45. This approach was designed to address one of the fundamental problems facing China's higher education institutions in the 1990s: a shortage of new talent to replace the older generation and a lack of academic leaders and young "backbone" talent.

While placing a premium on the recruitment of overseas scholars, early high-level talent programs also underscored the importance of cultivating domestic talent. After 2008, the Thousand Talents Plan and the Thousand Young Talents Plan were launched specially to attract high-level talent from overseas. Afterward, the National Special Support Program was formulated and implemented in conjunction with the Thousand Talents Plan, with a specific focus on cultivating domestic high-level talent in the fields of innovation and entrepreneurship.

Evolution of China's high-level talent programs in higher education

The quarter century since 1993 has witnessed various changes in China's high-level talent programs. While certain programs have remained in effect (with periodic amendment and refinement), others have either been terminated after achieving their goals or merged into new programs. This evolution can be characterized by the following five major traits.

Optimization of individual programs

The Changjiang Scholars Program is a case in point. Since its inception in 1998, the program has undergone four major amendments (in 1999, 2004, 2011, and 2018). While maintaining a consistent objective—"to attract and select young and middle-aged outstanding individuals and cultivate and foster a group of world-class academic leaders" (Ministry of Education of the People's Republic of China, 1998)—the program's standards for talent selection, grantee responsibilities, allowances and subsidies, regional balance, withdrawal mechanisms,[1] and other aspects have been updated in accordance with the changing landscape. Established in 1994, the

---

1 There are two types of withdrawal: mandatory withdrawal and individual application for withdrawal. Those who are investigated for criminal responsibility for violation of the law, who fraudulently obtain qualifications for admission, who violate teachers' morality, or who seriously violate academic ethics shall be forced to withdraw. Individuals may apply for withdrawal from the talent plan due to their departure from the original discipline for the post, inability to get to the post during the period of employment, or the deficiency of time on duty.

National Science Fund for Distinguished Young Scholars has been in effect for nearly 25 years. Its initial objectives were to promote the development of young talent in science and technology, to encourage overseas scholars to return to China to work, and to accelerate the cultivation of outstanding field specialists capable of competing with their international peers in science and technology (National Natural Science Foundation of China, 1995b). Among the initial 49 recipients, 26 were from higher education institutions (National Natural Science Foundation of China, 1995a). The scale and intensity of the program's funding and management, among other aspects, have been periodically adjusted, including through four rounds of amendments in 1997, 2002, 2009, and 2015.

Replacement, integration, and separation

China's high-level talent programs have undergone an array of structural changes. For instance, the Trans-Century Training Program Foundation for the Talents implemented in 1993 was replaced by the Program for New Century Excellent Talents in University in 2004, which, in turn, was incorporated into the Young Changjiang Scholars Program in 2015. The Hundred-Thousand-Ten Thousand Talents Project implemented in 1995 was integrated into the National Special Support Program for High-Level Talents (also known as the Ten Thousand Talents Plan) as a subprogram in 2012 (Eleven ministries and commissions including the Organization Department of the Central Committee of the Communist Party of China and the Ministry of Human Resources and Social Security, 2012). Likewise, the Young Elites Program was specifically established as a part of the Ten Thousand Talents Plan in 2011. Currently, the Young Elites Program, the Young Changjiang Scholars Program, the Excellent Young Talents Program, and the Thousand Young Talents Plan are collectively referred to as "the four youth-talent programs."

Preventing overlapping funding from talent programs

In recent years, there has been widespread criticism of scholars receiving overlapping funding from talent programs at the same level. This problem has been exacerbated by a lack of policy consistency and communication among different administrative departments. Many talent programs have now adopted measures to address this issue. For example, the 2018 revised version of *Administrative Measures for the Changjiang Scholars Program* explicitly states that "talent selection and cultivation should be coordinated to avoid overlapping with the support granted by other talent programs at the same level" (Ministry of Education of the People's Republic of China, 2018). The 2018 application announcement of the Ten Thousand Talents Plan stipulates that recipients of the Young Changjiang Scholars Program and Science Foundation for Excellent Young Scholars may not apply for the Young Elites Program under the Ten Thousand Talents Plan during the funding period.

Unbalanced impact on higher education institutions across regions

Due to regional disparities in China's economic growth, there is an ongoing flow of high-level talent from higher education institutions in the country's central and western regions to the more developed regions in the east. This has resulted in a decline in the competitiveness of institutions of higher education in the central and western regions. In recent years, the government has responded to this problem by loosening the talent program application requirements for applicants from central and western institutions, helping to reverse the flow of high-level talent from the central and western regions and preventing institutions in the east from "poaching" talent from the west. This trend in policy amendment is currently shared among all high-level talent programs.

Strengthened risk assessment for programs focused on attracting overseas talent

Although China's high-level talent programs are government funded, the actual applicants and users of the funds are institutions. While recruiting overseas talent over the past several years, a number of higher education institutions had an inadequate understanding of policies relating to intellectual property rights, confidentiality agreements, and noncompete agreements. This led to certain misunderstandings and conflicts of interests. This problem, however, has since been brought to public attention, and preventive measures have been adopted. For instance, the application procedures for all talent programs under the Thousand Talents Plan in 2018 include a requirement to incorporate risk assessments, which involve a comprehensive evaluation and review of the applicants' undertakings at their prior overseas workplaces, including an analysis of intellectual property rights, confidentiality agreements, and noncompete agreements.

Problems in China's high-level talent programs in higher education and trends in program reform

Since the 1990s, with support from high-level talent programs such as the Changjiang Scholars Program, higher education institutions in China have assembled a talented group of young and middle-aged scholars. As of 2017, the Changjiang Scholars Program had supported a total of 3,249 awardees, among which 2,298 were distinguished professors and 951 were chair professors [1]; the National Science Fund for Distinguished Young Scholars had funded 3,796 recipients. [2] With the deepening of policy implementation, however, certain negative impacts of these programs have also become gradually noticeable, as manifested in the following aspects:

Firstly, the original purpose of national "talent programs" (supporting the career development of high-achieving candidates) has been diverted, and these programs have gradually become mere labels of academic success. Being selected into a national talent program has become a symbol of academic achievement and a successful academic career. This drives scholars to invest time and effort into competing for a position in the talent programs at the expense of their teaching and scientific research. Secondly, successful candidates receive a substantial allowance and subsidy/grant for scientific research from the government, while enjoying benefits from specific institution-based supporting policies with respect to remuneration and welfare packages. Thus, selection into a talent program serves as "leverage" in salary negotiations within the academic labor market. Higher education institutions irrationally compete in "employee poaching" by offering higher salaries to lure the recipients of talent program awards. In addition, the structure of talent programs has resulted in the creation of a hierarchy among teaching faculty at higher education institutions based on the ranking of talent programs, which has widened the disparities in their status and income. Thirdly, policy coordination among different talent programs still has room for improvement. Due to the segregation of department duties, specific application procedures, and various administrative factors, many talent programs remain separated despite an increase in integration between certain programs. A viable, broad-reaching

---

1 Based on statistics from the past lists of selected candidates of the Changjiang Scholars Program.
2 Based on data from "Statistics on Application for and Funding of the National Science Fund for Distinguished Young Scholars" published by the National Natural Science Foundation of China in previous years.

solution is necessary for talent programs where shared objectives and regulations are lacking. Fourthly, although the risks involved in the recruitment of overseas talent have been brought to attention, an effective, comprehensive risk prevention mechanism has yet to be established.

Future reforms addressing China's high-level talent programs are likely to advance on three main fronts. The first is a move toward further streamlining and integration by substantially reducing the number of talent programs and by avoiding the launch of redundant programs from different departments that may result in wasteful, overlapping funding. The second is to eliminate the Matthew effect through which candidates of talent programs leverage their successful applications to obtain academic resources and to rectify the "academic hierarchy" that has been created by the talent program system. The third is to strengthen the protection of intellectual property rights and contractual obligations in connection with the recruitment of overseas talent. Given the increasingly globalized landscape, it is certain that a future direction will be to gain a better understanding of the systems of talent utilization policies across different countries while avoiding the risks involved in talent introduction. To reduce flexible talent introduction and enhance recruitment on a full-time basis will also become one of the main trends in the future.

References

Eleven ministries and commissions including the Organization Department of the Central Committee of the Communist Party of China and the Ministry of Human Resources and Social Security. (2012, August 17). *National Special Support Program for High-Level Talents* [in Chinese]. http://rsc.fafu.edu.cn/af/89/c7746a176009/page.htm

Ministry of Education of the People's Republic of China. (1998, July 13). *Changjiang Scholars Program* [in Chinese]. http://www.moe.gov.cn/srcsite/A04/s7051/199807/t19980713_162233.html

Ministry of Education of the People's Republic of China. (2018, September 21). *Administrative measures for the Changjiang Scholars Program* [in Chinese]. http://www.moe.gov.cn/srcsite/A04/s8132/201809/t20180921_349638.html

National Natural Science Foundation of China. (1995a). Result announcement of the National Science Fund for distinguished young scholars in 1994 [in Chinese]. *Science Foundation in China*, (2), 77–78.

National Natural Science Foundation of China. (1995b). Temporary measures for administration of the National Science Fund for Distinguished Young Scholars [in Chinese]. *China Scholars Abroad*, (6), 43.

Zhu, J., & Shen, Y. (2013). Status quo and problems of China's provincial policies on introduction of overseas talents and related suggestions [in Chinese]. *Journal of Shanghai Jiaotong University (Philosophy and Social Sciences Edition)*, (1), 59–63.

Recently, the Chinese government's consistent efforts to expand higher vocational education enrollment by one million students have significant implications for China's higher vocational education. The proposed "1 + X" model—which attaches equal importance to academic education and skill training—may represent the beginning of a new stage in the development of higher vocational education in China. This article explores the relationship between governmental policy and the development of higher vocational education in China. It begins with a textual analysis of dozens of policy documents on higher vocational education issued by the Chinese government since 1999. The article argues that the development of higher vocational education in China has mainly been policy-driven and can be divided into four stages. The transition between each of these developmental stages was marked by new policy initiatives undertaken by the Chinese government.

Policy-Driven Development and the Strategic Initiative of One-Million Enrollment Expansion in China's Higher Vocational Education[1]

Xiaoxian Fan

Since expanding enrollment in 1999, China has substantially developed the scale and quality of its higher vocational education sector. Higher vocational education has comprised roughly half of the higher education sector. According to data published by the Ministry of Education of the People's Republic of China (MOE), by 2018, there were 1,418 higher vocational and technical colleges, accounting for 53.2% of the total number (2,663) of higher education institutions in China (MOE, 2019). In 2018, higher vocational education had 3.6883 million newly admitted students and 11.337 million enrolled students, accounting for 46.6% and 40%, respectively, of regular higher education enrollment (Ma & Guo, 2019). Moreover, more than 90% of higher vocational education graduates found jobs within 6 months of graduation.

Thus, after two decades of development, China's higher vocational education has achieved the policy goals set for such indicators as scale, quality, graduate employment rate, and graduate starting salary. Playing a substantial role in the China's move to higher education massification,

---

1 This article was published on *ECNU Review of Education*, 3(1), 179–186.

higher vocational education has become a major component of the higher education system and a major source of the highly skilled and practical personnel. A number of competitive vocational colleges have also emerged, including A Hundred Model Schools, National Advanced Vocational Education Institutions, and National Model Higher Education Institutions of Innovation and Entrepreneurship. These achievements in higher vocational education are inseparable from China's continuous policy incentives.

Historical review of China's policy incentives for higher vocational education

Since the expansion of higher education enrollment in 1999, China has introduced more than 30 policy initiatives for enhancing higher vocational education. These policy initiatives have served as the institutional foundation, policy logic, and common guideline for developing higher vocational education in the country. Consequently, numerous vocational colleges have developed along similar trajectories. Under these policy incentives, higher vocational education has undergone a staged development with different focuses at various stages. This development can be roughly divided into four stages: Stage 1 (1999 - 2005), Stage 2 (2006 - 2010), Stage 3 (2011 - 2018), and Stage 4 (2019 - present). This section discusses these stages of development in greater detail.

During the initial development stage, Stage 1 (1999 - 2005), China introduced the "reform, reorganization, reinstitution, and supplementation" initiative. In January 1999, the MOE and the former State Development Planning Commission jointly issued the *Circular on the Issuance of the Opinions on the Trial Implementation of New Management Modes and Operating Mechanism for Higher Vocational and Technical Education* (document No. 2 [1999] of the MOE), initiating the vigorous development of higher vocational education. In January 2000, the MOE published the *Circular on the Issuance of the Opinions of the MOE on Improving the Talent Cultivation Work of Higher Vocational and Technical Education* (document No. 2 [2000] of the Higher Education Department of the MOE), which defined the guiding principle, priorities, and road map of higher vocational education. In 2004, the General Office of the MOE issued the *Circular on Implementing Comprehensive Performance Assessment of the Talent Cultivation Work of Higher Vocational and Technical Education* (document No. 16 [2004] of the Higher Education Department of the MOE). The nationwide implementation of performance assessments of higher vocational and technical institutions contributed to the sustainable and healthy development of higher vocational education.

The "reform, reorganization, reinstitution, and supplementation" initiative refers to the reform, reorganization, and reinstitution of the existing vocational colleges, independent adult colleges, and some technical colleges into vocational and technical colleges (hereinafter, vocational colleges). This initiative also supplemented higher vocational education by encouraging 4-year regular universities to set up vocational colleges, either independently or in cooperation with industry partners.

Moreover, under the premise of the overall coordination of local education resources, provincial governments were encouraged to allocate local resources to establish comprehensive and communal vocational colleges. The introduction of this policy by the Central Committee of the Communist Party of China (CPC) and the State Council, as well as the delegation of the authority to run vocational colleges to local governments, emphasized the importance of higher vocational education as a major component of higher education and defined the development direction of higher vocational education in the context of higher education massification. By 2005, China had more than 1,200 vocational colleges, including those set up by 4-year regular universities accounting for more than half the country's regular higher education institutions. The annual enrollment and graduate figures for higher vocational education accounted for more than half of those of regular higher education (MOE, 2005). As such, the goal of developing the scale of higher vocational education was achieved.

Stage 2 (2006 – 2010) involved improving the quality of higher vocational education and centered on an initiative to develop model vocational colleges. In November 2006, the MOE issued the *Decision of the State Council on Rapidly Developing Vocational Education* (document No. 35 [2005] of the State Council) and the *Several Opinions on Comprehensively Improving the Teaching Quality of Higher Vocational Education* (document No. 16 [2006] of the MOE). The policy focus shifted with the development of vocational colleges entering a transformational period centering on improving teaching quality. At the same time, the MOE and the Ministry of Finance (MOF) launched the "Program of Developing National Model Higher Vocational Colleges." This program supported the development of a hundred higher vocational colleges into national model vocational colleges, and another hundred higher vocational colleges to develop into national key vocational colleges. As such, the program sought to enhance reform and improve the overall quality of China's higher vocational education system through the demonstration and driving effect of model and key higher vocational colleges.

The indicator framework and method for evaluating the cultivating of talent by vocational colleges were adjusted with the publication of the *Circular of the MOE on the Issuance of the Scheme for Evaluating the Talent Cultivation Work of Higher Vocational Institutions* in April 2008. Led by education agencies, and participated in by society, these adjustments served to gradually develop a teaching quality assurance system for higher vocational colleges. The policy objective of talent cultivation established during this stage sought to develop hundreds of millions of high-quality personnel and tens of millions of highly skilled professionals to serve the needs of socialist modernization. Pursuing a "service-and employment-oriented" direction, China's vocational education sector was transformed from a plan-driven, examination-oriented sector to one that was market-driven and employment-oriented. Moreover, the role of the government shifted from direct involvement to overall guidance. Consequently, the system of modern vocational education, known as "modern vocational education system with Chinese characteristics," was formulated. The program for developing national model vocational colleges was launched to build the capacity and improve the quality of vocational colleges on a large scale.

Stage 3 (2011–2018) focused on capacity building—that is, on improving the capacity of the higher vocational education system to serve the needs of socioeconomic development. China has sought to transform its higher vocational education system to serve the economy, while maintaining its present direction and pursuing sustainable, healthy development. This can be observed in a series of policy initiatives introduced during this stage, including the *Outline of the National Medium-and Long-Term Education Reform and Development (2010–2020)*, the *Decision of the State Council on Accelerating the Development of Modern Vocational Education* (document No. 19 [2014] of the State Council), the *Circular of the MOE and Five Other Ministries on the Issuance of the Plan for Developing the Modern Vocational Education System (2014–2020)*, the *Circular of the MOE and the MOF on Supporting Higher Vocational Schools to Improve Their Capacity of Facilitating the Development of Professional Service Industries* (document No. 11 [2011] of the Vocational Education and Adult Education Department of the MOE), and the *Several Opinions of the MOE on Driving the Reform and Innovation of Higher Vocational Education to Steer the Scientific Development of Vocational Education* (document No. 12 [2011] of the Vocational Education and Adult Education Department of the MOE). The idea of enhancing "production-education integration and school-enterprise cooperation" was formulated to accelerate the development of a world-class modern vocational education system with Chinese characteristics. Particular focus was placed on the important role of higher vocational education in optimizing the structure of the higher education system. As such, with its hierarchical structure, institutional type, mission, tasks, road map, and assurance mechanism defined within the framework of the modern vocational education system, China's higher vocational education entered a new historical stage of development.

The current stage, Stage 4 (2019 – present), places equal emphasis on expanding the scale and improving the quality of higher vocational education. This intention is marked by the planned expansion of enrollment by one million students, as well as the initiative to develop the higher vocational education sector through institutional types and major clusters. Issued by the State Council in January 2019, the *Circular on the Issuance of the Implementation Plan for National Vocational Education Reform* (document No. 4 [2019] of the State Council) (State Council, 2019) clarified, for the first time, that "vocational education and regular education are two different types of education with equal importance" and proposed the further development of high-quality higher vocational education. The "1 + X" model, a graduation evaluation system with Chinese characteristics, was announced in this policy. In the "1 + X" model, "1" refers to the universal academic certificate for all students, while "X" refers to a number of skill certificates tailored to fit different students. In the future, "several skill certificates" will be a better indicator of the true value of higher vocational education graduates than an academic certificate, as these skill certificates will better differentiate the job competency and employment competitiveness of graduates. In this regard, the "X" is different from the existing professional qualification certification system supervised by the human resources and social security authority. Based on the top-level design of the MOE, a professional qualification certification system centering on the professional competency of students will be established under the supervision of the education authority. Higher vocational education will extend in two directions, each of equal importance: namely, academic education and vocational training. Vocational education and training will improve the employment competency of groups such as demobilized military personnel, laid-off workers, and rural migrant workers.

Another document, the *Opinions of the MOE and the MOF on Implementing the Program of Developing High-Standard Vocational Colleges and Specialties with Chinese Characteristics* (MOE, 2019), proposed launching a program to develop excellent vocational colleges and academic programs with Chinese characteristics. This initiative places a particular focus on developing about 50 high-standard vocational colleges and approximately 150 high-quality specialties, building platforms for the cultivation of technicians and skilled personnel, and thus fulfilling needs for technological and skill innovation. This will also serve to support the development of national key industries and local pillar industries, while driving the high-quality development of modern vocational education.

In the *Report on the Work of the Government Delivered at the Second Session of the 13th National People's Congress on March 5, 2019*, Premier Li Keqiang proposed to "reform and refine the examination and admission mechanisms of vocational colleges, to encourage more senior high school students, demobilized military personnel, laid-off workers, and rural migrant workers to apply, and to achieve a large-scale expansion of one million in student enrollments in 2019" (Li, 2019). As such, China's higher vocational education has entered a new stage that places equal emphasis on scale expansion and quality improvement.

Strategic initiative of one-million enrollment expansion

China's economy is undergoing structural adjustment and transformation. As a result of several internal and external factors, China's economy has been under significant pressure in recent years. This has resulted in a reduction in economic growth goals; for example, in the 2019 government work report, the GDP growth rate target was set in the range of 6%–6.5% (Li, 2019). The shortage of high-level technicians and skilled workers is a major factor affecting economic growth. In the report, Premier Li attached unprecedented importance to vocational education—establishing vocational education development as a major driving force for maintaining key economic indicators within a reasonable range. Therefore it is strategically necessary to expand the size of higher vocational education for the ongoing transformation, upgrading, and high-quality development of China's economy.

The enrollment expansion is also an important measure for the country's stabilization of employment. In 2018, a meeting of the Political Bureau of the CPC Central Committee (China Central Television, 2018) emphasized stable employment, finance, international trade, foreign investment, domestic investment, and expectation—with stable employment considered the top priority. Vocational education plays an important role in "modernizing the economy and attaining high-quality full employment." The expansion of enrollment by one million students was proposed in the paragraph centered on "using multiple channels to stable and increase employment," rather than on education issues. This indicates that the Chinese government considers the move from the perspective of addressing the employment challenge rather than education. Indeed, China's labor market still has prominent structural issues. The one-million enrollment expansion will encourage more senior high school students, demobilized military personnel, laid-off workers, and rural migrant workers to apply for higher vocational education, as well as train more high-level technicians and skilled workers, thereby promoting high-quality employment and easing the structural issues of the employment market. As employment is a basic need of human well-being and a matter of national stability and social harmony, the Chinese government is directing significant effort and attention to this sector.

Enrollment expansion is considered an opportunity to develop and improve a modern vocational education system with Chinese characteristics. For a long time, higher vocational education was considered a hierarchical level in the education system rather than an institutional type, usually regarded as inferior to undergraduate education. As noted, in the document of implementation plan for national higher vocational education reform issued by the State Council (2019) in January 2019, it was clarified that vocational education and regular education are two different types of education of equal importance. Moreover, vocational education is expected to play an increasingly significant role. Vocational education needs to operate in a model different from that of regular education and provide its own special programs. Thus, this strategic move of enrollment expansion offers an opportunity for the higher vocational education system to enhance the reform of its recruitment system, to develop clusters of academic programs, to optimize its institutional management systems, to improve the quality of student training, as well as to build and improve the modern vocational education system.

Last, local governments at all levels and vocational colleges have been closely connected to achieve the goal of expanding enrollment by one million students. To implement the national strategic move of enrollment expansion, local governments at all levels are mobilized and incentivized to increase investment in higher vocational education, develop diversified policy solutions, and design interdepartmental, intersystem policy coordination mechanisms.

Higher vocational institutions are also proactively implementing the planned expansion. They are searching for multiple solutions to address software and hardware difficulties such as lack of adequate facilities, applicants, and teachers, as well as the lack of a fit model of education and operation. In this regard, higher vocational institutions are seeking school-industry cooperation to solve the shortage of schooling space, and creating new teaching and management models to ease the shortage of teaching resources. They have also reformed recruitment practice by introducing a separate college entrance examination, an independent interview, a "three in one" comprehensive appraisal of student applications or on-demand appraisals by industry partners. Other methods include utilizing teacher resources from industries through school-industry cooperation, expanding enrollment in special programs with better employment prospects, strengthening the connection with secondary vocational education such as preschool education and elderly care, implementing vocational training in emerging industries and industries with shortages of technicians and skilled workers, strengthening the clustering of academic programs to improve the sharing of teaching resources, as well as improving school management systems through production-education integration and school-industry cooperation.

References

China Central Television. (2018). *CCTV quick review: Keep the economy stable and good* [in Chinese]. http://tv.cctv.com/2018/08/02/VIDEdTvquyWQ9cUl657WGYy1180802.shtml

Li, K. (2019). *The government work report delivered by Premier Li Keqiang at the second session of the 13th National People's Congress of the People's Republic of China on March 5, 2019* [in Chinese]. http://www.gov.cn/premier/2019-03/05/content_5370734.htm

Ma, S., & Guo, W. (2019). Insisting on the combination of academic education and vocational training to promote the reform of vocational education in the new era [in Chinese]. *Chinese Vocational and Technical Education*, (7), 13–18.

Ministry of Education of the People's Republic of China. (2005, December 6). *Higher vocational colleges in China have accounted for more than 50% of ordinary colleges* [in Chinese]. https://www.chsi.com.cn/jyzx/200512/20051206/271238-1.html

Ministry of Education of the People's Republic of China. (2019, February 26). *518,900 schools of all levels and types in China in 2018* [in Chinese]. http://yn.people.com.cn/n2/2019/0226/c378440-32683414.html

State Council of the People's Republic of China. (2019, February 13). *Circular of the State Council on issuing the implementation plan of the national vocational education reform* [in Chinese]. http://www.gov.cn/zhengce/content/2019-02/13/content_5365341.htm

Since the 1980s, *suzhi* (素质) has become a core word in contemporary China. *Suzhi* education as an education philosophy full of Chinese characteristics has been well known in China for generations. Particularly since 1995, culture-oriented quality education as an anchor and starting point of *suzhi* education implementation in universities, which integrates with general education and liberal education from Western concepts, triggered great changes in Chinese universities. This article aims to review the concepts of *suzhi* education, general education, and their practice in China and helps us to learn more about the relevant topics.

Suzhi Education and General Education in China [1]

Haishao Pang, Meiling Cheng, Jing Yu and Jingjing Wu

There are many related or similar concepts to general education in China. Some of them are very locally created, such as *suzhi* education, culture-oriented quality education, whole-person education, and all-round education, while others are borrowed from English terms, such as general education, liberal education, and so on. When the borrowed English terms were translated into Chinese, there were different Chinese characters owing to each individual translator's understandings, so *suzhi* education and general education are interpreted into different opinions; therefore, some of them are very easy to be confusing. This article clarifies *suzhi* education connotation of Chinese characteristics and the proper understanding of General education in Chinese universities.

The concept of *suzhi* education in China

Suzhi and *suzhi* education have gradually been known to educators as a core term all over China. The word *suzhi* is a Chinese concept full of connotations, which is difficult to define in one English word. It was ever expounded by many Chinese scholars, such as Zhou (2000), Pan

---

1 This article is the research result of the university *suzhi* education project "Research on the Education System Combining Morality, Intelligence, Physique, Aesthetics and Labor" (2019SZEZD01), which is set up by Chinese Higher Education Association. It was published on *ECNU Review of Education*, 3(2), 380–395.

(1997), Wen (1997), and C. Zhang (1996) in their academic articles and books. In summary, *suzhi* of a person refers to the relatively stable quality structure, which is due to one's knowledge internalization, based on the inherent gifts and physiology and deeply influenced by their education experience and social environment. A person has some kind of *suzhi*, which means they have certain values, cultural cultivation, physical and psychological quality, wisdom, and abilities.

Suzhi education is the education that helps one to improve their comprehensive *suzhi* by longtime personality edifying, knowledge accumulating, ability training, practice, reflection, and internalization, and so on. As Whitehead (1950) said, "The ideal of a university is not so much knowledge, as power … to convert the knowledge of a boy into the power of a man" (p. 49). Through *suzhi* education, one could have their own values, culture appreciation, physical and psychological quality, wisdom, and kinds of abilities such as independent thinking and judgment. The mission of *suzhi* education should instruct students not just knowledge, ability, and skills but also how to be good citizens, improving the comprehensive quality of all students. So *suzhi* education is a long-time education that runs through one's school days.

Then, in what background was *suzhi* education put forward? Why should China implement *suzhi* education? The former Premier Li Lanqing (2003) and former Vice Minister of the Ministry of Education (MOE) Zhou Yuanqing (2014) had given a definite discourse. *Suzhi* education was first raised in May 1985. Deng Xiaoping pointed out in the First National Conference in 1979 on Educational Work since China's reform and opening-up: "In China, the strength of our national power and the size of the economic development power more and more rely on the quality of laborers, the quantity and quality of intellectuals" (L. Li, 2003, p. 298). That means the aim of *suzhi* education is to improve the quality of the Chinese people.

Suzhi education was first implemented in primary and secondary schools in China in the 1980s. It mainly aimed at overcoming the shortcomings of examination-oriented education in basic education schools which were influenced deeply by *Gaokao* (the National College Entrance Examination). It emphasized that the basic education had to transfer from examination-oriented education to *suzhi* education in order to comprehensively improve the quality of citizens. In 1977, the Chinese government restarted the *Gaokao* system. Gradually, the scores of students gained in *Gaokao* each year had become the sole standard in recruiting new college students. It was also the most important factor in selecting talents in China. Since the students' future mainly depended on the only scores in each year's *Gaokao* system, the fierce competition led most schools and students to an overemphasis on higher scores of exams, rote in daily teaching and learning in basic education. The senior high schools were quite directly preparing students for colleges and universities by simply teaching them how to get high scores in various exams, but ignored the development of the students as the "whole-person" in moral, intellectual, physical, aesthetic, and personality. Therefore, *suzhi* education emerged aiming at changing such exam-based trends and fostering the comprehensive and personality development of all students.

The development history of *suzhi* education in Chinese higher education could be divided into three stages by 2000 and 2015.

Stage 1: Originating and popularizing before 2000

Its main feature was strengthening culture-oriented quality education, by integrating humanity education with education of science and technology. Humanistic and social science lectures, art education activities, and so on, were put to use in second class.

In the 1990s, advocated by the MOE, culture-oriented quality education as an anchor and the starting point of *suzhi* education was implemented in Chinese universities. In 1995 and 1998, the Higher Education Department of MOE (1998) issued two documents, that is, *Notice on Starting Pilot Work for University Students Culture-Oriented Quality Education and Several Viewpoints on Strengthening University Students Culture-Oriented Quality Education*. The main purpose of culture-oriented quality education was to balance the narrow specialized education and dissolving the phenomenon of the overemphasis on the education of science and technology at college education but ignoring the education of humanities and arts. It is required that students in science and engineering learn more courses in humanity, history, philosophy, and art, while students in liberal arts learn some natural science courses.

Led by the MOE, Chinese universities quickly started to hold a large number of extracurricular activities, such as humanistic lectures and artistic performances, which were collectively known as second class in China. These education styles were the main practicing methods of culture-oriented quality education in the first stage, which was a remarkable feature of Chinese *suzhi* education. The main reason is that it takes a long time to prepare general education courses while it is easier and more convenient to arrange extracurricular activities.

Stage 2: Reforming and exploring (2000 – 2015)

Its main feature was culture-oriented quality education fading while general education popularizing gradually. Universities established general elective courses and explored general education talents-cultivating mode by launching reforming and experimental classes.

In 1999, the CPC Central Committee and State Council issued *The Decision of Deepening the Reform of Education and Promoting Suzhi Education Comprehensively* and held the national conference on educational work, in which it called for promoting *suzhi* education. This meant *suzhi* education had entered a new stage. All schools in China began to develop *suzhi* education in the education system.

In 2010, the Chinese government issued *Outline for China's National Plan for Medium and Long-Term Education Reform and Development (2010 – 2020)* which affirmed *suzhi* education was the right developmental direction of Chinese education reform again. In 2011, the Chinese Association for *Suzhi* Education was established. [1]

At the same time, the concept of general education from Western countries was borrowed by some researchers and administrators again owing to China's reform and opening-up policy. Owing to the development of *suzhi* education and culture-oriented quality education, the general education concept was rapidly recognized by Chinese scholars and generally accepted by Chinese universities. Many universities learned from Harvard University, and MIT or other American universities then began to construct general education courses. Some top universities launched some experimental classes to practice general education cultivation mode, such as Yuanpei College of Peking University launched in 2001 and Fudan College of Fudan University launched in 2005 (Pang & Huan, 2015). General education seminars and exchanging activities spontaneously organized by universities increased during this stage.

Stage 3: Deepening and improving (since 2015)

Its main feature was both *suzhi* education and general education transformed from superficial prosperity to profound-level reforming, which triggered reforming of talents-cultivating system in Chinese universities. In March 2016, *The 13th Five-Year Plan for Economic and Social*

---

[1] See http://case.bit.edu.cn/fkgk/fkjj/index.htm.

Development of the People's Republic of China was issued. It proposed that universities should implement a cultivation system combining general education and specialized education, and improve innovative talents training ability. This was the first appearance of the general education in Chinese government documents and the new cultivation system construction was referred to.

At the same time, *suzhi* education was further emphasized and expanding. At the 19th Congress of the Communist Party of China in 2017 and the National Education Conference held in 2018, President Xi Jinping (Xi, 2017, 2018) emphasized that China must develop *suzhi* education, train socialist builders and successors with all-round development of morality, intelligence, physique, aesthetic, and labor. Along with the popularizing of Chinese higher education and change of external conditions of education, morality, aesthetics, labor, social responsibility, innovation spirit, and practicing ability all become the most important factors of *suzhi* education. Among these, ideological political courses, entrepreneurship education, and so on, were paid most attention by the Chinese central government.

Moreover, Shanghai and Zhejiang province pioneered experiments on reforming the *Gaokao* system in recent 5 years. In 2020, China will implement an entirely new *Gaokao* system, which brings significant opportunities to *suzhi* education. Comprehensive *suzhi* evaluation of students in senior high school will become a measurement in *Gaokao*. Universities will admit and classify students by general academic subjects rather than specific majors. General education will be more important for freshmen and sophomore students, while students could choose specific majors during sophomore or junior year. Through this reform, general education is strengthened, while traditional specialist cultivation mode and university management system are tremendously challenged.

In other words, *suzhi* education, culture-oriented quality education, and general education were mixed together and caused great changes in Chinese higher education. The main approaches included setting up elective general education courses, developing abundant extracurricular activities, paying more attention to the students' comprehensive qualities in specialized education. The ultimate goals were improving all the students' cultural tastes, aesthetic interests, and humanistic and scientific qualities.

Many scholars and administrators in education field such as Zhou (1996), S. Yang (2001), Q. Zhang (2003), Wang (2004), Hu (2004), and Pang (2015) explored the connotations, implications, and the practical ways of implementing *suzhi* education. They indicated a high-qualified talent should have harmony and unity in knowledge, abilities, and qualities. Knowledge teaching and ability cultivation only taught students "how to do," while *suzhi* education could help them "how to be." Culture-oriented quality education was a distinguished anchor of *suzhi* education (Zhou, 2000), and the general education curriculum is a very important way of implementing *suzhi* education.

The connotation of general education and its practice in China

When was the starting point of general education in Chinese universities? There were many opinions about its origin in China. Huang (1993) thought the traditional Chinese culture like Confucianism, Taoism, Legalism, and other ancient philosophers held the concept of general education. Feng (2004) sorted out the history of general education in modern Chinese universities from the late Qing Dynasty to the early years in the People's Republic of China. But we believed that although the concept of general education was borrowed from the Western countries, it was by chance very similar to the traditional Chinese education concepts that it had actually been put into practice twice in China.

The first time was from the late Qing Dynasty to the year 1952. The Chinese modern universities were modeled after Westerns at the end of the 19th century, aiming at learning the advanced science and technology for strengthening the national defense and developing the industry (Xiong, 1988). Before the 1950s, Chinese universities learned the idea about general education, especially from 1912 to 1949, some famous scholars, who were also presidents of universities, such as Yuanpei Cai in Peking University, Yiqi Mei in Tsinghua University, Kezhen Zhu in Zhejiang University, and so on, advocated general education (Feng, 2004). They not only advocated the idea of general education but actively carried it out in those universities. They believed that college education should "cultivate the students' whole-personality and balance moral, intellectual, physical and aesthetic education" (Feng, 2004, pp. 100 – 110). They claimed that "general education is fundamental and essentials in the students' cultivation, while specialized education is superficial and latter part" (Feng, 2004, pp. 100 – 110). However, different from the history of Western universities and the tradition of humanism, modern Chinese universities paid too much attention to their instrumental values and were all committed to the nation's politics and economy from the beginning in modern China. Thus, specialized education was more popular, and the purpose of education was always dominated by "the Social Standard Theory."

In the 1950s, Chinese universities learned from the Soviet Union System and set up the specialized talents cultivation mode in colleges and universities. From then on, general education had almost disappeared in China for 30 years. According to the central government's order, three strategies were carried out in the 1950s. And they affected Chinese education greatly in all aspects including the education philosophy, curriculum structure, organization structure, and so on.

The first strategy was the National College and University Adjustment. It was the reorganization of colleges, universities, and the departments along Soviet lines from 1952 to 1957. First, the Chinese government moved the same majors, similar specialties, and departments from several universities and put them into new colleges and universities. After being restructured, almost all the colleges and universities had a single category of disciplines. Only a few comprehensive universities were reserved. The number of colleges and universities of science and engineering had increased greatly, but the specialties of humanities and social sciences were severely weakened. For example, Tsinghua University was originally a comprehensive university. However, during the adjustment, its humanities disciplines were moved to Peking University. Then, it became an engineering and technological institute. While Peking University became a university which only had programs in basic sciences and humanities, due to its medical, engineering, and agriculture faculties all moving out to other specialized colleges and universities.

The second strategy was that the government ordered all the colleges and universities to adopt the Soviet Model in the education system. So from the idea to the content, from teaching to learning, the concepts, and teaching methods of Chinese higher education were all reformed aiming at training specialists.

The third strategy was that the whole education system was highly centralized management. From the management of all the specialties in colleges and universities, the teaching plan, the teaching program, teaching materials, to the teaching process, they were all unified, leading to the overuniform mode of talents cultivation and lack of personality in students' development (Hao et al., 2011, pp. 84 – 89, 100 – 117, 125).

Due to China's reform and opening-up policy in 1978, the general education concept from the Western world came into some of the Chinese researchers' and administrators' visions again. It was the second time that general education was practiced in China. In 1988, W. Zhang (1988) wrote *General Education in Higher Education* as his doctoral dissertation. In 1989, D. Yang (1989, pp. 11 – 17) published his book *On General Education*. M. Li (1999) had ever unscrambled the connotation of Western general education in detail in 1999. Later on, some leaders of the Chinese universities recognized the general education concept in international conferences. By the end of the 20th century, conferences and seminars on general education and cultural quality education had been held many times, which gave the Chinese administrators good opportunities for studying general education (Hu, 2002). This fostered the broadcast of general education in China.

However, since the specialized education has been implemented for almost half a century, higher education in China has had the characteristics of over-narrow specialized education, such as extreme weakness in culture nourishing, overemphasis on utilitarianism, and overstrong unification in administration (Wen, 2002). Graduates under over-narrow specialized education not only possessed a narrow range of knowledge but also lacked the necessary creativity. They were much difficult in adapting to the changing world in work field. So when general education was introduced in China the second time at the end of the 20th century, it had been understood quite differently.

Since 2000, more and more universities used general education concept (instead of *suzhi* education) in two situations. Many universities began to use the words "general education courses" and set up general education elective courses that are borrowed from the general education distribution elective courses of American universities. Some top universities declared that the undergraduate cultivation mode will implement the specialized education mode with a wide of knowledge based on general education. They launched some experimental classes to practice this mode. Chinese universities hope to overcome all drawbacks caused by the overspecialist education mode through general education. So the implementation of general education is not only setting up some courses in universities but also needs the complete revolution on education concepts, specialty settings, course designs, teaching methods, administration systems, and the way of talents cultivation.

Due to the unique situation and background, general education has become more localized in China. It is understood as an education idea; it has the same goals and similar philosophy as *suzhi* education. Sometimes this concept is considered equal to general education course. Sometimes it is regarded as a talent cultivation mode differing from specialized education.

Chinese *suzhi* education and general education practices

In the last 20 or 30 years, *suzhi* education and general education have given rise to a big change in Chinese higher education. All the Chinese universities practiced *suzhi* education by setting up general education courses and developing extracurricular *suzhi* education activities; some universities have explored many reforms on talent cultivation modes (see Table 1).

Table 1. Content system of Chinese *suzhi* education in higher education.

Suzhi education methods	*Suzhi* education content	
Method 1: Common basic courses—formal *suzhi* education curriculum	Common required courses/credits Total 54 – 60 credits	Ideology and Politics Theories, 16 credits; English, 8 credits; Academic Writing, 2 credits; Computer, 2 credits; Physical Education, 2 credits; The Military Training, 2 credits; Mathematics, Physics, Chemistry for students in Sciences, 22 credits; and Chinese for students in Humanities, 6 credits
	General education elective courses	Launching dozens or hundreds of courses, which are divided into different categories. In different universities and different majors, undergraduate students are required to study different credits, ranging from 6 to 22 credits
Method 2: Informal courses—extracurricular activities	*Suzhi* education activities	Extracurricular lectures, reading activities, scientific competence, recreation, sports, and community services
	Social practice	Volunteer services, social investigations, and social practice
Method 3: The cultivation mode reforms	General education talents cultivation mode reform to balance specialized education, such as general education experimental colleges (class), residential college, or Chinese *Shuyuan* ...	

Method 1: Common basic courses as formal suzhi education curriculum

Offering general education courses is the main approach to implement *suzhi* education. Generally speaking, BA courses consist of three parts: common basic courses (including common required courses and elective courses in general education), discipline-based courses (also called discipline platform courses), and professional courses. The total BA credit is 140 – 180, which depends on different universities and disciplines.

Take an engineering major at BIT (Beijing Institute of Technology) as an example. The overall requirement for BA is 170 credits. It consists of three kinds of courses and the distribution is shown in Figure 1 (Zhong, 2016).

Figure 1. The distribution of courses of BIT Engineering Major.

The common basic courses in Chinese universities, which usually take 25%–40% of a BA's total credits, could be regarded as general education courses in American universities. They are made up of four parts as follows:

1. Ideology and Politics Theories are equivalent to common core curriculum in American Universities. These include Morals, Ethics and Law, Principle of Marxism, Mao Zedong Thought and Theoretical System of Socialism with Chinese Characteristics, The Outlines of Modern Chinese History, and the Psychological Development of College Students. All undergraduates in all universities are required to study these common core courses. They are named as ideological and political education courses that are full of Chinese characteristics. The central government of China and every university have paid more attention to them, aiming at fostering students' virtue through these courses. The teaching and learning approaches of the courses are changing from lecturing-oriented ones to diverse methods, such as reading the classic texts, conducting social surveys, holding seminars, and so on.

2. College English and Computer Fundamentals are required courses as basic skills for modern social communication to all students. Besides, students majoring in science and engineering are required to learn mathematics, physics, and chemistry, while students in Liberal Arts are required to learn College Chinese.

3. Military Training and Physical Education are required courses that focus on the training of students' physique and willpower.

4. General education elective courses, borrowed from American general education courses and their requirements, have been set up for strengthening *suzhi* education since the 1990s. After 20–30 years' development, there are dozens even 200 or 300 elective courses opened in each university every year, covering humanity, social science, and natural science. Most universities adopt distribution elective courses. Table 2 presents general education elective courses of five universities.

Table 2. General education elective courses/credits of five Chinese universities (sorting out from the program for bachelors of universities).

Universities	General education elective courses/credits/categories
Peking University[a] The total BA credit: Science, 132–138 credits; Liberal Arts, 140 credits	Undergraduate *Suzhi* Education General Elective Courses, 12 credits, 6 categories A. Math and Science; B. Social Science; C. Philosophy and Psychology; D. History; E. Language, Literature, Art and Aesthetics; and F. Social Lasting Development
Tsinghua University[b] The total BA credit: 140 credits	General Education Core Courses, 13 credits, 8 categories A. History and Culture; B. Linguistics and Literature; C. Philosophy and Life; D. Technology and Society; E. Contemporary China and World; F. Art and Aesthetics; G. Law, Economy and Management; and H. Science and Technology
Beijing Institute of Technology[c] The total BA credit: 170 credits	General Education Elective Courses, 8–12 credits General Education Course of Culture Cultivation, 6–8 credits, including: A. Philosophy and History; B. Literature and Art; C. Health and Society; D. Economy and Politics; E. Science and Technology; and F. Innovation and Entrepreneurship General Education Course of Practical Training, 2–4 credits, including: A. Artistic Practice; B. Technological Practice; and C. Cultural Practice
Zhejiang University[d] The total BA credit: 160 + 4 + 5 credits	General Education Elective Courses, 16.5 credits, including 9 categories: History and Culture, Literature and Art, Communication and Leading, Economy and Society, Science and Research, Technology and Design, General Education Practice, Freshman Seminar and Subjects Introduction
Fudan University[e] The total BA credit: 151 credits	General Education Core Courses, 8–12 credits, 7 categories: A. Classics of Literature and History and Cultural Heritage; B. Philosophical Wisdom and Critical Thinking; C. Civilization Dialogue and World Vision; D. Social Studies and Contemporary China; E. Scientific Exploration and Technological Innovation; F. Ecological Environment and Life Care; and G. Artistic Creation and Aesthetic Experience

Note. [a] See http://www.dean.pku.edu.cn/userfiles/upload/download/201804242015094157.pdf. [b] See http://whsz.tsinghua.edu.cn/column/whszkc_xkyq. [c] Zhong (2016). [d] See https://wenku.baidu.com/view/f13e1511326c1eb91a37f111f18583d049640ff0.html. [e] See http://www.jwc.fudan.edu.cn/_upload/article/files/33/a4/cacc7f2b4b8a985f9299c79c1949/862a1ae4-127e-411eb515-4d3726a18065.pdf.

Method 2: Extracurricular activities as informal curriculum (Pang & Cheng, 2019)

Extracurricular activity is the second characteristic of Chinese *suzhi* education. It can be called informal curriculum, which is beyond teaching plan and aims at guiding and organizing students to develop types of meaningful and attractive activities. Extracurricular activities as part of culture-oriented quality education developed promptly. They are usually organized by the Department of Student Affairs, Youth League Committee, and Culture-Oriented Quality Education

Division. Styles of extracurricular activities include extracurricular lectures, recreation and sports, reading activities, community services, scientific competence, social practices, and campus cultural environment constructions.

Recently, many universities have formed their own activity brands. For example, Humanity Lectures opened in 1994 in Huazhong University of Science and Technology ever stroke a huge effect, which have been held more than 2,212 times by January 2018, attracting more than 500,000 students to join.[1] The series lectures Listening to Wisdom set by Beijing Institute of Technology attract more than 10,000 students to join every year. It is very helpful for improving students' comprehensive qualities and broadening their minds. Besides, Flowers in May is the most famous art activity founded by *Suzhi* Education Society in Chinese universities, which has become a China Central Television program. At the same time, Challenging Cup Extracurricular Scientific Competence for College Students, Humanity Knowledge Competence for College Students in Five Provinces of Eastern China (Cheng, 2015, pp. 290 – 300), and Humanity Social Science and Natural Science Competence for College Students in Jiangsu Province are famous activity brands (Ding, 2015).

Method 3: General education talents cultivation mode reform

The third practice is the implementing of the cultivation mode which is called Specialized Education with a Wide Range of Knowledge, based on general education. Some universities established experimental colleges (classes) to consolidate general education mode like Yuanpei College in Peking University, Xu Teli College in Beijing Institute of Technology, and Boya College in Sun Yat-sen University. These colleges recruit dozens of students each year. They will receive more general education in the first 2 years to broaden their vision. Then they choose majors freely according to their interests and learn their specialties in the last 2 years. Some universities like Qiushi College in Zhejiang University, Fudan College in Fudan University, and Xi'an Jiaotong University established residential colleges (Chinese *Shuyuan*), aiming at helping the freshmen adapted to new life in the university and strengthening the communications of students from different specialties through dormitory life and activities. The purpose of all these reforms is to establish policies to support general education.

1　See https://baike.baidu.com/item/华中科技大学人文讲座/4211315? fr=aladdin.

We have learned that the tension and conflict between liberal education college and specialized schools always exists because of the organizational reforms, which leads to uneven reforms in some universities. The operation of liberal education college still needs to adjust the traditional administration system.

Comparison and conclusion

Suzhi education as a Chinese education philosophy is the strategic direction of education reform in China. General education as a borrowed Western education concept is strengthened in Chinese universities. The two concepts, which are both rooted in their own cultural tradition and context, have different names but the same ideas. General education has been localized in China and has a different meaning and connotation from the West.

First, *suzhi* education is rooted in Chinese traditional culture such as Confucian idea of cultivating a gentleman and it also derives from the same origin of the Marxist theory of people's overall development. General education originated from liberal education in ancient Greek. General education in the U.S. has multiple meanings. According to the Report of the Harvard Committee (1945), Report of Columbia University (Bell, 1966), and Report of Chicago University (1992, p. 395), general education in America has two aims. One is to cultivate shared values for democratic society and to cultivate citizens full of social responsibilities at the same time. Another refers to general education contents to balance specialized education. Both are achieved mainly by the perfect general education curriculum system.

By comparison, we think that although the concepts of *suzhi* education (cultural quality education) and general education are different, their goals are the same, which concentrate on cultivating a whole-person and training comprehensive quality. Contents of these two educations are also similar, which encourage all students to learn humanity, social and natural science knowledge, and develop students' soft skills. But their practice paths, curriculum system, and education content have different characteristics.

Second, China and the U.S. have different university education concepts, which led to different systematic curricula structures and practicing characteristics. The U.S. has an excellent liberal education tradition and highly values general education. Its undergraduate course structure is *general education courses* + *major courses* + *elective courses*. The freshmen and sophomore students mainly study general education courses and choose or change their majors freely after that. General education courses play a significant role and take a large proportion during undergraduate education stage. Chinese universities adopted the Soviet education mode since the 1950s, which paid much attention to specialized education, aiming at cultivating specialists. The undergraduate course structure was *common basic courses + discipline basis courses + professional courses*. From the 1950s to the 1980s, there were hardly any general courses. Both common basic courses and discipline basic courses provided the foundation for latter specialized studies. After implementing *suzhi* education since the 1990s, Chinese universities supplemented general education elective courses, whose quality was not satisfying yet. Currently, ideological political courses and second class are playing a key role and become distinct characteristic features of *suzhi* education.

Third, because Chinese higher education was deeply influenced by specialist training and the Soviet model, *suzhi* education and general education are facing many difficulties in changing education ideas, reforming the teaching concepts and its methods, changing administrative systems, and organizing the new systems. We know that there always exists a fierce debate between individual-oriented educational goal and society-oriented educational goal. The most important issue for Chinese universities is to transfer the education aims from society-oriented to individual-oriented, to change the process of education to the individual-oriented and student-centered process and set up *suzhi* education and general education mode through the organizational adjustment and the system reform.

Therefore, according to the context, we believe that the connotations of *suzhi* education and general education in China can be understood in three aspects (see Figure 2).

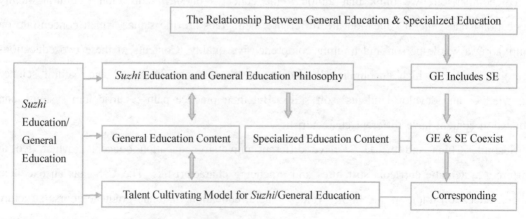

Figure 2. Three levels of *suzhi*/general education (SE/GE).

1. *Suzhi* education is an educational idea which aims at cultivating a whole person with specialized skills. From this aspect, *suzhi* contains general education and specialized education. *Suzhi* education should lead undergraduate education, not just as the supplement of specialized education. General education should be dedicate to solving the problems in higher institutions by stopping offering the fractures of knowledge, expanding the narrow minds of the students, improving their limited horizons, and correcting the extreme utilitarianism in higher education, which were caused by overspecialized education in the last century.
2. General education refers to the part of education contents, which means the general education courses and informal courses like extracurricular activities. Universities should offer both general and major courses. General education courses should integrate the knowledge of humanity, social science, and natural science in order to broaden the students' minds, develop their whole personality and soft skills, and help them make a solid foundation of specialties.
3. *Suzhi* education and general education can also be a kind of talent cultivation mode. It is not a standard cultivation model, but it emphasizes on building a system to guarantee general education to achieve its goals. From the institutional arrangement aspect, general education talents cultivation mode is quite different from specialized education talents cultivation mode. It requires the necessary reforms from the education concept, curriculum systems, course contents, and teaching methods to the supporting system, in order to meet the objectives of general education (Pang, 2009).

Acknowledgements

When writing the English version of this paper, a lot of advice was received from Professor Thomas J. Day and Guizhen Jin. We would like to express our sincere gratitude to them.

References

Bell, D. (1966). *The reforming of general education*. Anchor Books Doubleday.
Cheng, G. (2015). *Summary of college humanities knowledge contest for 2009 – 2012*. In D. Guo & H. Pang (Eds.), *Suzhi education and China dream* [in Chinese] (pp. 290 – 300). Beijing Institute of Technology Press.
Ding, X. (2015). Make knowledge contest as breakthrough push college cultural quality education ahead. In Y. Zhou (Ed.), *The idea of suzhi education* [in Chinese] (pp. 156 – 167). Higher Education Press.
Feng, H. (2004). *General education in Chinese modern universities* [in Chinese] (pp. 100 – 110). Wuhan University Press.
Hao, W., Long, Z., & Zhang, J. (2011). *History of higher education in China* [in Chinese] (pp. 84 – 89, 100 – 117, 125).

New World Press.

Higher Education Department of Ministry of Education. (1998). *Document of some decisions about strengthening cultural quality education for college students* [in Chinese]. http://old.moe.gov.cn/publicfiles/business/htmlfiles/moe/moe_734/200408/2982.html

Hu, X. (2002). *Lectures on general education courses and culture-oriented quality education* [in Chinese] (pp. 507–509). Higher Education Press.

Hu, X. (2004). Changing concept and strengthening cultural quality education [in Chinese]. In Y. Zhou (Ed.), *On culture-oriented quality education* (pp. 46–55). Higher Education Press.

Huang, J. (1993). *Philosophy and practices of college general education* [in Chinese]. Taipei General Education Committee.

Li, L. (2003). *Interview records of Li Lanqing education* [in Chinese]. People's Education Press.

Li, M. (1999). *General education—One kind of education philosophy* [in Chinese]. Tsinghua University Press.

Pan, M. (1997). On suzhi education [in Chinese]. *Education Review*, (5), 6–8.

Pang, H. (2009). *General education: Dilemma and prospect* [in Chinese]. Beijing Institute of Technology Press.

Pang, H. (2015). The connotation interpretation of general education [in Chinese]. *General Education Research*, (0), 23–35.

Pang, H., & Cheng, M. (2019). *The observation on innovation and development of higher education* [in Chinese]. Beijing Institute of Technology Press.

Pang, H., & Huan, X. (2015). Suzhi eduction and China university education reform [in Chinese]. *China Higher Education Research*, (9), 73–78.

Present and Former Members of the Faculty. (1992). *The idea and practice of general education: An account of the college of the university of Chicago*. The University of Chicago Press.

Report of the Harvard Committee. (1945). *General education in a free society*. Harvard University Press.

Wang, Y. (2004). Culture-oriented quality education should pay attention on educating [in Chinese]. In Y. Zhou (Ed.), *On culture-oriented quality education* (pp. 262–274). Higher Education Press.

Wen, F. (1997). On suzhi and suzhi education [in Chinese]. *China Higher Education Research*, (6), 19–22.

Wen, F. (2002). Culture-oriented quality education should have a whole-person concept [in Chinese]. *Journal of Higher Education*, (1), 27–30.

Whitehead, N. A. (1950). *The aids of education*. Ernest Benn.

Xi, J. (2017). *The 19th National Congress of the Communist Party of China. Achieve a complete victory in building a moderately prosperous society in all respects and fight for the great success of socialism with Chinese characteristics for a new era* [in Chinese]. http://cpc.people.com.cn/n1/2017/1028/c64094-29613660.html

Xi, J. (2018). *The national education conference* [in Chinese]. http://www.moe.gov.cn/jyb_xwfb/xw_zt/moe_357/jyzt_2018n/2018_zt18/

Xiong, M. (1988). *History of Chinese education* [in Chinese] (pp. 388–395). Chongqing Press.

Yang, D. (1989). *On general education* [in Chinese] (pp. 11–17). Liaoning Education Press.

Yang, S. (2001). Cultivating a person, not making tools [in Chinese]. *Journal of Higher Education*, (2), 7–10.

Zhang, C. (1996). Suzhi: What's in a person [in Chinese]. *Journal of Social Science of Hunan Normal University*, (4), 75–82.

Zhang, Q. (2003). Guiding of college culture-oriented quality education [in Chinese]. *China Higher Education Research*, (4), 3–5.

Zhang, W. (1988). *General education in higher education* [Doctoral dissertation, Hangzhou University] [in Chinese].

Zhong, S. (2016). *Beijing Institute of Technology course structure of the undergraduate programs*. Academic Affairs Office of

Beijing Institute of Technology.

Zhou, Y. (1996). Strengthening culture-oriented quality education and improving the teaching quality in higher education [in Chinese]. *China University Teaching*, (1), 4-7.

Zhou, Y. (2000). *Suzhi*, *suzhi* education and cultural quality education [in Chinese]. *China Higher Education*, (8), 3-5, 30.

Zhou, Y. (2014). *Suzhi* education: Origin, base and root [in Chinese]. *China University Teaching*, (5), 12-14.

After the concepts of first-class universities, first-class research disciplines, and first-class undergraduate education, China's Ministry of Education (MOE) proposed a new concept of first-class undergraduate major programs and also proposed policy initiatives for relevant selection and funding. This article provides an in-depth analysis of the motives, historical background, policy texts, core concepts, and unintended consequences of "The First-Class Major Programs" policy and proposes six criticisms. This article argues that the first-class major programs in undergraduate education include provincial-level points of these programs, which stealthily narrowed the scope for comparison from potentially the whole world to that of provinces. The policy also essentially strengthened the traditional concept of *zhuanye* (专业) as a physical unit and caused unintended consequences in its attempts to cultivate innovative talents and to adjust the *zhuanye* structure. The value of this study is to address a new education policy in China and its unintended consequences.

Review and Critique on the New Higher Education Policy Promoting "The First-Class Major Programs" in China [1]

Xiaodong Lu

An important concept for university education in China is students' *zhuanye* (major subject or specialized field of study). The *Dictionary of Education* states that this concept was translated from Russian and refers to "the various specialized fields in higher education for cultivating students in China and the Soviet Union. It is generally equivalent to a curriculum program as defined by the *International Standard Classification of Education* or a major in universities in the United States" (Gu, 1991, p. 26). This indicates that when graduates use the word *zhuanye* in their personal Curricula Vitae, it is equivalent to referring to their majors.

However, in the previous research, after having examined the organizational model of undergraduate education in China, I found the two terms were dissimilar. Specifically, *zhuanye* refers not only to a program but also includes a faculty organization such as *jiaoyanshi* (teaching and research unit) or *xi* (department) with a similar name. Students' identities are also tied to their *zhuanye*, and those in the same *zhuanye* form a collective. The courses of a specific *zhuanye*

---

[1] This article was published on *ECNU Review of Education*, 3(2), 338–345.

are usually taught by teachers who belong to the *jiaoyanshi* or *xi*, and students are very rarely allowed to choose courses conducted by other departments. In essence, *zhuanye* refers to a physical unit in a university (Lu, 2002).

With the reform and opening-up of China's education system, as well as increasing exchanges between China and foreign countries, some Chinese universities have introduced residential colleges as a new organizational model for undergraduate education. An example of this would be the Yuanpei College of Peking University, whose students are allowed to freely choose their *zhuanye* and any course offered by the university. In fact, even interdisciplinary *zhuanye*, such as Philosophy, Politics, and Economics (PPE), are being offered. As far as Yuanpei College is concerned, *zhuanye* refers to a group of courses, or in other words, a program. Explorations of such an organizational model for undergraduate education by Chinese universities have been ongoing for approximately two decades, with some preliminary results on the possibility of organizing *zhuanye* as majors on only a particular set of curricula (Tan et al., 2011).

At present, higher education in China faces two core issues. The first is the lack of high quality, and the second is the shortage of innovative talents. On May 2 and 28, 2018, General Secretary Xi Jinping delivered two important speeches that highlighted the directions for a new cycle of industrial transformation as well as scientific and technological revolution. During the Conference of the Natural Science and Engineering Academicians held on May 28, Xi stated that

> Global scientific and technological innovations have entered a period of unprecedented intensity and activity since the beginning of the 21st century. This new cycle of industrial transformation as well as scientific and technological revolution is reshaping the global innovation map and reconstructing the global economic structure. There are accelerated and breakthrough applications for a new generation of information technologies represented by artificial intelligence, quantum information, mobile communication, the Internet of Things, and blockchains. The field of life sciences is also nurturing new transformations represented by synthetic biology, genome editing, brain science, and regenerative medicine …There is a growing trend of cross-integration between disciplines, between technologies, and between the natural sciences and the social sciences and humanities … (Xi, 2018)

How can higher education reflect the aforementioned trend of cross-integration, and how can innovative talents in such cross-integrated disciplines be cultivated to meet the urgent needs of society?

Following Xi's speeches, the Ministry of Education (MOE) rapidly convened the Working

Conference on Undergraduate Education in the New Era. This was held in Chengdu, Sichuan on June 21, 2018. An important document was issued post-conference: *MOE's Opinions on Accelerating the Development of High-Quality Undergraduate Education and Comprehensive Improvements to Abilities for Talent Cultivation* (MOE, 2018). This document is also known as *40 Articles for Higher Education in the New Era* (henceforth, *40 Articles*).

Article 22 of 40 *Articles* was in response to the new cycle of industrial transformation as well as scientific and technological revolution.

> Article 22. Dynamic adjustments to the *zhuanye* structure: To deepen the supply-side structural reform of *zhuanye* in colleges and universities, establish a sound and dynamic *zhuanye* adjustment mechanism, as well as ensure the upgradation and improvement of *zhuanye*, incremental optimization, and margin reduction of old *zhuanye*; to actively plan the development of strategic emerging industries-related *zhuanye* in integrated circuits, artificial intelligence, cloud computing, big data, cyberspace security, eldercare, and pediatrics, as well as related disciplines that are urgently needed for the people's livelihoods; and to promote the improvement of a mechanism for forecasting talents resource demand and early warning of talents oversupply in all localities, industries, and departments, as well as the formation of a mechanism linking employment with enrollment planning and talent cultivation. (MOE, 2018)

In February 2018, the MOE proposed the new concept of emerging engineering *zhuanye*. From June 2018 onward, the MOE echoed the need for cross-integrated disciplines by proposing the additional concepts of emerging social science and humanity, emerging medicine, and emerging agriculture *zhuanye*. These were collectively referred to as the "four emerging *zhuanye*."

The *Circular on Printing and Coordinating the Overall Plan for Promoting Global First-Class University and Research Discipline* was published by the State Council (The State Council of the People's Republic of China, 2015). This circular officially introduced the concept of double first-class in higher education into China's higher education system. To prevent double first-class higher education institutions from over-emphasizing scientific research at the expense of undergraduate education, the Vice Minister of Education at the time, Lin Huiqing, specially penned an article titled *Developing a First-Class Undergraduate Education is an Important Task for Double First-Class Higher Education*, which was published in *Guangming Daily* in May 2016. This article introduced the concept of first-class undergraduate education into China's higher education system.

To date, there are three first-class concepts in China's higher education system: first-class universities, first-class research disciplines, and first-class undergraduate education. All these can essentially be supported theoretically. At the policy level, the first-class undergraduate education initiative is mainly implemented through Article 20 of *40 Articles*. However, another new concept appeared in that same article, namely, first-class major programs.

Article 20. Implementation of first-class major programs in undergraduate education through "The Plan of Twenty Thousand" major programs: *Zhuanye* is the basic unit of talent cultivation and the primary framework for developing high-quality undergraduate education and cultivating first-class talents. The goal is to develop a list of first-class major programs in undergraduate education that are future-oriented and can adapt to changing needs, lead development, contain advanced concepts, and are guaranteed to be effective. 10,000 state-level and 10,000 provincial-level first-class major programs in undergraduate education are to be developed to lead and support high-quality undergraduate education. Double first-class higher education institutions should take the lead in developing first-class major programs in undergraduate education; simultaneously, application-oriented universities should integrate their unique educational characteristics while working earnestly to develop first-class major programs in undergraduate education. (MOE, 2018)

On April 2, 2019, the MOE's General Office officially issued a *Circular for the Implementation of First-Class Major Programs in Undergraduate Education* (henceforth, *Circular No. 18*) (MOE, 2019). This was the formal launch of the Ministry's review of 20,000 first-class major programs in undergraduate education nationwide. In this study, an in-depth examination of the documents and contents of this policy revealed several potential issues, which have been elaborated below.

First, the concept of first-class major programs in undergraduate education is a comparative one that contains a scope and objects for comparison. For first-class universities and first-class research disciplines, the current implicit scope for comparison would be all of China or even the world. However, in reality, first-class major programs in undergraduate education include some provincial-level points, which stealthily narrows the scope for comparison from a potentially global or national one to a provincial one. What, then, are the exact objects for comparison? Considering that "major" refers to a group of curricula that may belong to multiple disciplines and academic fields, how should comparisons be made between the different courses and the knowledge contained therein? How are comparisons to be made to ascertain which of the various major programs are first-class, as opposed to being subpar? Furthermore, a major program comprises both specialized and general education courses, constituting 60 – 80 and 40 – 50 credits, respectively. General education courses are conducted by all departments and disciplines of a university and have significant impact on the cultivation of the quality of graduates. This leads to the issue of having to ascertain ways to determine whether the general education curricula are of first-class quality, which is an implicit problem regarding the objects for comparison among various first-class major programs in undergraduate education.

Second, *Circular No. 18* stated that multiple conditions are involved for the review of first-class major programs in undergraduate education. Among these, the fourth condition was "to have an abundant number of faculty members and to continuously strengthen the development of the faculty and basic faculty organizations, extensively carry out research on education and the scholarship of teaching, establish a rational faculty team structure for *zhuanye*, and maintain a high level of quality overall" (MOE, 2019). The supporting documents of this circular included the *Form to Collect Information Regarding the Development Points of First-Class Major Programs in Undergraduate Education at the State Level*. It is mandatory for first-class universities to provide data to the Ministry, including the total number of full-time faculty members, the student-teacher ratio, and a list of renowned faculty members. Such data requirements essentially strengthened the traditional concept that *zhuanye* is a physical unit. Students at Peking University's PPE *zhuanye* can build their own curriculum and knowledge structure by choosing courses from different departments. Basically, there are no full-time faculty members who only offer courses specifically for a single *zhuanye*. Therefore, it is difficult to accurately calculate the student-teacher ratio for the form.

Third, the "four emerging *zhuanye*" are, in essence, similar to PPE and other interdisciplinary *zhuanye*. *Circular No. 18* emphasized the active promotion of the development of the "four emerging *zhuanye*." It also emphasized "focused intensification of comprehensive *zhuanye* reform, optimization of the *zhuanye* structure, proactive development of new and emerging *zhuanye*, transformation and upgrade of traditional *zhuanye*, and the creation of specialty and advantageous *zhuanye*" (MOE, 2019). When comparing different first-class major programs in undergraduate education, it is necessary to know the number of full-time faculty members in each. This is hard to determine for the "four emerging *zhuanye*," making it difficult to accurately calculate student-teacher ratios. The treatment of this inherent contradiction during the actual review process is another issue that has yet to be addressed.

Fourth, in the aforementioned supporting form for *Circular No. 18*, it is mandatory to state the *zhuanye* graduates' employment or postgraduate education status for the past 3 years, as well as to track survey results and external evaluations regarding the quality of the graduates. Since the "four emerging *zhuanye*" are newly launched, only a few universities would have such graduates, rendering it difficult to provide accurate information. There is also an inherent contradiction between the data required by this form and the goal of "active promotion of the development of emerging engineering, emerging social science and humanity, emerging medicine, and emerging agriculture" emphasized in *Circular No. 18*.

Fifth, *Circular No. 18* stated that the review process for first-class major programs in undergraduate education requires "two steps." To begin with, a major program must first be ascertained as a state-level first-class major program in undergraduate education development point before it can be honored as a first-class major program in undergraduate education. The certification process for first-class major programs in undergraduate education is organized and conducted by the MOE. Only upon completion of certification can the next step be taken, which is to determine the list of state-level first-class major programs in undergraduate education. The *National Standards for Teaching Quality for Zhuanye Categories in Universities* (henceforth, *National Standards*), published by the MOE in April 2018, are the criteria used for the certification of first-class major programs in undergraduate education.

One method of classifying major programs would be the use of discipline-based standards. Based on this method, the primary categories would include single-discipline, interdisciplinary, and problem-centric major programs.

The "four emerging *zhuanye*" are primarily interdisciplinary in nature. Such *zhuanye* involve cross-discipline knowledge and courses that are extremely flexible and diverse. An example of this would be the group of emerging engineering majors developed by Stanford University in the last few years. Known as Computer Science+, the courses encompassed cross-integrated knowledge over a number of subjects; this number increased from 10 to 14 subjects between 2016 and 2019. Peking University's PPE *zhuanye* was introduced using Oxford University's PPE major program and University of Pennsylvania's PPE major as reference. However, this differs from Yale University's PPE major program, which includes Philosophy, Politics, and Ethics instead.

Being a formalized standard for quality, the logical basis of the National Standards does not accommodate knowledge and curriculum combinations that contain uncertainties, nor diverse and interdisciplinary *zhuanye* that utilize imagination. Such standards only lead to knowledge and curricula that are certain and increase the number of students with predictable behavioral outcomes. These are clearly not the creative talents that the "Four emerging *zhuanye*" are expected to produce. The introductions of the National Standards into the review process for first-class major programs in undergraduate education resulted in a contradiction between its internal logic and the goal of "active promotion of the development of emerging engineering, emerging social science and humanity, emerging medicine, and emerging agriculture."

Sixth, although special funds have been established for first-class universities and first-class research discipline initiatives, a separate special fund was also set up for first-class major program initiatives in undergraduate education. *Circular No. 18* stated: "Improvements to funding guarantees: Universities under the jurisdiction of the Central Government should make coordinated use of the Central Government's budgetary allocations (such as the 'Special Project for Educational and Teaching Reforms') and other various resources. All localities should coordinate the higher education funds in their respective local budgets with the funds granted by the Central Government to support the reform and development of local first-class major programs in undergraduate education, so as to support the development of these programs" (MOE, 2019). However, for universities that are already supported by the special funds for first-class universities and initiatives for first-class research disciplines, additional funding for first-class major programs in undergraduate education initiatives may result in resource duplication.

The initial findings of the aforementioned analysis indicate that the concept of first-class major programs in undergraduate education, which was introduced subsequent to first-class universities, first-class research disciplines, and first-class undergraduate education, may be difficult to establish theoretically. The related policies were also found to contain contradictions and issues at various levels of implementation. Universities are forced to participate and compete in first-class major programs in undergraduate education initiatives because it is considered to be a form of honor and has practical significance for future enrollment efforts. However, is it worthwhile to incur both direct and opportunity costs for assessing and determining the 20,000 development points of first-class major programs in undergraduate education? Further reflection and research should be conducted to assess the practical impact that policies regarding the first-class major program in undergraduate education initiatives have on higher education systems.

References

Gu, M. (1991). *The great dictionary of education* (Vol. III) [in Chinese]. Shanghai Education Press.

Lu, X. (2002). On connotation of *zhuanye* in university [in Chinese]. *Educational Research*, (7), 47–52.

Ministry of Education of the People's Republic of China. (2018). *MOE's opinions on accelerating the development of high-quality undergraduate education and comprehensive improvements to abilities for talent cultivation* (*Department of Higher Education* [2018] *Circular No. 2*) [in Chinese]. http://www.moe.gov.cn/srcsite/A08/s7056/201810/t20181017_351887.html

Ministry of Education of the People's Republic of China, General Office. (2019). *On the implementation of first-class major programs in undergraduate education* (*Department of Education* [2019] *Circular No. 18*) [in Chinese]. http://www.moe.gov.cn/srcsite/A08/s7056/201904/t20190409_377216.html

Tan, X., Qi, L., & Lu, X. (2011). The practice of professional independent choice and interdisciplinary professional construction: Taking Yuanpei College, Peking University as an example [in Chinese]. *China Higher Education Research*, (1), 54–57.

The State Council of the People's Republic of China. (2015). *The circular on printing and coordinating the overall plan for promoting global first-class university and research discipline* (*National Development Council* [2015] *Circular No. 64*) [in Chinese]. http://www.gov.cn/zhengce/content/2015-11/05/content_10269.htm

Xi, J. (2018). *Speech on the 19th conference of the natural science academicians and the 14th conference of the engineering academicians* [in Chinese]. http://www.gov.cn/gongbao/content/2018/content_5299599.htm

This study conducts a systematic review of policy reforms for the evaluation of scientific and technological research (E-STR) in China's colleges to identify changes to past policies and the objectives and realizability of the most recent policy reform. Initiated in the early part of 2000, China's latest E-STR policy reform constitutes an important turning point in the initiative to burst the research bubble and return to the essence of innovation. It uses content analysis method to analyze three important relevant policy documents from 2003, 2013, and 2020 as samples. Unlike previous attempts, the most recent policy reform has incorporated the lessons learned while introducing highly targeted measures and a monitoring mechanism. Such reform should accelerate the promotion of major original scientific research in China's colleges, enhance the contribution of scientific research to socioeconomic development, and strengthen support for the cultivation of undergraduate talents. This study contributes to the current understanding of China's latest E-STR policy reform.

Evaluation of Scientific and Technological Research in China's Colleges: A Review of Policy Reforms, 2000 – 2020 [1]

Junwen Zhu

In the mid-1990s, Scientific Citation Index (SCI) indicators were introduced into the evaluation of scientific and technological research (E-STR) in China's colleges. Subsequently, China's international publications have grown rapidly. But the original innovation performance has not improved accordingly. After 2000, the demand for reforming E-STR has grown. In 2020, the Chinese government released two policy documents that attracted widespread attention. The first was *Several Suggestions on Standardizing the Usage of SCI Papers and Related Indicators by Colleges and Establishing the Correct Approach Toward Evaluation*—jointly issued by the Ministry of Education (MOE) and Ministry of Science and Technology (MOST; MOE-MOST [2020] No. 2). The second was *Several Measures to Eliminate the Incorrect "Paper-Centric" Approach of Evaluating Scientific and Technological Research (Trial)*—jointly released by the MOST and Ministry of Finance (MOF) (issued by MOST [2020] No. 37). Both documents were immediately reported on and discussed by *Nature* (Mallapaty, 2020; Nature Editorial,

---

1　This article was published on *ECNU Review of Education*, 3(3), 556–561.

2020), while fervent debate occurred in China's mainstream media (Deng, 2020; Li, 2020; Zhao, 2020). This study provides a systematic review of E-STR reforms in China's colleges between 2000 and 2020. This systematic interpretation of how policy reform has changed over time offers valuable insights, including the identification of policy objectives and an evaluation of their realizability.

The differences between measures, 2000 – 2020

E-STR presents China's policymakers, colleges, and academic communities with a difficult and perplexing issue. Since 2000, there have already been three major E-STR policy reforms, including the current reform. This section explores the differences between the past and current measures.

In 2003, five ministries and commissions, including the MOST and MOE, jointly formulated *Decision on Improving E-STR Tasks* (issued by MOST [2003] No. 142). The policy identified several issues with E-STR, including the use of the same evaluation criteria for different types of STR activities, an emphasis on quantity over quality, and expert evaluations being influenced by personal relationships and connections. Further, the document clearly identified the need to properly examine the role of SCI, Engineering Index, and other databases in E-STR. The measure achieved some success, with the targeted approach and principles for category-based evaluation proposed in the document gradually becoming the consensus. However, there was no significant progress regarding the other stipulated requirements, such as prioritizing quality and addressing the shortsighted tendencies of seeking immediate benefits and fast returns.

This 2003 reform did not resolve issues with the E-STR system, including the emphasis on quantity over quality, singularization of evaluation indicators, and utilitarianism of evaluation results. Moreover, the measure failed to facilitate the conversion of STR achievements into practical applications and the use of science and technology to support talent cultivation. Consequently, the MOE's *Suggestions on Further Reforming E-STR in Colleges* was issued in 2013 (MOEMOST [2013] No. 3), which proposed the evaluation goals of "encouraging innovation, servicing demands, integrating science and education, and developing characteristics." It established the evaluation approach of pursuing innovation quality and contribution and stipulated detailed regulations for category-based evaluation. The document received widespread praise upon publication. Further, the proposed approach toward reform was acknowledged by colleges, which were granted sufficient space to respond flexibly and according to their characteristics.

Finally, the MOE began drafting its 2020 policy in mid-2019. Entitled *Standardizing the Use of SCI*, the document deals with displaced behaviors related to colleges' use of SCI papers as evaluation indicators in reviewing faculty members (job title and performance), talents, disciplines, resource allocation, and college ranking. For example, it mandated that SCI papers and related indicators no longer be used as the bases for MOE-organized subject evaluations. In addition to recommending against using such indicators as the basis for decisions regarding the granting of cash rewards to individuals, the measure denounced the practice of requiring graduates to publish a certain number of SCI papers to obtain their degrees.

The MOST's 2020 policy covers all types of STR units. Its primary policy points advocate the following: (ⅰ) encouraging to publish papers in high-quality local STR journals; (ⅱ) stipulating the maximum number of representative papers to be included in various types of evaluations; (ⅲ) formulating the scope necessary for the recognition of "three types of high-quality papers," as well as encouraging the publication of STR results in related journals; and (ⅳ) preparing a blacklist of journals that prioritize commercial gains and prohibiting the use of funding to pay for the publication fees of blacklisted journals.

A comparison of the policies underscores how the 2020 policy measures are highly targeted, with specific measures stipulating the actions that colleges should and should not undertake. Further, the 2020 policy required colleges to modify and delete any internal management regulations involving the use of SCI papers as indicators within a stipulated period, as well as promptly submit feedback to the MOE regarding the modification situation.

The targets of the 2020 policy reform

Another paper in this issue notes that the number of SCI papers published by China's researchers surpassed that of the United States in 2018, with China currently ranked first in the world (Liu, 2020). However, this number is not representative of innovation capabilities. In fact, the blind pursuit of publishing more papers hinders scientific progress (David, 2007; Génova et al., 2016; Nature Editorial, 2017). As such, China needs to actively burst the STR publishing bubble and return to the original intentions of science. This is the primary purpose of the 2020 policy reform.

In terms of general research, the 2020 measure emphasizes the pursuit of major original innovations. By eliminating the lopsided pursuit of the number of SCI papers, researchers are encouraged to concentrate on their research and the accumulation of achievements in the long term, focus on the scientific frontier and common challenges facing humanity, solve critical problems, and produce major original results. While the number of published scientific papers might decrease, the contributions to humanity and science will increase.

Regarding applied research and technological innovation, the 2020 policy reform encourages the pursuit of practical contributions to socioeconomic development. Removing the evaluation system based on SCI papers encourages researchers to solve the key technical problems encountered during socioeconomic development, as well as make practical contributions with significant application potential. This will result in real impact, including the realization of industrial applications through new technologies, products, and processes. This is in line with the MOE's approach as stated in *Several Suggestions on Improving the Quality of Colleges' Patents and Promoting Their Conversion to Actual Applications* (MOE-MOST [2020] No. 1). By eliminating the pursuit of the number of authorized patents, greater emphasis is placed on the quality of these patents and their conversion into actual applications.

To address the current emphasis on scientific research at the expense of teaching, the 2020 policy measure encourages the use of STR resources for talent training. China's colleges have long emphasized STR over teaching, reflecting the prioritization of previous evaluation systems. In addition to STR resources being unavailable to undergraduates, the latest STR findings were not incorporated as teaching materials on time. Indeed, renowned professors rarely taught undergraduate courses, resulting in undergraduate training not being supported by STR. The latest policy reform seeks to address these issues.

The potential impact of the 2020 policy reform

There are several possible reasons for why E-STR in China's colleges keeps changing and why progress has been so slow. First, various global ranking of colleges appeared successively from 2003, including the Academic Ranking of World Universities and Times Higher Education World University Rankings. As an internationally comparable indicator, the number of SCI papers became widely used in the ranking of colleges. Meanwhile, China accelerated its development of world-class colleges. Some colleges erroneously perceived ranking changes as reflective of their effectiveness at becoming first-class institutions and pursued higher numbers of published SCI papers to improve their ranking. However, these actions offset the effects of policy reform.

After the MOE released its 2013 policy reform, the government launched the "double first-class" program for higher education. Based on the SCI, the Essential Science Indicators index was an important reference factor in the selection of key colleges for the program. Further, the SCI indicator remained heavily weighted during the fourth round of evaluating the disciplines organized by the government. The lack of synergy among the various government policies undermined their ability to achieve the expected results.

Nonetheless, there are several reasons to look forward to the effects of the 2020 policy reform. First, China's government and colleges have reached a consensus on bursting the bubble of producing STR papers. Indeed, the government recognizes that the voluminous increase in the number of low-quality papers is just an STR bubble. Rather than being beneficial, this situation only serves to consume substantial amounts of STR resources and ruin the STR atmosphere. Further, colleges aiming to become world-class institutions have realized that they cannot enter the ranks of the world's top colleges by relying on increasing the number of SCI papers alone. After all, the number of SCI publications is not used to calculate colleges' contributions to the human sciences and the country. Second, the measures introduced with the latest policy reform are specific and clear: Colleges are required to provide feedback to the MOE regarding their revisions of internal rules and regulations by July 31, 2020. Finally, and most importantly, corresponding adjustments will be made to the system of indicators for the evaluation of disciplines organized by the MOE, including the removal of SCI papers as an indicator. The realization of these adjustments will be crucial to the effectiveness of the 2020 policy reform.

References

David, L. P. (2007). Stop the numbers game. *Communications of the ACM*, *50*(11), 19–21.

Deng, H. (2020, February 25). Dismantling the 'supremacy' of SCI papers and returning to the 'original purpose' of academia [in Chinese]. *Guangming Daily*, 9.

Génova, G., Astudillo, H., & Fraga, A. (2016). The scientometric bubble considered harmful. *Science and Engineering Ethics*, *22*(1), 227–235.

Li, J. (2020, March 3). Breaking the 'SCI supremacy' and finding ways to improve the evaluation of scientific research [in

Chinese]. *Guangming Daily*, 13.

Liu, W. (2020). China's SCI-indexed publications: Facts, feelings and future directions. *ECNU Review of Education*, *3*(3), 562–569.

Mallapaty, S. (2020). China bans cash rewards for publishing papers. *Nature*, *579*(7797), 18.

MOE. (2013). *Suggestions on further reforming E-STR in colleges*, MOE-MOST. [2013] No. 3 [in Chinese]. http://old.moe.gov.cn//publicfiles/business/htmlfiles/moe/moe_784/201312/160920.html

MOE and MOST. (2020). *Several suggestions on standardizing the usage of SCI papers and related indicators by colleges and establishing the correct approach toward evaluation*, MOE-MOST [2020] No. 2 [in Chinese]. http://www.moe.gov.cn/srcsite/A16/moe_784/202002/t20200223_423334.html

MOE, State Intellectual Property Office, and MOST. (2020). *Several suggestions on improving the quality of colleges' patents and promoting their conversion to actual applications*, MOE-MOST [2020] No. 1 [in Chinese]. http://www.moe.gov.cn/srcsite/A16/s7062/202002/t20200221_422861.html

MOST and MOE, Chinese Academy of Sciences, Chinese Academy of Engineering, National Natural Science Foundation of China. (2003). *Decision on improving E-STR tasks*, MOST [2003] No. 142 [in Chinese]. http://www.most.gov.cn/mostinfo/xinxifenlei/fgzc/gfxwj/gfxwj2003/201712/t20171227_137213.htm

MOST and MOF. (2020). *Several measures to eliminate the incorrect 'Paper-centric' approach of evaluating scientific and technological research (Trial)*, MOST [2020] No. 37 [in Chinese]. http://www.most.gov.cn/mostinfo/xinxifenlei/fgzc/gfxwj/gfxwj2020/202002/t20200223_151781.htm

Nature Editorial. (2017). Beyond the science bubble. *Nature*, *542*(7642), 391.

Nature Editorial. (2020). China's research-evaluation revamp should not mean fewer international collaborations. *Nature*, *579*(7797), 8.

Zhao, E. (2020, March 2). Evaluating innovation capacity and highlighting innovation quality and actual contributions [in Chinese]. *People's Daily*, 5.

In relation to the boom in China's SCI-indexed publications, this review piece examines this phenomenon and looks at possible future directions for the reform of China's research evaluation processes. The study uses bibliographic data for the past decade (2010–2019) from the Science Citation Index Expanded in the Web of Science Core Collection to examine the rise in China's SCI-indexed publications. According to the author, China has surpassed the U.S. and has been the largest contributor of SCI publications since 2018. However, the scale of this impact still lags behind that of other major contributing countries. China's SCI publications are also overrepresented in some journals. In all, this article will benefit the reform of China's research evaluation system.

China's SCI-Indexed Publications: Facts, Feelings, and Future Directions [1]

Weishu Liu

Previous studies have shown a rapid rise in China's SCI (SCI refers to Science Citation Index Expanded for brevity)-indexed publications in recent years (Liu et al., 2015). Most recently, China's Ministry of Education and Ministry of Science and Technology have jointly issued a document to stop the practice of SCI-based evaluation in scientific research. This document has stimulated a wide discussion in academic circles around the world (Mallapaty, 2020; Nature Editorial, 2020). Some people are in favor of the decision; others, however, are skeptical. Supporters argue that it will switch the research evaluation practice from counting the number of SCI papers and citations to evaluating the research itself. Others, however, suspect that the science and education ministries are trying to destroy an objective indicator but without establishing a new and more appropriate one. Consensus on this issue, however, does not appear imminent. In this opinion piece, the author tries to uncover the facts, feelings, and future directions in relation to China's SCI-indexed publications.

---

1 This article was funded by the Zhejiang Province Natural Science Foundation [Grant number #LQ18G030010]. It was published on *ECNU Review of Education*, 3(3), 562–569.

Three facts about China's SCI-indexed publications

Before any discussion about China's SCI-indexed publications, three recent developments should first be noted: China has been the largest contributor of SCI publications since 2018; while the impact of China's SCI publications is rising, it still lags behind that of other major contributing countries; and China's SCI publications are overrepresented in some journals.

China has been the largest contributor of SCI publications since 2018

According to the Statistical Data of Chinese S&T Papers released annually by the Institute of Scientific and Technical Information of China (hereinafter referred to as the ISTIC report), China has been the second largest contributor of SCI publications every year from 2009 to 2018. However, if we limit the document type to articles and reviews, which is a common practice in the scientometrics community (Bornmann & Bauer, 2015; Zhang et al., 2011), a different scenario emerges: China has surpassed the U.S. as the world's largest producer of SCI papers since 2018.

For comparison, this opinion piece also calculates the SCI publication outputs of the U.S. during the past decade (data accessed on March 5, 2020; only articles and reviews are considered). Figure 1

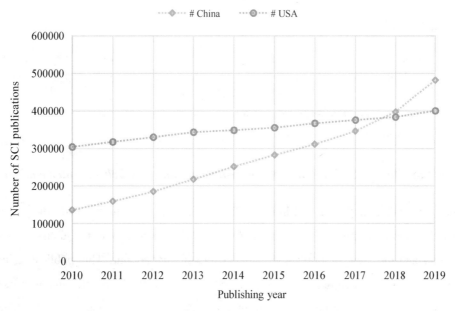

Figure 1. Numbers of SCI publications: China versus the U.S.

Note. Only articles and reviews are taken into account.

shows the annual SCI publication outputs of China and the U.S. The rise in China's SCI publications is very noticeable: from 137,000 in 2010 to 482,000 in 2019, an increase of 252%. The data also show that this rapid growth has actually accelerated in the last 2 years, which may be triggered by the Double First Class Plan in China (Liu, 2018; Wei & Zhang, 2020). In contrast, the output growth of the U.S. has been rather slower: from 304,000 in 2010 to 400,000 in 2019, an increase of 31%.

During the past 10 years, China has contributed 19.7% of the world's total SCI publications, while one quarter (25.1%) was contributed by the U.S. According to Figure 2, China's share of global SCI publication output also rose rapidly, from 12.2% in 2010 to 27.5% in 2019, while the United States' share has gradually decreased, falling from 27.2% in 2010 to 22.8% in 2019.

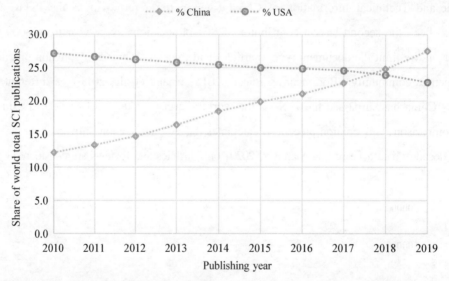

Figure 2. Relative shares of SCI publications: China versus the U.S.
Note. Only articles and reviews are taken into account.

The impact of China's SCI publications is rising but still lags behind other countries

Despite the significant growth in China's SCI publications, it would be misleading to conclude that China has replaced the U.S. as the world's leading scientific power. Quality matters more than quantity and the issue of publication impact remains paramount. This publication impact is usually measured by the number of citations. According to the ISTIC report, the average number of citations of China's SCI publications during 2009–2019 is 10.92, which is 9.2% higher than the data based on the period of 2008–2018 reported in the previous year. However, the average number of citations of China's SCI publications is lower than the world average (12.68), and China ranks only 16th among the 22 main producers of SCI publications. To sum up, the citation impact of China's SCI publications is rising but still lags behind the competition.

China's SCI publications are overrepresented in some journals

Table 1 lists the top 10 largest publishing outlets of China's SCI publications during the past decade. As demonstrated in Table 1, 6.67% of China's SCI publications during the past decade were published in the top 10 journals. The table also shows China's relative share of each journal's output during that decade. According to the data, 35.1% of the top 10 journals' publications were contributed by authors from China, which is 78% higher than China's average contribution to SCI publications globally (19.7%).

Table 1. Top 10 publishing outlets of China's SCI publications (2010–2019).

Ranking	Journal	Record count	% of China's total SCI publications	Total publications in each journal	China's share (%)	Publisher
1	PLoS One	33,274	1.20	204,900	16.2	Public Library of Science, USA
2	RSC Advances	28,991	1.05	55,582	52.2	Royal Society of Chemistry, England
3	Scientific Reports	28,783	1.04	100,537	28.6	Nature Publishing Group, England
4	IEEE Access	16,433	0.59	25,265	65.0	IEEE Inc, USA
5	Journal of Alloys and Compounds	15,673	0.57	31,246	50.2	Elsevier, Switzerland
6	ACS Applied Materials Interfaces	13,843	0.50	29,019	47.7	American Chemical Society, USA
7	Acta Physica Sinica	12,765	0.46	12,778	99.9	Chinese Physical Society, China
8	Chemical Communications	11,990	0.43	31,415	38.2	Royal Society of Chemistry, England
9	Applied Surface Science	11,799	0.43	24,356	48.4	Elsevier, Netherlands
10	International Journal of Clinical and Experimental Medicine	11,385	0.41	12,511	91.0	e-Century Publishing Corp, USA
	Top 10	184,936	6.67	527,609	35.1	N/A

Note. Only articles and reviews are taken into account.

However, China's relative shares among the top 10 journals vary significantly. The largest publishing outlet, PLoS One, has published 1.2% of all China's SCI publications, though China has only contributed 16.2% of all the publications in this open access (OA) mega-journal. However, China's contributions to each of the other nine journals exceed the benchmark value of 19.7%. It is worth noting that 91% of the publications in the OA journal *The International Journal of Clinical and Experimental Medicine*, published by e-Century Publishing Corporation, are contributed by China, while 65% of the articles published in *IEEE Access*, another OA journal produced by IEEE Inc., are also contributed by authors from China. The highest percentage contribution rate by Chinese authors is to *Acta Physica Sinica* (99.9%), but this is understandable since it is a local journal published by the Chinese Physical Society.

Some feelings about China's SCI-indexed publications boom

Introduced in the 1980s, the SCI-based evaluation system has enhanced the quality of basic science research in China (Gong & Qu, 2010). With the continuous investment of resources, China's scientific research capabilities have improved significantly over the past 30 years. At the same time, the SCI database has also significantly updated its content, including the introduction of more and more regional and OA journals. The limitations of SCI-related metrics still exist and have been widely discussed (Hu et al., 2018; Lariviere et al., 2016; Liu et al., 2016; Liu, Hu, et al., 2018; Liu, Liu, et al., 2018). As Goodhart's law states, "When a measure becomes a target, it ceases to be a good measure." Essentially, SCI-related metrics are still very useful but need to be used wisely. The famous Leiden Manifesto for research metrics also suggests that "quantitative evaluation should support qualitative, expert assessment" (Hicks et al., 2015).

In China, institutions at varying stages of development adopt different research evaluation strategies. Institutions weak in scientific research may judge the research outputs solely based on whether they are SCI-indexed. However, many institutions of medium scientific strength have adopted other indicators, such as journal impact factor quartile and number of citations, to assist the evaluation process of research output, while leading institutions tend to establish their own lists of recognized journals. Regardless of these different approaches, almost all institutions also use peer review to evaluate the research outputs, especially when promotion is being considered.

In China, many professions with strong practical attributes, such as clinicians, need to publish articles in order to meet the evaluation criteria. Young scholars in many middle-and lower-tier universities also need to publish as many papers as possible to improve their employment assessment and relieve economic pressure, while many graduate students need to publish SCI papers to meet graduation requirements. All this has contributed to the boom in China's SCI publication during the past decade. However, the issue of quantity versus quality remains and the boom in output has been accompanied by increasing problems in relation to research integrity in China (Lei & Zhang, 2018; Tang, 2019).

Publication output has also been boosted by some mega-journals, as presented in Table 1. The fact that more than 60% (and even 90%) of some journals' publications are contributed by authors from China is frankly astonishing. However, many of these journals charge high article processing fees, indicating the existence of possible conflicts of interest for both publishers and authors. In particular, the possibility that some publishers are being driven by financial reasons into lowering their acceptance standards needs to be considered.

Future directions

Evaluation is a difficult task and different institutions need to explore their own evaluation options in practice. Three directions may be considered in future evaluation practice.

First, various forms of contribution should be recognized, not just publication outputs. Different positions entail different responsibilities and therefore produce different forms of output and all contributions, in whatever form, should be recognized. In important cases, such as university promotions, stipulating SCI papers or national projects as an essential condition may not be appropriate.

Second, SCI-based metrics should be used wisely rather than abandoned. The Web of Science's citation indexes are powerful and invaluable; however, the SCI-based metrics should be used carefully in evaluation practice, with more focus on quality rather than quantity. Some SCI-based metrics, such as journal impact factor quartile and number of citations excluding self-citations, can act as important supporting indicators in the evaluation process. In practice, a blacklist or a grey list are effective ways of weeding out Web of Science-indexed papers and journals of questionable quality.

Third, the peer-review process needs to be optimized by combining quantitative and qualitative methods. While peer review is always an option for research evaluation, it is costly, time-consuming, and subjective. However, we should note that papers published in many prestigious journals have passed rigorous peer review. Evaluation management departments therefore need to pick appropriate and trusted experts and provide referees with both quantitative and qualitative information.

References

Bornmann, L., & Bauer, J. (2015). Evaluation of the highly-cited researchers' database for a country: Proposals for meaningful analyses on the example of Germany. *Scientometrics*, *105*(3), 1997–2003.

Gong, F., & Qu, M. (2010). A case study of Nanjing University: The influence of introducing SCI into assessment system on the quality of basic research in Chinese mainland universities [in Chinese]. *Higher Education of Sciences*, (3), 4–17.

Hicks, D., Wouters, P., Waltman, L., De Rijcke, S., & Rafols, I. (2015). Bibliometrics: The Leiden Manifesto for research metrics. *Nature*, *520*(7548), 429–431.

Hu, Z., Tian, W., Xu, S., Zhang, C., & Wang, X. (2018). Four pitfalls in normalizing citation indicators: An investigation of ESI's selection of highly cited papers. *Journal of Informetrics*, *12*(4), 1133–1145.

Lariviere, V., Kiermer, V., MacCallum, C. J., McNutt, M., Patterson, M., Pulverer, B., Swaminathan, S., Taylor, S., & Curry, S. (2016). A simple proposal for the publication of journal citation distributions. *BioRxiv*. https://doi.org/10.1101/062109

Lei, L., & Zhang, Y. (2018). Lack of improvement in scientific integrity: An analysis of WoS retractions by Chinese researchers (1997–2016). *Science and Engineering Ethics*, *24*(5), 1409–1420.

Liu, F., Hu, G., Tang, L., & Liu, W. (2018). The penalty of containing more non-English articles. *Scientometrics*, *114*(1), 359–366.

Liu, W., Hu, G., & Gu, M. (2016). The probability of publishing in first-quartile journals. *Scientometrics*, *106*(3), 1273–1276.

Liu, W., Hu, G., Tang, L., & Wang, Y. (2015). China's global growth in social science research: Uncovering evidence from bibliometric analyses of SSCI publications (1978–2013). *Journal of Informetrics*, *9*(3), 555–569.

Liu, W., Liu, F., Zuo, C., & Zhu, J. (2018). The effect of publishing a highly cited paper on a journal's impact factor: A case study of the review of particle physics. *Learned Publishing*, *31*(3), 261–266.

Liu, X. (2018). The "double first class" initiative under top-level design. *ECNU Review of Education*, *1*(1), 147–152.

Mallapaty, S. (2020). China bans cash rewards for publishing papers. *Nature*, *579*(7797), 18.

Nature Editorial. (2020). China's research-evaluation revamp should not mean fewer international collaborations. *Nature*, *579*(7797), 8.

Tang, L. (2019). Five ways China must cultivate research integrity. *Nature*, *575*(7784), 589–591.

Wei, F., & Zhang, G. (2020). Measuring the scientific publications of double first-class universities from mainland China. *Learned Publishing*, *33*(3), 193–348.

Zhang, L., Rousseau, R., & Glänzel, W. (2011). Document-type country profiles. *Journal of the American Society for Information Science and Technology*, *62*(7), 1403–1411.

This review demonstrates how to position Social Sciences Citation Index (SSCI) papers reasonably to promote the reform and development of the system for evaluating social sciences research (E-SSR) in China. This review analyzes documents pertaining to the E-SSR systems of more than 50 world-class universities with consideration to the inherent characteristics and historical mission of social sciences research in China. The study argues that the application of SSCI papers as an E-SSR tool is not common in world-class universities and proposes four deductive reform directions for China's E-SSR system. In all, although SSCI papers constitute an indicator of E-SSR system, their importance must not be overstated and the main purpose of the E-SSR system is to facilitate the development of social sciences with a style and characteristics unique to China. The findings of this study can serve as the basis for examining the future trends in the reform of the E-SSR system in Chinese universities.

Reflections on the Use of SSCI Papers in Evaluating Social Sciences Research in Chinese Universities[1]

Li Liu, Huilin Xue and Jing Li

The value of SSCI papers in China's E-SSR system

In recent years, Chinese universities have used institutional regulations to guide and encourage the publication of SSCI papers by their faculty members. Universities also use the number of papers as a yardstick to evaluate the academic levels of faculty members and disciplines. In the social sciences, SSCI papers have become the basis of talent recruitment, evaluation of professional titles, and awarding of scientific research grants.

Chinese universities have begun releasing the number of SSCI-indexed papers published by their various faculties and departments as well as the frequency with which these papers were cited. In China, the role of SSCI is not just a database for scientific researchers, but an important standard for the E-SSR system and related achievements (Dang, 2005). Moreover, many

---

[1] This article was funded by the National Social Science Foundation of China: General Program (BIA170162). It was published on *ECNU Review of Education*, 3(3), 570–575.

Chinese universities treat SSCI and CSSCI papers differently when awarding the publication of papers, such that "the award amount for an SSCI paper published in an international journal is usually several times, or even ten to twenty times, more than that for a local CSSCI paper" (Xu & Jiang, 2018, p. 49). This reflects the premium status of SSCI papers within the E-SSR system in Chinese universities.

Impact of introducing SSCI papers into China's E-SSR system

Although the SSR level of a country (or particular scientific research institution or scholar) cannot be accurately measured using the number of SSCI papers published, this indicator reflects its international status within a research field to a large extent (Kousha & Thelwall, 2007). As such, introducing SSCI into China's E-SSR system and encouraging faculty members to publish papers in international journals have contributed to the internationalization of SSR in the country. On the one hand, the international academic impact of Chinese social sciences has increased, facilitating the transformation of "silent China" into "China with a voice" (Liu, 2019, p. 111). The standardization of the country's academic research paradigm and improvement in the academic rationality of research have also contributed to this shift (Liu & Ding, 2014).

On the other hand, the excessive reliance on SSCI papers has created several issues that cannot be ignored, including a lack of in-depth research into Chinese real social problems. As Liu and Ding (2014) note, "When selecting topics to write papers for publication in SSCI journals, scholars from China were more inclined towards popular issues that western countries were concerned about" (p. 88). According to Qin and Zhang (2008), a desire to be published in English journals and to attract the attention of foreign academic journals resulted in three phenomena: First, Chinese scholars began researching topics currently studied by Americans; second, they began studying local issues of interest to Americans; third, they began interpreting local issues through direct recourse to Western theories. Consequently, many local studies have become a database for American research or evidence of the applicability of Western theories in the Chinese context. As a result, Qin and Zhang (2008) note, "the local issues that really need to be studied and solved were frequently ignored" (p. 8).

Therefore, although the publication of SSCI papers offers rich rewards for scientific research, research has failed to meet the country's social development needs. In this respect, emphasis on publishing SSCI papers has made "scholars mistakenly equate internationalization with a high quality level, thus weakening the role of scientific research at serving the country's development" (Liu & Ding, 2014, p. 91). Exaggerating the evaluative function of SSCI papers and placing this indicator at such a "supreme" position in the evaluation system have also led to a discrimination against the publication of papers in Chinese (Chou, 2014, p. 12).

Discussion

The world-class universities of other countries rarely apply SSCI papers as an E-SSR tool. A review of faculty member handbooks of 54 world-class universities, including Harvard University and Stanford University, reveals no mention of SSCI papers in respect to promotion, tenure, or performance assessment. In contrast, the corresponding guidelines for faculty members in the social sciences in Chinese institutions almost always include SSCI papers. Drawing on the experiences of other countries, as well as the developmental characteristics of the social sciences in China and the reality of its E-SSR system, this review proposes the following reform directions for China's E-SSR system.

Establish a pluralistic evaluation mechanism, with equal importance placed on SSCI papers and other research achievements

In world-class universities, both print and nonprint research achievements are considered for promotion, tenure, and performance assessment. In this respect, published papers are just one form of print achievements. For instance, Texas State University's College of Education considers 10 categories of print materials—including books, articles, conference proceedings, abstracts, reports, and book reviews—when evaluating promotions. Books comprise five subcategories: scholarly monographs, textbooks, edited books, chapters in books, and creative books. Articles published in both refereed and non-refereed journals are also included (Texas State University, 2018).

In addition to SSCI papers, the status of other forms of achievement—including academic monographs, consulting reports, textbooks, and translations—should be enhanced in the E-SSR system of Chinese universities. Instead of giving supremacy to papers, especially SSCI papers, a pluralistic evaluation mechanism should be established. As Chen (2011) argues, if Chinese scholars wish to step out onto the world stage without being overbearing or self-effacing, they must first "improve their personal abilities and strive to improve the overall academic level. They should remain patient, work hard, spend a decade boosting their strength, and another decade heeding lessons from the past and training conscientiously. By the time a large number of works embracing an international perspective and local sentiments have accumulated, the goal of internationalizing Chinese academia will be achieved naturally" (p. 66).

Apply SSCI papers as an E-SSR tool with caution and institute distinct treatments for various disciplines

In their empirical study, Klein and Chiang (2004) confirm that SSCI cannot accurately reflect the quality of published results as well as the existence of obvious ideological biases. As a result of the uneven distribution of disciplines, the use of SSCI has produced numerous biases in overall E-SSR (Chu et al., 2003). The SSCI contains the lowest number of ethnological journals, but the highest number of psychological journals. Indeed, due to its inclination and preference, SSCI cannot provide fair evaluations for academic research in the fields of modern languages and literature or theories of socialism with Chinese characteristics (Zhuo, 2011). It is necessary to recognize that the SSCI's uneven distribution of disciplines prevent its application to all disciplines in the social sciences. Accordingly, SSCI should be used discriminately according to the characteristics and particularities of individual disciplines.

Reduce the importance of language used and journal ranking, and emphasize innovation quality and actual contributions

This article reviews the recruitment and promotional literature of 54 world-class universities, finding that their evaluation standards primarily emphasizes originality, high accomplishment level and quality, as well as potential. For example, the criteria for lifelong tenure in Harvard University's Faculty of Arts and Sciences include scholarly achievement and impact on the field, evidence of intellectual leadership and creative accomplishment, potential for future accomplishments, and potential contribution to the university and broader scholarly community (Harvard University, 2012). The evaluation standards focused on faculty members' level of achievements in scientific research and the influence of those achievements. Essentially, these criteria have nothing to do with the journals in which faculty members' papers were published or the language in which they were written. According to Li (2020), "The specific journal that published the paper, the language of the paper, the amount of attention garnered after publication and the ways the attention was given—all these have no bearing on the scientific value of knowledge innovation, and should not be misinterpreted as standards for evaluating scientific research" (p. 13). Therefore, China's E-SSR system should downplay the language used and journal ranking, and shift the actual evaluation foci to innovation quality and practical contribution.

Establish China's standards of E-SSR with the aim of achieving an equilibrium between internationalization and localization

In terms of the nature of the various disciplines, the natural sciences constitute a pure knowledge system that emphasizes value neutrality. In contrast, the social sciences comprise a broad duality: namely, a knowledge system and an ideology (Yang, 2017). In this sense, there are "borders" within the social sciences (Zhuo, 2011, p. 9). The famous sociologist Xiaotong Fei advocated cultural awareness in later life. This idea is particularly important for the development of social sciences in China. Summarizing the course of cultural awareness, Fei (1997) claimed that "Every form of beauty has its uniqueness; it is precious to appreciate other forms of beauty with openness. When beauty is represented by diversity and integrity, the world will be blessed with harmony and unity" (p. 22).

In this respect, we need to identify the unique advantages and inherent characteristics of China's social sciences and develop these through self-reflection. Instead of blindly looking up to others, we should "step out" with our own unique stance. We must self-adapt to the global perspective, and engage in equal exchange and mutual growth with other cultures in creating a global civilization where "beauty is represented by diversity and integrity." China's E-SSR system should serve the purpose of "building social sciences with the characteristics and a style and imposing manner that are unique to the country, but are also of universal significance" (Yang, 2017). In the process of internationalizing the social sciences, China's ESSR standards should be formulated to achieve an equilibrium between internationalization and localization.

References

Chen, P. (2011). International horizon and local feelings: How to hold dialogues with sinologists [in Chinese]. *Journal of*

Shanghai Normal University (*Philosophy & Social Sciences*), *40*(6), 56-68.

Chou, C. P. (2014). The SSCI syndrome in Taiwan's academia. *Education Policy Analysis Archives*, *22*(29). http://dx.doi.org/10.14507/epaa.v22n29.2014

Chu, C. F., Liu, Y., & Xiong, X. (2003). The impact of SSCI indexed periodicals' discipline distribution on the social sciences research evaluation [in Chinese]. *Science of Science and Management of S.& T.*, *24*(11), 19-22.

Dang, S. (2005). Can the American standard be the highest evaluation standard for the achievements of Chinese humanities and social sciences? Using SSCI as an example [in Chinese]. *Tribune of Social Sciences*, (4), 62-72.

Fei, X. (1997). Reflections, dialogues and the consciousness of culture [in Chinese]. *Journal of Peking University (Philosophy and Social Sciences)*, (3), 15-22+158.

Harvard University. (2012). *FAS appointment and promotion handbook*. Retrieved March 8, 2020, from https://academic-appointments.fas.harvard.edu/4-tenured-professors

Klein, D. B., & Chiang, E. (2004). The Social Science Citation Index: A black box—With an ideological bias? *Econ Journal Watch*, *1*(1), 134-165.

Kousha, K., & Thelwall, M. (2007). The web impact of open access social science research. *Library & Information Science Research*, *29*(4), 495-507.

Li, J. (2020, March 3). Breaking "SCI first" and improving scientific research evaluation [in Chinese]. *Guangming Daily*, 13.

Liu, L. (2019). *The bibliometric analysis of SSCI articles in Chinese mainland from 1978-2007—A view on the internationalization of social sciences research* [Doctoral dissertation, Shanghai Jiao Tong University] [in Chinese].

Liu, Q., & Ding, R. (2014). Impacts of SSCI on the academic research of Chinese scholars: Taking education discipline as an example [in Chinese]. *International and Comparative Education*, *294*(7), 87-92.

Qin, H., & Zhang, R. (2008). Reflection on SSCI and evaluation of university seniority of social scientific research [in Chinese]. *Journal of Higher Education*, *29*(3), 6-12.

Texas State University. (2018). *TEXAS STATE VITA (with Fine Arts components)*. Retrieved March 8, 2020, from https://policies.txstate.edu/division-policies/academic-affairs/04-02-20.html

Xu, X., & Jiang, K. (2018). Humanities and social sciences academics' perceptions of incentive mechanism for international publications [in Chinese]. *Journal of Higher Education*, *39*(1), 48-60.

Yang, G. (2017, April 24). The particularity of social sciences [in Chinese]. *Guangming Daily*, 11.

Zhuo, W. (2011). Reflection on SSCI and academic evaluation of humanities and social sciences in colleges and universities using Xihua universityasanexample [inChinese]. *Journal of Higher Education: Chengdu*, (4), 12-14.

This article provides a policy review of the Greater Bay Area (GBA) development strategies and their relevance to higher education. It mainly reviews key GBA policies adopted by the central government of China and interprets higher education cooperation policies at provincial and national levels before discussing the opportunities and challenges for higher education. According to the study, the shift toward a high-tech service-led economy triggered by the GBA Development Strategy would hinge upon creating an effective partnerships platform between industry and higher education institutions, which would require greater institutional and professional autonomy for the academic research enterprises and more evidence-based policies by the Central and GBA regional governments. This study can be used to guide policies to promote higher education cooperation in the GBA in a more integrated, innovative, and internationalized way.

The Greater Bay Area (GBA) Development Strategy and Its Relevance to Higher Education[1]

Ailei Xie, Gerard A. Postiglione and Qian Huang

Introduction

The Guangdong-Hong Kong-Macao Greater Bay Area (GBA) comprises the two Special Administrative Regions (SARs) of Hong Kong and Macao and the nine municipalities of Guangzhou, Shenzhen, Zhuhai, Foshan, Huizhou, Dongguan, Zhongshan, Jiangmen, and Zhaoqing in Guangdong Province. It covers an area of 56,500 km^2, with a resident population of more than 67.65 million. Because of its geographical location and economic significance in China's social and economic landscape, the central government has initiated the GBA Development Strategy, which is China's first official bay area regional development strategy that has risen to the national level (Chen, 2018). As with other important policy initiatives, the GBA Development Strategy starts with a general framework and will be enriched by additional policy measures. The policy framework is ambitious, dynamic, and subject to interpretation and negotiation by policy

---

1 This article was funded by the Guangzhou Philosophy and Social Sciences Research Project under grant 2020GZGJ192. It was published on *ECNU Review of Education*, 4(1), 210–221.

actors at different levels.

This review introduces key GBA policies adopted by the central government and gauges their implications for higher education cooperation. It starts with an overview and an interpretation of strategical goals, followed by an analysis of current higher education collaboration in the GBA. Finally, it highlights future challenges and opportunities.

The GBA Development Strategy, its policy origins, and the three "I"s

The GBA Development Strategy aims to create a connected and unified bay area that is comparable to those world's leading bay areas in San Francisco, New York, and Tokyo in terms of economic competitiveness and technique innovations. Yet, the Strategy itself does not start from scratch. It is the result of a series of policy reforms and evolvement that targets at the economic and social cohesion in the Pearl River Delta. The GBA Development Strategy originated from *The Outline of the Pearl River Delta Reform and Development Plan (2008 - 2020)* issued by the National Development and Reform Commission (NDRC, 2009). The *Outline* is the first time that the nine cities of the Pearl River Delta and Hong Kong and Macao were included together in one policy initiative. In March 2015, the concept of the GBA was first proposed in *The Vision and Action for Promoting the Construction of the Silk Road Economic Belt and the 21st Century Maritime Silk Road* jointly issued by the NDRC, the Ministry of Foreign Affairs, and the Ministry of Commerce (Ministry of Commerce of the People's Republic of China [MCPRC], 2015). In March 2016, the concept of GBA appeared again in the *13th Five-Year Plan for National Economic and Social Development of the People's Republic of China* (State Council of the People's Republic of China [State Counci], 2016). Then, the GBA concept was included in the report of the 19th National Congress of the Communist Party of China in October 2017 and in the *Government Work Report* delivered by Premier Li Keqiang (March, 2018), which signified its rising, as a policy initiative, to the national level. In 2017, *Framework Agreement on Deepening Guangdong-Hong Kong-Macao Cooperation in the Development of the Greater Bay Area* was signed (NDRC, July 2017). In February 2019, the Central Committee of the Communist Party of China and the State Council released the *Outline Development Plan for Guangdong-Hong Kong-Macao Greater Bay Area*, which is to guide the GBA's development ahead to the year 2035 (State Council, 2019). The policy framework finally came into shape.

The GBA Development Strategy represents China's regional approach to develop its economy and is a part of its overall regional coordinated development strategy. Other regional development strategies include the Belt and Road Initiative, Jing-Jin-Ji Coordinated Development Initiative, the Yangtze River Economic Belt, as well as the Yangtze River Delta Regional Integration Strategy. All regional development strategies aim at achieving a high-quality development and narrowing regional gaps by joint collaborations between different areas (State Council, 2018). Yet, each strategy is also different in terms of approaches and pillars because of their own geographic locations and economic structure.

GBA progress is supported by a triple "I" helix strategy of integration, innovation, and internationalization.

Integration

The policy initiative aims to promote China's two Special Administration Regions' economic and cultural integration with the Chinese mainland under the "one country, two systems" framework. Deeper cooperation for Hong Kong, Macao, and the mainland will be mutually beneficial. As noted by Xi (2017) in the 19th National Congress of the Communist Party of China: "We will give priority to the development of the Guangdong-Hong Kong-Macao Greater Bay Area, cooperation between Guangdong, Hong Kong, and Macao, and regional cooperation in the pan-Pearl River Delta, thus fully advancing mutually beneficial cooperation between the mainland and the two regions." It will leverage the advantages of Hong Kong and Macao, support their development, and bring prosperity to China and the international community.

Innovation

The policy initiative constitutes part of a nationwide regional development strategy framework to build an innovation economy. China will pursue a structural rebalancing from a labor intensive, low investment, export-oriented economy to a high-tech manufacturing, and service-based economy that relies more on domestic consumption. The GBA is considered to be China'smost developed region with leading industries in the areas of manufacturing, financial services, and technological innovation which is key to its economic transition (Chen, 2018). It is no wonder that the GBA constitutes a new momentum for China's economic growth, a new channel for it to be engaged with the global economy and thereby a new engine for China's economic growth (Deloitte, 2018).

Internationalization

The GBA initiative serves as a catalyst for promoting China's economic internationalization. The 19th National Congress of the Communist Party of China stressed that "Openness brings progress, while self-seclusion leaves one behind" as well as "We must actively participate in and promote economic globalization, develop an open economy of higher standards, and continue to increase China's economic power and composite strength" (Xi, 2017). As Wang Yang (2018), the Vice Premier of the State Council, pointed out, it is necessary to deepen the openness of China's coastal economy and promote the deep structural adjustment of China's economy. A road map for opening up to the outside world in the coming period was drawn and a series of new tasks and new initiatives are planned (Xi, 2017). Among them are the Belt and Road Initiative and the optimization for an open regional layout. As the most open region to the outside world, the Greater Bay Area has an advantage in global economic positioning. As expected, it will play a key role in the Belt and Road Initiative and shoulder the responsibility of piloting more reforms to help China internationalize its economy.

Higher education collaborations under "one country, two systems"

The GBA has over 170 higher education institutions with a student population of more than 2 million. In addition, according to the 2021 QS world ranking, the GBA has five universities ranked among top 100 in the world (QS Ranking, 2021). The GBA colleges and universities will provide high-level human resources and become an engine for technical innovation. However, most higher education institutions are geographically concentrated in Guangzhou and Hong Kong. Their capacity to serve the GBA in an integrated way is a matter of concern. Another issue for stakeholders is that all five QS world ranked universities are located in Hong Kong. Since barriers to cross-system technology transfer and collaborations still exist, these top universities have some limitations in contributing to the structural rebalancing of the economy and to a high-tech drive in hinterland of the Pearl River Delta (Xie et al., 2019). There is a need for policy innovations that reduce the barriers hindering technology transfer and higher education collaborations at the institutional level.

The first modern university in the GBA was Lingnan University, established in 1888 in Guangzhou. Two decades later in 1911, the University of Hong Kong was founded. By the 1980s, Macao had opened its first university. Before 1978, the year when China began its opening-up and economic reform, there were a small number of Hong Kong and Macao youth who studied in Guangzhou (Zhang, 2002). Back then, the number of higher education institutions in Hong Kong and Macao was small and student mobility was restricted by Chinese government.

From 1979 to the 1997 reunification of Hong Kong with the Motherland, the educational and academic contacts, cooperation, and partnerships were encouraged and grew rapidly. After 1997, GBA cooperation grew at all levels and took various forms. The number of cross-border educational and academic exchanges in both directions grew rapidly. This included student exchange programs, research projects, joint research centers and laboratories, and industry-university-research bases. Since 2009, the Hong Kong SAR and Macao SAR governments with the support of the central government initiated joint venture campuses in the Chinese mainland.

By 2020, GBA higher education collaborations evolved to take various forms under different policy schemes.

Documents

Exchange programs based on the Memorandum of Understanding signed by the two SAR governments and the Ministry of Education (MOE) encouraged student exchange at university level or college/department level across the GBA borders with mutual recognition of credits and academic qualifications among universities.

Enrollments

GBA student enrollment includes the two-way recruitment by universities across GBA cities. Universities in the mainland recruit students from Hong Kong and Macao under three schemes: individual enrollment, joint enrollment, and recommendation enrollment. "Individual Enrollment" began in the 1980s. Approved by the MOE, a small number of mainland universities such as Sun Yat-sen University and Jinan University are authorized to organize their own entrance examinations for students from Hong Kong and Macao and recruit students independently. "Joint Enrollment" is a scheme in which students in Hong Kong take the Joint University Program Admissions System (JUPAS) examination in Hong Kong every May. Nearly 300 universities, including those in Guangdong, recruit qualified candidates, based on their performance achieved in JUPAS. "Recommendation Enrollment" targets mainly Hong Kong students. Their recruitment depends upon performance in the Hong Kong Diploma of Secondary Education Examination. Around 90 universities, including those in Guangdong, recruit part of their students through this scheme. In the meantime, universities in Hong and Macao recruit students from the mainland into their undergraduate or postgraduate programs through mainly two ways. First, after qualifying the National College Entrance Examination (NCEE), students who apply for the admission to undergraduate programs in Hong Kong take an "Independent Enrollment" test organized independently by each university. Universities in Macao recruit undergraduates based on their performance achieved in the NCEE. Second, all universities in Hong Kong and Macao admit postgraduate students by an independent application system that is similar to Western universities. Currently, there are 12 universities in Hong Kong and 6 universities in Macao recruiting students from the mainland.

Institutional cooperation

Joint cooperation in running of educational institutions, including academic programs, schools, and universities as early as 2006, included the University of Hong Kong's master of business administration program in Shenzhen with Peking University. As the cooperation in higher education increased, joint and independent campuses grew. In 2005, Hong Kong Baptist University launched the United International College in Zhuhai collaborated with Beijing Normal University. In 2009, with the strong support from the Chinese central government, a piece of land with an area of 1.0926 km^2 on Hengqin Island, which belongs to Zhuhai city adjacent to Macao, was approved for the construction of the new campus for the University of Macau. With the authorization of the Standing Committee of the National People's Congress, the Macao SAR was allowed to exercise jurisdiction over the new campus. In 2014, the Chinese University of Hong Kong (CUHK) established a joint venture university CUHK (Shenzhen) in collaboration with Shenzhen university. The students admitted to CUHK (Shenzhen) also register as students of the CUHK and will be awarded a degree from the CUHK upon graduation. In 2019, the Hong Kong University of Science and Technology also launched a joint venture university in collaboration with Guangzhou University.

Joint research

This form of collaboration developed rapidly is key to the GBA's future. Besides joint research projects carried out by scientists in higher education institutions in GBA, research collaborations also take the form of independent research institutes and joint key laboratories. For example, Shenzhen government has financed five universities from Hong Kong to set up research institutes in Shenzhen to facilitate technology transfer. In the year of 2016, the Department of Education in Guangdong Province began to promote the establishment of joint laboratories between Guangdong, Hong Kong, and Macao to promote science and technology innovation in the area.

Policy framework for higher education cooperation in the GBA

Higher education cooperation at institutional and system levels will continue to grow within the GBA (as well as globally). Currently, various types of higher education cooperation are under policy framework at such levels as governmental levels and institutional levels.

At the central government level, policies promote modest cross-border enrollment, academic exchanges, and cooperation in the running of educational institutions. These include, for example, *Colleges and Universities Regulations on Enrolling and Nurturing Students from Hong Kong SAR, Macao SAR and Taiwan Region* (MOE, 2016); *The Policy Provisions for Personnel Going to Hong Kong and Macao to Exchange*; and *Regulation on Sino-foreign Cooperation in Running Schools* (State Council, 2003), the issuance of the Employment Registration Certificates for Hong Kong students after graduation from mainland universities (MOE, 2017).

At the Guangdong government level, the relevant education policies and regulations include *Guangdong Province Higher Education Management Regulations and Outline of Educational Modernization in Guangdong Province (2004 – 2010)* (People's Government of Guangdong Province [PGGP], 2004), *Guangdong Province Medium- and Long-Term Education Reform and Development Plan (2010 – 2020)* (PGGP, 2010b), and *Letter of Intent on Qualifications Framework Cooperation Between Guangdong and Hong Kong* (RenminNet, 2019).

The Hong Kong and Macao SAR governments took measures to promote student exchanges and cooperation among the higher education institutions. This includes the recruitment of nonlocal students, especially those from the Chinese mainland to local higher education institutions. The Hong Kong SAR Government gradually relaxed the quota for admission of nonlocal students in its colleges and universities. However, higher education institutions in Hong Kong have limitations placed on the recruitment of undergraduate students at the time of a demographic shift to a shrinking college age cohort. This contributed to the closure of Centennial College. It also affects enrollments at other colleges.

There are also collaboration agreements and memos signed between the central government and the two SAR governments to support higher education cooperation between Guangdong, Hong Kong, and Macao. They include *The Mainland and Hong Kong Closer Economic Partnership Arrangement* (MOE, 2003), *The Mainland and Macao Closer Economic Partnership Arrangement* (MOE, 2005), and *Memorandum on Mutual Recognition of Higher Education Degree Certificates Between the Mainland and Hong Kong* (MOE, 2004).

In 2004, the Ministry of Science and Technology and the Hong Kong Trade and Industry and Technology Bureau signed the *Agreement on the Establishment of Science and Technology Cooperation Committee Between the Mainland and Hong Kong* (Xinhua, 2004) and established the Mainland and Hong Kong Science and Technology Cooperation Committee. A joint research scheme—*Guangdong-Hong Kong Technology Cooperation Funding Scheme* and the *Shenzhen-Hong Kong Science and Technology Cooperation Funding Scheme*—was created and led to the *Guangdong-Hong Kong Cooperation Framework Agreement* (PGGP, 2010a) and the *Guangdong-Macao Cooperation Framework Agreement* (PGGP, 2011).

The three "I"s: Opportunities and challenges for higher education in GBA

The GBA Development Strategy aims to build an integrated, innovative, and internationalized economy. It projects both opportunities and challenges for higher education institutions. There is an opportunity for universities to attract new funding opportunities as well as to prepare university graduates who can play a key role in the future of the GBA. The shift toward a high-tech service-led economy can be met by effective partnerships between industry and higher education institutions.

For higher education institutions in GBA, integration means deeper collaborations. The best picture would be that the higher education system will become a world-class one and function as a unified system which can respond well to the social and economic needs in GBA. Yet, although there are already policies encouraging and facilitating cross border academic and research collaborations, the higher education systems of Hong Kong SAR, Macao SAR, and Guangdong are still relatively separated from one another. Collaborations at the system level are alive and well, but the academic culture is not the same. This has important implications for student and institutional mobility. For example, studies suggest that there are increasing Chinese mainland students in Hong Kong universities. Yet, students reported acculturative issues because of Hong Kong's Western-style education model which emphasizes independent critical thinking, teamwork, creativity, and sophisticated research methods (Vyas & Yu, 2018). There is much academic cooperation across systems, but most of it is on an individual level, not an institutional level. For such institutional level collaborations as cross-border joint universities, the institutional distances including academic cultural recognitions usually constitute the barriers (Qin, 2020). Hong Kong's top universities will continue to maintain their competitive advantage by the predominant use of English in higher education instruction, retaining institutional autonomy, keeping transparency in administration and shared governance and involving academic staff in major development planning and key decisions (Postiglione & Jung, 2017). The strategies of universities in Guangdong may be less likely to be the same. That is why the policy designs and strategies for higher education collaborations in GBA are very limited and lack detail. The only commonality across the GBA systems of higher education is a market-driven environment. The GBA systems of higher education are very different in the extent to which their HEIs are mission-centered and market-smart. HEIs are a tool for improving human capital but identity and cultural production within a market-driven atmosphere are far more complex than ever. Challenges exist on how to define a common culture and identity and how are integrated into institution goals and the curriculum in a market-driven framework.

Policies of collaborations that lead to integration of knowledge networks require a higher degree of institutional autonomy and within-institutional professional autonomy. Both systems innovate in similar ways and different ways due to resources, policies, laws, work habits, academic leadership, the doctoral training received (in one system or in HK or overseas), etc. Yet, Hong Kong universities have legal autonomy to make decisions. Mainland universities often need approval from education department at the city or provincial level or MOE for such matters as international collaborations. For the academic staff—who become accustomed to operating in one system or the other and more senior staff may find it more difficult to change from one system to another, not only due to language but also governance style. A higher degree of institutional autonomy and within-institutional professional autonomy, therefore, is a key to more collaborations. They are also essentials for keeping the vitality of academic research enterprises and can stifle the capacity for innovation and worldwide impact (Postiglione, 2015).

Higher education institution in GBA can become world leaders in addressing problems like COVID-19, future pandemics, climate change, global poverty, equity and social justice, and sustainable development in innovative ways. They have begun to cultivate innovative talents with global vision and competitiveness, high-quality research, and industry-university cooperation. But their potential is limited by the awkwardness of their divergent frameworks for institutional governance in higher education. This is especially true with respect to internationalization. Qatar, Dubai, and Singapore all regarded the internationalization of higher education as an important strategy to attract and nurture international talents. China's SAR universities are well-seasoned in how to anchor globalization for economic and social development. In GBA cooperation, Guangdong's universities have to juggle internationalization along with limited institutional autonomy and a concern about the protection of its educational sovereignty.

There is no lack of ideas about how macro-policy designs can steer GBA higher education collaborations. Current policies are market-driven but not always market-smart. To maintain their integrity, institutions of higher education have to remain mission-focused, market-smart, and conscious of how to make the best use of their limited resources to raise their quality and relevance of their work. Higher education improves human capital and technical expertise, but it should avoid creating a highly stratified society. GBA HEIs have a challenge and an opportunity to appeal to the future generation of leaders by preparing them with the talent to innovate, the vision to think globally and act locally, and to be competitive in the international labor market.

References

Chen, G. (2018). *Guangdong-Hong Kong-Macao Bay area development report* [in Chinese]. Chinese Renmin University Press.

Deloitte. (2018). *From the world factory to the world-class bay area* [in Chinese]. http://www.199it.com/archives/766251.html

Li, K. (2018). *The government work report* [in Chinese]. http://www.gov.cn/zhuanti/2018lh/2018zfgzbg/zfgzbg.htm

Ministry of Commerce of the People's Republic of China. (2003). *The mainland and Hong Kong closer economic partnership arrangement* [in Chinese]. http://tga.mofcom.gov.cn/article/zt_cepanew/subjectaa/200612/20061204078587.shtml

Ministry of Commerce of the People's Republic of China. (2005). *The mainland and Macao closer economic partnership arrangement* [in Chinese]. http://tga.mofcom.gov.cn/article/zt_cepanew/afwmyxy/201511/20151101196720.shtml

Ministry of Commerce of the People's Republic of China. (2015). *The vision and action for promoting the construction of the Silk Road Economic Belt and the 21st century Maritime Silk Road* [in Chinese]. http://www.mofcom.gov.cn/article/resume/n/201504/20150400929655.shtml

Ministry of Education of the People's Republic of China. (2004). *Memorandum on mutual recognition of higher education degree certificates between the mainland and Hong Kong* [in Chinese]. http://www.moe.gov.cn/jyb_zzjg/moe_187/moe_410/moe_532/tnull_3392.html

Ministry of Education of the People's Republic of China. (2016). *Colleges' and universities' regulations on enrolling and nurturing students from Hong Kong SAR, Macao SAR and Taiwan region* [in Chinese]. http://www.moe.gov.cn/srcsite/A20/s3117/s6583/201701/t20170109_294338.html

Ministry of Education of the People's Republic of China. (2017). *Issuance of the employment registration certificates for Hong Kong students after graduation from mainland universities* [in Chinese]. http://www.ce.cn/xwzx/gnsz/gdxw/201708/11/t20170811_24944207.shtml

National Development and Reform Commission. (2009). *The outline of the Pearl River Delta reform and development plan (2008–2020)* [in Chinese]. https://www.ndrc.gov.cn/xwdt/dt/dfdt/200901/t20090107_974676.html

National Development and Reform Commission. (2017). *Framework agreement on deepening Guangdong-Hong Kong-Macao cooperation in the development of the Greater Bay Area* [in Chinese]. https://www.bayarea.gov.hk/filemanager/en/share/pdf/Framework_Agreement.pdf

People's Government of Guangdong Province. (2004). *Outline of educational modernization in Guangdong province (2004–2020)* [in Chinese]. http://www.edu.cn/edu/zheng_ce_gs_gui/shengji_zhce_fagui/guang dong_zhce_fagui/200603/t20060320_168052.shtml

People's Government of Guangdong Province. (2010a). *Guangdong-Hong Kong cooperation framework agreement* [in Chinese]. http://hk.mofcom.gov.cn/article/zxhz/zwqtjmjg/201005/20100506914145.shtml

People's Government of Guangdong Province. (2010b). *Guangdong province medium- and long-term education reform and development plan (2010–2020)* [in Chinese]. http://jw.scnu.edu.cn/a/20130909/74.html

People's Government of Guangdong Province. (2011). *Guangdong-Hong Kong cooperation framework agreement* [in Chinese]. http://www.xinhuanet.com/2018-07/21/c_1123158970.htm

Postiglione, G. A. (2015). Research universities for national rejuvenation and global influence. *Higher Education*, *70*, 235–250.

Postiglione, G. A., & Jung, J. (2017). The changing academic profession in Hong Kong: Challenges and future. In G. Postiglione & J. Jung (Eds.), *The changing academic profession in Hong Kong* (Vol. 19, The Changing Academy—The Changing Academic Profession in International Comparative Perspective). Springer.

Qin, Y. (2020). Same seed, different flavor? The institutional dilemmas of cross-border joint-universities in China, Tsinghua [in Chinese]. *Journal of Education*, *41*, 120–125.

QS Ranking 2021 [in Chinese]. https://www.topuniversities.com/university-rankings/world-university-rank ings/2021

RenminNet. (2019). *Letter of intent on qualifications framework cooperation between Guangdong and Hong Kong* [in Chinese]. http://hm.people.com.cn/n1/2019/0625/c42272-31189718.html

State Council of the People's Republic of China. (2003). *Regulation on Sino-foreign cooperation in running schools* [in Chinese]. http://www.gov.cn/zhengce/content/2008-03/28/content_5821.htm

State Council of the People's Republic of China. (2016). *The 13th five-year plan for national economic and social development of the People's Republic of China* [in Chinese]. http://www.gov.cn/xinwen/2016-04/13/content_5063729.htm

State Council of the People's Republic of China. (2018). *Opinions on establishing a more effective new mechanism for coordinated regional development* [in Chinese]. http://www.gov.cn/zhengce/2018-11/29/content_5344537.htm

State Council of the People's Republic of China. (2019). *Outline development plan for Guangdong-Hong Kong-Macao Greater Bay Area* [in Chinese]. http://www.gov.cn/zhengce/2019-02/18/content_5366593.htm#1

Vyas, L., & Yu, B. (2018). An investigation into the academic acculturation experiences of Mainland Chinese students in Hong Kong. *Higher Education*, 76, 883–901.

Wang, Y. (2018). *Promoting the formation of a new pattern of comprehensive opening-up* [in Chinese]. http://www.gov.cn/guowuyuan/2017-11/10/content_5238476.htm

Xi, J. (2017). *The report of the 19th National Congress of the Communist Party of China* [in Chinese]. http://www.xinhuanet.com/politics/19cpcnc/2017-10/27/c_1121867529.htm [in Chinese] and http://english.qstheory.cn/2018-02/11/c_1122395333.htm [in English]

Xie, A., Li, J., & Liu, Q. (2019). Collaborative innovation and development of higher education in Guangdong-Hong Kong-Macao Greater Bay Area: Background, foundation and path [in Chinese]. *Chinese Higher Education Research*, (5), 58–69.

Xinhua. (2004). *The agreement on the establishment of science and technology cooperation committee between the mainland and Hong Kong* [in Chinese]. http://www.china.com.cn/chinese/ChineseCommunity/566553.htm

Zhang, Y. (2002). *The higher education development history in Guangdong* [in Chinese]. Guangdong Higher Education Press.

The 8-year medical education program (EYMEP) is China's path to training high-level medical talents. In the new era of the reform and development of China's medical education, a systematic review of the development of EYMEP in China is of great significance to the promotion of high-level medical talent training in China. By analyzing relevant textual materials and policy documents dating back to the time of hosting of China's EYMEP, this study systematically reviews the developmental process of China's EYMEP. Based on some additional interviews and field trips, the study also discovers that 14 universities and institutes are hosting the EYMEP that approved by the Ministry of Education of the People's Republic of China, but differing greatly in training ideas and goals, enrollment processes, and training phases. According to the article, China's EYMEP is faced with some external threats and internal challenges. In the future, China's EYMEP should consider five aspects. Aside from its internal value, the exploration course of China's high-level medical talent training represented by the EYMEP may also be an enlightenment for other countries, especially developing countries like China, in their training of high-level medical talents.

Eight-Year Medical Education Program: Retrospect and Prospect of the High-Level Medical Talent Training in China [1]

Hongbin Wu, Ana Xie and Weimin Wang

Talents are the first resources for health services, and medical education undertakes an important mission of medical talent training. Since the introduction of contemporary medicine, China's medical education has made huge achievements under continuous exploration and reform. Currently, the core health indicators of China outperform those of middle-and high-income countries on average (State Council Information Office of the People's Republic of China [PRC], 2019). Among medical professionals, high-level medical talents decide the quality of medical services, medical science, and technology and guide the future development of medicine. In China, the path of high-level medical talent training, the 8-year medical education

---

1 This article was funded by the Key Project for Medical Education Research in 2018 of the Medical Education Branch of the Chinese Medical Association and Specialty Committee of Medical Education in China Association of Higher Education (2018A-N02095). It is partially based on the authors' recent study which will be published as a Chinese-language article in the *Chinese Journal of Medical Education*. The use of this version has been authorized by *Chinese Journal of Medical Education* and acknowledged by *ECNU Review of Education*. It was published on *ECNU Review of Education*, 4(1), 190–209.

program (EYMEP) is a crucial experimental field of top-notch medical innovative talent training (Lin, 2019). The developmental process of the EYMEP embodies China's exploration of high-level medical talent training. On July 10, 2017, the National Conference of the Reform and Development of Medical Education was held in Beijing, after which the General Office of the State Council of the PRC issued *Opinions of the State Council on Deepening the Coordination of Medicine and Education and Further Advancing the Reform and Development of Medical Education* (hereafter referred to as the *Opinions*). The issuance of the *Opinions* has strategic significance for China's medical education, which has entered a new era of reform and development thereafter (Shi et al., 2018). Against this background, the research questions of this article are what kind of development process EYMEP has experienced in China, what are the threats and challenges it faces, and how to develop it in the future.

Developmental process of the EYMEP

Since Peking Union Medical College ran the EYMEP in 1917, China's EYMEP has lasted over a century. The developmental process can be divided into five periods: the Only Host Period (1917–1978), the Duplication Pilot Host Period (1979–1987), the Expansion Period (2001–2004),[1] the Joint Exploration Period (2004–2018), and the In-Depth Promotion Period (2018 to present).

The Only Host Period (1917–1978)

In 1866, the establishment of Pok Tsai Medical School in the Canton Hospital started the developmental process of China's modern medical education. China's medical education is deeply influenced by churches and the international medical education (Li, 2015). Published in 1910, the Flexner Report led a trend in the reform and development of global medical education (Frenk et al., 2010). In 1914, the China Medical Board of the Rockefeller Foundation (hereafter referred to as CMB) was founded to support China's medical education. CMB acquired the Union Medical College Lockhart Hall hosted by churches, including the London Missionary Society, and renamed it as Peking Union Medical College (Zhang, 2009). After the field trip on

---

1 From 1988 to 2000, only the Peking Union Medical College held the 8-year medical education program.

China's medicine and medical education, CMB suggested that to train high-level medical talents, the enrollment conditions should follow the requirements of the American top medical colleges (Peking Union Medical College, 1987, p. 6). After relevant registration, in 1917, Peking Union Medical College began to enroll 8-year medical candidates who would be awarded the Doctor of Medicine (MD). This started the journey of China's high-level (modern) medical talent training. Considering China's national conditions and the standards of the Johns Hopkins University School of Medicine (the representative of the American high-level medical colleges then), the EYMEP in Peking Union Medical College upheld the concept of elite education with no more than 30 students enrolled per year (Wu & Dong, 2001, p. 10). From 1917 to 1978, Peking Union Medical College was the only institute to host the EYMEP throughout China. In more than six decades, the EYMEP in Peking Union Medical College experienced several changes. From 1917 to 1925, it hosted the 3-year premedical education program and the 5-year medical education program. From 1925 to 1941, and from 1948 to 1953, the college enrolled candidates who had finished the 3-year undergraduate education program for another 5-year medical education program. From 1959 to 1970, the National College Entrance Examination (NCEE) was held, through which students would receive a 3-year premedical education program in Peking University and then another 5-year medical education program in Peking Union Medical College. Besides, in the periods of 1941 – 1948, 1953 – 1959, and 1970 – 1978, the enrollment of the EYMEP in Peking Union Medical College was halted for the Second World War and some political reasons.

In the Only Host Period, the EYMEP in Peking Union Medical College produced a significant effect, and the college became a top medical school with a considerable influence in China and other parts of the world. Nearly half of China's medical disciplines were established and developed by the graduates from the EYMEP in Peking Union Medical College (Wang & Yin, 2013). It was the significant effect of the EYMEP in Peking Union Medical College that gradually developed people's awareness that this program is the path to training high-level medical talents in China (Yin, 2012).

The Duplication Pilot Host Period (1979 – 1987)

After the "Cultural Revolution" was ended in 1976, there was a lack in medical talents, and especially an extreme deficiency of high-level medical talents in China, which seriously affected the development of China's medical sciences (Zhu & Zhang, 1990, pp. 122 – 123). In 1979, the proposal of the former Tianjin Medical College (in short, TMU, Tianjin Medical University) was approved by the National People's Congress and the College won the right to host the EYMEP. Tianjin Medical College and Nankai University jointly offered the "pilot courses of the EYMEP" and started a small-scale enrollment at that year. Their training model of the EYMEP was a carbon copy of the model of Peking Union Medical College (Yin, 2012).

In 1980, China implemented the academic degree system, in which it took at least 11 years for a student to get their doctoral degree. That EYMEP enabled a candidate to get a doctor's degree in only 8 years was unacceptable to the interested parties. This greatly restricted the pilot host of the EYMEP in other colleges and universities. In 1985, the departments of the State Education Committee of PRC investigated and discussed the medical education system, which was regarded as the argument for expanding the hosting colleges and universities of the EYMEP. This argument ended up with the establishment of China's 7-year medical education program (Yin, 2012). In 1988, the State Education Committee of PRC issued the Circular on Pilot Host of the 7-year medical higher education program, standardizing China's medical higher education system and stipulating that a master degree of medicine will be awarded for those who finished the 7-year medical education program (State Education Committee of PRC, 1988). Tianjin Medical College's EYMEP was terminated due to the 7-year medical education program, while the program in Peking Union Medical College was preserved as a special case.

Tianjin Medical College's EYMEP had only lasted for 8 years, which did not reflect the expected result of talent training. During this period, the EYMEP in Peking Union Medical College was held as usual, whose basic training model was the NCEE enrollment, the 2.5-year premedical education program, and the 5.5-year medical education program.

The Expansion Period (2001 – 2004)

From 1988 to 2000, only the Peking Union Medical College held the EYMEP. The spread of the EYMEP in the 21st century can be credited to Peking University and Tsinghua University which were approved to host the EYMEP. There are two following reasons which allow the EYMEP to be hosted in other colleges and universities. Firstly, after issuing the *Outline of the Development for the Reform of China Medical Education* (Ministry of Health [MOH] of PRC & Ministry of Education [MOE] of PRC, 2001), China was fully aware of its shortage of high-level medical talents according to the national conditions and the development trend of world medicine and medical education. Secondly, in China's higher education structural adjustment, university mergers offered an opportunity to host the EYMEP (Hou et al., 2014).

While MOE of PRC approved Peking University to host the EYMEP, Tsinghua University, which has the same reputation as Peking University in China, but didn't own a good medical school, also won the right to host which greatly stimulated other colleges and universities who had long desired to host the EYMEP, and the cry to host the EYMEP was increasingly louder (Yin, 2012). For this reason, in 2003, MOE of PRC conducted the "Research on the Reform of China's Medical Education System and Degree." Based on the full review of literature from China and other parts of the world, as well as field investigation, the research group put forward the assumption and suggestion on the reform of education system with the EYMEP developing as a priority and the 5-year medical education program playing a dominant role (Wen, 2002). In May 2004, MOE of PRC and Department of Degree Management & Postgraduate Education (Office of the State Council Academic Degrees Committee) co-issued the *Circular on Increasing Pilot Schools of Pilot Host of the 8-Year Medical Education (MD)* (in short, the *Circular*) (MOE of PRC, 2004), approving five universities, videlicet, Fudan University, Sichuan University, Sun Yat-sen University, Huazhong University of Science and Technology, and Central South University, as the demonstration pilot universities to host the EYMEP (MD). MOE of PRC required the pilot universities to strictly control the enrollment scale and highlighted the hosting principle of "8-year consistency, integral optimization, foundation enhancement, clinic orientation, ability training and quality improvement." Each university can host the program practically and characteristically. Meanwhile, four military medical universities also won the right to host the EYMEP. In 2005, as Shanghai Second Medical University merged with Shanghai Jiao Tong University, Shanghai Jiao Tong University was approved to host the EYMEP. In the same year, Zhejiang University also launched the EYMEP (officially approved in 2011). By then, 14 colleges and universities had been approved to host the EYMEP, which lays the foundation for China's EYMEP, in other words, the basic pattern of high-level medical talent training in China.

The Joint Exploration Period (2004 - 2018)

Since the issuance of the *Circular* in 2004, China's EYMEP has entered the Joint Exploration

Period, which is intensively reflected in the holding of the China's 8-Year Medical Education Summit. In July 2004, Peking University initiated and held the 1st China 8-Year Medical Education Summit. The Summit had a heated discussion on the issues concerning the EYMEP and believed that the program is a key component of the reform of medical education, which helps improve China's comprehensive level of medical education. According to the Summit, it was necessary to set up a regular exchange mechanism by holding regular summits on the EYMEP (Medical Education, 2004). The basic information of successive China 8-Year Medical Education Summits is presented in Table 1.

Table 1. Basic information of China's 8-Year Medical Education Summits.

Order	Time	Organizer(s)	Topic
1st	July 2004	Peking University	Exploration of the EYMEP
2nd	July 2005	Central South University	Premedical Education in the EYMEP
3rd	July 2006	Huazhong University of Science and Technology	The Training Goals of EYMEP and Basic Medicine Education
4th	July 2007	Sichuan University	Basic Requirements and Degree Awarding Conditions of Graduates from the EYMEP
5th	August 2008	Fudan University, Shanghai Jiao Tong University, Naval Medical University	Curriculum System Building and Integration of the EYMEP
6th	November 2009	Sun Yat-Sen University	Training Goals and Basic Requirements in the Clerkship Rotation and Intercollegiate Exchange Student Training of the EYMEP
7th	May 2012	Zhejiang University	Retrospect and Prospect of the EYMEP
8th	October 2018	Peking Union Medical College	Retrospect of the Developmental Process of the EYMEP Conclusion of Successful Experience in International Medical Education Discussion and Suggestion on the Reform of 8-Year Medical Education

Note. EYMEP = 8-year medical education program.

Since the first Summit, the training phases or key issues of the EYMEP were discussed. The *Circular* issued in 2004 stated that "the teaching plan of the EYMEP is drafted on the situations of universities and colleges according to 'Basic Requirements for the EYMEP (doctor of medicine)' and 'Standards for Awarding the Degree of Eight-Year Doctor of Medicine (both further issued)'." But these two schemes have not been drawn up in the successive Summits.

Also, "Training Goal and Basic Requirements for Clinical Teaching of the EYMEP" proposed in the sixth Summit has not been officially issued by MOE of PRC.

Besides, after the seventh China 8-Year Medical Education Summit, the authority did not issue relevant documents on the EYMEP, instead the medical talent training model of "5+3" (5-year undergraduate and 3-year residency) and the standardized resident training system were implemented, which resulted in new difficulties and problems in the EYMEP. A discussion on whether the EYMEP should be continued was raised thereafter. In September 2017, the Department of Higher Education of MOE of PRC authorized the Working Committee for the Accreditation of Medical Education, MOE, to host the Forum of the EYMEP, aiming to discuss the future development direction and ways of reform. The Forum reached a consensus on persisting in the EYMEP.

In this Period, apart from the 14 approved colleges and universities, Nanjing University, Xi'an Jiaotong University, Jilin University, Shandong University, and Wuhan University also hosted the EYMEP in different forms. In this Period, in 2012, *Opinions of the MOE and Former MOH on Implementing the Comprehensive Reform of Clinical Medical Education* was issued, according to which several colleges and universities will become the demonstration pilot units of top-notch innovative talent training supported by the colleges and universities hosting the EYMEP. In 2014, MOE of PRC and other five departments issued *Opinions on the Coordination of Medicine and Education for Deepening the Reform of Clinical Medical Talent Training*, stating that it is necessary to reform and innovate the 8-year clinical medical talent training model as well as encourage colleges and universities hosting the EYMEP to explore effective methods to train multidisciplinary high-level top-notch innovative medical talents.

The In-Depth Promotion Period (2018 to present)

Since 2018, China's EYMEP has entered the In-Depth Promotion Period. To further implement the policies of the National Health Conference and *Opinions of the State Council on Deepening the Coordination of Medicine and Education and Further Advancing the Reform and Development of Medical Education*, according to *Opinions of the MOE on Accelerating to Build High-Level Undergraduate Education Programs to Comprehensively Enhance the Talent Training Capacity*, in October 2018, *Opinions of the MOE, National Health Commission, and National Administration of Traditional Chinese Medicine on Enhancing the Coordination of Medicine and Education and*

Implementing the Outstanding Doctor Education Program 2.0 was issued. It suggested deepening the reform of top-notch innovative medical talent training, promoting the reform of the EYMEP, laying a solid foundation for the candidates' comprehensive growth, improving their clinical capabilities, developing their potential of clinical scientific research, and broadening their international horizons so as to train fewer but better high-level quality and international leading talents in medicine.

After the eighth China 8-Year Medical Education Summit, Peking Union Medical College took the lead in drafting *Standards for the 8-Year Clinical Medical Education* (*first draft*) and *Guiding Opinions on Further Improving the 8-Year Clinical Medical Professional Talent Training* (*exposure draft*), but no consensus was reached on the two drafts, and the education authorities did not issue corresponding documents. In November 2019, the Chairman of Committee of Medical Education Experts of MOE of PRC and former Vice Minister of Education Lin Huiqing revealed that MOE of PRC will further strengthen the cooperation with NHC of PRC and Chinese Academy of Engineering. All sides have established a special research topic to conduct a systematical and in-depth study on the EYMEP, expecting to set the standards for degree awarding of the EYMEP as a reference for the reform of the EYMEP in relevant colleges and universities (Beijing Daily, 2019).

Status quo and characteristics of the EYMEP

Currently, there are 14 approved colleges and universities hosting the EYMEP in China, enrolling almost 1,000 candidates nationwide. Generally, the EYMEP follows the requirements in the *Circular* issued in 2004, aiming to train high-level medical talents, but in reality, differences exist in practice among colleges and universities (Wu & Wang, 2018). The core focus of the EYMEP lies in the talent training model, and the reform exploration and in-depth promotion of the program demands for a consensus on talent training. In accordance with the basic connotation of the talent training model and the practice of the EYMEP in China, this study built an analytical framework of the factors in China's EYMEP (see Figure 1).

Among the factors in the analytical framework, to analyze the status quo and characteristics of China's EYMEP, the most controversial and discussed components in this framework, including training ideas and goals, enrollment processes, and training phases, are selected.

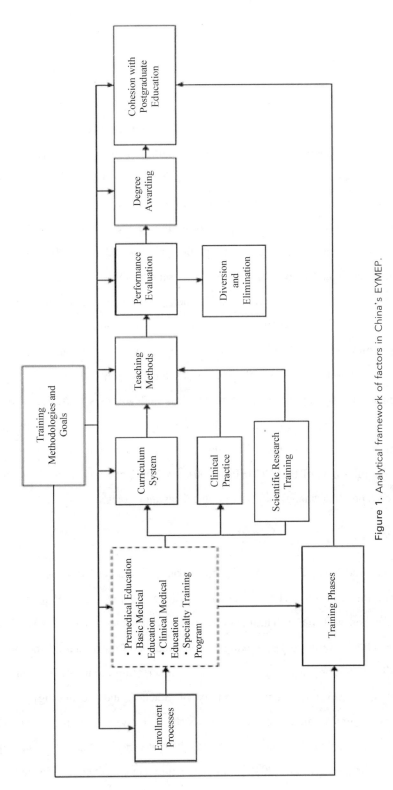

Figure 1. Analytical framework of factors in China's EYMEP.

Note. EYMEP = 8-year medical education program.

Training ideas and goals

Training ideas and goals of the EYMEP in different colleges and universities follow the hosting principle stipulated in the *Circular* overall; however, there are some specific variations. This study cited the training ideas and goals of several medical colleges as examples. The training goal of Peking Union Medical College is to lay a solid foundation for medical knowledge and proficient skills in clinical diagnosis and treatment and to develop innovative thinking and scientific research capabilities, so as to become a high-level medical talent with a doctoral degree in clinical medicine. Its methodology is to breed "medical leaders." Adhering to the thought of holistic education, Peking University's training goal is to train quality medical talents with a solid theoretical foundation, strong clinical capabilities, scientific research abilities, innovative spirit, good communication skills, team spirit, international outlook, and development potential. The training goal of Tsinghua University's EYMEP is to develop physician scientists.

By analyzing training ideas and goals of the EYMEP in different colleges and universities, it has been found that although the general descriptions are different, there are several common points. For example, in the expression of training ideas and goals, six medical schools use the key words "high-level," "innovation," and "future-oriented." In addition, since the pilot host of the EYMEP, most colleges and universities have adjusted their training ideas and goals. For example, since the pilot host of the EYMEP in 2001, Peking University adjusted its training plan 5 times, with corresponding changes in its training ideas and goals.

Enrollment processes

The enrollment processes of the EYMEP focus on the sources of candidates, enrollment methods, and enrollment quota. The enrollment processes of the EYMEP in 14 colleges and universities are detailed in Table 2. The major source of candidates for the EYMEP is graduates from senior high schools. From 2018, Peking Union Medical College started the pilot class and planned to enroll the seniors aspiring to a medical career from nonmedical majors in Peking University, Tsinghua University, and University of Science and Technology of China in a doctoral program in clinical medicine. In 2008, Sichuan University founded the "Eight-Year Innovation Class" to select outstanding students aspiring to a medical career, with a quota of no more than 20 per year (Peng et al., 2018). Shanghai Jiao Tong University selected and enrolled a few outstanding undergraduates from universities in the doctoral program in clinical medicine. Regarding the enrollment methods, graduates from senior high school are enrolled in line with their NCEE preferences, while the comprehensive enrollment processes are carried out via interview. In the enrollment quota, the three military universities set a relatively small quota, other colleges and universities enroll about 100 candidates, and Shanghai Jiao Tong University has relatively large-scale enrollment.

Table 2. Enrollment processes of the 8-year medical education program in 14 colleges and universities.

Names of colleges and universities	Source of candidates	Enrollment methods	Enrollment quota (persons)
Peking Union Medical College	Senior high school graduates	NCEE	60
	Seniors	Comprehensive enrollment	30
Peking University	Senior high school graduates	NCEE	140
Fudan University	Senior high school graduates	NCEE	150
Sichuan University	Senior high school graduates	NCEE	70
	Sophomores	Comprehensive enrollment	20
Sun Yat-sen University, Huazhong University of Science and Technology, Central South University	Senior high school graduates	NCEE	100
Southern Medical University	Senior high school graduates	NCEE	120
The Second Military Medical University	Senior high school graduates	NCEE	40
The Third Military Medical University, Air Force Medical University	Senior high school graduates	NCEE	20
Shanghai Jiao Tong University	Senior high school graduates	NCEE	160
	Graduates	Comprehensive enrollment	25
Zhejiang University	Senior high school graduates	NCEE	70
Tsinghua University	Senior high school graduates	NCEE	30

Note. The data are arranged according to the materials of different colleges and universities reported to the eighth China 8-year Medical Education Summit. NCEE = National College Entrance Examination.

Training phases

The training phases can be divided into premedical education (liberal education), basic medical education, and clinical medical education. The clinical medical education includes clinical medicine (including courses and the internship program) and clerkship rotation (general practice; Schwarz et al., 2004). For the EYMEP, colleges and universities may include the specialty training program to cohere with the standardized resident training in the postgraduate education. The training phases of different colleges and universities can be seen in Table 3. At each phase, no college or university lists scientific research training separately, which means the training "runs throughout" the whole program.

Table 3. Training phases of the 8-year medical education program in 14 colleges and universities.

Names of colleges and universities	Training phases (years)
Peking Union Medical College	2.5 (premedical education) + 1.5 (basic medicine) + 2 (clinical medicine) + 2 (clerkship rotation, scientific research training)
Peking University	1 (premedical education) + 1.75 (basic medicine) + 2.25 (clinical medicine, clerkship rotation) + 3 (specialty training program)
Fudan University	2 (premedical education) + 3 (basic medicine, clinical medicine) + 1 (clerkship rotation) + 2 (specialty training program)
Sichuan University	2 (premedical education) + 2.5 (basic medicine, clinical medicine) + 1 (clerkship rotation) + 2.5 (specialty training program, scientific research training)
Sun Yat-sen University	2 (premedical education) + 2 (basic medicine) + 2 (clinical medicine, clerkship rotation) + 2 (specialty training program)
Huazhong University of Science and Technology, Central South University, Southern Medical University, the Second Military Medical University, the Third Military Medical University, Air Force Medical University	2 (premedical education) + 3 (basic medicine, clinical medicine) + 1 (clerkship rotation) + 2 (specialty training program, scientific research training)
Shanghai Jiao Tong University	1 (premedical education) + 3 (basic medicine, clinical medicine) + 1 (clerkship rotation) + 3 (specialty training program, scientific research training)
Zhejiang University	4 (premedical education) + 3 (basic medicine, clinical medicine) + 1 (clerkship rotation)
Tsinghua University	3 (premedical education, basic medicine) + 2 (scientific research training) + 3 (clinical medicine, clerkship rotation)

Note. The training phases of Peking Union Medical College and Shanghai Jiao Tong University are for graduates from senior high school.

In the premedical education program, the training takes 1 – 4 years, mostly 2 years. The premedical education program in Zhejiang University takes 4 years. In the EYMEP, graduates from senior high school complete other courses and get a bachelor's degree in nonmedicine major before their 4-year medical study. Colleges and universities are focusing on the reform of the integration of basic medicine and clinical medicine; therefore, the training phases of basic medicine and clinical medicine in some schools cannot be clearly identified. Basically, the clerkship rotation lasts for a year. As for the phase of the specialty training program, the length of programs in Peking University and Shanghai Jiao Tong University is 3 years, and that in other colleges and universities is 2 years. Peking Union Medical College, Tsinghua University, and Zhejiang University have not included the specialty training program. A majority of colleges and universities include the scientific research training in the specialty training program. Tsinghua University offers 2-year scientific research training in the middle of the program. Besides, after the pilot host of the EYMEP, different colleges and universities have changed the duration of the training phases. For instance, before 2007, the premedical education program in Peking University lasted for 2 years.

Different colleges and universities are distinctive in training ideas and goals, enrollment processes, and training phases, but overall, they have the following common characteristics. Firstly, the goal is to train high-level, outstanding, and innovative medical talents; however, there is a divergence in training clinical physicians, medical scientists, or physician scientists. Secondly, they all uphold the concept of elite education and small-scale enrollment to ensure the outstanding sources of candidates. It can be argued that most outstanding candidates are enrolled in the EYMEP, and colleges and universities competent to host the EYMEP are deemed representatives of high-level medical colleges. For either colleges and universities or students, the EYMEP has become the symbol of the "elite." Thirdly, all colleges and universities are positively exploring reform of the EYMEP. They are especially attentive to the integration of foundation courses and clinical courses as well as scientific research training. Some students have already made high-level scientific research achievements. Fourthly, graduates can be directly awarded the MD, which saves considerable time compared to the general training of medical talents. Also, according to the schedule of the specialty training program, the graduates must finish the standardized resident training in some way.

External threats and internal challenges of the EYMEP

Twenty years have passed since the expansion of the EYMEP in 2001. In these 20 years, discussions and explorations on the EYMEP have never ceased. Through the analysis, current problems of China's EYMEP can be divided into external threats and internal challenges.

External threats

The external threats are reflected in the current policies and systems: to be specific, the standardized resident training system, the "5 + 3 (5-year undergraduate and 3-year residency)" model (hereafter referred to as the "5+3" model; Zhu et al., 2016), and the training system of MD candidates.

The standardized resident training is a vital part of China's postgraduate medical education, which is the only path to training qualified clinical physicians (Qin, 2017). To ensure a basic minimum of quality among doctors, in 2013, China embarked upon a nationwide reform of medical education, called "5+3," encompassing 5 years of undergraduate medical study and 3 years of residency. During the pilot host of the EYMEP, colleges and universities found that the standardized resident training after the EYMEP will reduce the program's attraction, which requires the cohesion between the EYMEP and standardized resident training. From Table 3, it can be seen that there are differences in the cohesion timing among different colleges and universities. The standardized resident training corresponding to the rotation of the specialty training program is a common ground between colleges and universities and the local health authorities. Some colleges and universities are exploring the issue of cohesion in postgraduate education by way of clinical postdoctoral system.

The "5+3" model refers to the transformation and adjustment of China's 7-year medical education program. The qualifiers in the 5-year undergraduate period directly enter the training phase of the 3-year program of professional master in clinical medicine, which coheres with the standardized resident training, and they will be awarded the certificate of the professional master's degree and the certificate of the standardized resident training after graduation (Zhu et al., 2016). In 2015, MOE of PRC issued *Circular on Improving the Reform of Shift from 7-Year Clinical Medical Education to the "5+3" Talent Training Model*, highlighting that from 2015. The length of the "5+3" model is 8 years, which unavoidably mixes up with the EYMEP.

According to China's academic degree system, there are professional doctoral degrees and academic doctoral degrees in the training of MD. For clinical medicine, the 8-year MD is faced with a pincer attack from Doctors of Philosophy (PhD) in Clinical Medicine and Professional

Doctorates in Clinical Medicine. The former focuses on scientific research capabilities while the latter on clinical skills. Regarding the training length, it takes 11 – 12 years to finish either doctoral program, which is obviously longer than the EYMEP. So, the EYMEP is not on a par with the program of PhD in Clinical Medicine for scientific research capabilities and does not rival the program of Professional Doctorate in Clinical Medicine in clinical skills. Moreover, there is the program of PhD in Basic Medicine in China. This topic also deserves further exploration to examine the distinction between the two programs.

Internal challenges

Regarding the EYMEP, internal challenges come from these aspects, like the goal and positioning, degrees, training phases, and administrative mechanism.

The prior internal challenge of the EYMEP lies in its goal and positioning. The *Circular* issued in 2004 indicated that colleges and universities should be realistic and distinctive in hosting the program. There are differences in the goal and positioning of the practice and exploration of the EYMEP among different colleges and universities. Such differences are mainly reflected in the training of high-level clinical physicians, medical scientists, and physician scientists, which, respectively, focus on clinical capabilities, scientific research capabilities, and the combination of both. In 2017, the *Opinions* issued by the General Office of the State Council of PRC described the training goal and positioning of EYMEP as to train compounded high-level medical talents with a solid theoretical foundation and strong clinical comprehensive skills. *Opinions of the MOE, National Health Commission and National Administration of Traditional Chinese Medicine on Enhancing the Coordination of Medicine and Education, and Implementing the Outstanding Doctor Education Program 2.0* described the training goal and positioning as to train high-level, high-quality, and international leading medical talents. Further studies on how to reflect such goals and positioning in the education plan and talent training model should be conducted. In practice, the training goals and positioning of the EYMEP in colleges and universities are influenced by their 7-year medical education programs and the reform and development of medical education in and outside China. Lacking unified standards and requirements, EYMEP in different colleges or universities are differentiated, thus leaving the impression of being disordered with no clear training goals and positioning in this program.

In degree awarding, according to the *Circular*, the EYMEP should award candidates MD degrees. How should colleges and universities train the candidates from such a doctoral program? What are the requirements of awarding degrees? Since the two documents mentioned in the *Circular* have not yet been formulated, there is controversy over the degree awarding of the EYMEP. In practice, although EYMEP award candidates the degree of Professional Doctorate in Clinical Medicine, it is not equal to the professional doctoral degree. It takes a candidate at least 11 years to get a degree of Professional Doctorate in Clinical Medicine since their graduation from senior high schools, while it only takes 8 years to study an EYMEP. The two programs are unavoidably different in the training requirements and results. The recent years' random inspection of dissertations showed that based on the current degrees awarded, the dissertations of 8-year medical doctors in many colleges and universities failed to meet the standards. This situation further reflects the issue concerning degree awarding of the EYMEP.

The training phases reflect the basic training models. At present, there are the "4+4" "1+4+3" "2+4+2" models of the EYMEP in different colleges and universities. As is mentioned above, there is more than one training phase. Different colleges and universities have different training stages, especially in the premedical education program and the specialty training program. Premedical education lasts 1 – 4 years, and it is adjusted continuously in the pilot host process. The 4-year premedical education program raises the question on the starting point of the EYMEP: Should the program start from graduates of senior high schools or graduates with bachelor's degrees? Considering the developmental process of the EYMEP and China's national conditions, EYMEP should develop students' solid theoretical foundation, and premedical education is a necessary step to lay such a foundation for them. In the specialty training program, the differences among colleges and universities are obvious. Such differences involve the cohesion with postgraduate education. Also, colleges and universities have different understandings of scientific research training. In addition, many of them are exploring the integration of basic medical courses and clinical medical courses, but the scientific and effective way is to be discovered.

Finally, the administrative mechanism, EYMEP, enrolls graduates from senior high schools. It is a long-term education program administered by the Department of Higher Education of MOE of PRC. However, EYMEP involves the postgraduate phase or the postgraduate education phase, which, on a macro aspect, leads to an unsmooth administrative mechanism of the EYMEP. Besides, the EYMEP is mainly hosted by universities. Nevertheless, before the *Opinions* was issued by General Office of the State Council of PRC in 2017, the administrative mechanisms of medical education were undefined and greatly differed between universities. Such a status results in the obvious differences in the administration of medical education among colleges and universities. In the implementation process, the involved administrative departments include teaching affairs offices, the education offices of the schools of medicine, medical education administrative offices, graduate schools, and undergraduate schools.

Future prospects of the EYMEP

Higher medical talents concern the implementation and promotion of a healthy China and scientific and technological power. *Opinions of the State Council on Deepening the Coordination of Medicine and Education and Further Advancing the Reform and Development of Medical Education* issued in 2017 and *Opinions of the MOE, National Health Commission and National Administration of Traditional Chinese Medicine on Enhancing the Coordination of Medicine and Education, and Implementing the Outstanding Doctor Education Program 2.0* issued in 2018 pointed the way for the reform and development of the EYMEP. With the developmental process, status quo, and characteristics, as well as the external threats and internal challenges of the EYMEP combined, the prospects of China's EYMEP are raised as follows.

Identifying the training goals and setting degree requirements

On the training goals, it is necessary to fully realize that the 8-year medical talents are distinctive in a solid theoretical foundation, strong clinical comprehensive capabilities, potential in clinical scientific research, and international horizons. They are high-level top-notch innovative talents with much potential who can drive and lead the future development in medical sciences. It is necessary to fully identify the goal of EYMEP to train high-level medical leading talents. EYMEP can stick to the hosting principle of "eight-year consistency, integral optimization, foundation enhancement, clinic orientation, ability training, and quality improvement" and set a specific training goal according to the target talents. In line with the requirements of the training goal, it is necessary to further innovate the training model, optimize the training plan, and reform the curriculum to continuously improve the quality of the 8-year medical talent training. The requirements of degree awarding of MD should be set according to the training goals of the EYMEP. The 8-year MD should be different from PhD in Clinical Medicine and Professional

Doctorate in Clinical Medicine. Under the existing conditions, the degree of MD can be awarded in-line with the requirements of degree awarding of Professional Doctorate in Clinical Medicine, but a transition should be made therefrom and finally the requirements of degree awarding of MD from the EYMEP should be adopted.

Upholding elite education and exploring diversified enrollment processes

According to China's current economic growth and social development, it is hard to comprehensively carry out elite education in medical education. Nevertheless, EYMEP must uphold the philosophy of elite education. The *Opinions* indicated that it is necessary to strictly control the college quantity and enrollment scale of EYMEP. Multiple measures should be taken to positively attract the most outstanding students. Given that China's graduates from senior high schools do not have a firm ambition or strong interest in medicine (Fan et al., 2017), it is acceptable to explore diversified enrollment processes. Based on current conditions, the enrollment process of graduates from senior high schools, as the primary methods, can be maintained, but the enrollment rules can be adjusted. For example, adding an extra examination to the NCEE mechanism to enroll appropriate candidates in the EYMEP. Also, explore the possibility of enrolling undergraduates aspiring to a medical career in EYMEP. For the enrollment processes of undergraduates, the enrolled students should be equivalent to those having finished premedical education in EYMEP in knowledge grasping and comprehensive quality.

Standardizing the training phases and encouraging characteristic development

According to the training goals, status quo, and characteristics of EYMEP, it is necessary to unify the requirements of the EYMEP in key steps to standardize the training phases. It is suggested that premedical education last no less than 2 years. It is necessary to fully realize the significance of premedical education in laying a solid foundation for the comprehensive growth of medical candidates and developing their multidisciplinary and innovative thinking. The curriculum of premedical education should focus on humanities and social sciences as much as possible, as well as strengthen students' scientific academic training and improve their natural scientific literacy. Universities should use their disciplinary powers to their full potential, and self-established medical colleges should be encouraged to join premedical education offered by high-level universities. The courses of basic medical education and clinical medical education should be fully integrated and cohered with clerkship rotation, all of which takes about 4 years, which is vital for the basic training of medical education for students. Students who fail to finish their study will be diverted. For the last 2 years, students can spend a year on the standardized resident training and another year on scientific research training and dissertation preparation. Undoubtedly, scientific research training should run throughout the process. For instance, it is necessary to cultivate students' interests in scientific research in the phase of premedical education. Apart from standardizing the training phases, colleges and universities can start from their own conditions to host characteristic and quality programs, following the principle of "a consistent goal, characteristic development, standardized phases and unified quality."

Allowing policy space and coordinating with existing systems

Since the EYMEP is inconsistent or uncoordinated with China's current policies and systems, the program's further development should focus on the developmental trend and future direction of international medical education. Certain policy space should be given for the program to coordinate with the existing systems. As is stated in "External threats," first, in standardized resident training, it is necessary to send graduates from the EYMEP to standardized resident training. Considering the particularity of EYMEP, it is necessary to raise the treatment for graduates in the standardized resident training by setting specific treatment standards, and then the coordination with the "5+3" model. This is mainly reflected in the enrollment processes, training models, and the cohesion with postgraduate education. In enrollment processes, it should be stipulated that the EYMEP should be different from the "5+3" model in the training phases and the curriculum system. In the cohesion with postgraduate education, the standardized resident training between the two types of graduates should be differentiated clearly. At last, for the coordination with the existing MD training system, firstly, we should identify the corresponding standards for each year of the EYMEP. For instance, the first to fifth year can be aligned with the undergraduate phase and the sixth to eighth year, the doctoral phase. Secondly, we should identify the differences among the 8-year MD, PhD in Clinical Medicine, Professional Doctorate in Clinical Medicine, and PhD in Basic Medicine and standardize the EYMEP according to its standards and degree requirements.

Establishing organizations and institutes and promoting mutual development

In the In-Depth Promotion Period, it is necessary to establish a relevant organization, such as the cooperative group or alliance of the EYMEP, to jointly promote the program. Depending on the organization, members can conduct peer reviews, consistent performance checks, and interacademic dissertation defense. Meanwhile, through the organization, members can draft the "Basic Requirements for the EYMEP (MD)" as well as "Standards for Awarding the Degree of 8-Year Doctor of Medicine," which are not formulated after the issuance of the *Circular* in 2004 and other necessary guiding opinions on the EYMEP. The organization aims to standardize the training model of the EYMEP, facilitate colleges and universities to organize and host the program in a proper way, as well as improve the quality of hosting the program, so as to push forward the healthy, sustainable, and orderly development of the EYMEP.

Conclusions

Among medical professionals, high-level medical talents play a vital role. The EYMEP, as the path of high-level medical talent training in China, has been conducted over a century. This study systematically reviewed the developmental process of EYMEP. The status quo and characteristics and threats and challenges were analyzed, along with the program's prospects. The process of EYMEP can be divided into five periods. Currently, there are 14 universities and institutes hosting the EYMEP approved by the MOE of PRC. As for EYMEP, the external threats are reflected in the current policies and systems, like "5+3" policy and the existing academic degree system in China. Meanwhile, internal challenges come from the goal and positioning, degrees, training phases, and administrative mechanism. At last, five prospects of China's EYMEP are raised. We believe in the new era of the reform and development of China's medical education, a systematic review of the development of EYMEP in China is of great significance to the promotion of high-level medical talent training in China. Also, the exploration course of China's high-level medical talent training represented by the EYMEP may be an enlightenment for other countries, especially developing countries, in their training of high-level medical talents.

References

Beijing Daily. (2019, November 26). *China will draft and release the degree awarding requirements for students from the eight-year medical education program* [in Chinese]. http://www.bjd.com.cn/a/201911/23/WS5dd8a38ae4b0e69db8165fcc.html

Fan, A. P., Kosik, R. O., Huang, L., Gjiang, Y., Lien, S. S., Zhao, X., Chang, X., Wang, Y., & Chen, Q. (2017). Burnout in Chinese medical students and residents: An exploratory cross-sectional study. *The Lancet*, *390*, S84.

Frenk, J., Chen, L. C., Bhutta, Z. A., Cohen, J. S., Crisp, N., Evans, T. G., Fineberg, H., Garcia, P., Ke, Y., Kelly, P. T., Kistnasamy, B., Meleis, A., Naylor, D., Mendez, A. P., Reddy, S., Scrimshaw, S. S., Sepulveda, J., Serwadda, D., & Zurayk, H. (2010). Health professionals for a new century: Transforming education to strengthen health systems in an interdependent world. *The Lancet*, *376*(9756), 1923–1958.

Hou, J., Michaud, C., Li, Z., Dong, Z., Sun, B., Zhang, J., Cao, D., Wan, X., Zeng, C., Wei, B., Tao, L., Li, X., Wang, W., Lu, Y., Xia, X., Guo, G., Zhang, Z., Cao, Y., Guan, Y., ... Chen, L. C. (2014). Transformation of the education of health professionals in China: Progress and challenges. *The Lancet*, *384*(9945), 819–827.

Li, J. (2015). The South China Medical College and the western medical education in modern China [in Chinese]. *Northwest Medical Education*, *23*(4), 667–670.

Lin, H. (2019, November 18). *Insist on reform and innovation, speed up the implementation eight-year medical education program reform breakthrough* [in Chinese]. http://medu.bjmu.edu.cn/cms/news/100000/0000000016/2019/11/23/a481772fb1fb48bc94171ef7f8413e7a.shtml

Medical Education. (2004). The first China eight-year higher medical education summit was held [in Chinese]. *Medical Education*, *23*(4), 65–65.

Ministry of Health of the People's Republic of China, & Ministry of Education of the People's Republic of China. (2001). Outline for the reform and development of medical education in China [in Chinese]. *Medical Rducation*, *20*(5), 1–6.

Peking Union Medical College. (1987). *History of China Union Medical College (1917–1987)* [in Chinese]. Beijing Science and Technology Press.

Peng, H., Li, Z., Jiang, H., Zhang, X., Wang, W., & Qing, P. (2018). The exploration and effect on the reform of the training model of eight-year medical program [in Chinese]. *Chinese Journal of Medical Education*, *37*(38), 325–329.

Qin, H. (2017). Present situation and prospect of graduate medical education in China [in Chinese]. *Graduate Medical Education in China*, *1*(1), 1–4.

Schwarz, M. R., Wojtczak, A., & Zhou, T. (2004). Medical education in China's leading medical schools. *Medical Teacher*, *26*(3), 215–222.

Shi, X., Cheng, H., & Wu, H. (2018). Policy significance, appeal and concept of China's new round of medical education reform [in Chinese]. *China Higher Education*, *53*(Z3), 61–63.

State Education Commission of the People's Republic of China. (1988). Notice on the pilot of seven-year higher medical education program [in Chinese]. *China Higher Medical Education*, *7*(2), 1–2.

The State Council Information Office of the People's Republic of China. (2019, September 16). To celebrate the 70th anniversary of the founding of the People's Republic of China news center held the press conference of the second [in Chinese]. http://www.scio.gov.cn/ztk/dtzt/39912/41837/Document/1665398/1665398.htm

Wang, D., & Yin, X. (2013). Thinking on the eight-year medical education [in Chinese]. *Chinese Journal of Medical Education*, *32*(33), 321–325.

Wen, L. (2002). Reflections on the reform of the academic system of higher medical education in China [in Chinese]. *Medical Education*, *21*(6), 3–5, 13.

Wu, H., & Wang, W. (2018). A review of world medical education and some thoughts on eight-year medical education program of China [in Chinese]. *Chinese Journal of Medical Education*, *37*(38), 641–645.

Wu, J., & Dong, B. (2001). *The road of talent cultivation of Peking Union Medical College* [in Chinese]. China Union Medical College Press.

Yin, X. (2012). *One schooling system and multiple modes: A study on the cultivation mode of eight-year medical education program in China* [Doctoral dissertation, Peking University] [in Chinese].

Zhang, D. (2009). Mapping modern medicine in China: Impact of Rockefeller Foundation [in Chinese]. *Studies in the History of Natural Sciences*, 28(2), 137-155.

Zhu, C., & Zhang, W. (1990). *History of medical education in China* [in Chinese]. Beijing Medical University, China Union Medical College Joint Press.

Zhu, J., Li, W., & Chen, L. (2016). Doctors in China: Improving quality through modernisation of residency education. *The Lancet*, 388(10054), 1922-1929.

Notes on Contributors

William Anderson is a full-time student at Middlebury College double majoring in Chinese Language and Literature and Economics.

Hui Dong is Associate Professor of the Faculty of Education at East China Normal University. He has published widely on Educational Management and Leadership, Educational Policy Analysis, Sociology of Education, and Educational Governance.

Shengzu Dong is Dean of the Institute of Private Education of Shanghai Academy of Educational Science. He has widely published on Private Education.

Guorui Fan is Professor of the Faculty of Education at East China Normal University. He has published widely on Basic Theory of Education, Education Policy, and School Change and Development.

Xiaoxian Fan is Dean of Center for Dissemination of Education Research of the National Institutes of Educational Policy Research at East China Normal University. Her research fields are Higher Education and Policy Study.

Yong Jiang is Professor of the Faculty of Education at East China Normal University. He has published widely on Basic Theory of Preschool Education, Preschool Teacher Education, and ECE Curriculum.

Kenneth King is Professor Emeritus at the University of Edinburgh. He was Director of the Centre of African Studies and Professor of International and Comparative Education at the University of Edinburgh till September 2005. His research interests over the years have focused on the history and politics of education, skills development in both the formal and informal sectors of the economy and on aid policy towards all sub-sectors of education, including higher education.

Tingzhou Li is Vice-Dean of the Research Center for Education and Social Investigation of National Institutes of Educational Policy Research at East China Normal University. His major research field is Education Policy, especially Teacher Policy.

Xiaoying Lin is Associate Professor of Graduate School of Education at Peking University. Her key research fields are Education Policy, Qualitative Research in Education, and School Assessment.

Notes on Contributors

Junyan Liu is Associate Researcher of the Faculty of Education at East China Normal University. Her key research interests are Shadow Education and Quantitative Research in Education.

Li Liu is Associate Professor of the School of Education at Shanghai Jiao Tong University. Her key research fields are Science and Technology Evaluation Policy in Higher Education and Higher Education Evaluation Policy.

Weishu Liu is Faculty at Zhejiang University of Finance and Economics. He has published widely on Knowledge Management, and Science and Intelligence.

Xiao Liu is Researcher of the National Institutes of Educational Policy Research at East China Normal University. Her key research interests are Public Policy, Educational Policy and Social Culture, and Social Issues and Policy Analysis.

Xiaodong Lu is Researcher and Professor of the Graduate School of Education at Peking University. His teaching and research interests are Higher Education Management, Comparative Higher Education, Education Finance and Institution Research, and Curriculum and Instruction Theory.

Haishao Pang is Professor of the School of Humanities and Social Sciences at Beijing Institute of Technology. She has published widely on Quality and Liberal Arts Education, University Faculty Development, Teaching and Learning Research, and Higher Education Administration.

Hanwei Tang is Professor of the Faculty of Education at East China Normal University. He has published widely on Moral Education, Educational Ethics, Educational Philosophy, and Basic Education Reform.

Tao Wang is Associate Professor of the Faculty of Education at East China Normal University. His key research fields are Basic Theory of Curriculum and Instruction, Teacher Professional Development, and Curriculum Design.

Hongbin Wu is Associate Researcher of the Institute of Medical Education at Peking University. His research interests are Medical Education, Student Development, and Economics and Management of Higher Education.

Zunmin Wu is Professor of the Faculty of Education at East China Normal University. His key research fields include Education Policy and Legislation, Basic Theory of Education, Research on Learning Society and Community Education, and Research on Contemporary Theory and Practice of Lifelong Education.

Ailei Xie is Associate Professor of the School of Education (Teacher College) at Guangzhou University. He has widely published on Social Development and Education Policy.

Shouxuan Yan is Professor and Vice-Dean of the School of Education at Liaoning Normal University. His main research interests are Curriculum Development and Teaching Reform, University Curriculum and Teaching Reform, Teacher Education, Life Education, etc.

Xiaozhe Yang is Associate Professor of the Faculty of Education at East China Normal University, and Executive Director of International Classroom Analysis Lab of the Institute Curriculum and Instruction at East China Normal University. His major research fields are Educational Technology, AI Education, and Curriculum Design.

Danqing Yin is a PhD student of University of Kansas. Her main research interest is Education Policy and Comparative Education.

Zhenguo Yuan is Professor and Dean of the Faculty of Education at East China Normal University (ECNU), and Vice-President of China's Society for Education Studies. Before returning to ECNU in 2014, he served as key policy planner at China's Ministry of Education for teacher education reform and Director of China's Institute of Educational Sciences (2007 – 2013). He has published widely on Education Policy, Comparative Education, School Leadership, and Quality Enhancement of Education.

Yuting Zhang is Associate Professor of Zhejiang Normal University. Her research interests include Education Policy, University Student Development, and China-Africa Education Partnership.

Bin Zhou is Professor of the Faculty of Education at East China Normal University, and Dean of the College of Teacher Education at East China Normal University. He has published widely on Classroom Instruction, School Change, and Policies and Regulations.

Junwen Zhu is Professor of the Faculty of Education at East China Normal University. His major research fields are Knowledge Innovation in Universities, Talent Policy of Universities, Scientific Measurement and Research Evaluation, and Transformation of Science and Education System.

Yiming Zhu is Professor at the Faculty of Education at East China Normal University. His research interests lie in Educational Evaluation, Teacher Education, International Education, and Education Policy.